THE LONGEST
ROPE HAS
AN END

THE LONGEST
ROPE HAS
AN END

C. and R. Gale

Charleston, SC
www.PalmettoPublishing.com

The Longest Rope Has An End

First Edition

Paperback ISBN: 978-1-68515-355-7
eBook ISBN: 978-1-68515-354-0

CHAPTER 1

There never was a plan to take Cali back to Marilyn's house, a stationary single-wide trailer in a mobile home park stuffed between Pulaski Highway and the train tracks. A hidden parcel of virtual wasteland smack dab in the middle of Baltimore County. The location could have just as easily been utilized as a junkyard. Like everything else that night, the decision to end up at Marilyn's home took shape on its own.

Marilyn needed a cigarette in the worst way. She knew it was bad for her singing voice but she allowed herself this one indulgence. She needed something to calm her nerves after her shows and alcohol never crossed her lips. Her performance had been a huge hit. The audience went nuts, like they were seeing the actual movie star in person. After all, Marilyn did have the iconic blonde hair, the formfitting shimmering gowns, the sparkling jewels. All those hours of practice paid off because she replicated the 1950's sex kitten's sultry moves and her throaty cooing as she made love to the microphone. Although her performance was scheduled to end at ten, she was late leaving the stage, the audience demanding not one but two encores from the Marilyn Monroe impersonator. After her show, she signed autographs for over an hour as she gratefully accepted generous tips from her slew of drunken fans, mostly female. Every last one of them white.

While driving with one hand, she used the other to dig around inside her imitation leather handbag for a good five minutes before admitting to defeat. She didn't want to do it but she needed a cigarette so she'd have to make a stop. Havre de Grace was at least an hour ride from her home and she couldn't wait that long, so Marilyn made the decision to pull off I-95. Jutting above the tree line, a colossal, yellow gasoline sign beckoned her up ahead.

Emerging from the convenience store, Marilyn poised a Berlin Menthol between her painted lips. Firing up her little silver lighter, she discreetly surveyed the scene around her. Thick false eyelashes were illuminated by the yellow flame as she scrutinized the never ending stream of cars, trucks, and tractor trailers pulling in and out. Families in cars weighed down with their possessions packed away in roof rack travel bins hastily piled out of their vehicles, making a mad dash for the public restrooms inside. In the shadows by the dumpster, a small figure crouched down. Probably scavenging for food.

Out of the corner of her eye, Marilyn kept her sights on a tractor trailer driver as he climbed down from his rig, his footsteps heavy and stiff. Beneath his red and black checked flannel, a pregnant belly strained against the buttons. He was the kind of man who boasted about wearing the same size jeans today that he wore back in high school, possible only by cinching the belt several inches below his rotund midsection. As he strutted past Marilyn, he pinched her ass hard, making her jump. The toothpick in the corner of his mouth remained perfectly balanced when he gave her an amused chuckle.

"Keep your big, hairy, paws to yourself," she wanted to say, yet no words escaped her lips. One day she was going to have the courage to stand up to people like him. Just not tonight. Bitterly, she watched him disappear inside the store. Out of habit, whenever she felt trouble lurking, Marilyn began to rub her snake ring, a precious gift from her grandmother long ago. Closing her eyes, she took a long drag on her cigarette while trying to ignore her aching feet. It had been a long day and she was dead tired. All she wanted was to smoke her cigarette and get back on the road.

Determined not to let the trucker get the best of her, Marilyn savored the nicotine smoke that filled her lungs. The menthol cooled her throat and she felt her body eventually relax.

Halfway through her cigarette, her peace was disturbed by a hand on her shoulder. Couldn't a girl just be left alone? Whirling around, an indignant Marilyn was ready for a confrontation with the greasy haired, red-neck truck driver.

Instead, she found herself staring down into into the very green eyes of a feral looking teenager. Marilyn noticed the length of sticker bush caught in the head of tangled hair the color of papaya. The petite girl's skin was covered in a multitude of scratches and bug bites. It didn't escape Marilyn's keen eye the way the knees of the girl's jeans were stained dark with mud.

Making no effort to disguise her annoyance, Marilyn gave her the once over before boldly shifting her position until she had turned her full back to face the girl. She flamboyantly blew a smoke ring above her head, watching it hover midair, all the while acting as though the teen didn't exist.

Marilyn tried her best to ignore the girl who called herself Cali but then she brought out that debit card, offering to fill her tank with gas. Havre de Grace was a long ride away from her home on Cherry Tree Lane and the gas gauge said she only had a quarter tank. She could use a full tank of gas, courtesy of someone else's wallet. Damn white people and their monies. It seemed whenever those people walked into her life, trouble was always quick on their heels.

Of course Marilyn made sure to make it worth her while. In exchange for giving the girl a ride in her car, she not only got a full tank of gas but also finagled a pack of Salem Light. Marilyn couldn't afford name brand cigarettes so she routinely made due with Berlin Menthol. Berlin Menthol tasted like smoldering tree bark.

The deal made, Marilyn sashayed to her light lavender Cadillac with a peeling and cracked landau roof. Her car was longer than a boat, certainly manufactured back when gasoline cost less than a dollar a gallon. Large, furry, black and white dice hung from the rear view mirror limiting the driver's vision. The headliner had come unglued years ago and sagged over the back seats obstructing even more of the driver's view. Rust desecrated the back quarter panels along the wheel wells. Obviously, no one had ever wasted a Saturday afternoon caring for this pimp mobile.

Sliding behind the wheel, Marilyn inched the car up to pump number ten. The loud rumble from a muffler with a hole in it caused more than one head to turn. Cali's immediate reaction was, this was not the ideal getaway car, but it had tires and a motor so she was thrilled to be its passenger.

Sitting in the driver's seat, Marilyn intently studied the girl in her driver's side mirror. While Cali pumped gasoline into the Cadillac, Marilyn suddenly began to have second thoughts about carrying a stranger in her vehicle. After all, her grandmother hadn't raised a stupid child.

When the pump clicked off, Marilyn made her move. Cali replaced the gas cap and before she could make it around the car to the passenger side door, the statuesque blonde unexpectedly exited the car and told her to stop where she was. Doing as she was told, Cali stopped dead in her tracks. In an instant, Marilyn was next to her, commanding her to put her hands over her head. Under the bright neon lights, Marilyn frisked the humiliated teenager like someone with great expertise. Ordering Cali to spread her legs, Marilyn slid her hands from inseam to ankles. Running both hands the length of one arm, then the other Marilyn concluded the search by patting down Cali's sides, her back, and abdomen.

Feeling all the blood rush from her head, Cali's vision blurred. Her throat constricted, making it hard to breathe. She feared she might faint when Marilyn suddenly commanded in her lilting, island accent, "Go on now, shift your carcass in. Can't be too careful. I can't have you pulling a gun or knife on me and stealing my car."

Stunned, Cali watched the glamorous woman in red stilettos saunter around to the driver's side of the car. The Cadillac thundered to life before Cali had the presence of mind to jump in and secure her seatbelt.

"So where might you be heading to, precise?" Marilyn asked.

"I'm heading south. To Baltimore," Cali answered.

The blonde shook her head before punching the accelerator. "Baltimore, huh? The city that bleeds."

CHAPTER 2

They rode for quite some time in silence before Cali noticed the dog-eared thesaurus laying on the bench seat, many torn bits of paper stuck between pages for quick reference. She picked it up, fingered the pages. It was dark inside the cabin of the car so she couldn't make out the many notations Marilyn had made in the margins. The book had the feel of being worn and well used like her grandparents' southern Baptist bible, where everyone committed certain passages to memory. Cali felt an instant connection to the eccentric woman since she too had been raised with a deep appreciation for the English language.

"It's old, but words stay the same. That book expands my horizon. I'm just trying to better myself, learning new words and such," Marilyn offered. "As a child we grew up speaking Creole, so English is not my native language."

Welcoming the conversation, Cali asked, "Are you from Jamaica?"

Shooting a disdainful look in Cali's direction, Marilyn scolded, "Not every chocolate girl with accent is from Jamaica." Marilyn prided herself for maintaining her West Indies island accent. Over the years she had made a great effort to never acquire what her grandmother had referred to as a fresh-water yankee inflection.

Feeling contrite, Cali took a minute before starting anew, "I have a thesaurus at home. I love words too. My Pop always says there're literally millions of words we can choose when expressing an idea. He's always told me the words we utter bear testament of our true inner self. Pop says the picking and choosing of our vocabulary serves as a fairly honest reflection of an individual's character. Or lack thereof."

"Your pop sounds like a man with great intelligence," Marilyn commented.

"Oh, he is. He's a circuit court judge back home in Georgia. I'm going to be like him and go to law school too one day," Cali spoke with undeniable pride.

"That's mighty big dreams for a girl living behind dumpsters," Marilyn didn't mince her words when she let it be known she had seen Cali hiding in the shadows.

"It's a long story." Overwhelmed by shame, Cali looked out her window at the endless stream of white headlights blazing against the black darkness of the night. Thousands of vehicles, it seemed, sped along the coast's I-95 north-south corridor which connects southern Florida to Maine.

"Plenty of time between Havre de Grace and Baltimore for your tale," Marilyn told her.

Squirming in her seat, Cali reluctantly began, "I actually live in Georgia with my grandparents. Last night when I got home from school there was someone waiting to talk to me. My grandparents hired him to lead an intervention because he said they're concerned for my well-being."

■ ■ ■

On cue, he cleared his throat, not because he had a throat irritation, but rather to make his presence known. Until that moment, Cali hadn't noticed the man with the ramrod posture seated near the stone fireplace. Cali knew all her grandparents' friends, the lawyers, and other judges from the courthouse. This man was a stranger.

First impressions would suggest he was the kind of nondescript person who could easily go through life unnoticed. Although he was probably in his early forties, his style of dress and haircut aged him considerably. His brown hair was combed into a side part with severely short sides. Heavy, black, horn rimmed glasses swallowed up his slender face. Cali noticed his white shirt was buttoned clear to the throat and was tucked tight inside the waist of tan khakis. His pants were hiked up much too high on his adolescent waistline. He crossed his legs at the knee like a woman to reveal argyle socks under a pair of brown suede oxfords.

On his lap, he held onto a black binder with both hands. A plain gold band on his left hand indicated he was married. Strangely, this anemic individual carried a great deal of clout, endorsed by his possession of the room's undivided attention. Caution flooded Cali's veins as she studied his every move.

Making eye contact, he rose, his hand already extended as he approached her. "I'd like to introduce myself, Cali. I'm a professional interventionist hired by your family who have all graciously gathered here this evening because they are deeply concerned for your well-being."

■ ■ ■

"What words of wisdom did this interventionist speak last night?" Marilyn asked.

"He mostly reminded me of the person I used to be. A girl who did well in school and had plans to go to college. Just a few months ago,

I was playing soccer and had lots of friends. I used to be happy. He's the reason my grandparents brought me to Maryland this morning," Cali lamented.

"Who is this girl you speak about? Certainly not the dirty girl I see now sitting in my car." The truth of Marilyn's words stung like alcohol poured into a fresh cut.

Cali's response was barely audible, "Marilyn, I'm trying my best to get her back."

"From what I see, you need to try harder."

CHAPTER 3

KT was the fourth of six children raised in poverty by the maternal grandmother who illegally immigrated to the United States from Trinidad. They didn't have much, but the grandmother managed to keep the ever expanding family under one roof and fed. The children's mother loved the act of creating life, but had zero interest in the end product. So apathetic toward the babies she was birthing, the mother ceased to even make the effort to give them names starting with the fourth infant, whose birth certificate read, KT, in the space provided for the name. No real name. Just two letters randomly plucked from the alphabet with no hidden meaning behind them. KT.

Children numbers five and six were also deemed unworthy of names, receiving the minimal effort of two initials for their self identity in life. At the insistence of the grandmother, all six children shared the surname, Shade. Since no two children had the same father, none of the brood looked alike. Hands down, KT was the prettiest with huge expressive eyes and delicate features.

As a child, it was the teachers at school who tried to force her into talking the way they did. Enunciating every syllable of every word until all that was left was as flavorless as a turnip boiled in a pot of unseasoned water. KT saw the teachers' sideways glances at each other because her way of speaking had a rhythm and a lilt they didn't like. They wanted her to be like everybody else, but the problem was, she wasn't like everybody else. KT was Trini to the bone. So every day after being subjected to six long hours in a classroom where she didn't belong, KT finally got to return to the safety of her grandmother's home where they were proud of their island roots and spoke only Creole.

KT was only eleven years old when her beloved grandmother unexpectedly died. Resembling a woman looking in the rearview mirror at her sixties, the fifty-four year old grandmother suffered from a heap of medical ailments, including morbid obesity and high blood pressure, which ultimately resulted in her fatal stroke. The children's biological mother hadn't been seen or heard from in many years, so the Shade children were farmed out to various family members. The Department of Social Services sweetened the pot, enticing reluctant relatives with a handsome monthly stipend, eventually finding homes for all six children. Altruism was trumped by greed. After the grandmother's passing from this earth, the siblings would never see or hear from one another again. Their common denominator was gone forever.

Only two days after the grandmother was laid to rest, it was some pasty white social worker who came knocking at the door. That lady didn't speak more than two words when she took eleven year old KT to the home of a short-tempered alcoholic woman who just happened to have the last name of Shade and her common law husband. The way KT figured, Child Protective Services must have put no more effort in finding her relations than to look in the phone book under the name, Shade.

Her grandmother dead, separated from her brothers and sisters, KT was taken to a stranger's house where she was banished to a dingy basement and told to be grateful to be sleeping on a stained mattress without sheets. Never once did that social worker lady come in and see what KT's living conditions were really like. The few times her job forced her to come to the house for a welfare inspection, she stood as close to the front door as humanly possible in her little navy blue suit with her brown leather briefcase pressed up tight against her chest. Her shiny patent leather high heels never set foot on those rickety steps that led down to a basement that smelled stink of mold. That lady never bore witness to the mattress thrown down on the floor where KT was left to sleep like a stray dog.

By the time she was fourteen, KT started running away. At the age of sixteen, she became a ward of the state after a long string of minor brushes with the law. Mostly playing hooky from school. She grew up fast. KT's years in juvenile detention gave her a clear understanding of the dog eat dog world. In order to survive, she learned quickly to look out for number one, first and foremost.

The girl without a name was an easy target for anyone looking to pick a fight and juvie jail was overflowing with angry adolescents. KT constantly attracted unwanted attention from the other kids by the way her slim hips naturally swayed when she walked. She was boldly mocked for the giddy way she adored frilly dresses. When her pinky finger habitually lifted when she drank from a cup, she became the brunt of all their cruel jokes. Her ultra-feminine ways became cheap fodder for hostile teens looking to unleash their anger. KT's life was pure misery.

Until the day that bazodee white boy, Skeeter Shiflett, was hauled in. Nobody messed with him. He was crazier than a rabid raccoon. Anybody with an ounce of common sense could see his black glassy eyes were filled with raw rage. All the little hairs down KT's spine stood erect the first time Skeeter's cold hard eyes met hers. If her grandmother had still been alive, she would've said those little hairs standing on end were a clear warning sign that boy'd unleashed a spirit to walk across her grave. KT's grandmother would've professed that the devil himself resided inside that boy. In KT's opinion, anybody could see something wasn't wired right in him so she tried her best to keep her distance. The problem with life was, things never turned out the way KT planned.

Weekends at the juvie lockup were the only time visitors were allowed. Since her grandmother's untimely death resulted in KT losing her entire family in one fell swoop, she had no one coming to spend time with her. For whatever reason, Skeeter's relations never once bothered to visit him either. When the other kids slumped in chairs and defiantly refused to communicate with families that sacrificed their weekends for a belligerent child in detention, Skeeter gravitated toward KT. Initially, KT did her best to try to avoid the boy who sent shivers down her spine but he had set his sights on her and she was powerless to stop it. It didn't take KT long to realize the advantage of a friendship with the crazy white boy. Since the other kids also feared Skeeter, they eventually stopped taunting her, making her days in juvie more tolerable.

An innate hunger deep down inside for some kind of human contact ultimately resulted in the two misfits sitting outside at one of the picnic tables surrounded by barbed wire fence. They were all they had. Skeeter was quick to reveal his long list of grievances against his mother, Peaches. Since KT was deservedly leery of Skeeter, it took quite some time before she let down her guard to reveal her secret talent to him. She had been gifted with a natural singing voice. She was visibly startled by the unexpected smile that erupted, looking as though it pained Skeeter's face the first time he heard her sing.

That was the moment she knew what she was going to do with the rest of her life the minute she was no longer incarcerated. She possessed a powerhouse singing voice ever since she was a little child. The kind of voice that caused goosebumps to rise out of people's skin the moment she opened her mouth. She saw how people's eyes filled up with tears when she sang. It was her God given talent. So, ever since that first time her voice made Skeeter's eyes soften just a little, she was certain of her destiny in life. KT set her sights on becoming a famous nightclub singer.

On February 15, 2007, the day of her eighteenth birthday, the panel of three men and two women granted KT her freedom. She was no longer a ward of the state. After landing a job at a clothing boutique in Fells Point where she worked on commission, KT bought herself a little trailer where she allowed herself the luxury of devoting one entire closet to an expansive wardrobe and coordinating wigs. KT knew if she wanted women with money to spend flocking in her direction for vogue advice, she had to look the part of a fashionista. So she dressed the part with flair. Without her discerning sense of style, they were just clothes on a rack. KT took pride in her ability to transform homely girls into little vamps. Her reputation at the boutique quickly became well known for creating one of a kind, sexy ensembles. The young and the beautiful looking for an exciting evening on the town sought her out, making her the top sales associate month after month.

Years went by and in spite of her best efforts, KT's true dream of becoming a stage performer didn't take root. Nobody wanted to pay money to hear her sing church hymns. Club owners repeatedly informed her singers were a dime a dozen. Time and again, KT was told to come back after she cultivated a unique hook. Her amazing voice, her God given talent wasn't enough they said. She needed a hook.

Everything changed one evening as KT was locking up the boutique at the close of business. That's when that white jarhead cop spotted her, called her that name. On that particular day, KT was wearing an expensive platinum blonde wig cut short along the neckline. No cost was spared on the soft, loose curls. It looked like human hair, not one of those cheap synthetic jobs. Her bright red stilettos made her tower close to six feet, highlighting long lean legs that were bare.

Her shiny black top was billowing and loose fitting in contrast to her skin tight, leopard print, mini skirt. Showing no emotion, she kept her eyes straight ahead, determined to pass the cop by like a full bus. If there was one thing her time in juvie had taught her, it was to never engage anyone itching for a fight. Yet, no matter how hard KT tried to avoid trouble, there was something about her that always encouraged trouble to redouble its efforts to find her.

"Well, well, well, if it isn't Marilyn Mon Yo in person," the cocky policeman smirked loudly as she walked past. "Tell me something, Marilyn, are diamonds really a girl's best friend?"

He made a deliberate show of watching her walk the length of a city block to her car as he twirled his nightstick, a shit-eating grin plastered on his face. Walking with purpose, KT fingered the snake ring her beloved grandmother had given her when she was a child. A ring meant to ward off evil.

The cop's words stayed with her for days, disrupting her sleep. It was impossible to count the number of people in her lifetime who had gone out of their way to be hateful to her, so why had that man's words singed her soul, refusing to give her a moments peace?

KT wondered, is that what people saw when they looked at her? Because she was a woman with a warm caramel-colored complexion and blonde hair, he felt righteous in his decision to call her Marilyn Mon Yo? That's when KT made up her mind to show the people what they expected to see. She had finally found her unique hook. For the next six months, she scrimped and saved. When she had sufficient funds, KT splurged her savings on her first of many evening gowns to come. The formfitting, red sequin gown with a plunging neckline and a slit up the thigh that left little to the imagination was an exact replica of the one worn in "Gentlemen Prefer Blondes". Assuming the name, Marilyn Mon Yo, she began a lucrative stage career as a Marilyn Monroe impersonator. At last, KT had a real name, Marilyn.

CHAPTER 4

During her time in juvenile detention, Marilyn had most certainly honed her street smarts. She prided herself on being able to quickly read situations and adapt accordingly, a lifeskill paramount for self preservation. Those survival instincts kicked in soon after they exited the ramp off I-95 onto Franklin Street. Heading west into the heart of Baltimore City, the lavender Cadillac with the peeling landau roof was quickly surrounded by a pack of young men on bikes. They came at the car from all directions.

Their heads were covered in black spandex skull caps in lieu of helmets. Males, some as young as nine, all the way to grown men sporting full beards surrounded the car on bikes. Scooters, dirt bikes, mopeds, four wheelers, and bicycles seemed to appear out of nowhere before engulfing the vehicle. There were easily two dozen of them. Either bare chested or wearing dingy, sleeveless, wife beaters, the aggressive males circled them like sharks in the open water. They zigzagged across the road slowing the Cadillac's progress. Marilyn knew better than to blow the car horn. Don't antagonize them, let them have their fun she thought.

To emphasize their presence, the males beat on the car doors or trunk with open palms as they made their passes. The car sounded like it was being pelted with rocks as the men slammed the vehicle each time they were close enough to make contact. Creating as much havoc as possible, they whistled, whooped, and hollered at the two females.

Deep voices overpowered the roar of the engines as they shouted, each trying to outdo the other, "Hey baby, want a piece of this?"

"Let me show you what a real man can do."

"I want you to be my baby momma!"

Cali rolled up the window and locked her car door. Her body liquified as she slid from her seat to the passenger side floorboard. Pulling her knees to her chest Cali huddled on the floor in a tight ball. She wanted to make herself invisible. Closing her eyes, she absently rocked herself from side to side trying to sooth her frayed nerves.

Irritated by her progress to no apparent destination being impeded, Marilyn was curt, "Hey, white girl. The longest rope has an end. This is where you asked me to carry you and you're down there on the floor hiding. This is Baltimore City. Get off that floor and take a look around. I know you're here for drugs. I see the track marks on your arms. These are the people who can help you. It's on every street corner. You can't give me an address to take you to, so how about I carry you to Catholic Charities on Mulberry and Cathedral Street? You're smelling stink of dirty sweat in my car. You got to go. They'll give you a bath and place to sleep. And you'll find your fix right outside the shelter's front door, that's for sure."

"No, please, Marilyn," a terrified Cali pleaded as exhaust fumes wafted up through the floorboard fueling her urge to vomit. "Please, you can't leave me here all alone."

"I'll not stay here. I got me a home. I don't understand any of it, I tell you. I carry you in my car to Baltimore, like you asked. Here you can find your heroin and all the men to pay you money to buy it. You're mighty skinny, but every bread has its cheese. Some like them fat, some like them thin. There will be some men who will part with their monies to lie with you. What more can I do?" Marilyn asked.

Marilyn drove aimlessly through the poorly lit streets, eventually picking up enough speed to lose the bike riders. She wanted to get rid of Cali and go home to her soft bed.

"No." Cali was perspiring profusely, her body's craving for heroin full-blown. Her heart pounded in her chest and temples. "No, you have it all wrong. I'm not a prostitute. I'm not. You have to believe me, I am not a prostitute. I'm a virgin."

Her fury ignited, Marilyn abruptly slammed on the brakes smack dab in the middle of an intersection, ready to confront her on this lie. Marilyn knew full well, no girl with a heroin habit was not turning tricks.

Gratefully, the hour was late so there wasn't any traffic behind her to plow into the rear of her vehicle. Enough light from the overhead street lights shined into the car enabling Marilyn to see the girl's face flushed red with embarrassment, her eyes downcast. Dumfounded, Marilyn actually believed the girl was being honest.

"If you're not turning tricks, then how're you paying for your habit, huh?" Marilyn asked skeptically.

"I have a debit card. Hey, I have an idea," Cali spoke with desperation, "I know what we can do. Marilyn, please, I know it's a lot to ask, but can you take me home with you?"

"Whoa, whoa. I don't care if Saturday falls on a Sunday. Do I look like a charity worker? What's in it for me?" Marilyn was annoyed.

"It won't be charity. It's not charity if I pay you. And it won't be for long, I promise. Just a few days, that's all. I just need a few days to get myself straightened out, call my family, then I'll catch a plane back home to Georgia. My grandparents and I can figure it out when I get home. But this, coming to Maryland has all been a big mistake," Cali tried to steady her voice as she made her plea.

Cali tried so hard not to cry, but the hot tears made streaky trails through the dirt on her face. She felt like she wanted to die, right there in that monster of a car. She needed heroin. Her insides were twisted in a tight knot. A headache that felt more like a butcher knife penetrated both eyes. All at the same time, she felt both cold as ice and also as if her body was burning up. Fire ants marched along every nerve ending. She viciously scratched at her skin and scalp yet was never able to alleviate the itch.

"Pay how?" Marilyn demanded.

"The debit card. The same card I used to buy the gas for your car and the cigarettes. Actually, if you'll just consider it for a minute, that's the perfect solution. It's extra money for you. I won't be a bother. I could sleep on the floor, if you want. You'll see, you won't even know I'm there. Please, let's go right now. We can find an ATM machine and I'll withdraw some cash. I can pay you if you will, please, take me home with you," Cali pleaded.

"Debit card. Debit card. And what happens when the police arrest you for being a thief? And I go down as accessorizing? Your father's dead and your mother's not born yet. How long you think you can use a stolen card before you get caught? In the meantime, I done used up most of my gas. This whole damn night's been a waste of my time and gasoline," Marilyn shook her head in disgust as she spoke.

"The card's not stolen. My father gave it to me," Cali insisted. She hoped to find a bathroom soon fearing her insides were coming out. She felt lightheaded. She needed to lie down. She needed heroin.

"You're bazodee," Marilyn snorted.

"Bazodee? I'm sorry, I don't know that word."

"Bazodee, bazodee," Marilyn used her index finger to make circles near her ear. "Bazodee. Crazy. That is what you are. Let me tell you, my grandmother didn't raise a stupid child. What father gives his child a debit card? You're a pack of lies."

"I'm telling you the truth, Marilyn. My father did give the debit card to me, to use any way I choose. He has plenty of money. He's a commercial airline pilot. This card's mine. Trust me, it isn't stolen." Cali could see Marilyn's expression soften somewhat. Some of the anger faded from Marilyn's eyes so Cali persisted, "Let's go buy some more gas and I'll get enough money to pay you for giving me a place to stay for a few days. Please, take me home with you. Let's get out of here, okay? I'm begging you. I'll be gone in a day or two and you'll never even know I was there."

CHAPTER 5

Marilyn's trailer was the last one on the left side of a poorly paved stretch of asphalt inappropriately named, Cherry Tree Lane. Not a single tree, cherry or otherwise, grew in the dilapidated trailer park. Weeds that replaced actual grass mercifully offered a vision of green to the undiscerning eye. Better than a brown dustbowl. Marilyn's trailer was a long white rectangle that used stacks of cinder blocks to reach the front door's threshold. No flowers. No shutters. No lawn furniture. The door was secured with three different deadbolts, which seemed to take forever to unlock.

Nothing could have prepared Cali for what lay beyond the front door. Inside, Marilyn had painstakingly recreated a flavor of her West Indies homeland. After much haggling, Marilyn had scored a mustard-colored sofa in perfect condition from the local thrift store for twenty-five dollars. Above the sofa was a full size red, black, and white Trinidad flag, neatly tacked to a robin's egg blue wall, making it the first thing visible when entering her home.

In a corner, she had hung a fuchsia macramé chair swing, wide enough to seat two. The swing, like the sofa, was piled high with pillows in shades of lavender and yellow. One wall was whimsically decorated with a white fishing net. Starfish, conch shells, and a large stag horn coral were smartly displayed on the net. The windows were covered with brown, faux wood, Venetian blinds. The floor was actual hardwood, whitewashed to complete the beachy feel. A small rattan rug was positioned in front of the sofa.

Much to Marilyn's chagrin, Cali needed to use the bathroom. Pointing her toward the rear of the trailer, Marilyn watched with irritation as Cali ran for her bathroom. It was spotless and smelled freshly scrubbed with scouring powder. Beyond the closed door, Cali could hear Marilyn's threats not to mess up her house.

Like the living room, the bathroom was painted a lively color. Vibrant lime green. It was small but the space was wisely utilized. Storage cabinets secured Marilyn's endless stash of cosmetics. There were eye shadows galore, and one pack after another of false eyelashes, eyeliners, mascara. Lipsticks were neatly lined up in a rainbow of colors, ranging from bright tangerine to blue. Products promising a better life through perfect hair. Pink foam curlers. Irons to straighten, curl, or smooth hair depending upon a particular day's desire. Drawers were stuffed with various gems, glitter nail polishes, feminine wipes, and an abundance of brightly colored costume jewelry. Perfumes and scented fragrances to capture any mood neatly lined the vanity countertop.

From the other side of the door, Cali heard Marilyn calling, "Are you making my bathroom a mess?"

"No, ma'am." Cali answered. "I promise, I'll leave it exactly as I found it. Spotless."

"I see you scratching like a dog with mange, maybe full of chiggers and poison. You need a bath before you sit on my furniture. Stay in there. Scrub from head to toe. I'll leave towels and clean clothes outside the door. When you're done, put your things on floor next to the hamper. I don't want yours mixed with mine," Marilyn instructed.

Stripping down to her bra and panties, Cali was startled by her image in the full length mirror which hung on the interior of the bathroom door. For the first time in three months, she took a long, hard look at herself. She was shocked by what she saw. She was filthy and sweaty from her long trek through the woods. Her neck had two angry slashes across her skin where thorny brambles had caught and torn her flesh. Both knees were skinned raw from tripping over fallen branches and rocks randomly birthed by the earth. Red streaks of poison ivy blistered the ivory skin on her arms where she had inadvertently brushed the oil from their leaves. Red insect bites were scattered about from the swarms of hungry mosquitos that had savagely feasted on her skin as colonies of dormant insects were roused with each step she took on layers of fetid leaves. They had flown in her ears and up her nostrils. Her hair was wild, ripped from the ponytail. Bits of brittle twigs and leaves nestled in her hair like a wild bird's nest.

She was a mere shadow of herself. Just two days ago, Cali had blatantly lied when she told her MomMom she weighed one hundred and eight pounds, a healthy number for her five foot three stature. Cali was genuinely startled this morning when the nurse at the drug rehab confirmed her weight at a meager eighty-eight pounds. Every rib was visible. Her hip bones protruded. Her grandparents' sorrow would have been unbearable had they known she no longer had menstrual periods since she had lost all the fat cells that once stored estrogen.

For the first time, she realized not only had her strawberry blonde hair lost all its luster but it had also begun to fall out at an alarming rate. She was disheartened to be able to see her scalp in more than one spot. Her once bright emerald green eyes were sunken and dull. Her peaches and cream complexion was no more. It had been ages since she had gone with MomMom to get her nails done. Ugly chips of pink polish clung to jagged nails.

With great deliberation, Cali rotated her arms until her palms were facing the mirror. To her horror, she saw what her grandmother had seen two days ago. The memory filled her with an urgent sense of dread.

■ ■ ■

As was their nightly ritual, Cali and MomMom were in the kitchen cleaning up after dinner. Like most nights here of late, Cali had hardly eaten. It didn't go unnoticed by MomMom, Cali shuffling her food around on her plate, very little actually making it into her mouth. Although she had not yet had a conversation with her about it, MomMom suspected Cali had begun to wear baggy clothes, long pants, and long sleeve shirts in an attempt to hide her rapid weight loss.

Then, while rinsing the dishes, Cali inadvertently pushed one sleeve of her shirt above the elbow to keep it from getting wet. The entire length of her arm was covered in bruises in various stages of healing. Her skin was decorated in a variety of sickening shades of yellow, green, and purple. Small scabs scattered about an arm more suited to a small child than a sixteen year old adolescent.

Visibly alarmed, MomMom took Cali by the shoulders, turning her until they faced one another. Cali's back rested against the sink. Spellbound, MomMom slid the sleeve up on her other arm to reveal it too was bruised and battered. Tracing the swollen discolorations on both arms with her fingertips, MomMom had never felt so frightened.

Her eyes welled with tears as she whispered hoarsely, "What in the world has happened to you, Cali?"

Cali offered, "It's okay, MomMom. Really, it's nothing to be worried about. We had our annual blood drive at school last week. The nurse there wasn't very experienced and she said I was dehydrated. She had to stick me over and over again before she got any blood."

"*Didn't they feel you're too thin to donate? Back when Pop and I were young enough to give blood, The Red Cross had a minimum weight requirement. Cali, just look at you. Why are you so thin? I watch how you hardly eat anymore.*" MomMom searched Cali's eyes for a glint of deception.

Cali spoke with conviction, "*I'm healthy as a horse. I probably look thinner than I am. I'm one hundred and eight pounds. Really, MomMom, it's okay. It doesn't hurt. Please, don't worry about me. I'm fine.*"

Except she wasn't fine.

CHAPTER 6

Cali emerged from Marilyn's bathroom clean, her wet hair wrapped in a towel. She was grateful to be wearing Marilyn's Bob Marley T-shirt that fell to her knees. Immediately outside the bathroom, the door to the only bedroom was ajar. Cali quickly peeked in from the small hallway. Unlike the festive island vibe in the rest of the house, this room was subdued, painted a light gray. As was Marilyn's daily habit, the queen size bed was neatly made with a pretty, paisley print bedding. Marilyn never left her bed unmade, didn't understand people who did. No clothes were strewn about. An expensive looking, thick, hand woven, wool rug completed the room's warm and relaxing feel.

Cali walked past the bedroom to find Marilyn busy in her tidy kitchen. Every surface was wiped clean. She certainly was an ambassador for the motto, "A place for everything. Everything in its place."

"Your home is lovely. I especially like your flag. I apologize for assuming you were from Jamaica. Now I know you're from Trinidad. The colors represent each of the elements of fire, water, and earth," Cali said while standing in front of the sofa, admiring the flag.

Marilyn turned from the stove, where the enticing aroma of sautéing garlic, onion, tomatoes, and peppers originated. "How do you know?"

Cali noticed she had replaced her red stilettos with a comfy pair of pink terrycloth, Hello Kitty slippers. A white chef's apron protected her outfit from splatters.

"From school. We learned what various flags represent when we study about different nations in geography. That's a Trinidad flag," Cali stated as she pointed to the wall above the yellow sofa.

Marilyn's pride was captured in her voice, "What you say is true, but it goes deeper. Fire stands for courage. White's for purity. Black earth shows dedication. My home here is nice, yes. I work plenty hard for it. Most days, I work two jobs. It's plenty big enough for one. I don't believe in hanging my hat where my hand can't reach."

Two places had been set at the formica counter but Cali chose a seat on the sofa. Marilyn turned down the heat under her frying pan.

"You live far from the kitchen. A sack of bones, you are. I am Trini to the bone, so this here is island foods. Curry goat. Roti. Callaloo rice. Come and eat. It will make you healthy," Marilyn invited her guest to sit at the counter with her.

"I appreciate all you've done for me, Marilyn. Honestly I do, but I can't eat. I can pay you whatever you want but I have to go back to the city tonight. I need...my body needs. Marilyn, I'm sick," Cali confessed.

"It's coming. We stay put right here. I didn't want to do it, but I can't be driving all over, all night long. I got with this guy I knew ten years ago. While you were in the bath, we conversated and he's got what you want. I'm warning you now, you best have the monies because he's as mean as a rattlesnake. He won't take to skylarking. Thirty minutes he'll be here."

"Thank you," Cali replied.

"Don't be thanking me for helping you kill yourself," Marilyn didn't try to hide her displeasure.

Cali gingerly tucked her bare feet under herself as she unsuccessfully tried to ignore her body aches. The deep, visceral stomach pain, her jittery muscles, and the pounding in her chest rendered her help-less. She was at the peak of drug withdrawal and the symptoms were unbearable. Someone was coming in thirty minutes, she silently repeated her mantra. Someone was coming in thirty minutes.

Marilyn couldn't ever recall a time when she offered to give away a cigarette but Cali wasn't looking too right. Even for a white person, her color was alarmingly ghostlike. Like most island people, Marilyn was deathly afraid of spirits. She began to finger her snake ring.

"You want a cigarette? You can go outside the door to smoke," Marilyn offered.

"Thank you, but I don't smoke," Cali said as a sharp knifelike pain seared her insides. Cali's bowels violently twisted for what felt like the hundredth time that day. Looking at the clock on the wall over the stove, she silently reassured herself she could hang on for twenty-eight more minutes.

"Liquor does not cross my lips so I have none to offer," Marilyn declared.

"That's okay because I don't drink," Cali managed.

Until tonight, Cali had no idea how excruciatingly painful heroin withdrawal was. She was consumed with fear as her body revolted against her. Cali desperately craved the feeling of warm honey flowing through her veins that only heroin provided.

As a rule, Marilyn never ate late at night. The food settled in her dreams and on her thighs. For the time being, this girl disrupted any chances of sleep, so Marilyn made herself a plate. She had her meal at the kitchen counter just a few feet from Cali. The entire time she ate, her gaze was fixed fast on Cali.

"Skipped all that and went straight to heroin? I don't understand any of it," Marilyn declared. "My eye tells me you are new to this. Your teeth are white like sand on a beach, not rotten yet. You say you do not sell your body to men. That will change when the debit card runs out of monies."

"Marilyn, please. I'm sick so I'm not very good company right now," Cali begged.

"Are you better company with a needle in your arm?" Marilyn saw the immediate flush of embarrassment on Cali's face. "Your eyes will not make that clock move. We have only time. Plenty of time to talk. Tell me about this debit card of yours."

Twenty-two minutes to go, every minute seeming to last an hour. A cold sweat formed on Cali's forehead. Her insides were on fire, while her limbs were filled with frigid ice.

"My father gave it to me," Cali told her hostess.

"I see. A father gives a debit card to a girl. Why, I ask? That girl uses the debit card monies to poison her body with heroin. Did you run from your home to escape your father's hands? Then you say you not know man. New broom sweeps a room clean but old brooms know all the corners," Marilyn thought aloud, unwilling to ignore the discrepancies in the teen's story. "No. No, you have it all wrong. My father would never, ever lay a hand on me. I don't even live with my parents. Ever since I was born, I've always lived with my Pop and MomMom," Cali defended herself.

"Your parents did not want children?" Marilyn questioned while picking at her meal.

"Not exactly. I have an older sister and brother. My brother's away at college. Abigail still lives at home with Maggie and Robert," Cali said, trying her best to ignore the cramping in her gut.

"Who are all these people you call by name? Abigail, Maggie, Robert?" Marilyn asked for clarification.

"Abigail's my older sister. Maggie and Robert are my parents," Cali answered, her eyes on the clock. Nineteen minutes.

"It is just you they not keep?" Marilyn asked. "Why?"

Cali recalled the conversation she had with Robert after her knee surgery before giving Marilyn the abbreviated version.

■ ■ ■

Robert felt a pang of shame for having never shared her story with her before. "You know, you're named after Pop. Cali's a female, abbreviated version of Calhoun, which goes back for generations in our family. Anyway, after you were born, you and your mother both came home from the hospital. It was probably no more than two days when your mother suddenly started hemorrhaging. We rushed her back to the hospital for an emergency hysterectomy. She had lost so much blood and they couldn't get her fever under control. It was touch and go for a couple of weeks there. Your brother and sister were older and pretty easy to take care of. But you were just a little tiny baby. Remember, you were five weeks premature. You were so little. I didn't know how to take care of you and your mother was so sick. So, your grandparents took you home with them."

The air in the room shifted, making it a little more difficult to breathe. Robert's face looked as though he had just confessed to the worst crime possible. Acknowledgment that he and his wife had forfeited raising their youngest child from the time she was a newborn. Robert's parents took Cali home with them and he and Maggie were satisfied to leave her there.

■ ■ ■

Cali explained to Marilyn, "Maggie got sick after giving birth to me so my grandparents took me home with them. Ever since I was born, I've always lived with my MomMom and Pop."

Realizing their conversation seemed to return a little color to the girl's face, Marilyn continued her questioning, "So, why does a father give a debit card to his child?"

Inhaling deeply, Cali began, "In March, my grandparents were away on a cruise to celebrate their sixtieth wedding anniversary. Because I'm in high school, I wasn't allowed to stay in the house by myself. I had to go to Maggie and Robert's house for the entire month. That very first day, I wound up injuring my knee playing soccer and had to have surgery." Hiking up the Bob Marley T-shirt, Cali revealed the scar on her right knee.

Cali seemed to run out of steam, however Marilyn encouraged her to continue, "Still time to pass."

With twelve more minutes to endure, Cali picked up where she left off, "A couple of days after my surgery, he gave me the debit card. I told him I didn't need it because I have a job waitressing on the weekends, but he insisted I take it. Honestly, I have no idea why he gave it to me. Marilyn, you have to believe me, he gave it to me. I didn't steal it."

Having finished her dinner, Marilyn began to clean up her kitchen while intently listening to Cali's every word. Her hand on the refrigerator's door handle, she paused to ask, "Does your father know his monies pay for your drugs?"

True to his word, in half an hour, an irritated pounding on the front door announced the guy's arrival. He beat the door with his fist as though he was trying to scare someone out of hiding rather than someone who had been invited to the premises. Startled, Marilyn peeked through the Venetian blinds before unlocking the three deadbolts, finally allowing entry to a hard looking man, appropriately described as mean. However, Cali quickly realized, Marilyn omitted other defining characteristics, such as ugly with skittish rodent eyes. Shuddering, Cali was acutely aware of the dangerous air about him.

Introduced informally as Skeeter, the five foot seven man had the kind of sallow complexion that proclaimed he had never eaten a fresh vegetable or fruit in his entire life. This was an individual who survived on a consistent diet of potato chips, fast food, and soda. His dietary practices took root long ago as a malnourished child whose mother's idea of dinner was either fish sticks covered in an effortless homemade sauce of mayonnaise and ketchup or boxed macaroni and cheese, the cheese originating from an orange powder in a packet. He had the resemblance of a scarecrow. Hollowed out cheeks. Sharp, pointy features. Dark, black eyes that didn't miss a trick.

His straw colored hair shaved into a jailhouse stubble, Skeeter looked like a criminal years before he ever had his residence, O'Donnell Heights, inked across his scrawny chest. So many tattoos on a guy who looked like he barely had enough money to eat. Wasted dollar bills decorated unhealthy looking skin with intimidating images. He not only looked dirty, he smelled dirty. Cali was very certain, Marilyn wouldn't pressure him into bathing before taking a seat on her furniture though.

"You got my money?" He revealed a mouthful of neglected teeth. Unable to stand still, Skeeter rocked from one foot to the other. He was a jittery, raw nerve. His very presence emitted a sense of wrongdoing.

"Yes," Cali whispered, pulling a neatly folded, Hello Kitty, fleece blanket from the back of the sofa, wrapping herself up tight.

Marilyn's reaction was quick, immediately removing the pink blanket from Cali's shoulders, with, "Uh-uh, not that one," before replacing it with an eggplant colored throw. Marilyn slid past the agitated man and safely tucked her Hello Kitty blanket in her bedroom, taking care to shut the door before returning to the living room.

"This here's grade A, quality heroin. On the street, they grind up drywall, rat poison, even. Just about any shit they can get their hands on and mix it with a little of the H. Take a little and make a lot. Make a bigger profit that way. Lately, it's all laced with fentanyl, too. I ain't tellin' you nothin' you don't know. People are dyin' by the truckloads. I ain't gonna do you no wrong. But you pay for what you get, understand me?" The muscles in Skeeter's jaw balled into a tight knot.

Wide-eyed, Cali nodded. Her friend Blake had never said anything about rat poison or people dying by the truckloads. At that moment, her body in excruciating pain, she felt she had no choice but to trust the most untrustworthy person she had ever laid eyes on.

"And I figure it's only right I get a inconvenience fee. I was enjoyin' a quiet evenin' in my den," he spat the words at her. "I gotta make it worth my while, drivin' all the way over here, ain't that right? It's twenty-five a capsule, but that gets you a clean needle, too."

Marilyn was unable to disguise her shock, but when she met Skeeter's cold eyes, she knew better than to utter a word. A single capsule of heroin normally went for ten dollars on every street corner in Baltimore, yet Skeeter was demanding more than double that price. Wholeheartedly, Marilyn regretted telling him about taking the girl to the ATM machine. With his price gouging, he ran the risk of ruining her golden opportunity to make a few dollars in rent.

Without a second thought, Cali reached into her bra, timidly handing the skittish man twenty-five dollars, but not before he promised to return tomorrow.

CHAPTER 7

He was just a little kid when Peaches learned him the art of distraction. His mother would take him into a store where she'd cause a big scene by arguin' with an unsuspectin' store clerk or another customer. When everybody was distracted by all the commotion, Skeeter's job was to lift a wallet from a purse left unattended in a shopping cart or grab a carton of cigarettes, preferably his old lady's favorite brand, from behind the counter. From an early age, Skeeter learned how to stuff high dollar items down the front of his pants they could later sell on the street, such as razor blades or cosmetics. Peaches was such a world class actress, she had people bendin' over backwards, apologizin' to her for doin' nothin' wrong.

While other kids were practicin' their times tables, Peaches was learnin' him how to jimmy a lock. Breakin' and enterin', snatchin' pocketbooks from old ladies on the first of the month, shit like that. Only once did he try carjackin'. It never occurred to Skeeter there might be a kid in the backseat, strapped in some carseat like he was headin' into outer space. That crazy woman slashed him across his chest with some pointy metal somethin' or another before she nearly blinded him with half a can of pepper spray. That chick was bat-shit crazy for her kid.

Hell, in the same situation, his mother woulda gladly gave the carjacker the keys to her car, told him to go ahead and take the kid too so she could of collected on the insurance.

Sadly, Skeeter wasn't far off from the truth. His mother, Joyce Melton, AKA Peaches, had tried to abort the fetus, but like everythin' else in her life, it was too much trouble to go to the clinic for a pregnancy test. So by the time she finally made her way to the doctor's, motivated only by the loss of her curves, her pregnancy was too far along to terminate it. The whole time he was growin' up, Skeeter had often heard his old lady sum up her thoughts on motherhood by describin' the experience as nothing more than, " changin' a bunch of shitty diapers."

She was the reason Skeeter was sent away to juvenile detention in the first place. What kinda mother has her son beat the livin' crap out of the wife of a man she was prostitutin' with? Peaches, that's who. At the urgin' of his mother, Skeeter launched a particularly brutal attack on the short, bullish looking wife with deep frown lines etched into her face. The attack was in retaliation for the wife previously whoopin' her ass. All over a man.

Peaches regularly supplemented her tips as a barmaid at The Piney Tavern by turnin' tricks in the ladies' room. It all came to a screechin' halt the day the longshoreman passed along the clap to his wife. Showin' up at the tavern a few hours after the doctor informed her why it hurt so bad to pee, the wife beat Peaches to a bloody pulp. Since much of the brawl took place behind the bar, several hundred dollars worth of liquid inventory was destroyed. In exchange for keepin' her job, Peaches agreed to pay restitution.

Although the beatin' made the wife feel some kind of vindication, Peaches ain't never learned her lesson. She continued to turn tricks. She also made the decision to send her son to pay the longshoreman's wife a little visit. Several days later, Skeeter met up with the wife while she was hauling the trash cans to the alley before turning in for the night.

Them psychotherapists back in juvie were quick to call him names like sociopath, maladjusted, antisocial personality disorder. The doctors said he consistently displayed self-serving behaviors. He lacked empathy and was incapable of remorse, they said. He perfected the art of manipulation, ignoring the concerns of everyone else. Aggressive. Arrogant. Willing to engage in behaviors that were harmful to others. Will stop at nothin' to get what he wanted.

Yeah well, they ain't never met Peaches. If they had to live with her, day in and day out, they'd lack empathy too. Truth was, Skeeter doubted anybody really had a conscience if nobody was watchin'. In his opinion, conscience was all a big put on. Ain't nobody out there who won't do whatever it takes to look out for number one.

Hands down, his favorite word them psychiatrists used to describe him was a misogynist. He usually wasn't much for big words, but he liked the sound of that one. So, he learned it. Misogynist. A woman hater. Hell, yeah, he was a woman hater. Peaches made sure of that.

He could tolerate women for certain things, but they had to be set straight right from the get go. They had to earn their keep. Like cookin' a meal that didn't come out of a cardboard box. Naturally, Skeeter wanted a woman in his bed to service his manhood. Any broad he wound up with better know how to clean house and wash clothes. But that pretty much was the extent of their value. Otherwise, women were way more trouble than they were worth.

Not only was it a woman who sent him on over there to teach a lesson to that little pit bull broad married to a loser longshoreman, but that same woman ain't bat an eye when they hauled her only son off to jail. When they shuffled Skeeter into the courtroom, his wrists shackled to a chain around his waist, he walked right past Peaches perched up in the gallery. Had no idea that was his mother. A woman who usually wore very little clothing, at least two sizes too small, was dressed up like a Catholic school nun. One thing was for sure, she musta gone down the Goodwill and found that getup. Skirt hem down below her knees and a blouse buttoned clear up to her chin. She barely had on any makeup, neither. What happened to all the hairspray, blue eyeshadow, and bright pink lipstick?

When it was her turn to testify, his old lady sat up in that witness box and blubbered all about being a single mother devoted to a difficult child. The old phony used up a whole box of tissues, tellin' about how she was a saint, who had no idea the dude she was doin' on a regular basis in the ladies room at The Piney Tavern was married, much less that her sixteen year old son was goin' to retaliate against his wife. Lyin' bitch.

That lecherous old judge swallowed her performance up, hook, line and sinker. His keen eye could tell beneath all that clothin', Peaches was a hot little number. Way back then, she kept herself nice, not like the pig she eventually turned into.

More than once, the judge told his liar mother to, "Take your time, Ms. Melton. This is my courtroom and I have all day."

His court appointed lawyer only made the mistake of askin' Skeeter to sit up straight at the defense table once. Skeeter shot him a look of pure hatred that resulted in the lawyer scootin' his chair as far away from his client as possible. Skeeter's anger took form in his knee, workin' up and down like a piston in an engine. Slumped down at the massive defense table, head bent over, he peered out in distrust at a strange world he didn't fully understand. Skeeter's blood was boilin' good by the time the judge threw the book at him. He was committed to the Maryland State Department of Corrections, Juvenile Division until his eighteenth birthday.

Course, he ain't helped hisself none when he sprung on up to his feet and started yellin' about how his mother was lyin' through her teeth. He couldn't help hisself, though. A few minutes before, the judge actually stopped everything while the bailiff brung her a glass of water. A glass of water, like she was in some damn restaurant or somethin'. That was it, the final straw. Skeeter was like a mad man, screamin' and cursin'. He was deranged, foamin' at the mouth.

Hauled off to kiddie jail for two years for a crime his old lady put him up to, and ain't once did his heartless mother show up for visitation. Two years was a long time for a mother not to visit her only child. Payback's a bitch. One day, he vowed, she'd get hers.

That's how he done got hooked up with KT. Ain't nobody gave a shit about her, neither. The whole time she was locked up, nobody came to visit. Even after they both got their walkin' papers, Skeeter always figured they'd reconnect one day. He was right. It took ten years, but tonight was the night when KT's voice was on the other end of his phone. KT done got herself a new name, callin' herself Marilyn. She said she was makin' a little pocket change, lettin' some chick named Cali sleep on her couch. Cali was lookin' for smack.

CHAPTER 8

Marilyn had no emotional ties to the stranger sitting on her couch, yet she didn't want to bear witness to her self-destruction. It was one thing to know what Cali was doing, but actually watching it was something else altogether. Leading Skeeter outside, Marilyn was mindful to pull the door shut behind them to keep the cool air inside. She decided she'd give Cali the same amount of time it would take her to smoke a Berlin Menthol, then she was going to bed. Although Cali had bought a pack of Salem Light for her a few hours ago, she knew better than to smoke them in front of Skeeter. She had no doubt, he would bum at least one cigarette off of her. No way was he getting the name brand.

The sun was long gone. Marilyn looked up at the sky as she blew cigarette smoke through her nostrils. Any stars in the sky were concealed behind the thick, Maryland humidity that settled in her hair, made her clothes cling to her sticky and damp. To add to Marilyn's misery, a stealthy mosquito landed on her shoulder sucking the blood until a welt bubbled under her skin. This was going to be one fast cigarette or else I'll surely be eaten alive by the bugs, she thought.

When Skeeter spoke, his black eyes shone, "You look a little different from the last time I seen you." When Marilyn didn't reply he asked, "So, how'd you find her?"

"She found me. I stopped for gasoline and she asked me to carry her to Baltimore," Marilyn explained, eager to return to the air conditioning. She scratched at the bug bite on her shoulder wondering if she had any rubbing alcohol or calamine lotion to take the itch out.

Skeeter had been paying very close attention to the girl's every move. Every word that came from hers or Marilyn's lips, he committed to memory. He was a hoarder of minute details. Ever since he was a little kid, he had a habit of squirrelin' away tidbits of useless information because you never knew when stuff like that might come in handy. He had perfected the art of devisin' a way to use those little facts to his advantage.

"You said she's payin' a few notes to sleep on your couch, ain't that right?" Skeeter inquired as he grabbed the pack of cigarettes from Marilyn's hand, helping himself.

Marilyn didn't dare stop him. During the two years they were incarcerated together, Marilyn had seen firsthand his uncontrollable fits of brutality without the slightest hint of remorse. Many nights, she'd lain awake in her bed, recalling the utter bewilderment on the boy's face in the seconds before Skeeter pushed him down the flight of steps. So much blood gushing forth from his disfigured nose when he splayed limp across the landing far below.

He sucked on the cigarette as though he was taking his last breath. Marilyn looked away, refusing to let the conversation go down that road. She knew better than to discuss money with him.

Regretting her decision to initiate contact with Skeeter after all these years, Marilyn held out hope the next puff of her cigarette would calm her jittery nerves. She'd worked hard to create a personal life of total privacy, building an impenetrable fortress around herself, the mortar consisting of equal parts distrust and fear. Yet it was by her very own invitation that Skeeter was led to her door. She had no one else to blame for failing to protect her tender self.

"So, let me get this here situation straight. You hooked up with her at a gas station, ain't that right? But my question is, where'd she come from?" Skeeter wouldn't let it rest.

"She says her grandparents carried her to a drug rehab this morning. She made the decision to leave. From the looks of her, she traveled through bush and trees. She can stay with me for a few days. The matter's fixed. That is all there is to say," Marilyn filled him in before abruptly declaring, "I need to find sleep."

Bending over, Marilyn ground out her cigarette before climbing the cinderblocks to her front door.

"Yeah, sure. Hey, one more thing. Where was this gas station at?" Skeeter persisted.

Her hand on the doorknob, Marilyn hesitated opening the door just long enough to give him his answer, "Havre de Grace."

Skeeter jumped in his car with a renewed purpose. He was going home to look up drug rehab centers in Havre de Grace. Gather a little intel. He hoped that ancient piece of crap computer somebody sold secondhand to Ol' Peaches years ago would be cooperatin' tonight.

Hunkered down in front of the computer with a bag of cookies and a can of warm grape soda, he was able to find only one drug rehabilitation facility located in Havre de Grace. New Light Treatment and Recovery. He leaned in closer to the screen, carefully studying their website, liking what he saw. He especially enjoyed the pictures.

New Light Center's physical layout was designed after a typical college dormitory. Women, housed two to a room on one side of the building, men on the other. A private bath was attached to every room. Purposefully, there were no televisions in the entire facility. There was much personal growth to be done and it was believed television posed an unnecessary distraction.

Skeeter was astounded. No TVs nowhere. Now ain't that a load of crap. Whoever heard of such a thing? What the hell did they do all day if there ain't no TVs to pass the time? He ain't never heard of nobody who didn't watch TV on a regular basis.

Shit, he wished he ain't have to share a bathroom with Peaches. Half the time, she only bothered to flush the toilet when she took a dump. Just once, it'd be nice not to have to stare into a sink fulla her globs of dried up spit and toothpaste clingin' to the porcelain. Like it'd break her damn arm to turn on the water and rinse her slobber down the drain.

Sleeping quarters were strategically separated by a centrally located reception area. It was strictly forbidden for members of the opposite sex to ever venture past the large common area into the opposite side of the building. Physical intimacy among the patients was not tolerated. Depending upon the infraction, expulsion from the program without reimbursement of fees was a possibility.

The word, fees, piqued Skeeter's interest. Now we're gettin' somewhere. He could care less about the rest of this crap. Bottom line, he wanted to know how much it all cost.

Three smaller buildings located on the ten acres were used throughout the day for various classes and meetings. Every patient received an individualized plan of care addressing his particular needs. Cookie cutter treatment plans were historically found to be ineffective, thereby not utilized by New Light however, some form of exercise was strongly encouraged. A fully stocked gym containing free weights, stationary bikes, and treadmills was accessible all hours of the day and night.

What a waste, he thought. Probably the same genius who came up with the no TVs idea came up with this one. Ain't none of them crack heads locked up in this place were wastin' time workin' out. They should give them weights to somebody who'd put them to good use. Like him, for instance. He'd gladly take them weights off their hands for hisself if he had the chance.

The combination of soda and cookies caused Skeeter's stomach to loudly protest. Realizing he was hungry, he got up long enough to look for something to eat. Course there ain't nothin' in the fridge 'cause old lard ass Peaches ain't never cooks nothin' he thought angrily. Opening a can of spaghetti and marinara sauce from the dollar store, he heated it in the microwave before returning to the computer screen, fork and bowl in hand.

Skeeter found himself deeply annoyed by the section which discussed forms of alternative medicine. Devoted to a holistic approach to wellness, the staff explored countless modalities for recovery. Nutritious meals were prepared by a chef. Massage therapy as well as yoga and meditation were daily activities.

They did yoga there. And got massages. This place ain't no rehab, he thought. Where were the pictures of people curled up in a ball on the floor, pukin' up green bile, ready to sell off a kidney for their drugs? This New Light place was nothin' like any drug rehab he'd ever heard about.

Practitioners were discouraged from prescribing drugs to reduce the harrowing symptoms of withdrawal. It was the center's core belief, addiction to methadone was as damning as addiction to illicit drugs. Replacing one drug dependency with another was not an option. The goal was drug free. Complete liberation from all substances.

Wiping his mouth on the back of his hand, Skeeter let out a rank smelling, explosive burp before taking his fork to scratch at a zit in the center of his back while continuing to read.Hot damn, now that's one swanky joint! They had chefs and massages. A medical clinic right there on the property. Hastily scrolling through the computer screen, Skeeter looked for the most vital information of all. How much did a place like that cost? Naturally, they ain't put that on the website but he figured it had to cost at least twenty, maybe even thirty grand. Imagine that, thirty thousand bucks for three lousy months in a joint that ain't even givin' you a TV. He was grinning from ear to ear as he continued to read.

New Light had a dedicated staff with impressive credentials because they were well compensated for their long hours and hard work.

"Yeah, like I done already asked, how much does it cost?" he practically growled at the computer but of course the fees were not readily available. Well compensated. Ain't that just a fancy way of sayin' they make a shitload of money?

The website said a nominal amount, if any, was covered by the majority of medical insurances. Payment in full was expected during the intake process. Papers were signed stating both parties agreed that absolutely no portion of the fees was refunded if a patient refused to complete the program.

Every member of the staff was driven by a single goal. Giving people their lives back. Short term achievements were deemed failures. Long term sobriety was their benchmark for success. Well, la-di-da. With a heart full of pure spite he thought, I guess this Cali girl who done run away ain't met your benchmark for success, ain't that right? At least thirty thousand bucks down the drain.

Shutting the computer down, Skeeter climbed in bed, images of dollar bills paving the way to his dreams.

CHAPTER 9

Yesterday, from the moment Cali opened the door to her home, she knew something was amiss. Somehow, the air in the house felt different. An unfamiliar energy signaled something was out of order the same way victims report sensing their attacker moments before the actual assault. She checked her watch, noting it was fifteen minutes before her ten o'clock, school night curfew. Dropping her backpack in the foyer, she darted into the living room, eager to make sure her grandparents were okay.

The man cleared his throat before rising from his chair to introduce himself as a family interventionist. The word interventionist attached itself to Cali's viscera like a leach making her feel naked, exposed. He was there on her behalf. Because of her. Crimson colored heat quickly rose in her face, neck, and ears. Acutely aware everyone in the room was staring at her, Cali's first instinct was to run and hide. She was having a fight or flight reaction. But her muscles betrayed her rendering her unable to move. She stood alone on display, paralyzed, wondering how long before her legs would buckle under her weight.

MomMom's whisper became her life preserver, "Cali, come here, please. Come up here and sit with us."

Barely turning her head, out of her peripheral vision, she saw her grandparents shift apart on the sofa to create a safe haven for her. In one swift motion, Cali burrowed between them, flanked on either side by the two people she most adored.

The elderly couple fought for composure as they felt her body quiver involuntarily. Her tiny body pressed between theirs, her skeletal frame hidden beneath layered clothing was unmistakable. She was literally skin and bones. Her grandparents stole a glance at one another over the top of Cali's head. No words were necessary. Their eyes said it all - Pop and MomMom were terrified. Mournfully, Pop was dumfounded at how quickly their beautiful granddaughter had become a mere shadow of herself. In that moment, a wave of fear that they might actually lose her washed over him.

"I'd like to start by saying your family invited me here this evening because they're genuinely concerned about your health and well-being. In no way does anyone in this room intend to embarrass or falsely accuse you. There's absolutely no one here tonight who doesn't have only your best interests at heart. The people who love you are looking for a way to facilitate honest conversation in an effort to help you. You should know, when speaking to me, they used the phrase, grave danger, more than once when referring to your situation." He took his time before adding, "The reason we're all here this evening is because we're hoping you'll enlighten us as to what's going on in your life."

Cali stared at this stranger with raw fear. He knew. Subconsciously creating a protective shield, she wrapped her arms around herself. Kicking off her shoes, she brought her knees to her chest.

Clearing his throat, he started anew, "I was given written permission by your family to access your school records because those records actually contain much more information than mere grades."

He took a seat on an ottoman just a few feet from Cali and her grandparents. Opening the black binder, he leafed through the pages as he spoke, "From them, I was able to ascertain a stellar academic career. Impressive GPA. National Honor Society. Your ability to excel in several advanced placement classes reinforces the fact you're a serious student, not just someone cruising through. Looking through all these notes from your academic advisor, I know you have a very focused goal for law school, in particular Stanford, University of Chicago, or Duke. You participate in after school activities. In fact, I see you were instrumental in forming a mock trial club at your school. Your soccer career mirrors your academic career. Also impressive. Several college scouts have had you on their radar for some time now."

He looked straight into Cali's emerald green eyes and stated matter-of-factly, "It all changed about three months ago. To say the changes have been drastic would be an understatement. Just looking at the grades and various annotations from teachers and school administrators, one would think we were discussing two separate students. Is there some insight as to what's going on with you that you'd be willing to share with your family tonight?"

Unbeknownst to Cali, the interventionist was actually holding his breath. Regardless of the adage, strength in numbers, it was this frail teen who had ultimate control over this entire situation. At any moment, she was free to physically get up and leave, thereby putting an end to the intervention.

Although she had yet to speak, he was very pleased she remained seated. He patiently allowed a tense, full six minutes without any input from Cali. The silence in the room was deafening.

Opening the floor to discussion, he finally turned to Cali's parents, Maggie and Robert. "Are there any concerns you'd like to voice?"

Not wasting time on pleasantries, Maggie jumped in with both feet, "Did you take my spoons from my house when you were staying with us? And your grandmothers?"

"Yes, ma'am," Cali answered, truthfully.

The annoyance was written all over Maggie's face as she stated, "I find that absolutely ridiculous. And would you mind giving me a list of everything else that's missing so I don't drive myself completely crazy trying to inventory our possessions?"

"You won't find anything else missing. I apologize for taking the spoons," Cali spoke with sincerity.

"Am I to believe our jewelry and other valuables were not also taken? Our money? It was spoons you were after, is that right?" Every syllable Maggie spoke was filled with accusations.

"Yes, ma'am. That's the truth," Cali answered.

"Oh, the truth? I see. Am I to assume that you collect spoons? Are you seriously going to sit there and tell us you felt compelled to break into our home and take spoons? I find that hard to believe, young lady. And while we're on the subject, exactly how did you break in? I've had the security company out more than once to check all the windows and doors, but they can't find how you did it. I remain baffled." Maggie seethed, her posture ram-rod straight.

Cali shook her head and said something that Maggie couldn't hear.

"Could you repeat yourself, please? I didn't hear a word you mumbled," Maggie reproached Cali.

"Yes, ma'am," Cali increased her volume. "I said, I didn't break into your house. I have a key."

Maggie's eyebrows shot up and her eyes widened into saucers as her voice shot up an octave, "You have a key? Since when do you have a key to my house?"

Robert interjected, "I gave Cali the key a couple of days after her surgery. She was staying with us for an entire month and she needed a key. I told her to keep it, just in case."

Maggie was incredulous, but made the conscious decision to bite her tongue.

In that brief exchange, the interventionist gained a wealth of knowledge he quickly parlayed into his next series of questions, "Cali had surgery?"

"Yes, sir. She had quite the knee injury playing soccer. That was back in March when my wife and I were away for our wedding anniversary," Pop offered in his slow southern drawl. "Cali had to wear a knee brace up until fairly recently."

Flipping thought the binder, the interventionist began to put the pieces of the puzzle together. "March correlates to the drastic change in Cali's school performance. I assume she was prescribed pain killers after the surgery?"

Robert answered this one, "Yes. Oxycodone and oxycontin."

"Now, we're getting somewhere," the interventionist declared. "These are powerful narcotics. Oxycodone and oxycontin are synthetic opioids, meaning they're manufactured in a laboratory, rather than made from naturally occurring agents. The fact they're synthetic makes them highly addictive. For some individuals, addiction can take place in a shockingly short period of time, only days or weeks. The latest research suggests a hereditary component meaning parents who abuse alcohol or nicotine may have children who are more prone to addiction. The other thing I want to point out is, females typically begin using substances at smaller doses but can escalate into addiction much more rapidly than their male counterparts."

The therapist took his time laying out the groundwork, "Let's just say for the sake of argument, shall we, that Cali's body began to crave the narcotics pretty quickly. Several days or even a week or two. The narcotics interfere with production of two naturally occurring hormones in the brain that activate the pleasure response. A deficiency in these hormones is linked to depression and anxiety. People develop a physical dependency on opioids because the body eventually gets to the point where the drugs are the only triggers for the brain to release the pleasure hormones."

"But her surgery was three months ago," MomMom offered.

The therapist didn't consider himself a gambling man, but things were progressing well enough for him to take a chance. "Cali, this might be a good place for you to explain why you took the spoons."

The room fell silent as all eyes were on Cali. When she refused to take the bait, the interventionist finally provided the answer for her, "It's been my experience, spoons are used to cook heroin."

Just like that the word, heroin, buried them alive like a truck load of wet cement. The word, heroin, rung in their ears. They all focused on breathing, maintaining a heartbeat, staying alive. The ugly beast was let loose. It wormed its way into everyone's realization.

Up until that very moment, Cali's family had naively hoped all their fears were for naught. There was certainly some other plausible explanation for expected adolescent transgressions. Heroin? That had never once crossed their minds. Heroin. There it was, big as day.

Pop's hands were visibly shaking as he clumsily removed his glasses, nearly breaking off an earpiece. He set them on the arm of the sofa before closing his eyes and rubbing the bridge of his nose. Hot tears spread across his lashes. Leaning to one side, he reached into the back pocket of his trousers pulling loose an ironed white handkerchief. Wiping one eye, then the other, he struggled for composure.

For the first time in his life, Robert watched his father cry. Pop tried to conceal the steady stream of tears which spilled down his exhausted face. A face suddenly so old. Robert knew at that moment, he would soon bury both his parents if something wasn't done to save their Cali Girl.

The interventionist had been speaking for some time before Pop became aware of his voice, "That's where inpatient drug rehabilitation centers become absolutely necessary. I'm a firm believer in a minimum forty-two day stay. Not only does the drug need to be cleared from the system, but the brain has to be given an opportunity to begin production and regulation of those hormones I mentioned. Shorter therapies have staggering relapse statistics. Keep in mind, if Cali expresses a desire to stop taking illicit drugs, it would certainly be favorable to her outcome. She would benefit from a program that also focuses on social and behavioral modification. With time and distance, we also have the opportunity to disband the relationships where she's been able to obtain these illicit drugs."

MomMom asked for clarification, "Forty-two days? What about school? Do they have tutors there?"

He welcomed the questions. "I think we've all seen, school hasn't been much of a priority for Cali since her drug usage began. Rather than continuing the destruction of her academic career, my advise would be to put it on hold for now and have her return to her school work with a renewed desire for education after she successfully completes a drug rehab program. That being said, I'd suggest being open to the possibility of repeating a grade. To answer your question, Mrs. Hasting, no, there will not be any tutors. My recommendation is to send Cali to a facility in Havre de Grace, Maryland. New Light Treatment and Recovery. It's rather expensive, but I think you have the resources. It's well worth the investment."

He paused to let them digest the words.

"Maryland!" Cali blurted out, her gaze quickly swinging from the interventionist to her grandparents. "Pop, please, don't make me go to Maryland. Why can't I go to rehab in Georgia?"

Pop blew his nose in his handkerchief before speaking, his voice cracked, barely audible, "Forgive me, I have to agree, sir. That seems like a mighty far distance. Georgia's a big state. What kind of rehabilitation facilities are here?"

"Georgia does offer quite a number of rehab facilities. But the ultimate goal here is to achieve success the first time. The National Institute of Health reports a forty to sixty percent relapse rate within five years post treatment. Across the board." The interventionist noted the look of surprise on everyone's face before telling them, "Overall, the statistics are pretty dismal, but this particular facility in Maryland has one of the most impressive records in the country. They have an eighty percent success rate five years post completion. The state of Maryland is leaps and bounds ahead of the rest of us. Their governor just declared the 2017 State of Emergency regarding opioids, heroin, and fentanyl deaths. For all the reasons I've already mentioned, I strongly endorse New Light Treatment and Recovery for Cali."

"Please, Pop. Can't I get treatment in Georgia, please? Maryland is, well, it may as well be on the other side of the world. I want to stop, so I know I'll have success. He said Georgia has treatment centers right here," Cali urgently tried to persuade her grandfather.

Not to be deterred, the therapist pushed his conviction, "The truth is, there isn't a lot of time to make your decision. Once again, the numbers speak for themselves. One hundred and seventy-five Americans die every day from opioid overdoses. The drugs are being mixed without the user's knowledge. Heroin, in particular, is being laced with a deadly drug called fentanyl. You're educated people. I know you've read about the heroin epidemic and the staggering numbers of deaths from fentanyl. The longer we wait to get Cali into a reputable treatment program, the higher her risk of becoming one of those statistics. I'm urging you to act quickly. If you like, I can arrange her admission as early as tomorrow."

Pop cleared his throat before beginning, "Now, Cali, honey, we have to get you far away from these scoundrels who've been selling that dope to you." Pausing momentarily to put his glasses on, his words grew more confident, "Your MomMom and I have entrusted an expert in this field with finding the best possible solution. It's his belief this New Light Facility in Maryland has a mighty fine reputation. After listening to what he's presented here tonight, I also believe they will offer you your best shot at getting off the drugs."

Addressing the interventionist, Pop stated, "Sir, tomorrow sounds fine."

CHAPTER 10

Thankfully, Marilyn had the entire following day off. Thursdays were her scheduled day off at the boutique and for the first time in months, she didn't have a nightclub engagement. It was well past three in the morning by the time Skeeter left and the girls finally fell into an exhausted slumber. The sun was already high in the sky when they awoke. After preparing breakfast, which she didn't touch, Cali went outside to get some air and attempt to clean up Marilyn's yard.

Standing at the top of Marilyn's makeshift cinderblock porch, Cali surveyed her surroundings. The thing that struck her about Marilyn's place was the absence of birds. Unlike MomMom's gardens at home which were teaming with a variety of birds from hummingbirds to woodpeckers and everything in between, Marilyn's tiny yard didn't attract a single feathered friend.

In contrast to the inside, the outside of Marilyn's home was a mess. Cali really appreciated everything Marilyn was doing for her so she wanted to do something nice for her in return for her hospitality. To show her appreciation, Cali set her sights on tidying up the yard. In spite of feeling sick, she welcomed the solitude and the way the work made her feel connected to her grandmother. She tried her best to ignore the waves of nausea and her aching muscles as she pulled the ankle high dandelions. Tugging at the climbing poison ivy that snaked around the back of Marilyn's trailer, Cali felt the cold sweat forming on her skin, signaling her body's desire for heroin. Knowing she'd be lost in a haze for hours, Cali was trying her best to finish the task at hand before using the drug. She kept working, sparing the wild honey-suckle, clover, and chickweeds, preferring them over a yard of brown dirt since there wasn't any actual grass to speak of. Cali decided some weeds were better than a barren yard. She filled a total of six plastic grocery store bags with the foliage before setting them in a straight line next to the mailbox.

The last thing anyone needed this morning was Skeeter's presence. He barely looked in Cali's direction as he exited his car and jogged up to Marilyn's front door. Letting him inside, Marilyn deeply regretted her phone call to him last night, but what choice did she have when the girl was in such bad shape from drug withdrawal?

"So, I been thinkin', if you want, I can dump her under 83 on my way home. I gotta charge a small fee, of course, understand? Twenty bucks sounds reasonable, don't it? Not a bad price to haul away your garbage, ain't that right?" Skeeter's smile was menacing.

He stood at the kitchen window, watching Cali's every move as she slowly bent over to pick up wind blown trash that gathered around the wood lattice skirting at the base of the trailer. Earlier in the week, one of the neighbor's garbage cans was knocked over and since they hadn't bothered to clean up the mess, most of their litter had eventually blown in front of Marilyn's place.

Nothing about Cali escaped Skeeter's keen eye. He saw the way she struggled to steady herself when she rose from a squatting position. He didn't try to disguise the devious smirk on his face as he watched her suddenly stare into space with vacant eyes. He didn't miss a trick. The strange blotchy mottling of her skin. The tremor in her hands. He'd been around long enough to recognize the telltale signs of a junkie going through withdrawal.

"No, she's no trouble. We made a deal. I'm letting her stay a few days more. After, she'll travel back to her home." Marilyn was still in her bathrobe, a magenta wraparound that fell below her knees and her pink Hello Kitty slippers.

"Go home? Nah, she needs to stick around for awhile so me and you can make a little pocket change," Skeeter insisted.

It was barely eleven o'clock in the morning and Marilyn desperately wished Skeeter would leave. It was more than she could bear, dealing with him so early in the day after such a late visit last night.

Her show last evening in Havre de Grace was a huge hit. Although her performance was scheduled to end at ten, she was late leaving the stage because the audience demanded not one but two encores from the Marilyn Monroe impersonator. She had to admit, she was great. Choosing "Diamonds Are a Girl's Best Friend" to open the show and "Happy Birthday, Mr. President" as her closer. She did three costume changes. Her fans absolutely adored her. Once her performance ended, she posed for photographs and signed autographs for over an hour as she gratefully accepted generous tips from her fans. During that one hour alone, she made ninety-seven dollars in tips.

Then after picking Cali up at the gas station, they aimlessly rode around the streets of Baltimore City for almost an hour before finally coming home. She had her fill of Skeeter last night when he drastically overcharged Cali for the heroin.

Switching gears, Skeeter tried to convince Marilyn to see things his way, "I think you're makin' a big mistake. Right now, she's got a few bucks for smack but as soon as that's gone, bam, she'll be turnin' tricks on your couch."

He walked past Marilyn as she perched on a stool at the kitchen counter sipping a cup of ginger tea. Uninvited, he uncovered a plate wrapped in plastic next to the stove and began shoving the leftovers from breakfast into his mouth. Cali had surprised Marilyn with pancakes, made from scratch, with maple syrup for breakfast. The mouth-watering aroma had lured a very sleepy Marilyn from her deep slumber.

Marilyn was tired. Letting down her guard, she unintentionally let the words slip out, "No need for worry, she's a virgin."

Seeing the fire ignited in Skeeter's eyes, she immediately regretted that statement.

"What?" Skeeter was instantly animated, practically leaping across the kitchen to the stool next to Marilyn's. Chewed pancake spewed from his mouth as he mocked this fact, "Seriously, are you are pissin' up my leg and tellin' me it's rainin'?"

He plopped down on the stool next to hers. Averting her eyes, Marilyn barely disguised her annoyance when she told him, "She told me by her own mouth. She does not know man." Marilyn wished Skeeter would move, his breath was horrid. When was the last time he changed his clothes?

"Then you tell me, how's she comin' up with all this cash to buy H? Hey, you got anything to drink around here?" A foreigner to social graces, he opened Marilyn's refrigerator and began moving items of food around.

"There's mango soursop or ginger tea," Marilyn spoke with an undeniable sharpness as she rose from her seat and gently nudged Skeeter away, closing the refrigerator door. He smelled terrible. Looked even dirtier. Did he ever take a bath, she mused? Marilyn made a mental note to wipe down the inside of her refrigerator as soon as he left.

Thankfully, the kitchen was too small to comfortably accommodate them both at the same time so Skeeter retreated into the living room. Standing in the middle of the room, he picked at a scab on his forearm, finally satisfied when it started to bleed.

Without bothering to look at her, he mumbled, "I ain't drinkin' that crap. Ain't you got a Pepsi or some orange soda, at least? So, where's she getting the money at?"

"She carries a debit card," Marilyn's tone was clearly annoyed as she checked the clock on the kitchen wall behind the stove.

"A debit card? Yeah well, a stolen card's only good for so long. Where'd she get it at?" Skeeter asked nonchalantly as he sucked the blood from the open wound on his forearm.

Marilyn was busily wiping down her stove and countertops, ignoring Skeeter. Trying to drown him out, she clicked on the transistor radio above the sink to Morgan State's cool jazz station.

She just about jumped out of her skin when he appeared at her side, rambling, "I just thought of somethin'. Do you got any idea what kinda money we can get for a virgin? I know me some guys. In fact, I can make some phone calls, right here, right now. We can probably get a thousand bucks for her. It's a one time deal 'cause after the first time, she ain't technically a virgin no more. Hell, if she didn't look so damn boney, we could probably charge around two thousand bucks, ain't that right?"

"Does your brain listen to your mouth? That's rape. And she's a child." One hand on her hip, Marilyn stared Skeeter squarely in the eyes, saying, "I turn my back on that idea, boy."

"Who shoved a stick up your ass?" Skeeter tried bullying. "It's easy money."

"I was not invited to the wedding, so don't ask me to the funeral," Marilyn stood firm.

"Whatcha so worked up for? It's a brilliant idea, if I do say so myself," he fought back.

"What I have, you let burn your eye. I say no, and it will never change," Marilyn's words held no trace of their normal, languid melody. Her tone became hard, the words rapid fire. She firmly crossed her arms across her chest in a no nonsense stance.

"Okay, okay. Don't be gettin' your panties all in a twist. Anyways, I ain't wastin' my day here, I got stuff to do," he yelled, throwing his hands in the air before storming out the door to his 1978 Chevy Chevette.

Four letter insults thrown over his shoulder at Marilyn continued long after he closed the car door. Although neither she nor Cali could hear his cursing, they both cringed in disgust, fully aware of the offensive words. Making no effort to disguise his irritation, he pulled away in the style befitting road rage. Grinding the gears of the four speed manual transmission, the harvest gold, two door disappeared down the street at a velocity more than three times the posted speed limit.

Cali hurried into the trailer, afraid he might decide to return. She didn't want to take the chance of being caught in the yard all alone with him. She had no firsthand experience with anger. Pop and MomMom had never, ever raised their voices to one another. To anyone, for any reason, whatsoever. They weren't cut out for anger.

Pop had zero tolerance for cursing. He said it showed how small a man was when his misguided intent by using offensive obscenities was to prove himself formidable. Pop never wavered in his belief that there were literally millions of words to choose when expressing an idea, therefore, allowing foul language to dominate a man's vocabulary was a quick indicator of his lack of intelligence. Anyone brought into his courtroom who dared use profanity was guaranteed the stiffest penalty allowed by the law.

Genuinely concerned for Marilyn's welfare, Cali wrapped her arms around Marilyn without giving it a second thought. "Are you okay? He didn't hurt you, did he? He was so angry when he left."

Cali's embrace caught Marilyn off guard since the last person to hug her with pure intent was her grandmother, many years ago.

Flustered, Marilyn abruptly pulled away. "If anger was made of gold, that would be a rich man."

CHAPTER 11

After Skeeter's theatrics, both Marilyn and Cali were reluctant to venture outside the trailer. Neither of them wanted to be caught outside with him should he unexpectedly return. Securing all three locks on the door and pulling the Venetian blinds closed, the two girls were content to spend the remainder of the day indoors. Marilyn was genuinely perplexed by her impromptu house guest. She had crossed paths with more than her share of drug addicts in her day, but Cali didn't fit the mold. In an attempt to discover some sort of truth about the girl, Marilyn passed the hours presenting an endless stream of questions.

When Cali wasn't lost in a drug-induced haze, she did her best to answer Marilyn truthfully. After spending the entire day revealing her most recent transgressions, Cali was filled with equal measures of embarrassment and remorse. Up until the moment she was introduced to the interventionist, Cali had no idea her grandparents thought anything was awry. It would have crushed Cali's soul to know the lengths her MomMom had gone to in an effort to uncover the truth about their granddaughter.

■ ■ ■

On Tuesday morning after Cali left for school, MomMom headed for the restaurant where Cali waitressed on the weekends. She made it seem as though she just happened to be stopping by for a leisurely lunch. Nothing out of the ordinary. Although she had no appetite, she ordered a sweet tea and the chicken fried steak, which came with a side of fried green tomatoes and cornbread. Her plan was to request a doggy bag and take it all home for her husband's dinner. There wouldn't be time to fix supper tonight.

Once the hostess told him Mrs. Hasting was there, the manager stopped by her table to greet her. He was both the full time manager, as well as the successful business owner, who turned his privately owned eatery into a gold mine despite the competition of the more powerful chains. Essentials of customer service were his forte, such as making the effort to personally speak with his patrons. Make each and every customer feel valued. He always greeted his clientele with a smile and an unhurried demeanor. His name recall was uncanny as he, more often than not, addressed people by name. He lived by the statistics which read, if a diner is pleased with her experience, she will eventually tell three friends about it. If dissatisfied, ten acquaintances will instantly know.

"It's nice to finally make your acquaintance, Mrs. Hasting," the manager said as he shook MomMom's hand.

"The pleasure is all mine. Please, call me Caroline."

Speaking with the manager, Caroline was immediately relieved to learn Cali was a good worker, someone who received frequent comments on her behalf to the manager on her wonderful service. He expressed how impressed he was with how quickly she caught on to the art of meeting the needs of the customers while being friendly without interfering with their dining experience. Really particularly challenging for a girl who looked like Cali because she had the capacity to unwittingly disrupt an evening out for a couple by having the boyfriend or husband pay attention to her, making the date feel snubbed.

Unlike every other girl her age, who thrived on a constant diet of being the center of attention, Cali tried unsuccessfully to downplay her natural beauty. She never wore makeup. Her waist length hair always tightly pinned in a matron bun at the nape of her neck. She was effortlessly beautiful.

A quick study, Cali always stood directly behind the men, maintaining direct eye contact with the women. No giggling, no conversations about herself. She was approachable, yet all business. She possessed a mature social skill whereby she gently redirected the conversation back to the customers when she was met with inquisitive remarks about herself. Not an easy skill to learn.

"Cali still has her regular clients asking for her to be their server. But, after her knee injury, she said it was nearly impossible to be on her feet for eight hours. I have to tell you, I really hated to lose her," the manager said.

"Pardon me? Lose her? Yes, I...lose her?" her words drifted off, unable to formulate a complete sentence, Caroline's mind bombarded with so many thoughts. She felt her arms go numb. Her mouth unable to speak. Like a punctured balloon, she felt her body begin to slowly deflate.

"Ma'am, are you okay? Do you think you're having a stroke? Should I call an ambulance for you?" the manager knelt at her side, taking the elderly woman's hand in his, nervously patting her in an effort to keep her revived.

Quickly regrouping, Caroline shook her head as she responded, "No, no. I'm fine, thank you so much. I'm so sorry. I didn't mean to frighten you. I skipped breakfast this morning, so my blood sugar is probably a little on the low side. That's all."

"Get us something to drink and a basket of rolls over here right away," he jumped to his feet, yelling to a middle aged waitress who'd lost her figure long ago after her first child. The waitress who loved a little drama in her otherwise dull life, sprang into action. In no time at all, the pear-shaped woman delivered the food to Caroline's table.

"My husband's a diabetic. Eat this," the waitress ordered while slathering too much butter on a warm roll. "You'll feel better in no time."

Caroline knew she wasn't having a stroke. Her blood sugar was not the culprit. She did not have diabetes. Her mind simply needed a moment to process the disturbing information she had just received. Cali no longer worked at the restaurant. However, she had no choice but to acquiesce, taking two bites of the roll dripping with butter under the scrutiny of the restaurant owner and his waitress.

"Thank you. I'm so sorry to be a bother. Thank you both for your kindness. Actually, this did the trick, I feel so much better now," Caroline managed when in fact she felt as though she needed to vomit.

Forcing a smile, Caroline looked at the terrified restauranteur, asking, "May I ask you for one more thing, sir? Am I correct, you did say Cali no longer works here?"

"Yes, but her job is waiting for her anytime she's able to come back," a low level of panic was detected in his voice. It would be really bad for business if emergency medical responders were blocking the entryway to his restaurant. Rumors of food poisoning and such.

"I thank you for that. If you could be so kind, for the sake of keeping her records straight for income taxes, could you give me the exact date of Cali's last shift? I can stop back later today if this isn't a convenient time."

"That's not a problem at all, Mrs. Hasting. You sit right there. Drink your tea, eat another roll. Anything at all you need, just let us know." Turning his head, he bellowed, "What's the hold up with Mrs. Hasting's food?"

Clearly feeling rattled, he continued, "I have all my staff's schedules on a spreadsheet.

It'll be easy to look up. Give me a minute and I'll get that information for you lickety-split. You stay right here and get that blood sugar up now."

Up until now, Caroline had never known an occasion when Cali had been dishonest. Clearly, she was not coming to work during her long absences from home every weekend. If not here, then where did she go? What was she doing for the nine to ten hours she was away from home?

"Enjoy your meal, Mrs. Hasting." In a flash, the waitress delivered a heaping plate of steaming hot food, as well as a neon pink sticky-note, the date of Cali's last shift neatly written in black ink.

Reluctantly, Caroline looked at the date on the pink paper. Twelve weeks ago. For three months, Cali disappeared from home, her whereabouts unaccounted for. The last time Cali had come to work was right before she and Cal took their European river cruise.

Grabbing the edge of the table, Caroline attempted to slow both her thoughts as well as her racing heartbeat. As in any crisis, she strove to remain cool, calm, and collected. She needed to remain focused and objective. Separate fact from speculation.

But that was why she was here, wasn't it? The truth. Truth was the catalyst for her early morning call to Cali's high school, requesting a meeting with the principal. Concrete information propelled her to swallow her pride by making an unexpected appearance at her daughter-in-law's home just about an hour ago, where she was never welcomed. This was the focus of her day, to gather factual information to present to her husband later that evening.

Removing a small spiral notebook and pen from her purse, she began to make a list. With trembling hands, she wrote Cali's last day of work. Below that she wrote the words, missing spoons.

The waitress was blatantly staring at her from across the dining room. Trying to keep her at bay, Caroline made a production of nibbling on a fried green tomato as she replayed last evening's events in her mind. The happenstance discovery of the condition of Cali's arms. Arms the size of a young child's covered in tender bruises revealed only by Cali absently pushing up the sleeve of her shirt while they washed the dinner dishes. Caroline made the immediate decision not to express her skepticism concerning Cali's weight. Clearly, she was skin and bones, no where near the one hundred and eight pounds she claimed to weigh.

At that moment, she had an epiphany. There were many aspects of her granddaughter's well-being that had been niggling at the back of her mind. Excessive credit card bills for gas, of all things. Unexplained weight loss. Arms covered in bruises. Reticent behaviors. Chronic fatigue. Things, small things, missing from their home. Last night, Caroline silently vowed to do a little probing first thing in the morning, starting with the restaurant.

Keeping an eye on the time, Caroline noted she still had time to place a phone call before heading to her one forty-five appointment at the high school. Pushing her plate of chicken fried steak to the side, she removed her cell phone from her purse. Caroline jotted down the number for the American Red Cross in her spiral notebook. Dialing the number, she dreaded what she may discover, but she was determined to turn over a few stones.

Like a solid blow to her gut, she learned Cali did not qualify for the minimum weight requirement of one hundred ten pounds to donate blood. No exceptions for underweight minors wishing to donate blood were ever granted by the Red Cross.

The person on the other end of the telephone assured Caroline of their steadfast policy that no phlebotomist ever stuck someone more than twice. If it necessitates, a second phlebotomist may try one time. If she, too, is unsuccessful, the person is disqualified from donating at that particular time. Therefore, no one is ever subjected to more than a maximum of three needle sticks.

Asking for her check and forgetting all about the doggy bag, Caroline devised a new plan. Slipping a twenty dollar bill in the waitress's hand for a twelve dollar meal, she thanked her for her kindness before hurrying to her car.

Making a quick detour, she swung by a local bakery for four dozen cookies. Four plain white boxes, tied closed with red and white twine, contained an assortment of snicker doodles, macaroons, chocolate chip, and old fashioned oatmeal raisin cookies.

Carrying the boxes of cookies in both hands, her purse hanging from the crook of her arm, Caroline Hasting climbed the brick stairs leading into Martin Luther King Jr. High School, a well maintained three story house of learning. An American flag suspended forty feet in the air slapped gently against the aluminum pole. Double front doors constructed of shatter resistant glass were positioned centrally in a hallway too long to be able to visualize either end.

The first thing she was acutely aware of, was the intermingled smells of chalk, cafeteria meat loaf, art supplies, and gym lockers. Cinder block walls were painted a pale sage. Endless rows of metal lockers fortified both sides of the hall. Banners constructed by talented art students were suspended from the ceiling advertising an upcoming pep rally. White poster board sign up sheets for prom committee volunteers were hung on the walls with tan adhesive tape.

Voices of teachers, intermittent collective bursts of laughter from students, sounds of student participation drifted from behind closed doors. One got the immediate impression that learning was taken seriously inside these walls.

An oversized, glass showcase outside the principal's office was packed with trophies and pictures of student athletes. There was Cali, smiling alongside all her girlfriends, wearing green and white jerseys, a black and white soccer ball on the grass in front of them.

Squaring her shoulders, Caroline entered the front office where she was greeted by the receptionist. Since she was a few minutes early, she was offered a seat and a cold drink. She gratefully accepted a bottled water before she opened one box of cookies, presenting them to the secretary. The secretary's craving for cookies outweighed any desire she may have had to stand without first prying her saddlebags free from under the armrests of her chair.

"I realize you're a very busy woman. Would it be too much of a bother to give me the date of your last blood drive?" Caroline asked after taking a much needed drink of water.

"No bother at all, sweetie. Just give me one little second," the receptionist cheerfully replied while staring at her computer screen and chewing on a moist macaroon. "You know when computers first came out, I was plum set against them. But now, I wonder what I'd ever do without them. My husband and I even bought one for our home. At first, we both said, computers are going to take the place of our brains. We have to use our brains to keep sharp. But honestly there are so many things you can learn from a computer. Oh, here it is. December tenth. Right before Christmas break. Our next blood drive, in case you're interested, is in two weeks. There's a sign up sheet in the hall next to the girls' bathroom. You know, our student body is amazing. Our goal is to supply the American Red Cross with fifty pints, but in December, we more than doubled that quota. We collected one hundred and one pints of blood. Would you mind if I tried one of those snicker doodles?"

"No, of course not. Please, help yourself." Caroline set the open box of sweets on the woman's desk. "I must have written it on the wrong page in my calendar. Sometimes, I think my age is catching up with me. So, you didn't have a recent blood drive in the last week or so?"

"Positive. It's all documented right here, in my mechanical brain. Our next blood drive is coming up two weeks from tomorrow." The pudgy secretary smiled brightly, examining the latest cookie in her fingers when the phone on her desk buzzed.

Replacing the receiver, she beamed. "It's your lucky day. The principal will see you now, fifteen minutes ahead of schedule. Go on through that door, right over there. And don't forget your goodies here." She lifted the box in outstretched arms, but not before she plucked out two chocolate chips, her all time favorite.

The principal looked like he enjoyed his wife's cooking. He wore a brightly colored dress shirt that strained against his middle complimented by a color coordinated, plaid bowtie. His navy blue jacket hung neatly on the back of his ergonomically designed chair. The walls behind his desk were covered in framed diplomas, verifying his right to occupy this office. Caroline guessed him to be in his mid-fifties from the gray hair which he combed men's hair color through, from time to time. Today was not one of those days.

He was warm and cordial. After all, he was in charge of the number one high school in the state of Georgia. His students routinely recruited to top notch universities, not to mention the Air Force and Naval Academies after graduation. This was the birth place of countless doctors, authors, engineers, and top government officials.

Once they were both seated, he jumped right in, "Let me start by saying, I am most grateful you requested this conference. I've personally left numerous messages with, let me see here," he opened a file on his desk, "Maggie Hasting. That's Cali's mother, am I correct?"

"Yes, it is."

"I know Cali normally resides with you and your husband, The Honorable Calhoun Hasting, but there's been a great deal of confusion concerning her parental supervision since her knee injury. This is as good a time as any to clarify that issue. Does she live with you or her natural parents?"

"Cali lives with my husband and myself. She always has, her entire life, since birth. My husband and I had taken an extended vacation at the time of Cali's injury, so she was temporarily staying with her parents. As soon as we returned from our trip, Cali came back home with us," Caroline spoke clearly, watching him make notations in his folder.

Setting his pen down, the principal began, "Let me start by saying I take pride in getting to know about all our students here at Martin Luther King. Cali, in particular, has always been one of our brightest and most talented, student athletes. Her teachers and guidance counselor have all taken a special liking to her. If it's appropriate to say, she has always been what we used to call back in the day, a teacher's pet. There's always been something rather special about your grandchild. She has a magnetic quality about her that makes people feel better about themselves when they interact with her. Whatever it is, I've seen it with my own eyes, people walk away from Cali smiling."

Caroline squeezed the strap of her purse, daring to hope all was well at school.

He cleared his throat, leaning back in his chair, creating a little more distance between them. "Which brings us to the matter at hand. My background is in childhood development, as you can see from all those pieces of paper hanging on the wall, so I'm keenly aware of the challenges facing adolescents and the pressures they feel. It's really not that uncommon to have rather wide swings in a student's behavior. But her recent behaviors are so far out of character for a girl like Cali, I thought it best to address them with a parent, or in her case, a grandparent.

"I'm concerned if we can't get Cali back on track, she may miss out on scholarship money she's clearly entitled to, up until now. More importantly, if she continues to miss classes and her grades continue on this downslide, she may not be considered for acceptance to the colleges she has expressed interest in. In fact, it's highly unlikely any

school, even our local community colleges will consider her. Since day one, her ultimate goal has been law school. As I am quite sure you are aware, being the wife of a judge, law schools have very stringent acceptance criteria and it's extremely competitive. I'd hate to see a student with such an impressive academic career, up until recently, have it all slip away."

Caroline felt as though she were drowning as she continued to hear the principal use phrases like, "missed opportunities...problems at home...seeking help from a therapist...class attendance is impera- tive...incomplete assignments...boyfriend troubles."

The dismissal bell rang and the halls magically filled with a palpa- ble energy as five hundred students were granted permission to freely talk. The noise level was barely muted by the principal's heavy wooden door as energetic teens called to one another over the sound of metal locker doors slamming shut.

By the completion of the meeting, Caroline desperately wanted to go home, curl up in her bed and sleep. Every ounce of energy had been sucked out of her. She wondered how she had been so blind. She had always taken pride in being a woman of substance. If ever Cali needed her, whether she knew it or not, it was now.

Exiting the front doors of the school, she walked past the visitor parking lot and headed straight for the sports fields out back. The green space was swarming with students participating in a vast num- ber of after school activities, as well as friends hanging around, killing time. Ever so grateful to make it to the soccer field before the start of practice, Caroline hastened her steps.

Kennedy was the first to spot her, yelling, "MomMom Hasting's here! MomMom Hasting, we've missed you so much!" which quickly resulted in her being swarmed by Cali's teammates. Kennedy flashed an easy smile of perfectly straight teeth, her reward for four years of painful orthodontics.

Simultaneously, the cluster of girls gushed how much they missed seeing her and Judge at their games. Caroline easily kept their attention by opening the boxes of cookies, encouraging the girls to help themselves.

"Where's Cali? Aren't girls on the injured list still required to make it to practice to help support their team?" Caroline asked innocently.

The mood shifted noticeably as all, but three girls, ran off to begin their warm up routine.

A blonde with striking features boldly announced with pleasure, "Cali quit the team."

Scarlet was unmistakably the school's queen bee. She was the kind of girl who practiced her countenance in front of a mirror while applying that third, heavy coat of mascara. For most people, it was unimaginable that beneath that little kewpie doll face lived a stewing pot of jealousy and pettiness.

"Shut up, Scarlet!" Kennedy hissed.

"Suit yourself, but you know it's true," she shot back. "Toodles."

Realizing she had pushed far enough, Scarlet grabbed her girlfriend's hand to retreat, shooting Kennedy a cheeky grin over her shoulder as they ran to the middle of the field, the tails of her twin French braids flying behind her.

"I have to go, too. Practice and all, " Kennedy said, no longer able to make eye contact. Her head tipped over as she studied the ground.

Caroline timidly reached out, gently taking Kennedy's hand in hers. "Kennedy? Please, sweetheart, I know you love Cali too. You two have been like sisters since you were barely old enough to walk. Something's terribly wrong and I need you to tell me what you know so I can try to help her. Please, before it's too late. I'm begging you, Kennedy."

A lone tear made its way down the girl's freckled cheek.

"She would help you, don't you think?" Caroline felt her chest tighten, her throat swell.

In a torrent, all those weeks of suppressed grief came pouring out as Kennedy told Cali's MomMom every rumor she'd heard circulating in the halls of Martin Luther King High. In disbelief, Caroline listened as her heart shattered beyond repair.

Trudging back to her car, she fought for composure. Her voice must sound rock steady when she made the call to her husband. She was determined not to cry. For what seemed like an eternity, she sat in the sweltering car, too preoccupied to even turn on the air conditioning.

At last, she dialed the number, "Cal? Our Cali Girl's in trouble."

CHAPTER 12

After breakfast on Friday morning, Marilyn determined she had exactly three hours before she had to leave for her shift as a salesperson at a chic clothing boutique in Fells Point. She decided to treat herself to a luxurious bubble bath. There was time to pamper herself a little since Cali was the one making breakfast and cleaning up the kitchen afterwards.

With bubbles to her chin, she closed her eyes while making plans for her ensemble. Once her retail shift was finished, she had another Marilyn Monroe impersonator gig later tonight at some swanky joint over in Federal Hill. There was a great deal of preparation involved in packing her show costumes. Pricey gowns and wigs were transported in expensive garment bags and wig boxes. Matching the correct look with a particular song. It all took time.

Perhaps she would wear the black jumpsuit with the extra wide legs to the boutique. Pair it with big, chunky, turquoise and silver jewelry. Maybe wear the purple wig. Marilyn was actually looking forward to going to work at the boutique today. With the money Cali paid her for sleeping on her couch, she planned to buy that adorable orange sundress she had her eye on for weeks. Orange was her color. It complemented her warm caramel complexion. Pair the dress with an extra-wide, purple, leather belt. With Cali's cash and her employee discount, she could finally afford it.

Surprisingly, after spending the entire day with Cali yesterday, she had no apprehension about leaving the girl alone in her trailer. Marilyn's gut instinct was, Cali wasn't interested in stealing anything. Marilyn surprisingly decided she trusted Cali. It was Skeeter who caused her concern. She was annoyed with herself for telling him too much. She knew better than to let the left hand know what the right hand was doing. She didn't want him inside her home. Skeeter knew the girl had money. No doubt, he would return today. As she was leaving for work, Marilyn paused long enough to caution Cali against the wisdom of inviting a thief to watch a house.

Exiting the trailer park, Cherry Tree Lane ultimately dumped into Pulaski Highway, also known as Route 40. At the crossroad of Cherry Tree Lane and Pulaski Highway, drivers were forced to make a right turn only, heading eastbound. Lanes traveling westward were positioned on the opposite side of the concrete jersey barriers. In order to head west, a driver had to take an exit ramp three miles down the road and re-enter Route 40 in the desired direction.

Skeeter prided himself on always being one step ahead of everyone else. First thing this morning, he called the boutique to inquire what time Marilyn's shift started. Fully aware of the time Marilyn would need to leave for work, Skeeter came up with an idea. Knowing she would be forced to take the right hand turn when entering Pulaski Highway, he found the perfect observation spot. Located off to the side of Pulaski Highway was a Tacos To Go.

Once Marilyn left her house, she had no choice but to pass by this fast food restaurant. After ordering three bean burritos and a large soda at the drive through window, he pulled his Chevy Chevette in the shade, on the far left of the parking lot. Taking up two parking spots, the nose of his car sitting on an angle, Skeeter faced the on-coming traffic. From that vantage point, he could see cars cresting the hill a mile down the road. Hunkered down low in the front seat, he patiently waited.

He had nothing better to do with his time. He ate his food, drank his soda. When he was finished, he threw the brown paper bag and soda cup on the passenger side floorboard. It landed on top of a mounting pile of other fast food containers, soda cans, empty potato chip bags. The interior of his car was a dump.

Finally, he spotted the furry, black and white dice dangling from the rearview mirror. There she was, at last. Sunglasses on. Purple hair he could see a mile away. The lavender Cadillac Coupé de Ville, in all its glory, unknowingly drove past Skeeter.

A man of little self control, he almost immediately started the car and pulled onto Route 40, rather than patiently giving Marilyn a few minutes head start. Because he had a lead foot, combined with Marilyn's habit of driving under the speed limit, Skeeter had to apply his brakes a total of five times in the fifty-five miles per hour traffic to avoid winding up directly behind her. His patience pushed to the limit, Skeeter finally veered off, allowing them to go their separate ways.

In less than ten minutes, he was in front of Marilyn's trailer. The girl was no where in sight. He started for the front door but as an af-terthought, he spun around and headed back to his car. Opening the passenger side door, he scooped up all the trash and threw it on the back seat and floor. If Cali hadn't been out there yesterday morning pickin' up garbage, he coulda dumped it all in Marilyn's front yard. But since little miss homemaker tidied up, he couldn't very well do that now. A lotta girls would make do and put their feet on the empty bags, but he had a feelin' not this one.

Clearing his throat, he stood tall as he knocked. A jovial, door to door salesman kind of knock. Rat-a-tat-tat. When Cali answered, he slunk right past her, letting himself inside.

"Oh, hi, Skeeter. Marilyn's not home right now." Cali remained at the open door while Skeeter plopped down on Marilyn's mustard-colored couch. He pulled one of the colorful throw pillows from the sofa and began to nervously twirl it in his hands. Cringing, Cali was certain Marilyn would instantly smell his offensive odor on her sofa. "And I'm not allowed to have any visitors when she's not here," Cali explained.

"I know she ain't here. That's why I come on over. Plus, I brung your China white."

Skeeter noticed how the girl took a step nearly outside when he suddenly stood. Under normal circumstances, that little reaction would of ignited his anger, causin' him to grab her. But not right now. He had to give it to hisself, he was doin' a pretty good job with self control. He backed up, puttin' a little more distance between them in an attempt to draw her in.

"I seen you workin' in the yard yesterday mornin' and it got me thinkin'. I was wonderin', who learned you all about plants and weeds? Hey, you washin' clothes?" Skeeter turned his head in the direction of the laundry area.

Before leaving for work, Marilyn had once again graciously loaned Cali a clean pair of black stretch pants and a black Rolling Stones T-shirt, depicting the famous red lips and tongue in red glitter. As soon as Marilyn left for work, Cali started a load of laundry. The flowery fragrance of detergent filled the small home, as the muffled, chug-chug-chug sound of the agitator softly hummed in the background.

She just stared at him like he was some kinda freak. He wanted to slap her for not answerin' none of his questions. Like he gave a rat's ass about plants or washin' clothes. It was a matter of respect, and he wasn't about to let her disrespect him like that, ignorin' him. But he did that deep breathin', count to ten crap they shoved down his throat durin' all them years of therapy. One, two, three, four, five, six...

Forcing composure, Skeeter asked, "So, like I done already asked, you know about plants, huh?"

"My MomM ..." the word stuck firmly in Cali's throat, refusing to cross her lips. This creepy little person didn't deserve knowledge of the intimate intricacies of her cherished relationships. She sucked the name, MomMom, back inside her throat, starting anew, "my grand-mother's a very big gardener. She knows a lot about plants and birds, so she's taught me a few things."

If not for her body's craving for heroin, Cali would have actually enjoyed working outside yesterday morning. It was the first time she felt even the slightest bit of joy since she was brought to Maryland against her will. Working in the summer heat reminded her of the many hours she and her MomMom spent in their lush garden, overflowing with tranquility. She missed her grandparents so much. While pulling weeds yesterday, she decided perhaps just one or two more days and she was going home.

"She learned you that, gardenin', huh? You and her spend a lot a time doin' that kinda stuff? I'll bet that's how you know about washin' clothes, too. Ain't I right?" Skeeter's attempt to look friendly was in vain. His face wasn't designed to smile.

"Yes, you're right. We do spend a lot of time together because I actually live with my grandparents." Cali answered, ever mindful of her manners. She secretly wished she was more spunky like her best friend Kennedy and had the courage to demand he leave.

"No shit! Me too. My old lady was always makin' babies that she ain't wanted to keep. So all six of us lived with my grandmother. She died when I was still a kid though, rest her soul. Tough break, ain't that right?"

Cali nodded in an effort to appease him.

"So me and you, we got a whole bunch in common. Both raised by our grandmothers and all. I bet we could be friends, ain't that right?" Skeeter lied.

Not a word of this was true. Skeeter told Cali the personal history of Marilyn's childhood, making it his own. His lies were based upon the things Marilyn had revealed to him way back when they were incarcerated together as teens. Conveniently, throughout the years, he assumed parts of Marilyn's identity as it suited his needs. In reality, Jimmi Shiflett, AKA Skeeter, an only child, lived in a disgustingly filthy, subsidized housing unit in O'Donnell Heights with his very much alive mother.

Cali recoiled at the suggestion of a friendship with Skeeter. It didn't go unnoticed.

"Oh, yeah, I get it, okay. I ain't good enough for you. I ain't all hoity toity like you, right?" He stopped short of saying, *I ain't the one injectin' heroin in my veins, you skinny little slut.* He ain't never put none a that shit in his body. He kept his mind sharp at all times. Skeeter's anger boiled just beneath the surface.

Backpedaling, she tried to smooth things over before he lost his temper, saying, "It's just that we're not really the same age. I'm still a kid in school and you're an adult."

His chest inflated. He liked the sound of that. "True that. Very true, I am an adult. That's good you recognize that. My point is, with me and you havin' so much in common, it makes you feel like we can trust each other, don't it?"

He took a step toward her. Reacting quickly, she exited the trailer, taking a seat on the bottom cinder block step, putting as much distance between them as possible without actually running away. She was most grateful to see the neighbor across the street was outside working on his car. Granted, his head was buried beneath the open hood, but if she needed to scream, she was confident he'd hear her. Perhaps come to her aid.

Skeeter followed her outside, jumping the four feet from the threshold to the ground. Treating her with kid gloves, he positioned himself several feet away, close to the street.

"I guess you heard me and Marilyn's little disagreement yesterday mornin', huh?"

Cali looked away.

"Well, like you done already said, I'm the adult, and sometimes adults who been friends for a long time need to clear the air every now and then. When you're growed up some more, you'll see how it is. Anyways, me and Marilyn, we're cool." Casually lighting a cigarette, he kept his eyes trained on Cali through the flame.

No, that's not the way friendships work, she wanted to say. She and Kennedy had been friends their entire lives and they never needed to clear the air by screaming at one another. In fact, she didn't know a single person who behaved that way. If she only had the courage to confront him. To tell him he needed to work on his interpersonal skills, from A to Z.

A cunning fox, relentless in the pursuit of his prey, Skeeter persisted, "Anyways, I figured you'd wanna do somethin' nice for her birthday tomorrow, after all she's did for you. Buy her a flower, maybe. But if you ain't interested, I get that. A lot a people are only out for themself. If that's how you want it, see you later. I'll be back again tomorrow with your junk."

"Tomorrow's Marilyn's birthday?" Cali exclaimed, springing to her feet. "Oh my gosh, I had no idea. I have to do something for her."

Reeling her in, he continued, "Yup. Course, there ain't no place way out here you can walk to. If you wanna get a present or a cake or somethin', seein' I'm a good guy, I figured I'd give you a ride."

Gettin' her in his car was like takin' candy from a baby.

CHAPTER 13

Once they were seated in Skeeter's car, he headed west on Pulaski Highway, toward Baltimore City before saying, "I can't help but notice, you talk kinda funny, don't cha? Like a hillbilly or somethin'. Where you live at?"

"I suppose you mean I have a southern accent. But to me, you sound like you have an accent, too," she said flatly, her eyes wide in disbelief. Who was calling who a hillbilly, she wondered in amazement?

"Nah, I ain't the one with no accent. You talk funny, not me. You gonna answer me or what? Where you live at?" Skeeter demanded.

"I live in Georgia." Cali turned her head, searching the vehicle for the malodorous source. As best as she could tell, the rancid odor seemed to originate in the back seat. She rolled down her window, attempting to dilute the smell.

"Hey, I got the air conditionin' on," Skeeter protested. Clearly on its last leg, the air blowing full blast from the vents did nothing more than stir the egregious odor inside the vehicle.

"Would you mind if I open my window? There's an odor and I think the summer breeze will help settle my stomach," Cali asked as she licked her lips. Her face had turned a pale green color.

"Whatever. Suit yourself, just don't be pukin' in my car," he smirked as he turned off the air conditioner. This chick was a royal pain in his ass.

"If you live in Georgia, what're you doin' all the way the hell down here in Maryland for?" Skeeter inquired.

Obviously he had no idea how the two states were positioned to one another geographically.

"My grandparents brought me here for rehab. They thought it was the best move at the time. The place they sent me has one of the best reputations in the country. But I need to go home. I really do want to stop taking drugs, but not here. I want to go to a rehab in Georgia so I can be close to my family," Cali explained.

He let out a long, low whistle before saying, "Best reputation in the country. Whoa, baby. That musta cost a pretty penny. A fancy place like that probably costs twenty or even thirty thousand bucks a pop, ain't that right? So, they musta hocked all their stuff to send their little princess to the best rehab in the whole country, huh?" Skeeter poked at her.

Pop sometimes did call her a princess. But the manner in which Skeeter said the word, princess, turned a term of endearment into an insult. He made her skin crawl. Her head was throbbing. All her muscles ached as though she had the flu. It had been way too long since she last used. She wanted to get this little outing over with as quickly as possible so she could get back to Marilyn's trailer and heroin.

She quickly decided there was no way she was going to tell him his arbitrary guess of thirty thousand dollars was a far cry from the one hundred ten thousand dollars Yeo Ming told her New Light charged.

Closing her eyes, she tried to shut him out. Gingerly laying her head against the headrest, she replied, "My grandfather's a circuit court judge. No one had to hock anything."

Because her eyes were closed, she didn't witness how Skeeter suddenly sat taller in the driver's seat. Cali paid no attention to his body language when he muttered, "You ain't lookin' so good. You ain't used in a few hours, huh?"

He reached across her lap to open the glove box. Her eyes flew open when his arm brushed against her leg. There was nowhere for Cali to move away from him. Grabbing a clear plastic baggie from the glove box, he threw it on her lap. It contained three, small, white pills.

"Those're benzos. Take the edge off. I got a bottle a soda in the back somewheres. Or, you can take them dry. Whatever, suit yourself, ain't make no difference to me," he added.

While driving, Skeeter lifted his rear end off his seat, twisting his torso in order to fish around the garbage dump in the back. Cali heard cans and papers being pushed about. Victorious, he sat down as he handed her a plastic bottle containing a small amount of dark liquid that was left inside. The entire car stank like a wet dog. She was more grateful than ever for the hot summer air blowing in her face. Taking slow deep breaths through her mouth, Cali resolved not to throw up.

"Thank you," she said, taking the bottle from him, choosing to swallow the pills dry rather than put her lips on anything his disgusting mouth had touched. "I decided I'm going home the day after tomorrow, so I've been trying to wait as long as I can between using. I have to make sure my body isn't withdrawing when I'm flying. I can't exactly take heroin to the airport, so I feel terrible. Anyway, thank you for the pills."

Skeeter became unusually quiet, absorbed in his own thoughts. Cali was grateful for the silence. They drove aimlessly for what seemed forever through the streets of an inner city before Skeeter said, "Hey, you got enough cash for a birthday present or what? And your smack. It ain't free you know."

"Oh, no, I don't. Would you mind stopping at an ATM so I can withdraw some money, please? It sure is taking a long time to drive to this grocery store," Cali said.

"It ain't stole is it? I don't wanna be goin' down for being with you while you use a stole card," he scolded her.

"It's not stolen. My father gave it to me," her voice was smoothed over, the effects of the pills having taken hold.

Cali looked out the window at the throngs of people waiting on corners for public transportation buses to come. Others sitting on front steps outside their apartments, preferring the summer humidity to the stifling heat of high rise buildings without adequate air conditioning. As the miles drifted by, more and more people took shape as the streets filled with mostly men gravitating from who knew where. Groups of men who were tired of being caged up inside with nagging women and rowdy kids congregated together. They came seeking camaraderie. A familiar face. News relevant to their lives.

"You done got your stories all mixed up. You ain't being straight with me, are ya? First, you said your grandfather's a judge. Now you say your father. Which one is it?" A hard knot in his jaw formed.

"My grandfather's the judge. The honorable Calhoun Hasting. My father is Robert Hasting. He's a commercial airline pilot," the syllables lingered a little longer on her tongue, the pills making her words stick together.

The pills made her so sleepy and it seemed so long since she had had a decent night's sleep. Gratefully, Cali let her head fall back against the headrest. A delicious haze settled over her. It was impossible to keep her eyes open. Crossing her arms over her chest, she let her mind take her back to the time she showed up at Blake's house, uninvited. The kindness his family extended to her was betrayed by her ill intentions.

■ ■ ■

For the longest time she stood outside the brick colonial, all the while telling herself it was okay to show up at his house, unannounced and uninvited. The thing that caused hesitation for her were the windows. Tall windows, framed by working shutters, that glowed with a warm lighting from inside. Her position allowed her clandestine glimpses of Blake's family moving about their home. A real family, living a real life, that she dared to intrude upon. It was a bold move indeed, showing up at Blake's house, her presence unsolicited. Cali had been raised better than that. Down here in the south, phrases like, please, thank you, yes ma'am, or no sir, were milestones achieved long before a toddler learned to walk on steady feet. Social etiquette was not a mere courtesy, it was a reflection of proper upbringing. The dividing line between the refined and the ill-bred. Mountains were moved with a hefty dose of southern charm and gentility.

At last, she mustered the courage to ring the doorbell. Rich baritone chimes echoed throughout the house. It was Blake's mother who came to the door and invited her inside. She had no more than stepped inside the foyer when a little girl carrying a naked baby doll in one hand appeared. Cali guessed her to be around four years old. Using her free hand, she wrapped her arm around the inside of Blake's mother's leg. She studied the unexpected visitor from beneath thick chestnut bangs cut much too short above her eyebrows.

"I hope I'm not interrupting your supper." Cali was demure.

The foyer held the savory scent of fried chicken and collard greens.

"Not at all. We've already finished and the kitchen's put back together. Please, come inside. It's always a mother's delight to meet her children's friends. It's so nice of you to come calling. May I have your name, dear?" Blake's mom was a pretty lady dressed in a polka dot summer frock.

"Hi. I'm Cali Hasting, ma'am," she said, taking a half step forward as she offered her hand, which Blake's mother embraced with both of hers. Such grown up manners for someone so young.

"Hasting," Blake's mom mulled over the name. "My mother plays bridge with a Caroline Hasting."

"Yes, ma'am, that's my grandmother," Cali said.

"Oh my, what a small world. It's such a pleasure to make your acquaintance. You come from such lovely people. And which of my children have you come to see this evening?" the mother asked.

"I was hoping Blake might be home. It's Friday evening, so I realize now, he might be out with his friends. But I was hoping. He's very smart and I need help with my chemistry homework." The words seemed to get stuck in Cali's brain, coming out in short bursts.

"Are you and Blake boyfriend and girlfriend?" the four year old asked. Both she and the mother looked to Cali for her answer.

Shaking her head, Cali giggled. "No. We're just regular friends from school."

The pretty little girl sprang into action, running up the stairs as fast as her little legs would take her, an exact replica of her American Doll swinging wildly from her left hand. During her entire ascent, she yelled at the top of her lungs, "Blake! Blake, come on down here!"

For a little girl, she had quite a loud voice, the stairwell adding to the amplification.

The mother's eyes widened, but her tone remained soft, "Hazel Mae, you come down here this very instant."

Her tiny feet made a sudden U-turn on the stairs. Crestfallen, the little girl promptly did as she was told, returning to her mother's side.

The mother knelt down so she was eye level with her daughter before asking, "Is that how a young lady asks someone to come downstairs? Screaming and hollering?"

"No, ma'am," Hazel Mae's reply was contrite.

"Now you go on to the kitchen and invite Cali to follow you. Ask your daddy to get out some milk and brownies, while I go upstairs and get your brother, the proper way." The mother kissed her cheek.

Hazel Mae's eyes shone with excitement for her assignment.

Grabbing Cali's hand with her chubby little fingers, she led the way while hollering, "Daddy! Momma said for you to give me and Blake's girlfriend some brownies and milk."

■ ■ ■

While Cali dreamt of happier times, Skeeter's brain was firing away, processing all this new and invaluable information. A judge. An airline pilot. Both them people made bank, that's for sure. My, oh, my, Skeeter Shiflett hit the jackpot here. It was about damn time things went his way.

His brain was busy. At that particular moment, he wasn't sure how, but he was working out a way to parlay this information to his benefit. He might not have much of a brain for school assignments, but when it came to deviousness, he was the master. He might not be able to recall all that useless crap teachers wanted him to know, like what the Emancipation Proclamation was, but when it was to his advantage, he had a pretty impressive memory. Silently repeating the words over and over, he committed two names, Judge Calhoun Hasting and Robert Hasting the airline pilot, to his memory bank.

When the car engine died, Cali woke with a startle. Since she had insisted upon riding with the windows open, Skeeter had pushed up the long sleeves of his cotton hoodie. For the first time, when Cali finally opened her eyes, she saw some of the frightening images tattooed on the length of his arms. Dragons. Guns. Devils. Tombstones.

She knew it was rude to stare, yet her eyes were riveted to his arms. Sitting so close in the passenger seat, she could clearly see the words inked in blue, above his left wrist, Death Before Defeet, directly below a silhouette of a man hanging from a noose.

By the time they made it to the ATM on Gay Street, the benzos had eased some of Cali's withdrawal symptoms. She was less jittery, able to concentrate a little better. But then she began to complain about the heat. He was hot, too, but you didn't hear him whinin' about it. And besides, it was her damn idea to open the car windows.

The car was rank with his sweat, his apparent habit of omitting deodorant, and the festering pile of rubbish in the back seat. Had it not been for the pills, Cali most certainly would have vomited.

He parallel parked between a white pick up truck and a crotch rocket, directly in front of the ATM. Before Skeeter stepped out of the car, he pulled his red Bulls cap down low on his forehead, the upper half of his face lost in a dark shadow. He slid the sleeves of his hoodie to his wrists. To Cali's surprise, he came over and opened her car door before impatiently yanking her by the forearm to get her out. Nudging her in the back, he walked on her heels to the ATM.

Aware of the security camera, he deliberately positioned himself directly behind her, making sure he kept his head tilted on a downward angle at all times. It seemed past experience had taught him how to make sure his face was never visible to the camera. Skeeter kept his eyes glued to the keyboard with the intent of getting her pin number. Unaware of Skeeter's plan, Cali started to punch in the four digits the exact way Pop had taught her. Out of habit, using her left hand, she formed a cup over the keypad obscuring his ability to make out the sequence of numbers.

Pissed off, he pounced like a snake. The little bitch thought she was smart. He'd show her. Reaching in front of her, Skeeter roughly smacked her cupped hand away.

Cali was stunned. No one had ever hit her before.

After she had withdrawn a fistful of cash, he drove to a corner mom and pop grocery store. Skeeter impatiently sat in the car, double parked at the entrance, while she ran inside. By the time Cali emerged, a bouquet of purple and yellow flowers in one hand, a red velvet cake with the words, Happy Birthday Marilyn, written in yellow icing in the other, Skeeter had hatched his plan. It was second nature to him. Scheming. Conniving. Plotting.

Always the gentleman, Skeeter helped carry her purchases into Marilyn's trailer. Placing a capsule of heroin on the kitchen counter, he refused her money. It was on the house. No charge. Really. He insisted. They were friends now, after all.

He mumbled something about, "usin' the head before I hit the road."

Behind closed doors, Skeeter unlocked Marilyn's bathroom window. Fishing around in Marilyn's vanity, he found a stray bobby pin. Snapping it in two, he forced the bobby pin inside a tiny hole in the window latch, preventing the mechanism inside from locking. Twice, he made sure the window smoothly slid up and down before finally pulling it in the closed position.

Satisfied, Skeeter flushed the empty toilet, grinning as the clean water swirled around in the bowl before going down the drain.

CHAPTER 14

"Dude," the voice on the other end of the phone belonged to Nick, Walter's longtime friend and partner. "Celeste says she's running out of girlfriends. You know she's probably picking out baby names by now. It's been your longest stretch so far. What, four months?"

"Sure, about that. Three and a half, four months," Walter agreed.

"I'm just saying, no one's perfect."

Walter had Nick on speaker phone while he shaved. He wanted to get that over with this morning, knowing he'd be pressed for time later. He was using the day for his annual fitness training. The two couples were going out for crabs at six, but he had things to do today and if he was cutting it close on time, he could still grab a quick shower before picking up Chloe Rose.

First on his long to-do-list was target practice at Free State in Middle River, an indoor gun range. Square up to the target using an isosceles stance with his body weight evenly distributed on both legs. Feet shoulder width apart. Breath in slowly, let it half way out, hold your breath. Sight alignment, sight picture. Squeeze. Five pounds of pressure is all it takes. Both arms in full extension, one hand on the handle of the weapon with the index finger on the trigger, the second hand supporting the weight of the gun. Thirteen rounds, two hand, strong hand. With one round in the chamber, a hot reload. Followed by fourteen rounds, two hand, weak hand. One round in the chamber, a second hot reload.

Although his arms would be shaking from fatigue, he'd discharge eight rounds using only his weak hand. Walter never skipped the one hand training because if he ever found himself in a firefight and he sustained a hand injury, being able to shoot with his weak hand could mean the difference between life or death. His life or death.

"Not true, my man. Celeste. Celeste is perfect. Take one for the team, you've had her way long enough. I deserve to be happy for awhile. We'd make a great couple, Celeste and me," Walter teased.

Secure in both his marriage to Celeste and his longtime friendship with Walter, Nick laughed too, but couldn't help but add, "Asshole. She'd probably love to pair up with a ginger."

Nick's unexpected jibe caught Walter off guard. The sudden up-swing of his cheekbones when he broke out in laughter caused him to cut himself. The bright red blood mixed in the shaving foam before sliding in big globs to the sink. He shrugged it off, a man who never let the little things in life bother him.

Shaving was a priority for Walter ever since his days at Curley High School. He learned the hard way as a sophomore, the easiest way to get a Saturday detention was to present in homeroom with a scruffy face. It didn't seem to matter how the students smelled, they just had to give the outward appearance of cleanliness. The entire all boys school reeked of raging hormones, body sweat, and obscene amounts of cheap cologne.

The Catholic high school was run by friars, clad in long black robes with hoods that fell halfway down their backs, woven ropes tied around their waists, and sandals on their feet twelve months of the year. When Brother Benedict wasn't teaching advanced math, he spent much of his free time roaming the halls at change of class, trying to hand out detention slips. Brother Benedict was charged with keeping the grounds clean, in particular, the green space outside the fence that bordered the school property. Trash and litter constantly blew along Sinclair Lane and Erdman Avenue, seemingly pulled to the wrought iron fence surrounding the school's property like a magnet.

Armed with white trash bags, purple latex gloves, and janitorial trash grabbers, fourteen year old Nick and Walter struck up a friend-ship that made them seem more like brothers than classmates. After graduation, they attended the same college, and later, both were re-cruited by The FBI. It was recognized early on, each man possessed an exceptional level of intelligence, but the two partnered together created an Einstein-like genius. Criminals, beware.

"Ah, the real question is, is he really a redhead? Only one way to find out for certain," Walter used a line from his teen years he often heard escape the lips of other adolescent counterparts.

Sticking a wad of toilet paper to the razor cut, Walter scrutinized himself in the mirror, turning to check first the right side of his face, then the left, making sure both edges of his short boxed beard were evenly matched. He was indeed a ginger, but thankfully not the orange colored hair of a cartoon character. Rather, he was a handsome mix of his Irish mother and his burley, olive skinned, Greek father. He kept his dark clay colored hair cut two finger widths in length, which he never combed. He had his father's warm Mediterranean complexion and his mother's clear blue eyes. Eyes the color of a blue jay, hooded by his father's thick black eyelashes, that were the first thing that caught ev-eryone's attention. They shone with adolescent mischief behind his steel framed eyeglasses.

If anyone were to ask him to describe his outward appearance, his response would have been, "I look okay. I have the kind of face people would want to be friends with." Women had a different opinion, dreamily describing him as a gorgeous hunk of man.

Grabbing his phone and heading to the bedroom, Walter began throwing on his clothes. Unlike Nick, who looked like the kind of guy who ironed his pajamas, Walter was never outed as law enforcement at first sight. His preferred style of dress was a T-shirt and jeans. He usually looked a little rumpled since he liked activities that made him sweat such as jogging, mountain biking, and doing yard work for his dad. If any of his buddies needed help moving a piece of furniture or relocating an entire household, he was their guy.

"So, what's up with Chloe Rose?" Nick inquired as he took a bite of something crunchy. Walter moved the phone from his ear, putting it on speaker, hoping to dull the chewing sound.

"Have you met her?" Walter's eyebrows lifted.

"No." Nick took another bite. It sounded like toast. "Celeste says she's cute, in shape, educated. A local TV personality. Basically, a loser."

Walter let the sarcasm roll off.

"Tonight, then," Walter said as he turned his purple and orange running shoes over in his hands, looking at the worn tread. "Great girl, no doubt. But the question is, is she right for me, or better suited to someone else? Let's leave it at that and you can form an opinion for yourself, because frankly, I haven't really figured that one out for myself yet. You're my closest friend, so I'm looking forward to your take on her. And us, as a couple."

"Absolutely," Nick agreed. "But just remember, your parents were not the norm."

Walter laughed that hearty laugh of his, full of joy. Eyes closed, head thrown back, all teeth showing. His mind instantly conjuring the image of his parents, who used to hold hands and touch one another like affectionate honeymooners after thirty years of marriage. Walter wanted what his parents had. More than anything, he wanted to find the one woman he could love with reckless abandon.

He was perhaps in ninth grade when he got up the courage to have an adult conversation with his father about the sounds coming from his parent's bedroom at night.

His father grabbed him in a great big bear hug and told him, "Son, I'd walk through fire for your mother. She's the love of my life. Your curse is living with two people who treat their marriage like God meant it to be. The most sacred possession they have." Respecting the courage it took his son to come forward with his concern, his dad added, "I'll try to keep the volume down from now on."

And it was the first time his father took a step back and shook Walter's hand, man to man.

The next day, Walter arrived home from school to find all the furniture in his bedroom rearranged. His bed was no longer situated against the interior wall he and his parents' bedroom shared. His bed was moved clear across his bedroom, the headboard resting against an exterior wall. In the middle of his bed was an eight inch by eight inch package, wrapped in plain, brown paper, the kind grocery bags are made of. Using a black magic marker, his father had written a note on the brown paper wrapping in his careful, block print. Inside the box, a portable CD player, six music CD's, and a set of headphones.

"They set the bar high, my friend," Walter agreed.

Walter grabbed his car keys and headed for the door. As an afterthought, he turned around taking a minute to backtrack to his office. Walter fondly studied the message inside the eight by eight frame hanging above his desk. Walter smiled realizing that even as an adolescent, he had felt compelled to save his father's words of wisdom. The brown wrapping paper with his father's careful block print was preserved forever. "One Day I Hope You Have The Good Fortune To Be In This Same Predicament With Your Son. Love, Dad."

"Okay. Meet you at Jimmy's Seafood at six."

"Later, Dude."

And the men hung up their phones.

CHAPTER 15

Marilyn's place was the perfect location for the commission of a crime. Situated on the absolute last parcel on a dead end street. A neighbor on one side, a chain link fence separating the train tracks from the community on the other. The Department of Public Works and Transportation felt Cherry Tree Lane was adequately lit when they installed the last street light on an existing creosote pole three houses down. If the lights were out inside her home, Marilyn's trailer was barely visible after dusk.

Waitin' for nightfall, Skeeter had a long list of things to do. The first thing he had to do was find out if this Judge Calhoun Hasting guy actually existed. See if Cali was just a little, schemin' bitch who made the whole thing up. It took several hours on the computer and countless phone calls where people kept transferrin' him to 'someone in that department' before finally locatin' the old grandpa in Gwinnett County, Georgia's judiciary system. Lo and behold, a judge by that name actually existed.

Taking it one step further, Skeeter looked up the wealthiest places to live in Georgia. Berkeley Lakes was ranked as the wealthiest city in Georgia, which he had no doubt was where the girl lived. Searchin' the real estate listings for Berkeley Lakes, he determined the shittiest places were listed for around eight hundred thousand bucks. A place where a judge lived went for three, four million, easy.

I'm gettin' me some of that, he thought. He pictured himself in a five bedroom one with at least four bathrooms. If he had to go, he wouldn't need to walk up any steps, he could just take a piss on every floor if he felt like it. Maybe get a pool, too. He'd have all kinda babes sunbathin' at his place. Girls who never, ever gave him the time of day would be beggin' for a chance to massage his back, bring him a cold drink. No more bumpin' uglies with dog-faced welfare whores neither. This here was his big chance to become a real player in life. No more scraps for Skeeter. Nope. No more scraps for Mister. Jimmi. Shiflett.

The courthouse didn't accept phone calls after five pm, at the end of the business day. Since it was Friday, if he didn't get the ball rollin' today, he'd have to wait 'til Monday to talk to the old judge. Skeeter figured he'd make the call now. So what if things were a little out of order? It ain't make no difference because that old grandpa down in Georgia ain't got no idea where the hell the girl was.

It took awhile, but he was steadfast in his goal of talking to Judge Hasting. Then after all that effort, people still tried to get in his way. People always underestimated him. Thought they were better than him. But he done showed them who was in charge. Like that guy who answered the phone.

"Yeah. I need to talk to Judge Calhoun Hasting," Skeeter said, his call answered on the third ring.

He locked the door to his bedroom before turning on the TV. He'd try his best to keep his old lady from eavesdroppin'. She was always tryin' to stick her big nose in his business.

The man cleared his throat before responding, "The Court does not accept telephone calls, sir. You need to have your lawyer contact him."

"I ain't got no lawyer. This here is personal business, okay." Skeeter paced back and forth in his eight by ten bedroom. He increased the volume on his TV another notch to drown out his conversation from his mother.

"If you cannot afford a lawyer, one will be appointed for you," the man spoke with an even tone.

Interrupting the man mid-sentence, Skeeter asked, "This here's where Judge Hasting works at, ain't it?"

"The Honorable Calhoun Hasting does indeed preside at this particular courthouse. It's a matter of public record, sir." The young lawyer loosened his tie, unbuttoned the top button of his dress shirt. It had been a long day and he silently vowed to be on the road within the hour.

"Then do like I already done told you and get him on the phone," Skeeter's words were laced with intimidation.

Who did this clown think he was, demanding to speak with a justice in the same manner he'd call a retail store and ask to speak with the manager? Silence filled both ends of the call as the harried lawyer busied himself with looking for a case file in the first of several daunting stacks. He needed to get home in time for dinner with his wife tonight. He had barely seen his new bride in the last two weeks and they were both beginning to feel the strain. Resisting the urge to hang up on the caller, he decided to give him another five minutes of his time.

"Hey, you still there?" Skeeter made no attempt to disguise his irritation. His minutes were being eaten up on his burner phone.

"As I have already instructed, your lawyer will need to handle any communication with The Court on your behalf."

"Hey, you got a name?" The words seeped out between Skeeter's clenched teeth.

Gladly. The man identified himself as Anthony Rock. He graduated second in his law class and was currently employed as Judge Hasting's law clerk. He had to stifle a laugh when the caller asked him to spell his name. His wife was going to love hearing about this over dinner tonight.

"I wanna make sure you get all the credit for this here phone call, understand? Listen up, Anthony Rock, you can kiss your fancy ass job good-bye when the judge finds out you ain't lettin' me talk to him about Cali. It's your call, pal, you decide," Skeeter laid his cards on the table.

Now he had Mr. Rock's attention, not because of the idle threat to his job. He heard empty promises like that all the time when people didn't get the reaction they wanted. It was the mention of Judge Hasting's granddaughter that was arresting. He stopped looking for the file. "May I ask your particular connection to Cali, sir?" The law clerk inquired while jotting down the exact time of the call on a legal pad.

"You put him on the phone right now, got it?" Skeeter was done being jerked around. He paced like a caged animal at the foot of his bed as he began to pick at the ever present scab on his forearm.

In less than one minute, a male voice with a deep syrupy Southern accent answered the phone. His was the voice of an older man, "This is Judge Hasting. To whom am I speaking?"

Briefly tongue tied, it took a beat for Skeeter to speak, "I got your granddaughter, understand? Me and you are gonna work out a deal for you to get her back, ain't that right?"

Judge Hasting felt all the blood drain from his head. Reaching back, he lowered himself into a dark brown leather chair that had been around the court house as long as he had. The skin on the old man's face glistened against a sickly colored pallor as he broke out into a sweat. His law clerk stood, mouth agape, watching his mentor apparently have a heart attack right before his eyes.

"Are you alright, sir?" Anthony Rock rushed to his side.

The judge shook his head, waved him off. Doing as instructed, Mr. Rock backed up a few steps but remained in the room, his eyes riveted to the judge.

Skeeter thoroughly enjoyed the commotion on the other end of the phone. No doubt, the judge was takin' him serious now.

"Cali tells me you're pretty rich, bein' a judge and all. A millionaire. So, if you want her back, five million sounds like a pretty cheap deal, ain't that right?" Skeeter spoke with authority.

"That's a rather substantial sum of money, sir," Judge Hasting calmly replied as he began rooting around in his desk for a bottle of baby aspirin. Placing two orange tablets in his mouth, he chewed them dry in hopes they may alleviate the oppressive heaviness in the center of his chest. On a yellow legal pad, he scribbled with trembling hands, call Sheriff Mathias. Paper in hand, Mr. Rock turned on his heels and ran from the judge's chambers. Although he was unable to hear the caller's voice, from Judge Hasting's end of the conversation, Mr. Rock was able to deduce this was quite possibly a ransom call involving the judge's granddaughter.

"This's how it's goin' down. You and that airline pilot father are gonna get to get it, understand? Do whatever it takes. Ain't my problem how you do it, just get it done," Skeeter demanded, thoroughly enjoying the feeling of calling all the shots.

Judge Hasting kept his wits about him, saying, "Cali's just a child. She has no idea whatsoever what my finances are. She has no real concept of money. I can assure you, sir, there is no way I could ever meet a demand like that. If we are to both get what we want, we have to come to a more reasonable agreement. I want my granddaughter returned to me, unharmed. For that, I'm willing to do my best to give you what you want, within reason."

Without further negotiation, Skeeter reduced his demands for ransom considerably. "One and a half million dollars. That's it. Take it or leave it."

"It's going to take me several days to have one point five million dollars in my possession." The judge's heart was thundering away in his chest.

"Don't be doin' none of that crap now, you hear me? No one point nothin'. I said one and a half million dollars. If you try to trick me with that one point five crap, the girl ain't gonna make it back to you, understand?" Skeeter's voice was angry.

"Yes, I do understand. From one gentleman to another, there will be no tricks. You have my word. One and a half million dollars, sir. Not a penny less. I'm sure you understand, I'm going to need some kind of assurance we are indeed speaking of my granddaughter."

Skeeter'd been called a lot of things in life. Most of them foul. This was the very first time anyone ever tried calling him a gentleman.

Before abruptly ending the call, Skeeter said, "Yeah, yeah, sure, I get that. I tell you what, judge, how about if I strip her down, bare ass naked, and look for a mole or somethin', how about that?"

CHAPTER 16

Sheriff Mathias's action was swift. Flashing lights and siren cleared the roads as his cruiser sped to the courthouse the moment he received the call concerning his lifelong friend, Cal. A man without ego, Earl Mathias immediately knew this was bigger than his ability to handle. Placing a call to the FBI, the sheriff gratefully handed over the investigation to the appropriate agency. There was no room for error. Cali's life was at stake.

As a result of the sheriff's call, law enforcement personnel quickly descended upon the building. The halls of the courthouse and the judge's chambers were instantly filled with commotion as federal agents swarmed about. Feeling the need to be of some kind of service, Anthony Rock brought the judge a pitcher of ice water in the same helpless spirit someone is sent to boil water as a baby enters the world.

Reluctantly, the agent in charge allowed Judge Hasting, Sheriff Mathias, and the law clerk to remain in the chambers once he began his interviews. If they didn't want to be separated, they had to abide by one stipulation, they speak only when directly addressed. The lead investigator wanted to give each person involved an uninterrupted opportunity to speak. Experience had taught him a case is often solved by the smallest of details. He didn't want to chance leaving out a single observation, often the result of having a train of thought cut short by somebody else's well intended interjections.

Judge Hasting was the first to detail his recollection of the telephone call. His voice somewhat shaky, he spoke thoughtfully and concisely. He reported the call lasted only a few minutes. Perhaps two to three minutes, at the most. He believed the caller did, indeed, have his grandchild, simply because he knew he was her grandfather. He also possessed the knowledge that Cali's father is an airline pilot. The caller initially demanded five million dollars. When the judge expressed doubt about being able to obtain that amount of money, the caller instantly reduced the ransom to one and a half million dollars. No haggling. No back and forth. The new ransom became one point five million dollars. The math stood out in the judge's mind. Notably, the caller was unable to reconcile one and a half million to one point five million dollars. The kidnapper's mood escalated when he felt his intelligence was being manipulated.

Drained, the judge leaned back in his chair to signal he had told his story completely.

"Please forgive me for my frankness, sir. Difficult as it may be, I have to ask the next question. Do you have any reason to believe your granddaughter is still alive?" The agent was stone faced.

"Yes, sir, from the things the caller said, I do believe she's alive," the old man replied while removing a handkerchief from his back pocket to wipe tears from his eyes. "I can't say he actually reported that fact, but we spoke about me getting her back, unharmed, if I pay the ransom."

Giving Judge Hasting a moment to collect himself, the agent asked if anyone else had spoken with the kidnapper. Anthony Rock came forward, offering a more detailed account. He verified the caller's probable lack of education. His repeated usage of the word, 'ain't'. Improper enunciation of the suffix, 'ing', omitting the 'g' sound. Slurring words together such as 'wanna' instead of, 'want to'. He used double negatives. In general, very poor grammar. Once he identified himself to the caller, he was asked to spell both his first and last names. Mr. Rock's final assessment, the kidnapper was globally unintelligent.

"Wonderful detail, Mr. Rock. Anything else you noticed, such as extraneous background noises? His accent? Any slip of the tongue to help identify him?" The federal agent questioned.

"There was either a radio or a television playing in the background. A man's voice was announcing the battle of the beltway, starting at seven-O-five tonight." Mr. Rock racked his brain. "As far as his accent, I don't know where he lives, but it's definitely not a southern state. I'm positive, he's not a native of Georgia."

A diehard baseball fan, Earl Mathias offered, "The battle of the beltway is what the folks up north call it when The Baltimore Orioles face up against The Washington Nationals. It's easy enough to verify if and where there's a scheduled game tonight at seven-O-five. Somebody can look on the MLB website for game times."

Turning his attention back to the judge, the FBI agent summarized, "As you're well aware, this suspect is going away for a very long time, Your Honor. Kidnapping. Ransom demands in excess of one million dollars from a sitting judge, no less. Transportation of a minor across state lines from Georgia to, possibly, either Maryland or the nation's capitol."

Shaking his head, Cal Hasting sat upright in his chair. "I need to clarify your last statement. The kidnapper didn't transport Cali to Maryland." He stoically met the eyes of Earl Mathias, who was the only person other than his wife who knew why Cali was in Maryland.

Then he nodded at Anthony Rock, who was about to be let in on a well kept secret. "On Wednesday morning, my wife and I flew Cali to

Maryland. Our granddaughter was checked into a long term rehabilitation center for drug dependency. Cali's been hooked on heroin for about three months now. On the advise of a professional in this area, we chose a place in Maryland because it has one of the best reputations in the country."

In a show of support, Earl walked over to place a hand on his friend's shoulder, while Mr. Rock's feet remained firmly planted in place. He was mindful not to avert his eyes in shame. Nor did he allow his face to betray one fraction of the shock he felt. Mr. Rock's gaze was steadfast, poker straight, while his insides reacted with an overwhelming sense of doom.

Springing into action, the lead investigator began yelling out orders to his agents, "Somebody get that rehab center on the phone now. I need to find out if the girl is still there and this whole thing's a hoax. If she is missing, what kind of Mickey Mouse operation doesn't immediately notify the family? Did anybody verify the battle of the beltway yet? I want that information now. Who's working on the telephone lines? Did we have any success tracing the call? My guess is, he probably used a burner phone, but it's still worth a try. I want that drug rehab on the phone right now."

The administrator on call at the rehabilitation center was forthcoming. She claimed she was relieved some kind of law enforcement agency was finally taking her missing person report seriously, although she didn't expect the FBI's involvement. Once it was disclosed the missing individual was an inpatient at a drug rehabilitation center, all sense of urgency was lost by the local police department. Cali's worth was diminished by prejudices surrounding drug addiction, which in her opinion, is unfortunately shared by the masses.

On the other end of the call, the lead investigator could hear the tapping of her computer keyboard. Reading from notes made to carefully document her response to Cali's disappearance, she noted Cali was discovered missing at approximately seven ten yesterday morning when she failed to present to yoga/meditation class.

The lead investigator was unable to stop himself as he yelled, "Yesterday? She's been missing since yesterday?"

The administrator's voice quavered as she explained at that time personnel were dispatched to Cali's room, the dining area, the restrooms, all common areas. When Cali wasn't immediately located, a more comprehensive search of all the buildings and the grounds ensued. Protocol was followed to the letter. She pointed out, the facility sits on ten acres, four of which are heavily wooded. The clients are not incarcerated and are, therefore, allowed to wander about the grounds during their free time. Cali Hasting was assigned to a seven a.m. yoga and meditation class, followed by prayer, then breakfast.

By ten-thirty, the local police department had been notified of her disappearance. No officer actually came to the facility in person. After making an official report with the police over the phone, the administrator placed the first of twenty-eight phone calls to the contact number in Cali's file. All the calls went directly to the mother's voice mailbox. At no time, did Maggie Hasting either answer her phone or return any of the urgent calls which she personally made.

"We take every precaution. At our organization, we're fully cognizant we are caring for a vulnerable population. Criminal background checks are done on every employee, from the staff directly involved in patient care, all the way to housekeeping, kitchen staff, maintenance. There's an automatic electronic record of every employee's entering and exiting our facility because they have to swipe their name badge to clock in and out in order for it to reflect in their paychecks. Anyone using somebody else's badge to falsify time records is automatically terminated. That being said, I feel confident you won't find any of our personnel are involved in any way," the woman vouched for her staff with the same vigor a mother would defend her children.

The FBI agent said, "We need you to fax over a list of all your employees. I want a second list of the names of anyone working during Cali Hasting's stay. I need those records in the next fifteen minutes."

Ending the call, he turned to the visibly shaken judge, "It's my belief that your grandchild, most likely, remains in Maryland. I'm turning this investigation over to the Maryland division. I can follow up with loose ends here, but if we're going to have any communication with the kidnapper, Maryland has to take the lead. Every minute counts, Your Honor."

CHAPTER 17

Nick could not suppress his grin, "You chose steamed crabs on purpose, didn't you?"

"Gotta see what's under the wrapping," Walter confirmed Nick's speculation as the men held the doors, allowing the ladies to enter the restaurant. "This place is a landmark. They have the best seafood in Baltimore."

It was Friday night and the place was kicking. People out for a good time and good food. Jimmy's Famous Seafood was divided into two very distinct areas. Directly to the left of the entrance was the bar area which was loud, with eight flatscreen televisions mounted high on the walls. Every TV was programed to a different sports channel. Staggered between the flatscreens were neon bar signs advertising Natty Boh, Coors Light, Corona, Flying Dog Ale. The crowd at the bar was three deep. One female and two male bartenders were constantly on the go, racking up enough tip money to pay for a four year college education.

A kid who looked to be around fifteen more than earned his cut of those tips as their bar-back. The kid was a muscular machine, humping cases of beer and twenty pound bags of ice, keeping the bar well stocked and the bartenders happy.

Groups of guys in T-shirts and ball caps were laughing with girls in tank tops and cut off shorts. In an effort to be heard, everyone was talking at full volume over everyone else. Classic rock alternating with top country was piped in from the ceiling. Because seating in the bar was reserved for those eating steamed crabs, all the tables were covered in heavy brown paper. In the center of each table sat a blue plastic bucket. From time to time, the people eating crabs would scoop the mounting piles of empty crab shells into their plastic buckets which would be quickly whisked away and emptied by a busboy. Scattered about the tables were wooden mallets, thick steak knives, and rolls of paper towels. The aroma was mouth watering. Old bay, rock salt, steamed crabs, beer on tap.

This was where Walter had made reservations a week ago for the two couples. A casual evening in the bar area. The plan was to hang out, give Nick an opportunity to meet Chloe Rose and form some kind of opinion. The two couples could spend a great evening Baltimore style, feasting on steamed crabs and corn on the cob dripping with melted butter while watching the O's sweep the Nationals. Hopefully, they'd drink enough beer to warrant an Uber ride home.

Suspicion took hold the moment the small group emerged from their vehicles and discreetly inventoried their attire. The couples' initial greeting took place in the Holabird Avenue parking lot. Walter was casual in loose fitting cargo shorts and a slightly rumpled Beatle's Abby Road T-shirt. He left his contacts at home and opted for glasses to protect his eyes from flying crab seasoning. In an effort to show support for his hometown ball club, he wore his favorite baseball cap adorned with the famous toothy smile of the Oriole bird.

Nick wore a short sleeve polo neatly tucked inside chino shorts. His wife, Celeste was cute in a racer back floral romper complimented by strappy, flat sandals that showed off her Ravens purple nail polish.

In stark contrast to the others' casual dress, clad in all white, Chloe Rose had chosen a sleeveless silk blouse over skinny jeans. Gold geometric earrings matched the thick Bvlgari 14 K gold necklace which disappeared inside the neckline of her blouse. A single pop of color was added with her choice of dusty rose Kate Spade sandals, featuring an ankle strap and two inch heels. In a few words, Chloe Rose was dressed to kill.

Clearly, someone dressed in white was not prepared to eat steamed blue crabs harvested just a few hours ago from the Chesapeake Bay. It is a well known impossibility for anyone's clothes to remain stain free when cracking the rock hard claws open with the wooden mallets. Dark orange seasoning sprays the air, ultimately landing on the diner's clothing or in the worst case scenario, in an eye. There's absolutely no way to eat steamed crabs without surrendering to hands covered in a spicy coating of seasoning, as well as the delicious, warm, yellow mustard found inside the crab. All that goodness washed down with an icy cold beer is heaven on earth for many native Baltimoreans.

But not so for Chloe Rose. While she absolutely loved crab cakes, she wasn't a fan of eating messy steamed crabs that resulted in multiple tiny cuts on her fingers. She absolutely abhorred eating anything with her fingers.

Being the traffic girl for the local Fox channel afforded her many considerations, so she was accustomed to getting her way. It never once crossed her mind that she was inconveniencing others when she made a fuss about the steamed crabs. Additionally, the two friends had been raised by their mothers to be quintessential gentlemen. In the time it took for the hostess to fetch their glasses of ice water, the heavy hearted decision had been made to request seating elsewhere, for Chloe Rose's sake.

"Oh, that's no problem at all. Around here, people will practically kill each other for a chance to eat crabs in the bar. Trust me, your table won't go to waste. Follow me," the perky high school girl led them to the opposite side of the restaurant, chatting nonstop the entire way. "There's no waiting line for a table in here. But in the bar when the O's are playing, the only way to get a table in there is with a reservation at least a week in advance. Or if somebody dies. Just kidding. But, you probably already know that, right? Your waitress will be right over. Enjoy!"

Walter's eyes met Nick's. Strike one. Turning on a dime, Chloe Rose suddenly became the only member of their group appropriately dressed. The couples settled themselves in the subdued dining room which was the antithesis of the bar area. White cotton tablecloths, stainless cutlery, and soft overhead elevator music filled the space. There was nothing energizing about this room. It was a room for romance, marriage proposals, first dates, or anniversary celebrations. For a fleeting moment, Walter felt like a kid who had contracted chickenpox the first day of summer vacation, quarantined behind his bedroom window, enviously watching all the other kids ride their bikes.

Although it got off to somewhat of a rocky start, everyone loosened up after a cold beer or in Chloe Rose's case, a chardonnay. All was not lost. Maybe after dinner, they could make their way into the bar and catch the last few innings of the ball game in a room where, no doubt, there would be standing room only. Every so often, loud bursts of cheering drifted from the other side of the establishment. Clearly, the Orioles were well on their way to defeating the Nationals for a third game in this series.

It was more than Walter could take. He wanted to be in the bar, watching the Orioles sweep their nemesis, but Nick had started to poke the sleeping bear, so Walter stayed put for the time being. The baseball game would have to wait.

"What about you, Chloe? Are you a traditional, two children, a nice home in the suburbs kind of girl?"

"Oh, it's actually Chloe Rose," she flashed a million dollar smile in Nick's direction.

"My apologies, I stand corrected. Chloe Rose," Nick lifted his drink in a toast.

"I think that's something my future husband and I should decide together," she gave the perfect answer. Just as he predicted, Chloe Rose reached over and threaded her fingers through Walter's.

"I'm an only child. What about you, do you have any siblings?" Nick was on a roll.

Celeste knew perfectly well what her husband was doing. Interrogating her girlfriend under the guise of friendly conversation, but she had grown used to it. She just hoped, finally, Chloe Rose was that special someone who deserved the coveted seal of approval.

"Actually, yes, I do," Chloe Rose thoroughly enjoyed the attention. "I have a sister, who is two years older than me."

"Hey, if she's local, I think it'd be fun for all of us to get together. I can check the schedule at Merriweather, see if there's a band playing that we all like. You should invite her and her husband. Is she married?" Nick continued to ply vital information from the unwitting woman.

"Oh, yes. Married. Mother of three, the whole shebang," Chloe Rose sighed. "We don't really have that kind of a relationship though. We're more of a, see you at Christmas or Thanksgiving kind of sisters."

Walter was paying very close attention now.

"Wait a minute. I didn't know you have a sister," Celeste offered. "All these years, I've never heard you mention a sister."

"That's because we're polar opposites. She's all mother earth. Making her own baby food. Hiking in the mountains. That's really not my thing." Celeste made a face of disgust.

By comparison, Walter and one of his two sisters were on the phone almost daily. They were always mothering him, fretting over his personal safety when he had field assignments, preferring he and Nick were confined to offices and computers to track their various villains.

Once a month, he'd take his sisters to lunch, get the lowdown. Feed all the good information to his dad, while holding anything of concern close to the vest. Both girls adored their dad, but ever since their mom passed away last year from cancer, they gravitated to Walter for subjects they may have normally discussed with their mother. Their mom's death had taken its toll on their father, so they spared him any news that may have caused him the least bit of angst.

Walter desired a serious, committed relationship. His personal goal was to get married and raise children. He had serious doubts about a longterm relationship with a partner who didn't have close family ties. Strike two.

They had all finally placed their dinner orders and the way Walter figured, it would be at least thirty minutes before their meals arrived. That was more than enough time to get a quick peak at the score. The ladies were engaged in some conversation about fashion. Now was the perfect time to make his move.

Walter caught Nick's eye, mouthing the words, men's room, which, of course, Nick knew was a ruse. And he was out of his seat. Toward the rear of the dining room, only to make a sharp left, by-passing the men's restroom altogether. Walter quickly headed directly for the bar area.

The room looked like Mardi Gras, people cheering, a few men whistling loud enough to herd cattle. Girls danced in place, oblivious to their beer sloshing over the rims of thick beer mugs onto the sticky floor. It was an explosion of energy. Eventually, he squeezed his way into the room by twisting and turning his body as he inched his way along the congested maze of bodies. He was propelled along the waves of people until he was somehow standing behind an older couple sitting at the bar. A flat screen tuned into the ballgame directly in front of him, he couldn't have asked for a better vantage point. The crowd burst into cheers.

"Ahhh, I missed it! I can't believe I missed it. What just happened?" Walter exclaimed to himself, so excited to be in the midst of the celebration, no longer an outsider.

The old man turned in his seat, his flabby neck stretching to look at whoever was behind him. His glassy-eyed wife followed suit, turning her stool until she faced Walter. Already one drink too many, he enjoyed chastising the tall guy in the Beatles T-shirt, "You're kidding, right? You'd have to be blind and deaf to miss that. You gotta pay attention, son. Pay attention."

The gray haired woman nodded her head, echoing her husband's sound advise, "Gotta pay attention."

As the man and his wife turned back to their beers, Walter glanced at the person who bumped into his left shoulder while his hand instinctively felt for his weapon concealed in the pocket of his cargo shorts. He came face to face with the most exquisite creature he had ever laid eyes on. A gorgeous face framed by a wild mane of black tresses that cascaded down the middle of her back. For a fleeting moment, he caught himself inappropriately wondering if her loose curls felt as soft as he imagined.

"The O's made a six, four, three double play," she looked directly into his eyes while she spoke. "Oh, you have a little cut right here." She touched her finger to her own face to mirror where Walter had nicked his face shaving.

He smiled and responded with nothing. Not a single word formed when he opened his mouth to speak. He stared at her like an idiot, his brain losing the connection between itself and his mouth. He just stared at the most beautiful woman he had ever seen, not a single utterance escaping his lips.

Thinking her statement needed further explanation, she spoke again, this time leaning in a little closer so Walter could hear her over the sound of a successful business, "The Orioles made a double play. The Nats were up to bat. Their batter hit a ground ball to our short-stop in the hole. The shortstop made the first out by throwing to second. Once he got the out, the second baseman pivoted and fired to first, making a double play."

Her hair smelled like honeysuckle and sunshine. Walter was grateful for the deafening noise level.

She had an accent. Italian, he guessed. The way she curled the sounds in the back of her throat made every word seem exciting and fresh. Around here, there were Highlandtown accents, Greek, and Spanish. But Italian, never. He was intrigued. This woman was alive. It was jumping off her skin. Walter found himself trying to discreetly check her left ring finger but so far he was unable to get a good look.

"You know your baseball. I guess your husband's a diehard fan."

She smiled, slightly cocking her head to the side, "My father and brothers deserve the credit. It was for my own survival since birth. I had to learn baseball or live a very lonely life as a child."

Elated, he gave her every opportunity, but no mention of a husband. Just a father and brothers. He loosened up, daring to take a glimpse at the height of her heels. She had on Adidas running shoes. She was all of five feet, ten inches. Legs that went on forever.

She laughed, "Yes, I see you noticed I am rather tall for a woman." Walter leaned in close as he studied her face, noting she wore no makeup except some lip gloss. "Also compliments of my father."

"If I had to take a guess, I'd say you look like you've been bike riding," Walter wanted to know more about her. She was wearing black, skin tight Spandex under florescent lime green running shorts. A matching sleeveless cycling jersey, with a logo Walter couldn't read from that angle, revealed sunburnt shoulders.

"Hi, beautiful," the bartender's face lit up. "What'll it be? Natty Boh? My treat."

"Grazia. You are most kind," the woman said.

"Make that two, please, my man," Walter quickly added.

The bartender's unprovoked evil eye did not go unnoticed.

For the barkeep, the rest of the universe ceased to exist. In a bar jam packed with thirsty patrons, he suddenly had all the time in the world to chat with this stunningly beautiful woman. Jealousy took hold in two middle aged women, dressed like two twenty year olds showing way too much cleavage, when he leaned between them. Half his body stretched across the bar as he handed the exotic woman an open bottle of Natty Boh. He made a half-hearted delivery of Walter's unopened can of beer by placing it on the bar, clearly out of his reach. Walter had to reach between the two women who didn't mind one little bit.

Drinks delivered, the bartender still didn't go away. Annoyed by his physical presence, splayed across their territory, the two twenty year old wannabes began to loudly protest about the perceived delay in the next round of orange crushes, even though they hadn't yet finished the drinks in their hands.

Making no effort to disguise his misuse of power, the bartender eyed them before saying, "You two just might be at the legal limit. Hate to cut you off so early in the evening," which immediately resulted in their being content.

Practically climbing over the bar, the bartender took full advantage of the Italian woman's attention, "You rode all thirty miles?"

The bartender smiled, which made his physical appearance less appealing. To put it kindly, it was good he worked in an environment of dim lighting.

"Thirty-five," she corrected.

"Rode thirty-five miles? On a bicycle?" Walter put in his two cents.

"Si. It's a benefit ride my friends and I do every year. It's the silliest name, called Tour Dem Parks, Hon. The route takes us all over Baltimore. Patterson Park. Druid Hill. Dickeyville. Did you know there's an actual waterfall behind a neighborhood in Dickeyville? We even rode to Fort McHenry. So many amazing sites to see on a bicycle that we would have missed traveling by car."

Getting back into the conversation, the bartender asked, "Two dollars per mile adds up to seventy dollars." He was a mathematical genius.

"Oh, that is most generous. If you will be so kind to make your check payable to St. Jude Children's Research, per favore," she requested.

The bartender raced to his backpack tucked in a corner, ready to make out the check.

She was amazing. Striking beauty, yes, but so much more. Anyone who rode thirty-five miles in a day certainly bike rides on a regular basis. Walter was an avid cyclist. Obviously, she was someone with a loving heart, doing it for the sake of a children's charity. He loved kids.

"Ahhh shit!" the old man directly in front of Walter yelled. "They got a guy on third and that's never a good thing." Craning his neck, he asked, "You paying attention back there, son?"

"Too many ways to score," Walter agreed as he gave the man's shoulder a friendly pat.

"Wild pitch," the gorgeous woman offered as she and Walter faced one another. She was close enough to kiss.

"Balk," Walter added.

"Passed ball," she said. Walter was in awe. Here he was, talking with a breathtaking woman who really understood baseball. "Oh, and not to forget, catcher's interference."

She raised her beer bottle. Walter tapped his can against it producing a low thump which delighted her.

Walter stuck his hand out, "I'm Walter Kostos."

She slipped her warm hand inside his, completing the handshake, "Piacere, which in my language means, nice to meet you. I am..."

"I'm Chloe Rose," the blonde in two inch Kate Spades appeared out of no where. There was no mistake, she was making a display of ownership as she threaded her arm inside Walter's elbow and pressed her body close. Her tone was borderline aggressive, "And how exactly do you two know each other?"

The woman's voice remained kind, "Your husband was explaining a baseball play to me."

Walter opened his mouth to rectify the presumption of marriage, but Chloe Rose beat him to it, "He's always rescuing damsels in distress. But that's why I love him."

The woman was unfazed. She smiled warmly and said it was her pleasure to make their acquaintances. At that very moment, the bartender reappeared, check for seventy dollars in hand. He was ecstatic to see a good-looking blonde tightly clinging to the handsome guy, thereby putting an abrupt end to his conversation with the gorgeous brunette. A woman he had been trying unsuccessfully to date ever since he first laid eyes on her two years ago. Sure, she was way out of his league, but you can't blame a guy for trying.

Hey, wait a minute. Hold everything. Wasn't this the blonde traffic girl on Fox news standing here in person? His face glowed with pleasure. It took every ounce of willpower for him to resist yelling out in delight, "Busted!" He didn't care how many tips he lost, he wasn't moving. Determined not to miss a thing, he stationed himself directly in front of the threesome, arms folded across his chest, thoroughly enjoying the show.

Taking the check, the woman who just participated in the Tour Dem Parks, Hon Bike Ride thanked the bartender before turning to Walter and Chloe Rose, offering a warm farewell, "Ciao."

He should have run after her. Asked her name. Asked her for a chance to get to know her. In that moment, Walter made the worst decision of his life as he watched the woman of his dreams walk away, because what chance did he ever have of meeting her again?

CHAPTER 18

Skeeter wasted no time moving to the next step in his plan. Crawling on his hands and knees to the back of his bedroom closet, he pulled a small metal lock box from behind a loose wall panel. He counted his stash of money. After stuffing two hundred twenty bucks in the front pocket of his grimy jeans, he returned the remainder of the money, closed the box and safely tucked it back in his secret hiding spot. No way he was gonna leave his dough out for his mother to steal when he wasn't lookin'.

At the convenience store down the street, he purchased two pay as you go mobile phones with untraceable cash. He was way smarter than those chumps who made buys with credit cards.

Returning home, he began to search his room for the key to the lock. Where was it? He hadn't looked for it in a really long time. Without hesitation, Skeeter ransacked the eight by ten bedroom. Pulling underwear, socks, and shirts from drawers, he let them land on the floor next to the mounds of dirty clothes. No key. Dumping his bedside table drawer onto the center of his unmade bed, he quickly rooted through the contents. Half empty packs of cigarettes, loose candy covered in lint, pennies, a few nickels, one quarter, and a balled up receipt from his last burger spilled on top a bed that was a tangle of one army surplus blanket and sheets that hadn't been changed in well over seven months.

Pushing a collection of dumbbells out of his way, he was mindful not to knock over any of the coffee cans he kept on the floor by his bed. Too much trouble to walk the ten feet or so to the bathroom in the middle of the night, Skeeter routinely relieved himself without getting out of bed. Three plastic coffee cans filled to the brim with his urine rested against one wall.

Getting down on his hands and knees, Skeeter pulled a shoebox from under his bed. Rooting through his most valuable possessions, he found his knife and a small silver colored key. Since the knife might come in handy, he shoved it in his pants pocket before grabbing the key, just in case.

Making a bee line for the alley, he flung the battered tarpaulin off the dirt bike. Slits and gaping holes did little to protect the bike from the elements. Although it hadn't run for a couple of years due to neglecting to change the oil, Skeeter kept it secured to a metal pole declaring, No Parking, with a four foot length of chain. From the looks of things, he guessed nobody'd want to steal it. It was rusted through in a couple of spots. Both tires were dry rotted, flat as pancakes. The gas cap was missing.

The chain and lock weren't in much better shape, but he didn't care. They would still serve his purpose. So much corrosion and dirt plugged the lock's key hole, Skeeter had to run back to his house, returning with a bottle of corn oil from the kitchen. Using his jagged fingernails and the tip of his knife, he scraped away the debris. He then poured several drops of the cooking oil into the hole. Forcing the key inside, he impatiently worked it back and forth, back and forth until it finally came free.

Behind the closed door to his bedroom, he tucked the lock and chain, a hammer, and two bandanas in a cheap plastic, undersized, gym bag. Putting the cart before the horse, he made the call to the grandfather. The timing was all off but he wanted to get the girl after dark and if he wanted to connect with the old man before the weekend, he had to do it before the end of the business day. It didn't matter because the old grandfather had no idea where she was. Cherry Tree Lane or West Lafayette Street, so what did it matter?

When evening fell, that's when he finally made his move as he headed back to Marilyn's trailer. This time he drove well under the speed limit which was a rarity for Skeeter. He didn't want to take any chances of being pulled over by the police for speeding. It was vital to blend in, fly under the radar, not be noticed.

Tracking down the judge was the hard part of the whole operation. The rest was second nature for someone who'd been breaking into houses since he was nine or ten years old. Just as he expected, the trailer was barely visible from two houses down. Taking his time, Skeeter made a three point turn at the end of the dead end street so when he parked, his Chevette was pointing in the right direction for a quick getaway.

A very dim light shone through the cracks of the closed Venetian blinds where the living room area was located. The rest of the windows were completely dark. Hustling to the far end of the trailer, he crouched down between it and the chain link fence. He waited a beat or two before trying the bathroom window. It slid open without a hitch. That broken bobby pin shoved in the lock did the trick. Hoisting himself the six feet from the ground onto the sill was no problem for the man who almost daily lifted weights until his muscles cried out for mercy. His body was hard and strong, without any visible layers of fat.

Walking on light feet, not making a sound, he passed Marilyn's dark bedroom and stopped at the end of the hall, gazing into the tropical themed living room and kitchenette. The place was empty. In disbelief, he rushed into the living room and did a quick spin.

It was no wonder he almost completely missed her. She was curled up on the near end of the couch like a baby kitten, the eggplant colored blanket pulled over her body and the greater part of her head. Only her nose, mouth, and chin were visible. He could see her hands were tucked under her chin like a small child praying. The small mound looked like nothing more than a blanket tossed on the end of the sofa. Something about her innocence stirred a deep resentment in Skeeter's chest. His hands automatically clenched into tight fists as he stared at her with eyes filled with hate.

Getting her in the car was a piece of cake. She was so out of it, so drugged up, she did whatever he commanded without question. Tucked safe and sound in the passenger seat of his Chevy Chevette for the second time that day, Cali leaned her head against the seat and closed her eyes. She missed the miles of condemned brick row-homes with the words, No Trespassing, stenciled across the fronts. With every mile Skeeter drove, their surroundings filled with images of spray painted bubbled graffiti as rival gangs staked out their territories. There were no signs of life beyond mutant size rodents roaming about. As far as the eye could see, Skeeter and Cali were swallowed up by the crumbling red brick colosseums found deep inside the streets of West Baltimore.

Even when he took the hammer to the wood that blocked the entryway to the condemned building, she didn't budge. In less than ten minutes, he was in. It was the perfect location because the walls adjoining the other houses on either side remained intact. There was a large, exposed, cast iron pipe that once carried water, or gas, or something in the front room. He really didn't care. All that mattered was the pipe was securely in place.

Skeeter helped her up the steps. Told her to sit down next to the pipe. It wasn't until he secured the chain around her ankle, the other end to the pipe, that she came to life. She kept objecting, pleading, squealing like a newborn puppy, saying, "no, no, no, and please," until he wanted to either punch her in the face or give her another hit of H just to shut her up.

Instead he got down on his hands and knees so they were face to face. Separated by inches from one another, she felt his hot breath on her face. His uncontrollable rage emanated from him like an exposed electrical current. Trying to create distance between them, Cali scrambled backward on all fours until she was pressed up against the wall, trapped. There was nowhere for her to go.

"You better hope your grandparents give a shit about you. 'Cause if they ain't willin' to pay up to get you back, you're gonna rot in here, understand? In case you got any ideas about screamin' for help, these here streets are gonna fill up with men who will take turns on you. One after another, all day long. Or you can keep your trap shut and lay low 'til I get my ransom money. Ain't make no difference to me, you'll still be right here waitin' for me when I get back, one way or the other," he threatened.

Skeeter stood, walked to the doorway. He heard the light clatter of the chain as it shook against the pipe from her uncontrollable trembling. The faint sound of Cali's cries, muffled by her own hands clamped over her mouth infuriated him.

"That's right, not a peep. Thing is, you never know if I'll be the one standin' right outside this here door, listenin'. The way I see it, if I come back and hear you in here makin' a ruckus, I got no choice except to shove a rag down your throat before I duct tape your trap shut. Then I'd have to tie your hands up," Skeeter intimidated her, his dark eyes shining. "Is that what you want?"

"No, please don't do that, Skeeter. You'll see, I won't make a peep. You have my word," Cali begged.

He hesitated for what seemed an eternity. His were the fiery eyes of a soulless fiend. Trembling with terror, Cali lowered her head onto her bent knees. Closing her eyes, she prayed he would leave.

"Don't make me come back here and hurt you," he leveraged a final threat before shoving the plywood securely over the entry way.

CHAPTER 19

Some people would say they were like an old married couple, able to finish each other's sentences. Celeste thought they had the ability to read one another like identical twins. A glint of an eye. A barely detectable furrowing of the brow. Each one knew what the other was thinking without a single word being spoken. So attuned to each other's psyche, Celeste often joked that her husband and his partner shared the same DNA. Not just identical twins, she decided. More accurately, they were siamese twins joined at the heart.

Walter didn't have to tell Nick the phone call was from their chief. He already knew from Walter's expression, the way he excused himself from the table as he listened intently for a full seven minutes to the other end. The way he ended the call with, "Yes, sir." Nick was pulling out his credit card long before Walter announced to the table they had to leave because they were on assignment, effective immediately.

"Seriously? This is a little beyond the call of duty, don't you think? I'm famished. We're all starving and besides she just took our order," Chloe Rose protested. "What's an hour, give or take? You have time to eat before you go. Just say you were somewhere an hour further away. You could tell him you were in D.C."

Nick handed Celeste his credit card and the keys to the car, "I love you, baby. Be careful driving home." His wife lifted her face to receive his kiss.

Walter removed one hundred fifty dollars. Chloe Rose refused to accept it, petulantly hiding her hands in her lap beneath the table. She had already begun to sulk.

"This should cover our meals and a taxi home for you." He kissed the top of her head as he set the money on the table.

"What kind of job expects its employees to just abandon everything at their whim?" Chloe Rose was indignant as she watched the men's backs as they hurried out the door. In her petty frame of mind, they looked comical, Nick's slightly chubby five foot ten frame overshadowed by Walter's muscular six three stature. She took a rather un-ladylike swig of her chardonnay.

Celeste smiled warmly as she explained, "They're FBI agents, Chloe Rose. It's a different world they work in. Listen, if you want to have a meaningful relationship with Walter, if you really want this to work out with him, you'll have to get used to it. They can't go out there and safely do the things they do, if they don't have our full support. Nick needs to be fully engaged in his job at all times and he can't do that if he's worrying about me. Their jobs are extremely dangerous and I don't want a mishap ruining our lives because he wasn't focusing on whatever bad guy they're confronting. Walter deserves that too, don't you agree?"

Begrudgingly, Chloe Rose nodded as she admired her reflection in the mirrored wall directly across from their table. It's just that she was used to getting her way. That's the way it was her entire life. First it was her father. True, she had to admit she was a tad bit spoiled being a daddy's girl but that wasn't her fault. For the most part, it was hard going anywhere in public because people naturally fawned over her being a television celebrity. A loyal fan base religiously watched her live morning traffic reports. Could she help it if she was drop dead gorgeous and was accustomed to men bending over backwards trying to please her? Her whole life, her good looks parlayed into a ticket for a free ride.

But that wasn't the case with Walter and she didn't like it one little bit. No question about it, that one was a challenge. The first and only man she couldn't control with a tilt of her head or an adorable little pout. The thing was, she couldn't make up her mind if she found his behavior irresistible or infuriating.

It wasn't that she wanted him to get hurt, but the fact that he didn't even bat an eye when he recognized her displeasure was what needled at her. Any other man would have at least seriously weighed the option of disappointing her against immediately reporting to work. But without a second thought, Walter was gone in a flash. Although she was attracted to his intriguing line of work for the FBI, must he treat every assignment as though it were a life or death situation?

Jumping in Walter's car, the men headed to headquarters while Walter filled Nick in on what information he knew, "We have a sixteen year old female kidnapping victim. The grandfather, who's a presiding judge in Georgia received the ransom call a little over an hour ago. The caller's demanding one point five million in cash in exchange for her return."

"If the grandfather's in Georgia, why is Maryland involved?" Nick asked.

"On Wednesday morning, the girl was admitted for inpatient drug treatment at New Light Treatment and Recovery. It's located somewhere just south of the Delaware line. Feds in Georgia got the initial call. They initiated contact with the treatment center's administrator who claims she made twenty-eight telephone calls to the mother since yesterday morning. Not one of those calls was answered," Walter kept both hands firmly planted on the steering wheel at ten and two, a definite giveaway that his mind was somewhere other than his driving.

Flipping open a small notepad, Nick began to take notes, "Twenty-eight phone calls from a drug treatment center were ignored, huh? Makes me wonder where the mother was that she was so busy she couldn't answer her phone. Maybe she isn't keen on having a kid with a drug addiction. One point five million would make a nice rainy day fund, while she's at it. Parents have been known to snuff out their offspring for a lot less. What do you think, suspects number one and two, the parents?"

"I agree," Walter nodded.

"Does this sixteen year old girl have a name?" Nick asked, pen poised over paper.

"Cali Hasting. She didn't show up for a scheduled therapy class yesterday morning, so the staff members searched the grounds. By ten thirty, the administrator claims she made a missing persons report with the local police department."

"Easy enough to check out," Nick said as his encyclopedic brain began to spout out statistics while making entries in his notepad. "I don't have to tell you, time is of the essence. We both know about fifty percent of abductions are by family members so that reinforces our decision to keep the parents on our radar. When was the last time anyone actually laid eyes on Cali?"

"Wednesday evening, around nine."

"Forty-six hours. That puts us way behind the eight ball. We've already missed a significant window of golden opportunity because the majority of children who are murdered are dead within the first three hours of being taken. It's not looking good," Nick reflected.

Walter never treated any of Nick's information with skepticism. Years of experience had taught him, his partner's data was always spot on.

Exchanging a look with Nick, Walter noted his concern. "Most kidnappers don't have us on their tails. Do you have a preference, the family or the rehab center?"

"How about if you take the family? If they have something to hide, you're like a bloodhound on a scent trail. You can smell a lie a hundred miles away." Nick didn't hesitate to recognize his strength was analytical, whereas Walter's forte was psychosocial.

"In the meantime, I can get a car from headquarters and head up to New Light. I want to check the security cameras, employee time clock, get a list of all their vendors who have access to the grounds. Run people through NCIC for past criminal histories. Talk to the local police who took the missing person report." Nick was already making a mental list of duties for himself. "It's all going to take a day or two. The hard part will be trying to convince the other patients to come forward if they have any information."

Walter smiled for the first time since he spoke with the breathtaking brunette clad in cycling gear. "You'll get them to talk. Pour on the charm, my friend. Pour on your charm."

Prior to receiving the call from the bureau's chief, Walter was somewhat preoccupied with thinking about a return trip to Jimmy's Seafood the next evening. Solo. He wanted to coax the hostile bartender into giving him some information about the exotic woman who understood baseball.

Walter's sister had been right all along. Chloe Rose wasn't the one. While in the mystery beauty's company, he finally understood what his baby sister had been talking about all this time. Standing next to the stunning woman with the Italian accent, he felt his pulse quicken. Suddenly, all his senses were keenly alive. He wanted to be swallowed up whole in this woman's world. Up until tonight, no woman had ever made him feel like that before. He wasn't about to let her slip through his fingers without a fight.

However, once the work call came through, everything in his personal life became secondary. For the time being, the woman of his dreams would have to be securely tucked away in the recesses of his mind. His central focus became accomplishing the assignment at hand. Right now, his only priority in life was a girl named Cali Hasting. According to Nick's statistics, the girl's life was in grave danger. Unlike Nick, who uttered his game plan aloud, Walter formulated his plan of action in his head. While driving to headquarters, an extensive inventory of questions evolved.

Why did the kidnapper contact a grandparent rather than her parents? What was the connection between a judge in Georgia and an abductor in Maryland? In the past, had Judge Hasting presided over a trial involving Cali's abductor and the kidnapping was in retaliation? Were the parents able to account for their whereabouts for the past two days? What prompted the family to choose New Light Treatment and Recovery Center in Maryland, rather than a place in Georgia? Did the judge and the kidnapper establish an agreed upon time for their next exchange? Walter fretted, what trails were left for him to follow?

CHAPTER 20

In order to effectively orchestrate the ransom demands, Walter needed the judge to be physically present in Maryland. Utilization of local, as well as national television coverage needed to be strategically timed so as not to unhinge the abductor. His first plan of action, once he and Nick arrived at headquarters, was to speak directly with the agent in charge in Georgia.

Once the case was determined to fall under Maryland's jurisdiction, Judge Hasting was immediately delivered to his home by the sheriff. Prior to exiting the courthouse, Judge Cal Hasting somehow had the wherewithal to ask a stunned Mr. Rock to please clear his docket indefinitely. On the ride over, Sheriff Mathias dispatched a call to his deputies ordering them to add the Hasting's homestead to their daily run sheets on an hourly basis. It was the least he could do, keeping an eye on his childhood friend's place in case the scumbag kidnapper showed up.

■ ■ ■

Judge Cal Hasting and Sheriff Earl Mathias shared a long history. Almost forty years ago, it was Cal who came to the sheriff's aid in his time of need. The two men had an isolated evening sitting in the Hasting's den sharing a bottle of bourbon. Cal almost never drank, but he liked to keep a bottle tucked away on the top shelf of the coat closet in case a situation warranted it. His taste for alcohol was so infrequent, he had to use the palm of his hand to clear away the fine dust that had settled on the bottle before breaking the seal.

Earl was looking for a little solace in the bottom of that bottle. Earlier, he had gone home to discover his wife of twelve years had left him. No disagreement. No warning. Nothing.

Cal was his most true and loyal friend. Friends since childhood, Earl had no hesitation whatsoever trusting him with his darkest secrets.

"She didn't take any of the furniture we picked out together. Not even one lousy picture to remind her of us. She left it all. Crazy as it sounds, that makes me feel worse. It's like she wants to act like we never existed." The man took his big paws to smooth back hair over the beginning of a bald spot.

"Let's think about that for a minute, now. What you're telling me may actually be a good sign. How do you know she didn't just want to get away for a few days? Needed a little time to clear her head?" Cal remained the voice of reason.

"Her wedding band on top a handwritten note wishing me a happy life, is why," Earl said before taking a big swallow of his whiskey, wincing from the burn down his esophagus. Dismay hung heavy in his tone, "That's what it said, 'Best wishes for a happy life'. Like she was signing my high school yearbook or something."

■ ■ ■

After all these years, it was finally Earl's turn to repay the favor. Depositing his lifelong friend in his leather recliner, Earl Mathias intercepted Caroline as she headed to the den to greet her husband. He was pretty lithe for an old guy. Ushering her to her own kitchen, he asked Caroline to have a seat at the kitchen table before he gave a brief synopsis of the situation. Earl was most grateful Cal's wife of sixty years was made of sturdy stock. Right now, the behavior of a hysterical wife would certainly send his friend to his grave.

Without a second thought, Caroline picked up the wall phone and requested Robert and Maggie's immediate presence at their home. As Cali's parents, it was only right that they should know what was going on. In person, the circumstances much too dire to disclose over the telephone. There was an urgent situation. She would explain when they arrived.

After ending the call, Earl asked Caroline to make one more quick detour before running to her husband's side. The FBI would need a picture of Cali. Hurrying to their bedroom, she pulled two picture albums from the top shelf of their closet. Albums stuffed with countless photographs of their Cali Girl. Her radiant beauty jumped off the pages. One photograph after another captured a vivacious girl with a winning smile. A healthy, exuberant teen before heroin ravaged her body. With a heavy heart, Caroline realized she didn't have a recent depiction of the gaunt, lifeless girl they so adored to show the FBI.

Robert and his wife arrived mere minutes before the call came through from Special Agent in Charge Walter Kostos. For the next four hours, he spoke with each member of Cali's immediate family. He was left with one troubling impression. He was never given a satisfactory explanation as to why Cali didn't reside with her parents. The same parents who willingly raised two older children, a daughter and a son. This same mother blatantly ignored twenty-eight telephone calls over the course of two days, as well as their subsequent messages from a drug rehabilitation facility where her daughter was being treated. In another state, no less. He made a mental note to keep a close watch on Maggie and Robert Hasting.

Checking in with Nick, Walter discovered there weren't any surveillance videos of Cali exiting the grounds with an employee. Security cameras monitored all five parking lots. To Nick's dismay, none of the entrances to any of the buildings on the property were videotaped. Food was delivered twice a week, on Tuesdays and Saturdays, so those deliverymen were eliminated for the immediate time being. Laundry was done on the premises. Nick made plans to have the grounds professionally searched with the assistance of the local police department first thing in the morning when there was light.

"Basically, I got one big goose egg. How'd you do?" Nick yawned into the phone.

Expressing his concerns about the parents, Walter delivered his thoughts, "The family dynamics between the girl and the parents doesn't feel right to me. The father gave Cali a debit card but the curious thing is, it was on the sly. Apparently, he wasn't forthcoming about the card with his wife. In fact, she didn't know anything about it until tonight. The mother was pretty quick to recover, but her immediate reaction when her husband came clean about the card, she was not happy."

"Another red flag," Nick confirmed. "Whoa, wait a minute. Are you sure it was a debit card and not a credit card?"

"He definitely said it was a debit card. Why?"

"When the patients arrive, the treatment center routinely confiscates anything that the patients might use to buy drugs with. I checked the locker with Cali's personal effects. It had her driver's license, a credit card, and her cell phone. There was one credit card in the locker, no debit card," Nick explained.

"Merry Christmas," Walter smiled into the phone. "I'll call the father back. See if he has the debit card number. It would be a huge break if she's somehow in possession of that card. I'll call you right back as soon as I talk to him."

"Hey buddy, do you think we could wait until morning to call? It's almost one a.m.," Nick yawned again as he checked his watch. "We can take a look with fresh eyes in the morning."

Without realizing it, the agents had worked tirelessly for hours. Nick was no more good. Reluctant at first, Walter finally agreed to go home, grab a little sleep and start fresh in the morning. At the very least, a shower and change of clothes, a cup of steaming hot coffee after a few hours shut eye would revitalize Walter.

CHAPTER 21

Skeeter didn't answer the first four times Marilyn's number lit up the screen on his phone. It wasn't until the phone went silent for a full ten minutes that he felt the beginnings of concern. He didn't want her to go and do somethin' stupid like show up at his place, let his greedy mother find out what he was up to. His old lady was always stickin' her big nose in his business, where it didn't belong and he wasn't about to give her any of his dough. He ain't trust Marilyn when she got all wound up like that. He wouldn't even put it past her to call the cops. Mess up his big plan. Ruin his big payday.

There was a big chip on his shoulder when Skeeter returned Marilyn's call.

She answered on the first ring, demanding, "Where did you carry her?"

Mirroring the feeling in her gut, her tone was wound tight. She ignored the collection of prized Marilyn Monroe gowns that she had worn earlier as they slid off the edge of the bed into a heap on the floor.

"I don't know what you're talkin' about," Skeeter said.

"I come home and she's not here. I smell me some fish, boy. You tell me now where you carried her!" Marilyn was nearly screaming.

Skeeter pulled the phone away from his ear, shocked by the intensity of Marilyn's outrage.

Still, he lied, "Like I done said, I ain't got no idea what you're talkin' about."

"That store you make groceries on Montford Avenue? A tag on the cake box is from that very store. Only way she could get there is you carried her in your car, I know. It is not my birthday. What tales did you tell her? You let what I have burn your eye."

"Talk English. I ain't in the mood for none of your voodoo talk," Skeeter reproached her.

"You look at what I have with a jealous eye," she clarified.

Under normal circumstances, Marilyn spoke fast, but now her words were rapid fire. Her melodious island lilt replaced with a quick barrage of choppy words.

"I been home all night. I ain't done nothin' wrong. Maybe she went on home to Georgia. I ain't her keeper, got it?" Skeeter was only half listening.

When Skeeter didn't come clean with the truth, a fire in Marilyn's gut burst into an inferno. "Did you sell her to mens? You think because the dog does not bark, it does not have teeth. I am Trini to the bone, boy. I will bang on every door. I tell you, the dead will climb out of the grave looking for some peace when I get there. I'll scream your name and I will not stop until you carry me to her this night!"

He ain't wanted to do it, but he didn't have much choice. Begrudgingly climbing out of bed, Skeeter picked up an irate Marilyn. She was sure as shit goin' to make a federal case out of this whole thing if he didn't.

Marilyn may have gotten her way this time, but she was keenly aware that didn't necessarily mean they had reached a resolution. She wanted to say more. Express her outrage. Chastise him for breaching her boundaries. After all, she was the one who found the girl. Cali was paying money to sleep on her couch. She was doing chores around the house. Skeeter had no place taking bread out of her mouth.

But they shared a common history of survival. It was just twelve years ago when she and Skeeter first met in juvie lockup. That's when Marilyn saw firsthand the end result of pushing his anger beyond its limits. He was nasty. To the undiscerning eye, his vengeance was like a small boil on the surface of the skin. A slightly reddened area, an innocent irritation. Nothing to cause alarm. But beneath the surface lies a pocket of putrid, infected pus secretly invading tissue and bone.

So, Marilyn kept her mouth shut. She dared not push him any further. The silence in the car was deafening but she reassured herself her eardrums always pounded for a few hours after her club performances. Stealing furtive glances, she noted the way Skeeter massaged the steering wheel. Marilyn's nerves frayed when she witnessed the steely penetration of Skeeter's eyes beyond the headlights.

Entering the hallowed out structure, they found Cali collapsed against a crumbling section of wall, sitting in a corner right where Skeeter had left her just hours earlier. At the sight of Marilyn, the girl burst into tears. Her ankle chained to the pipe, Cali was prevented from running to Marilyn but that didn't stop her from crawling on her hands and knees across the filthy floor in her direction. Her anguish was etched across her face.

Crouching in front of her, Marilyn allowed a distraught Cali to grab onto her hands as she hysterically pleaded about ransom money and never breathing a word to a living soul and giving the debit card to Skeeter. Just please don't leave her there. It was dark beyond imagination. She was terrified.

Marilyn did her best to reassure her, "His mind is made up. That is all there is to it. I cannot change it. You need to stay quiet. There will be men out there who need the feel of a woman. Every day, we bring food and drink. You'll be on a plane home in no time. The longest rope has an end."

Peeling the girl's grip from her hands, Marilyn stood, tapping a bright green fingernail against her temple, repeating, "The longest rope has an end."

Wanting some kind of guarantee the girl'd stay quiet, Skeeter tossed a baggie at Cali's feet before telling her, "Keep your trap shut like you already been told and there'll be more where that came from."

Cali pressed the plastic bag containing heroin and all its paraphernalia to her heart.

Before Skeeter could even put the key in the ignition, Marilyn started, "What ransom does she speak of?"

Pulling away from the curb, he headed to Marilyn's place. This time he drove with his usual reckless disregard for posted speed limits.

"You're in or you're out, but either way, it's happenin'. I got me an idea. This here is my big ticket in life, understand? You wanna make somethin' outta yourself, you gotta be smart like me. We're in this together, me and you. Let's get one thing straight right off the bat, I'm the brains of this here operation and what I sez goes, got it? I brung you here so you can see for yourself, ain't nobody done nothin' wrong by her." Skeeter's tone was testy. "That girl in there, she's our cash cow."

"How much monies? Where did you get it?" Marilyn bordered on hysteria.

A wicked smile spread across Skeeter's face, "Now we're talking, right? It's all taken care of. I listen when people talk. So you know what I heard when she said her grandfather was a judge? Cha-ching. Me and the old grandpa already worked it all out. I figure we'll split it, me and you. We each get half. Two fifty each."

Marilyn clearly was on edge as she repeated, "Two fifty? All this trouble for two hundred fifty dollars? You're bazodee, boy! You're bazodee!"

"You think I'm some small time nobody? I'm gonna learn you how smart I am right now. No two hundred fifty nothin'. Two hundred fifty thousand. You got that? Thousand." Skeeter resented Marilyn's underestimation of his prowess, but he thoroughly enjoyed the look of admiration on her face when he rectified her ignorance. "Yup, that's more than enough dough to head on over to Trinidad and live like the queen of England, ain't that right? Or buy your own clothin' store. So, you better shut your damn mouth before I shut it for you."

The first streaks of pink colored the sky before he finally got home and laid across his bed, staring at his ceiling. It was nearing dawn but Skeeter was way too fired up to sleep. Unbelievably, everything went as planned. A brilliant plan that hatched as it went along. Once he found out about her rich family, there was no turning back. No way was he letting an opportunity like that slap him across the face and not take full advantage of it.

Disablin' the lock on Marilyn's bathroom window was ingenious. He coulda knocked forever and Cali woulda never answered the door. She was high as a kite. Knockin', trying to arouse her, all that commotion mighta led a neighbor to investigate. Or worse, call the cops. Nope, easy peasy. Slipped right inside the bathroom and there she was, passed out on that baby-shit yellow couch. It turned out, the girl was no problem at all. Cali barely weighed nothin'. Once she used, she was effortless to control. Hell, he coulda set her in the middle of the freeway if he wanted to and she wouldn't of objected. In fact, there was no need to tie her up with the bandanas after all. She was a little lamb bein' led to the slaughter. His little lamb.

Marilyn was way more hysterical than he anticipated. He kinda figured she'd have somethin' to say. But demandin', actually threatenin' him if he didn't take her to the girl tonight, after he had just left her, he did not plan on. It took a lot of convincin', but he got Marilyn to see things his way in the end. After all, he didn't earn the self appointed title of, Master Manipulator, for nothin'. Sure, sure, he'd give her a slice of the pie, but he was the brains of this here operation, so he rightfully deserved the bigger half. He might need her help, so he'd go ahead and give Marilyn the two hundred fifty G's. Give a little. Take a lot. That's the way life worked, ain't it?

CHAPTER 22

Pressed face down onto the dirty hard surface, Cali was roused by a violent hacking. Her sides ached as she struggled to roll onto her back in an effort to catch her breath. It felt like her windpipe was crushed. Every time she inhaled, the back of her throat felt like it was being scraped raw with sandpaper. She desperately needed a sip of water. Not a single drop of saliva lined the inside of her mouth. Her lips curled inward and stuck to her teeth. When she stretched her mouth to free them, they cracked and began to bleed, leaving behind the bitter taste of iron on her tongue.

She fitfully awakened from the deep disconnect that heroin provided to the smell of dirt. An ancient, filthy grime that births disease filled her lungs. The kind of dirt the body naturally rejects with uncontrollable fits of cough if accidentally inhaled. Dirt that evolved from years of sediment or asbestos dust that settled on rafters. Wet basements invaded by black mold spores. Attics strung with cobwebs. The unclean end product of decay. Not at all related to a black earth necessary for life and growth, the kind of nutrient-filled soil cultivated in MomMom's amazing flower gardens. Or the rich organic fragrance found inside the lush hollow that had become hers and Blake's secret meeting spot.

Blake. If she could only turn back time. Cali wondered sorrowfully, how much of their lives had she and Blake wasted hiding in the woods behind school, doing shameful unfathomable things? How did their lives get so off kilter?

■ ■ ■

By the time Pop and MomMom returned from their trip, the surgeon had given Cali permission to stop wearing the knee brace. So over-joyed by being reunited with Cali, the grandparents failed to notice her slight limp. They had no idea she had been hurt. While driving home from the airport, Cali eased into the story of her soccer injury. Downplaying the extent of the damage to her knee, she revealed for the first time that she had had surgery. She wasn't quite sure what kind of reaction she expected, but when MomMom burst into tears, Cali was crushed by overwhelming guilt.

It should have been the perfect opportunity to tell them every-thing. Reveal it all. How she had suddenly lost all ambition ever since her knee was crushed playing soccer. How she had somehow become enslaved to her pain medication. That she was way in over her head, her days consumed with thinking of nothing other than taking her next oxycodone. But at that moment Cali couldn't bear to disappoint them any more than she already had. Driving her grandparents home, Cali made the split-second decision not to tell them about the hold the pain pills had over her.

Before meeting the nurse at the hospital, Cali had never given any thought to her grandparents' age before. But the nurse was right, they were up there in years. There was no way she was going to burden them with her problem, jeopardizing their health. After all, at sixteen, she was certainly old enough to solve her own problems. At that mo-ment, Cali decided not to tell them the truth. Somehow, one way or another, she'd have to figure out a way to get her life back on track without their help.

Although it had always been her intention to stop taking the pills, day after day, she and Blake had met in their usual spot after school, the dense woods that surrounded the school's sports complex. A public high school that boasted the highest standardized test scores in the state, as well as many of the sporting championship titles. State of the art turf constructed from granular rubber to minimize joint damage. Digital score boards. All surrounded by enough seating to accommodate one thousand students and parents, who religiously turned out to watch their sons and daughters compete. It was a well known fact, in the south, sporting events were treated with the same reverence as Sunday morning worship.

Just twenty or so steps past the tree line and they were completely hidden from view. Brambles, tall grass, trees thick with leaves created a lush hollow. Cali was the first to arrive and for a few, uninterrupted minutes, she watched her friends and former teammates complete conditioning drills. Scarlett and her friend were huddled together complaining, as usual. The rest of the girls had fallen into line for killer shuttles. Although you were supposed to dread this drill, Cali actually enjoyed it because she loved to run. She was fast and almost always came in first.

That's why her best friend, Kennedy, starting calling her Lightening Hasting. It was obvious from her face, Scarlet hated it when Kennedy called her that. Suffice it to say, Scarlet's most notable personality trait was the green eyed monster, jealousy.

Peering out from the woods, Cali was quietly cheering for Kennedy, her attention on her best friend's every move when he came up behind her.

"Hey," he greeted her.

Round spots of sunlight filtering through the canopy of trees sprayed him like shotgun pellets.

"Oh, hi, Blake. I was just watching soccer warm ups. I can't wait until next season. I'm going to be back out there," Cali spoke with confidence in her words.

Cali stole one last look at her friends chasing soccer balls on a field flooded with sunshine. Bright green uniforms, pony tails bouncing, tanned legs flying across lush fields.

Just a few months ago, that used to be her. Carefree. Athlete. Member of The National Honor Society. Happy. Now, her afternoons were spent sneaking inside the chilly shade of a damp and musty woods, shamefully buying illicit drugs.

Blake nodded, his large brown eyes filled with empathy before he dug to the bottom of his book bag, saying, "So, I have ten."

She reached into the front pocket of her jeans for the wad of money as he handed her a zip-lock baggie. Cali's eagerness was instantly deflated by the unfamiliar pills. They were too big. Instead of being round, these pills were oblong.

"What are these?" Cali asked as she hugged herself trying to rub away the sudden burst of goose bumps that settled on her arms.

"Hydrocodone."

"Hydrocodone? I've never taken these before," she said.

He nodded, saying, "I know."

She looked from Blake to the baggie in her hand, then back to Blake as she shoved the cash back into her pocket. She looked away not wanting Blake to see the surge of tears that filled her eyes. Embarrassed, Cali knew her face looked as though she might start to cry.

"Trust me, they're basically the same thing as oxycodone," Blake's voice was soft, barely audible. He looked paler than usual.

"I don't want you to think I'm being ungrateful because I'm not. I really appreciate everything you've done for me, Blake. Why can't I have the oxycodone?" she managed.

Cali was startled at her unexpected sensation of panic. Her breathing became noticeably more rapid. She needed those oxycodone. She had taken her last one hours ago.

"They're the real deal, trust me, Cali," Blake tried to persuade her.

Cali spoke with conviction, "Oh, I do trust you, Blake. Completely. I won't need them much longer. It's only because the surgery was so extensive. The doctor said my knee was one of the worst tears he had ever seen. So, you know, if you can just help me out a little longer."

Blake took a seat on a rotting log, stretching out long, lanky legs. His shoulders slumped over in defeat. He was so skinny. When had he become so thin? He looked exhausted. He ran his hands through his thick, dark, shoulder length hair.

"We've known each other our entire lives. We're friends, right? If anyone else had come to me asking for pills, I'd have told them to get lost. But you're different. A really nice girl. Genuinely nice, not some big put on like Scarlet. You're not like anyone else I've ever met. You have to know, I'd never do anything to hurt you. Here, let me see them," he requested, his hand extended.

Cali gave him the baggie. When Blake removed a pill and swallowed it, an involuntary gasp escaped her lips. She wiped the sweat from her palms on the front of her jeans while resisting the urge to grab the baggie from Blake before he swallowed any more of her pills.

"See, it's all good." Blake looked into his classmate's face.

Her eyes were wide, her mouth agape, not because he ingested the unfamiliar looking pill, but because now there were only nine remaining. Now there were only nine pills left for her. They were at a stalemate. Cali wanted the pills Blake always supplied but today, he had only these for sale.

"I don't mean to seem ungrateful, because I'm not. It's just, I don't understand. Where did you get these?" she persisted, trying to keep her voice steady.

He closed his eyes, hung his head as he talked, "What difference does it make?"

"Blake? You know you can tell me anything," Cali reassured him.

"I'm afraid you'll hate me if I tell you," Blake practically whispered.

She saw the unmistakable anguish on his face before he ducked his head to hide the expression.

Cali slid onto the log next to Blake, the length of their upper arms and thighs pressed against one another. Her right knee ached in that position but she stayed put. Sitting so close to the ground, the odor of mushrooms and rotting vegetation wafted around them.

"Are you kidding me? Blake, you're the sweetest boy I know. You have to know, I could never hate you. Ever. You should trust me," she said in a soothing voice.

He studied her hard with huge brown eyes that looked like they hadn't known a restful night's sleep in a very long time. Looking at her, he wished things were different. He wished they were sitting in the sunshine, instead of hiding in the shade of the woods. He imagined a different life where he'd dare to kiss this girl who was a rare combination of brains and beauty while making plans for Saturday night. He wished he could turn back time and erase that day he stole his dad's pain pills for the first time.

"Okay, I'll tell you. But, please, don't look at me while I say this. I don't want to see the look of disappointment on your face," Blake said mournfully.

His Adam's apple jumped as he swallowed hard.

When she tried to object, he hardened his jaw and squeezed his eyes shut. Impossibly, he seemed to shrink a little more. Obeying his request, she turned her head away, fixing her gaze on a small brown bird skittering around a patch of wild ferns a few feet away. Her heart pounded in her ears as she waited for him to begin.

"I didn't want to go into all this detail but here goes. You know how we learned in biology that animals and people can contract similar diseases? Like feline leukemia or diabetes?" he asked.

She nodded. "Yes."

"That means animals can take some of the same medications that humans do. Like, my mom's cat, for instance. Mister Pickles has diabetes so she has to give him insulin twice a day. The same insulin that people take," Blake explained.

"Are these insulin pills for your cat?" Cali asked, confused.

"No. Insulin's an injection. But the insulin for cats is the exact same insulin injection that people with diabetes take. That's my whole point. Animal and human medications can be exactly the same." Blake paused for a very long time as he measured each word he was about to utter.

Cali patiently waited in silence.

Before beginning again, he took a big breath, filling his lungs with air, then slowly blew out through his mouth, "Which leads me to my dog. He was hit by a car a couple of days ago."

"No! Oh my goodness, Blake! I'm so sorry to hear that. Why didn't you tell me? Is he okay?" she blurted out.

Unable to disguise her shock, Cali turned to Blake. Eyes filled with genuine concern searched his face.

"Please, Cali. I asked you not to look at me. Or, I won't be able to say any of this," he repeated as a lone tear found its way down his cheek. Before Cali looked away, she slid her hand inside his. This simple act of compassion caught him by surprise, making him feel worse. He was a monster that didn't deserve anyone's compassion for what he'd done.

"He ran out of the house and was hit by a car. His leg was broken, but he's okay. These are his pills. The same hydrocodone pain pills people take. The only difference is, they were prescribed by a veterinarian. That's why they look different. But they have the exact same active ingredient as the oxy. They're still opioids."

"I can't take these. Doesn't your dog need the pain medicine for his broken leg?" Cali shook her head.

"I want you to have them. I have him covered. I've been giving him a baby aspirin twice a day for pain. Look, it's all on the internet if you want to research it for yourself. But, this is all I have right now. So if you want them, go ahead and take them," Blake urged her.

Cali covered her face with her hands, her voice anguished, "But these are for your dog....his leg.....it has to be very painful. Your dog needs them. Oh, Blake, what's happened to me? I'm completely out of control."

Unable to hold it inside any longer, Blake's buried grief erupted. Bursting into tears, his chest heaved as he gasped for breath as the ugly truth came spilling out, "Trust me, I understand being out of control. You want to know what really happened? Here's the whole disgusting story, if you really want to know the truth. My dad had some dental surgery about a year ago. They did a bone implant and he said the pain was unbelievable. My dad, he's a big guy who never complains about anything. But this was different. He was in agony. I remember watching him take the oxycodone pills and it was like magic. All the pain disappeared and it was like he was floating on a cloud or something. So, out of curiosity, I swiped two or three from his bottle so I could see for myself what it was like. Then later, I took some more. My mom wound up calling the dentist and got a second prescription. But after I took half that bottle, she told my dad he was going to get addicted. She threw the rest out in the trash, which of course, I took for myself. She never knew I was the one taking them, not my dad."

Lost in his story, Blake squeezed her hand until it felt like the bones in her fingers were being crushed. Ignoring the pain, she dared not pull away for fear of breaking the spell. Blake had something very important to say and she wanted to hear every word.

She'd never seen anyone cry with such abandon. A violent trembling from his body radiated into the log, causing it to rock back and forth. Gulping for air, Blake seemed to be suffocating from his despair. His loss of control terrified her.

Speaking between sobs, spittle flew from his mouth as he continued, "I mean, I come from a really nice family. My parents don't deserve this. I used to be a top student. You know that, you're my lab partner. AP chemistry. AP calculus. Look at me now. I hardly ever make it to class anymore. I'm failing almost everything. All I can think about is getting pills, pills, and more pills. I'm done with the pills ruining my life. This is it, no more pills for me. I mean it, I'm quitting the pills."

Using the sleeve of his shirt, he wiped his nose, smearing snot across his face before confessing to the worst sin imaginable, "Never in a million years did I see this coming. Never did I think I'd turn into some bastard who'd deliberately run over my own dog to score some pills."

Cali jolted around to stare at Blake's exhausted face. A face consumed with fear and self loathing. Without hesitation, she grabbed her friend and pulled him close, clinging to him as they both cried for the lives they had lost.

CHAPTER 23

The orthopedic surgeon had finished his last case hours ago. He could have been home, barbecuing steaks, enjoying a cocktail with his wife. Instead, he chose to stay. The sixteen year old soccer player in the emergency department needed an MRI of her knee, tonight. From the report the emergency room attending gave, Cali Hasting would be on his operating table tomorrow and he wanted an MRI done before he left for the day. The hold up was locating the patient's parent.

It took nearly four hours for the emergency room nurse to finally contact the girl's mother. For almost four hours, the nurse redialed the number every fifteen to twenty minutes, only to leave yet another voice message saying, "Please contact us immediately."

The mother's cell phone was on vibrate buried deep inside her eight thousand dollar Hermes Birkin handbag. Maggie Hasting was spending her afternoon pampering herself at a day spa. Facial, deep tissue massage, French tip mani-pedi. Always French tip. Two glasses of wine, well, actually four, but who's counting?

By law, the medical staff was extremely limited in their ability to adequately treat the injured teenager. She lay on a stretcher, writhing in pain. The only treatments a minor was able to receive without parental consent, a simple ice pack, a knee immobilizer, and her mangled leg elevated on two pillows. Deeply frustrated, the doctor's hands were tied as he could neither prescribe pain medication nor order the much needed MRI for a patient under the age of eighteen without the permission of a parent.

Another forty-five minutes went by before the surgeon got word the mother finally showed up. At a quarter of nine, a glowing and slightly tipsy Maggie Hasting finally walked into the ER, addressing Cali from the door in an exaggerated Georgian accent, "Bless your heart, today is day one. So, young lady, is this what the next four weeks are going to be like? You and I are going to have the best time together, don't you agree?"

Within minutes, the MRI was completed. The orthopedic surgeon headed to the radiology department to review the results. In layman's terms, Cali Hasting's knee was demolished. There are four major ligaments in the knee. Their purpose is to connect the large thighbone to the shinbone, also known as the tibia. These ligaments allow stability to the joint, as well as making movement possible. The MRI showed all four ligaments were torn. Of particular concern were the areas where fragments of bone sheared off while still attached to the ligament. Cali had two such avulsion fractures.

Her knee was unstable. It was impossible for her to walk since the leg was no longer able to support her weight. Immediate surgery was imperative. She could go home for the night with crutches, a knee immobilizer, and instructions that no weight was to be placed on that leg.

The doctor placed two phone calls on his way to his car. The first was to the ER physician with instructions to have the mother bring the patient back first thing in the morning. He had a full surgical schedule tomorrow, so he'd have to work her in as an emergency case. Next, he called the operating suite scheduler. Before pulling off the hospital's parking lot, the doctor's plans for Cali Hasting's surgery were set in motion.

The next morning, Maggie Hasting and her daughter Cali presented to the surgical suite at six as instructed. After gingerly, but truthfully, explaining the dire status of Cali's knee, the orthopedist asked if either Cali or Maggie had any questions.

Without hesitation, Maggie spoke up, "There is one tiny little problem. I'm a realtor, doctor. Weeks ago, I scheduled a closing today on a two million dollar property. The clients are extremely prominent figures. You would be impressed if I could tell you who they are, but rules are rules, so my lips are sealed." The mother put her fingers to her lips and locked an imaginary key. "Honestly, these aren't the kind of people used to being disappointed. I'm sure you understand, I absolutely cannot postpone their settlement. It shouldn't take much longer than an hour or two. Two and a half tops. Would it be a problem if I dash out for the closing and hurry right back after? Normally, we have a celebratory champagne luncheon after these types of transactions, but I can skip that, if you think it best."

Maggie did an impressive job of continuing to smile when the surgeon replied. Maintaining her decorum, she stood tall in her expensive, sapphire blue, silk blouse with matching peep toe mules and white linen slacks. Her only hint at discomfort was when she began to absently play with the three long strands of pink cultured pearls that hung from her neck.

He already had a hard on for the woman when he realized her daughter lingered unnecessarily for hours in pain in the emergency department because she wasn't answering her cell phone. He didn't mince his words. He looked directly at her perfectly made up face as he informed her that any parent who leaves the hospital while her child is undergoing a surgical procedure would be promptly reported to the authorities for child endangerment and abandonment.

Maggie wasted no time setting up shop in the family waiting room. Clearing off a table meant for magazines and hospital brochures, she typed away on her laptop. She spread out a stack of legal documents as she talked nonstop on her phone. Why couldn't she find a nurse to bring her a fresh cup of coffee? And turn off those obnoxious reality shows on the television. Couldn't people see she was trying to concentrate?

It may be illegal to physically leave the hospital, however, there were no rules forcing Maggie to remain at Cali's bedside. Cali was left alone in the cold, sterile, surgical prep area. The sixteen year old was stoic as surgical residents poked and prodded her knee. She was a champ when the nurse started her IV.

When the nurse said she was going to administer some IV narcotics for the pain, Cali asked for five minutes so she could send a text to her grandparents.

"Of course, sugar." The twenty something year old nurse smiled broadly at her patient. "I'm very close to my grandparents, too."

"They're in Europe, on a four week river cruise to celebrate their sixtieth wedding anniversary. Their ship's sailing down the Rhine River through Holland, Germany, France, and Switzerland. I want to wish them a wonderful trip," Cali told her nurse.

"Sixty years together, bless their hearts. That's an accomplishment you don't hear everyday. A lot of folks have trouble making it through the first year," the pretty nurse remarked.

"They never properly celebrated their golden anniversary because my Pop couldn't take all that time off from work. This time, MomMom made all the plans for their trip because she said she wanted them to go while they're still young enough to enjoy it to the fullest."

The nurse giggled as she inquired, "How old are they, if you don't mind my asking?"

"Wow, I guess I never really thought about it before. If they've been married for sixty years, I suppose they must be in their late seventies, maybe even eighty. But let me tell you, they're not the average seventy year old. I actually live with them, ever since I was born. If you met them, you'd never guess their ages," Cali confided.

The nurse noticed the dark circles under Cali's beautiful green eyes. She adjusted the pillows under her patient's leg.

"So, you said you live with your grandparents, not your mother? Then, who's your legal guardian?" The nurse was suddenly worried that the mother didn't have the legal right to consent to Cali's surgery. She needed to inform the surgeon, right away.

Cali said, "Oh, even though I live with my grandparents, my parents, Maggie and Robert, never gave up their guardianship rights. It's okay Maggie signed the consent form."

"Whoa! And just how do you know so much about legal issues?" the nurse was clearly impressed.

"My Pop's a judge. I'm going to be a lawyer one day, too," Cali winced from the pain.

"If you don't mind my asking, why don't you live with your parents?"

"I've never lived with them and I like it that way. I've never given it much thought because I'm really happy living with my grandparents. Maybe on some level, I've always been afraid to ask because I don't want anyone to tell me I have to go to their house to live," Cali realized aloud.

"Okay, then. Now that we have all that figured out, I'm going to get that pain medication for you, so you go ahead and send your text message," the nurse said before she disappeared.

After sending a message to her grandparents that revealed absolutely nothing about her injury, Cali sent a second text to Kennedy, her best friend since preschool. Kennedy was worried sick about Cali after that big girl named Monica hurt her. It was Kennedy's opinion, she did it on purpose. Both Cali and Kennedy were keenly aware of Monica's father's unleashed hostility throughout the entire soccer match.

It was mind boggling, but somehow, through the cacophony of cheers pouring out from the fans along the sidelines, the father's baritone aggression resonated above all the rest, "Monica, shut her down!"

Monica wondered why he couldn't see, she was trying her best to stop her? Boiling resentment replaced the blood in Monica's veins as she recalled the ride home after their last game, her father's cruel words, "Get your head out of your ass, girl. She's half your size. I didn't come all the way out here, after a long day at work, to watch you get beaten on every play by some little Barbie doll. Act like you want to be out there."

Monica did want to be out there. More than anything. Soccer guaranteed her a sense of belonging in the savage jungle known as high school. The sport exonerated her from a life of social isolation. If it wasn't for soccer, Monica was the kind of girl who would be banished to eating alone in a crowded cafeteria, while being the brunt of unkind jokes, or worse yet, treated as if she were invisible. Life wasn't fair for a girl like her. A big girl with big, man-size feet, dull brown hair, and a bad complexion with obscenely huge pores.

Monica couldn't help but wonder, was it sheer coincidence the girl wore Mia Hamm's number nine? What did she ever do to deserve the honor of wearing the same number as the most famous woman in all of soccer? Monica bitterly questioned why she couldn't be the one wearing Mia Hamm's number on her jersey. Little Miss Petite Number Nine was everything Monica wished she was, but would never be. Head turning beauty. Strawberry blonde hair. Perfect skin. Emerald green eyes. She had no doubt, her father had an endearing pet name for her, like Princess or worse, Kitten. The only thing Monica's father had ever called her was a clumsy oaf.

Past history filled Monica with animosity long before she set foot on the field. As half-time approached and the score was tied, Cali made an unbelievable play. She had seen it done on TV while watching the World Cup last year. A move called a bicycle kick. Although Cali had never practiced it before, desperate times called for desperate measures. The ball arced through the air in her direction. With her back to the goal, Cali thrust her body backwards off the ground as she used both legs to pedal, kicking the ball over her body and head while suspended horizontally mid air. The position of her body was that of a pole vaulter at the instant she cleared the bar.

The roar from the field took on a life of its own, wafting over the trees, past the school, settling on the surrounding neighborhood. Fans obliged to do their part to drive their team to victory began using their feet or open palms to bang on the metal benches. The air was deafening. People were deranged. A handful of teenagers actually began to jump up and down, causing the bleachers to shake. No one told them to stop.

Suspended horizontally midair, Cali was defenseless. At that moment, Monica decided no more left overs for her, no siree. What did she ever do to deserve the short straw in life? For once, she wanted to be the girl with the charmed life, even if it was only for a fleeting moment. It was her turn. Monica's turn. All that resentment for the number nines of the world erupted as she deliberately barrel rolled into the petite girl in the green jersey while she was most vulnerable, lifted high in the air.

Neither girl saw the ball strike the inside of the mesh net, giving the Knights the half-time advantage. Neither girl was aware when the noise decibel impossibly increased as both sides cheered in amazement for the outstanding play. They were both oblivious to the referee thrusting the red card above his head, thereby ejecting Monica from the remainder of the game, as well as suspending her from playing the next.

Both girls focused only on the sickening crunch of bone and cartilage, the tear of ligaments. The instant, uncontrollable face of agony. The way Cali's leg lay cockeyed on the ground when they landed, Monica splayed across her torso. Green eyes overflowing with tears meeting brown eyes filled with sweet revenge.

Ejected from the field, Monica made a deliberate show of pointing to her father in the stands. Her face lit up as he gave her a double fisted pump signaling his approval for the way she took care of business. Like a proud peacock, Monica strutted off the field. It was going to be a great ride home tonight.

Returning to her bedside, the pretty nurse told Cali, "Okay, sugar, this is going to make the throbbing pain in your knee go away," just before she injected the medication in her IV.

Those were the last words Cali heard before she woke to a knee on fire. The pain was agonizing. The surgeon and Maggie were standing at the foot of her bed. Through a thick fog, she heard fragments of the doctor's explanation.

The four hour surgery stretched into six. Considerable damage to the knee. Open reduction and internal fixation. Hardware in her knee. Pins, screws, and titanium plates. Metal anchors used to reattach ligaments to bone. Extensive trauma caused bone to sheer off. Avulsion fractures. Cadaver implants.

There was a high pitch to Maggie's voice that bordered panic, "What do you mean I'm supposed to take her home tonight? I can't possibly manage all this by myself. Wouldn't it be best to admit her to the hospital for a few days, or maybe a week, until she's back up on her feet again? We have excellent health insurance through my husband's employer. He's a commercial airline pilot for one of the major airlines."

Ignoring Maggie's pleas, the orthopedic doctor forged ahead, "Mrs. Hasting, your daughter will need aggressive rehab. It'll take ten months, possibly a year before her knee is anywhere near normal again. I'd like your permission for the anesthesiologist to insert a peripheral nerve catheter in Cali's groin area. The catheter will be attached to a pain pump that will continuously deliver numbing medicine to the nerves in Cali's knee. Without the pump, her pain will be excruciating. It will be impossible to control her pain with oral narcotics alone. In three days, when the medicine in the pump runs out, you'll simply remove the catheter."

"Does this pain pump come with a private duty nurse?" Maggie was aghast.

"No, Mrs. Hasting. The nurses will give you detailed instructions about the pump before I discharge Cali home," the physician's voice was devoid of all emotion.

"No, no, and no. I cannot give permission for something like this. No pumps. I faint at the sight of blood, so I can assure you, I will not be pulling anything out of anyone's groin. I am beyond exhausted. I have been confined to that dreadful waiting room of yours for almost seventeen hours." Maggie was incredulous. "She can take pain pills like a normal person. No pain pumps."

She was not a woman used to hearing the word, no. Making a fuss all the way out the door, Maggie reluctantly took a very groggy Cali home.

CHAPTER 24

Walter was beyond exhausted. It had been a long day, beginning with the firing range, followed by a four mile trail run through Gunpowder, then dinner at Jimmy's Seafood. Except, they never did have dinner. They were put on assignment before they had a chance to eat. Their desperate search for Cali Hasting had begun. Normally, it would have been pointless trying to sleep when he was starving but he had no trouble passing out as soon as his head hit the pillow.

Walter's fitful dream vividly conjured up a particularly painful event from his childhood. It was a memory that hadn't crossed his mind in twenty-five years. Forever etched into his subconsciousness, the event was the one and only recollection Walter ever had of disappointing his father.

■ ■ ■

Walter was about eight years old and his family was living in North Carolina at the time. Like every Sunday, he had gone to church with his parents and his two sisters. After the service, his parents stood on the steps speaking with the pastor. His sisters stood quietly at their mother's hem. Like many of the other ladies, his mom wore a wide brimmed straw hat that kept the sun off her face. She was dressed in a pretty cotton dress with short sleeves. She held the strap of her pocketbook with hands covered in wrist length white gloves.

His daddy wore his best suit. In spite of the August humidity and oppressive heat, he never once considered removing his jacket or loosening his tie even a fraction. Beneath his suit jacket, sweat had morphed his dress shirt into a darker shade of blue. From time to time, Walter glanced at his parents as he ran around the front lawn with the other children. As was tradition, members of the congregation lingered on the church steps, greeting one another after the service.

It was then Walter spotted the older boy. It was quite unusual for an older boy to dismiss the time honored pecking order and fraternize with someone younger, yet he didn't chase Walter away. In fact, the boy, two years Walter's senior, challenged Walter to a spitting contest.

Walter basked in the attention of an older peer. The older boy flamboyantly boasted, he could spit further than anyone else in fifth grade. In fact, he could spit further than anyone in the entire school. Having his share of testosterone, Walter simply could not let a braggart go unchallenged. So, on that hot August day, he made the conscious decision to be too big for his britches.

As men and women dressed in their Sunday best watched in veiled disgust, Walter snorted every ounce of phlegm from his sinuses and hocked it across the lawn. This was followed by the older boy's equally disgusting ball of snot shooting through the air. One by one, the boys took turns trying to outdo one another. Slimy, thick spit rolled off their tongues as mothers hurriedly grabbed their children by the hand and whisked them away. Walter didn't notice many of the older church goers glaring condescendingly.

He was oblivious to a few of the men gathered, murmuring, "That's LaRue Kostos's boy, isn't it?"

"Dirty Greeks."

His parents stood proud, continuing their conversation with the pastor, acting as though unaware of their son's behavior. When at last they descended the church steps, Walter ran off to join his family as they headed for their car. He jumped in his spot in the back seat, just as he always did, behind his father. He rolled down his window before scooping his baseball glove from the floorboard, holding it in his lap. Yes indeed, after breakfast, he and his daddy were going to work on his curve ball. They were going to walk over to the high school so there'd be a real home plate and pitchers mound. Life was grand.

He closed his eyes and watched the kaleidoscope of orange and dark green through his lids as the car moved from bright sunlight to shade. The hot air blew across his face. He loved his life.

Pulling up to the house, his daddy told him to wait in the front yard while mom and his sisters went inside to start breakfast. It was too good to believe. He didn't have to set the table. He could hardly believe his good fortune. Sunday breakfast meant homemade biscuits, scrapple, grits, and sunny side up eggs. He was starving.

He watched in eager anticipation as his father came around the side of the house from the shed. Only eight, Walter was too young, too naive to recognize the heavy shoulders or his father's trudging gait was that of a beaten man. LaRue Kostos carried a metal bucket. A bucket of balls. He'd certainly have his curve ball perfected by the end of the day.

His dad's voice was soft in contrast to the hard look in his eyes, "I saw your little spitting contest after the service. That boy won't have anything on you by the end of the day. Fill it up."

He set the empty bucket at Walter's feet before turning to go in the house.

■ ■ ■

The sound of his phone vibrating on his bedside table jarred him awake. Walter's mouth was as dry as a desert. The dream left him prickled with shame as he vividly recalled his father's mournful look of disappointment so many years ago.

Fumbling for his phone, Walter checked the time. He had barely gotten four hours rest. It was only a few minutes past five. During college, middle of the night phone calls usually meant a party somewhere, however after the age of twenty-two, calls in the wee hours were almost always a signal of bad news. Having just crawled into bed a few hours ago, he momentarily felt disoriented.

"Did I wake you?" the woman's voice on the other end whispered.

Walter cleared his throat, trying to find his voice. He lied, "No, I was already up. What're you doing up so early?"

His voice was raspy from sleeping with his mouth open while dreaming of filling a metal bucket with spit. He needed a drink of water, but he didn't feel like walking to the kitchen. Besides, nothing in there was where it should be because he and his dad were renovating his kitchen in Walter's spare time, which wasn't much. All his dishes were packed in boxes. At that moment, he had no idea in which box the glasses were. The work zone had been in progress for six months now, without an end in sight.

"I couldn't sleep last night. I'm just being selfish, Walter. I know I woke you but I just needed to hear your voice." Her melancholy was undisguised.

He'd slept like a maniac, his dream igniting an inner turmoil. All the covers were askew, the fleece blanket keeping the floor warm while he froze in the bed. His feet were ice cold. They must have been uncovered all night. The few hours of sleep he managed were haunted by the ugly memory of his behavior in the church yard. After reaching over to turn on the light, he tried to straighten out his bedding somewhat. A lot of guys he knew slept with their socks on, but he didn't like the feel of his feet being restricted while he slept. He was a T-shirt and boxer briefs kind of guy. Years ago, he knew a guy who complained about his wife's flannel pajamas but in the same breath he disclosed that he never took his socks off in bed. Not even while making love. What a dope.

"You know you're my number one girl. You can always call me anytime, day or night, you know that." He balled his pillow under his head, propping himself up on a slight incline.

"I'll bet you say the same thing to all the girls," she pouted.

"Say what to all the girls?" he teased.

"Don't even try to pretend you don't know what I'm talking about, mister." she giggled. "Do you call them your number one girl, too? Are you toying with my heart?"

She dared not mention Chloe Rose. There were boundaries she knew not to cross. Or maybe she just didn't want to hear his answer. Why couldn't he see she was all wrong for him? She lived by the philosophy, if you don't want to know the answer, don't ask the question.

"Never!" he tried to make his voice sound indignant. "I only tell you that because it's the truth. You are, and always will be, my number one girl. You have nothing to be jealous about. Hey, if you're home alone, I can come over for a little bit if you want."

"No, he's home. He doesn't go back on nights until next week. He's still upstairs sleeping."

She had told him many times, her husband could sleep through a hurricane. They could talk all night long and he'd be none the wiser.

Walter could hear the anguish in her voice. He knew her too well. He imagined her sitting alone in the kitchen, her bare feet pulled under her as she perched on a kitchen chair. Her hair would be that crazy, beautiful tousled mess that is only caused by a pillow. Her husband blissfully asleep upstairs in their bed.

He made small talk, patiently waiting for her to unburden her troubles in her own time, "Are you still wearing that blue robe I gave you about a hundred years ago?"

She brightened for a minute, "You know I am. He's always buying me a new one for my birthday every year, but this one can't be replaced. The fabric's worn just right, so it feels so soft. He says I'm like Goldilocks, who finally found the perfect bed."

"Or, Linus, carrying around a ratty blanket," he played along.

"I had my OB/GYN appointment yesterday afternoon," she finally said it. The other end of the phone was silent, but she knew Walter was still there.

She hated herself for crying. She wanted to be brave when she told him the news, but all that raw emotion stored up inside her heart broke wide open. Over the past couple of years, she had perfected the art of crying, without making all those blubbering noises. It was the one thing that made her proud of herself. She closed her eyes, resting her forehead on the kitchen table, grateful Walter couldn't see her. Her suffering was visual, so the phone mercifully spared him that misery.

"You know, I love you," Walter whispered.

"I know," her words were barely audible.

"It'll take the next time, baby sister."

"Next time," she managed before ending the call.

His eyes barely open, Walter stumbled to the bathroom to wash his face. He needed a minute to compose himself. While splashing cold water on his face, Walter decided to call Cali's parents first. It was no surprise when Robert answered on the first ring. The elderly Hastings were so distraught, Robert and Maggie had made the decision to spend the night with his parents. While the rest of the household feigned sleep, Robert had spent the entire night searching Cali's bedroom for drugs and paraphernalia. They were just now pulling into their own driveway. Walter heard their car doors slam, followed by keys jingling as the front door of their house was unlocked.

Walter wasted no time. He needed Robert to verify the whereabouts of that debit card he had given Cali. Rushing into the guest bedroom, Robert reported the debit card was missing from the bedside drawer. This was followed by the sound of typing as Robert accessed his banking files on the computer. Within minutes, he was able to provide the FBI agent with the card's digits.

Walter was well aware, he would be stonewalled if he tried to call and inquire about the card's most recent activity. Most certainly, he'd be required to secure a search warrant which would monopolize time he could put to better use. Telling Robert he'd call back within the hour, Walter asked him to contact the twenty-four hour customer service for the debit card to ask about any transactions incurred in the last three days .

Twenty minutes later, Robert reported the card had been used a grand total of four times. The first transaction was for the purchase of a bottle water at the airport. This was followed by activity on Wednesday evening at a gas station in Havre de Grace, approximately five miles south of New Light Treatment and Recovery Center. The card showed activity a third time to pay for gas and a withdrawal of one hundred dollars on Pulaski Highway. Less than twenty four hours later, the card was used a final time to withdraw two hundred dollars from an ATM owned by Old Town Liquors. Then the trail went quiet.

CHAPTER 25

"I done heard you on the phone yesterday. What was that all about, huh? I'm guessin' you done figured you could drown out your conversation with the T.V. on and all that. So what was such a big secret you didn't want your own mother to hear it none?" Peaches said between bites of food.

She was eating a pie with a soup spoon. Not a slice of pie. She was eating an entire blueberry pie, right from the aluminum tin it was packaged in. A fork, like a regular human being couldn't get it in fast enough, so she chose a miniature shovel instead. Purple, blueberry filling caked in the corners of her mouth. On the front of the men's, double extra large T-shirt she was wearing was a bright purple stain where a glob of pie landed when she missed her mouth. He stared at the blemish in disgust. Following Skeeter's eyes to the front of her shirt, she used her fingers to rescue the stray dropping, shoving it in her already overstuffed mouth.

Underneath the T-shirt, she was braless. Massive, pendulous breasts sagged clear down to her navel. When she waddled in his direction, her cow udders swung back and forth.

He was repulsed by her. Narrowed into dangerous slits, his eyes studied his mother. Still, he ignored her inquiry.

"What? You want some?" She held up a spoonful of pie in his direction. He recoiled, as though he had touched a hot stove.

"What're you so jumpy at? So, you gonna tell me or what? This here is my house so I got a right to make sure nothin' that ain't legal is goin' down," she spoke absently as she used a sausage index finger to wipe up the spills in the aluminum pan. She licked her fingers before saying, "If I ain't lookin' out for me, then who's gonna?"

His mind flooded with a lifetime of past hurts. Yup, his mother was the poster child for law abidin' citizens alright. When ain't she looked out for herself? If she ever cared about anybody else, it was way before he was ever born. He drew the short straw with her, that's for sure.

Skeeter despised her. She was a pig. She had no couth. All she had to do all day long was sit around this dump, waitin' for her welfare check. And eat. It was hard to believe when he was a kid, she made a livin' turnin' tricks. He wondered if she still occasionally supplemented her monthly government checks with whorin' around. He pitied the poor bastard who dared to let her wrap those ham hocks around his back. Her massive thighs could crush a man to death.

He ain't never had the best recall for words, so he couldn't remember the name of the creature. He'd seen it hundreds of times in the cartoons he loved to watch from the corner of the couch on Saturday mornings. For the most part, the couch was a saggin' sorry crap piece of furniture because of her lard ass. But if he tucked up close to the armrest, he was able to avoid the springs that jutted through the cheap fabric. Besides, he could balance his bowl of Fruity O's on the armrest while he zoned out on his cartoons. It was his version of breakfast in bed.

Anyway, in the cartoons, the head and chest was a man, while the lower half of the creature from the waist down was a horse. A centurion, centaur, or somethin' like that. That was his mother. A big, fat slob. Half pig. Half cow.

But cow or no cow, she was his mother. In a few days, as soon as the old judge paid up, he was takin' off for good, never to look back. After much debate, he finally set his sights on Florida. Watching her eat her pie, the thought suddenly came to him. He should give her a goin' away gift. A gratitude, thanks for all you've done for me sort of thing. He figured it was the least he could do, to give his mother a final, so long sucker present. Skeeter could think of nothin' more better for a heifer like Ol' Peaches. A long stay at a fat farm.

What was that voodoo crap Marilyn was always sayin'? Oh, yeah. "You never miss the water till the well runs dry." Ha! She'll see how much she misses him when he leaves her here to rot and he's the one livin' large. If she thinks her place stinks like rot now, just imagine how rank it'll be when he ain't around to haul out the garbage. Wait 'til she finds the little surprises he left for her in the coffee cans in his bedroom.

For a flashing moment, he allowed himself the luxury of that fantasy. Old Peaches carelessly kickin' over the coffee cans filled with his urine. Stale, cold piss soakin' her feet as a little payback for all the times she clipped her filthy toenails, lettin' them fly recklessly through the air. Sweet revenge for the pain she caused him when his bare feet stepped on one of her crescent shaped, shard of glass toenails.

Lookin' back, it's a good thing him and Marilyn did become friends back in juvie, or else he'd of never run across Cali. He ain't no dummy. When she brung out that twenty-five bucks to pay for her heroin, right then and there, that's when he made up his mind, he was goin' to get me some of that.

He had to make his move real fast before she got the chance to go on back to Georgia, so he'd forgot about a few things. Like, where the hell was she going to go to the bathroom? Later, he'd have to swing by one of them dollar stores and grab her a bucket. On the way, he'd make a pit stop and get somethin' for her to eat. A bag of candy, or chips. Or maybe he'd splurge on a slice of pizza behind the hot case at the gas station. If she thought he was gonna be runnin' all over town like her personal delivery boy, that shit ain't gonna happen. She'll get what she gets.

He hated wastin' his time checkin' in on the girl when he was dead tired from runnin' back and forth to his hidin' spot all night long. First to take her there, then a second time to shut Marilyn up. He wound up not gettin' hardly no sleep last night.

What he needed to do was come up with a solid plan to get his dough from the grandfather. Maybe have the old judge leave a sackful of money in the woods somewhere. He should come up with a disguise, maybe grow a Fu Manchu mustache so nobody could recognize him. He seen a movie once where this guy come by boat to pick up a suitcase full of cash left on the end of a pier. Only problem was, he ain't have a boat. Didn't know nobody who did. Anyway, after he made sure the suitcase was filled up with cold hard cash, one and a half million dollars to be exact, he'd make one last call to let the old man know where Cali was holed up.

But Marilyn, sure as shit, made a federal case out of his plan. Probably jealous she ain't thought of it first. She was small time, collectin' a few notes so the girl could crash on her couch. Not him. When he seen her hand over twenty-five bucks for one hit of brown sugar, he seen the potential for a big payday. But ain't many people smart like him. That made him smile. A smile that morphed into a cynical sneer, as he vividly recalled the power he held over the snivelin' girl he left chained to a pipe.

CHAPTER 26

Under normal circumstances, Walter's superiors described him as driven, tenacious, and unrelenting. Once he discovered the victim was a child, Walter's only focus in life became getting Cali Hasting back alive. Chloe Rose had a slightly different opinion to describe Walter's behavior, feeling he was possessed. By day two of the investigation, a resentment had taken ahold of her. When she arrived home last night, he hadn't sent flowers in an effort to make up for their botched dinner plans. Instead, after Walter hung up with Robert Hasting, Chloe Rose got one measly five minute phone call where Walter was so distracted, he barely paid attention to anything she was saying. She wasn't used to playing second fiddle and, frankly, it didn't sit well with her.

According to their website, Old Town Liquors on Gay Street, opened at six a.m. Feeling sluggish, Walter determined he had time for some coffee and a long, hot shower before heading over there. Since the renovation on his kitchen began, he had a bachelor fridge, with little more than condiments, milk, and cheese inside. Starving, he decided he'd stop somewhere for breakfast. Besides, he needed a few minutes to formulate his strategy for following the breadcrumb trail that debit card was leaving.

Working backwards, Walter started his investigation with Cali's final transaction. Pulling up to the liquor store, Walter noted the ATM was positioned on the outside of the brick building, allowing access around the clock, anytime, day or night. Initially, the proprietor tried to play hardball, refusing to allow Walter to view the security footage without a warrant. When the FBI agent suggested the establishment appeared to have blatant liquor board violations, Walter was begrudgingly given free access to the bank machine's security tapes.

He felt his heart skip a beat. There was no mistaking the strawberry blonde hair. It was Cali Hasting. A man standing directly behind her had taken great pains to conceal his identity. His face was shadowed by a ball cap. The hood of his sweatshirt pulled over the ball cap further concealed his head and neck. But then, three seconds in, he made a fatal error. It was so fast it could have gone undetected by someone less astute. Walter's sharp eye caught it. The kidnapper briefly reached around Cali Hasting with his left hand as she was entering her pin number. In that fraction of a second, the sleeve of his hoodie rose above his wrist, revealing a tattoo. The image was grainy but it appeared to be three words. Squinting at the image, Walter was unable to make out the words. Revealing those words was imperative to identifying the kidnapper.

Studying the ATM video over and over, Special Agent Kostos gradually noted something in the background. Parked in front of the ATM, the camera had captured the front quarter panel of a vehicle. It was a long shot, that vehicle being connected to the girl, but it was certainly a stone worth overturning.

Confiscating the video, Walter headed to the site of the debit card's second transaction on Pulaski Highway. The cashier had his feet propped up on a counter while a pint-size TV with aluminum foil waving from the rabbit ears kept him company. Confined to a booth encased in heavy wire fencing, he seemed content to spend his work day in a cage. So engrossed in his television program, the middle aged man didn't even look up when Walter opened the door. The place stunk like incense.

There weren't any security cameras on the premises, the owner reported. The posted signs were for show only. They had been robbed at gunpoint twice in the past eight months and other than taking the initial report, he had never heard another word from the Baltimore City Police Department. He got rid of the cameras because what good would it do for his wife to have his murder captured on film, if it ever came to that? He put what little money he had into the wire fencing since he couldn't afford bullet proof glass. It was the best he could do to protect himself.

Walter noted the ATM tucked in the corner behind a display rack of grab and go snacks. Unlike the owner of Old Town Liquors, this proprietor willingly surrendered the ATM security video. This time, the footage showed Cali Hasting was alone.

Leaving with the second ATM video in his possession, Walter drove the forty-five miles from the gas station on Pulaski Highway to the gas station in Havre de Grace. One fact was glaringly obvious, she didn't walk that distance. Walter knew if he could somehow find footage of the vehicle used to transport her, their case would break wide open.

Once again, Cali Hasting was clearly visible on the third ATM's security camera footage. Like the video preserved at the Pulaski Highway establishment, the only image caught on camera was Cali's.

It was a big blow to learn all security videos monitoring the premises, both inside and out, were recorded over every twenty-four hours. Any images of Cali Hasting getting into a vehicle heading southbound to Baltimore were forever erased.

None of the employees had any recollection of seeing the girl. Strategically positioned off the I-95 interstate, the volume of vehicles coming and going was astronomical. Open twenty-four hours a day, an average day registered one thousand transactions. A never-ending stream of people entered through those doors on a daily basis. No one remembered the petite strawberry blonde.

Three ATM surveillance tapes in hand, Walter headed for the Marine Corps Base in Quantico, Virginia, the home of the FBI's forensic lab. It took the remainder of the day but the tattoo was finally deciphered using the latest, high powered imagery system. The three words inked on the left wrist of the hooded individual reaching around Cali Hasting, Death Before Defeet, spelled with two e's.

Pushing his luck a little further, Walter wanted to know if anyone at the crime lab was able to identify the make or model of the car in the background. He knew he was grasping at straws. Only the front quarter panel was visible, but it was worth a shot.

One of the many strong suits of an agent who graduated from the FBI academy the class before Walter and Nick's was vehicle recognition and identification. The only problem was, the agent had two days approved vacation leave. They'd put the tape on his desk, asking him to make it a high priority first thing Monday morning.

One thing he felt confident of, Cali Hasting was in Baltimore City. An elated Walter checked in with Nick as he finally headed home after another long, yet productive day. After arranging for cadaver dogs to search New Light's grounds, Nick was able to definitively clear room one ten as a crime scene once no blood was detected using luminol and a UV light. His interview with Cali's roommate, Yeo Ming Hung, came up empty. She insisted they had spent only a few hours together and had exchanged only a handful of words. According to Yeo Ming, she had absolutely no knowledge of Cali's whereabouts. She offered no insight into Cali's disappearance.

After hearing about Nick's progress at New Light Treatment and Recovery, Walter placed a second call to FBI headquarters. In the morning, he needed assistance from the Baltimore City Police, specifically the southeast district since the ATM transactions on Gay Street and Pulaski Highway were located inside that district. He needed the higher ups to pave his way before he arrived at the Southeast District first thing tomorrow morning. There was no time for red tape.

CHAPTER 27

It was the beginning of another intolerable day for Cali. Swallowed into a black hole, she startled awake and stared into a vastness without reward. She rubbed her eyes, blinked hard, but still, she couldn't see anything. It was pitch black all around her. Fear, magnified ten fold by the darkness, consumed her as she quickly tried to get her bearings.

Her situation was unfathomable. Chained to a pipe like a savage beast in a city where no one even knew she existed. All this mess because she chose to take heroin. Heroin. The reality shocked her. What kind of person has heroin for a goal? For the first time, she wondered what had happened to her. She barely recognized herself anymore. Always surrounded by adoring friends, she was now kept at arm's length. The girl who once got straight A's in school now barely attended class.

Law school was the perfect dream for the girl who was a natural born rule follower. Cali never once cheated on an exam. Never missed curfew. She was one of the few students in eleventh grade who had never even tasted alcohol or smoked a cigarette.

But over the past three months, her life had taken a dark and unforeseen twist. She had turned into someone she barely recognized.

And she was deeply ashamed of herself. For the life of her, she couldn't understand how or why things had spiraled so out of control. How had she gotten involved with drugs in the first place? Heroin, no less.

Not that long ago, her days were filled with school projects, athletic competitions, spending time with her friends and family. When she wanted to purchase a used, candy apple red Jeep, her grandparents agreed to let her take the weekend waitress job. She had it all. Now her life was consumed with stopping at almost nothing to get her next fix.

Pop and MomMom sacrificed everything to pay for her treatment at New Light. According to Yeo Ming, they paid one hundred ten thousand dollars to get her the help she needed, yet she didn't make the minimal effort to complete even one day of the treatment. One hundred and ten thousand dollars thrown in the trash without a second thought.

■ ■ ■

Cali's room was number one ten. She followed the winding hallway until she came to her destination on the left. Since the door was wide open, she was able to peruse the space before entering.

On the bed under the window sat a jet black haired, petite girl with alabaster skin. Because of the stark contrast between her fair coloring and her midnight black hair, her skin almost appeared as if it were radiating a light source. Her features were so delicate, she put to mind a porcelain doll. She was clothed all in black. Black T-shirt, black skinny jeans, black ankle high boots, although it was clearly flip-flop season. A stainless steel bar pierced a thin eyebrow over almond shaped, dark eyes that were heavily painted with black eyeliner. Putting her journal face down on her bed, she gave Cali the once over.

"You may as well come in and make yourself at home. As much as you can without any of your personal belongings," she invited with a mild hostility. "It will take most of the day before you get your suitcase back. They go through it inch by inch, looking for drugs and paraphernalia. I hope you didn't bring expensive luggage because they will ruin it. When they searched mine, they actually tore the lining out before removing the handles and the wheels. By the time they were done with it, my bag looked like it was thrown out of an airplane, then run over by a tractor trailer."

Cali giggled nervously.

"You often find the purposeful destruction of another's personal property amusing?" the girl shot.

"I was thinking about those old-timey suitcase commercials where even a gorilla couldn't harm the suitcase. Maybe they need a commercial for a suitcase that can make it through the rehab admission process," Cali remarked.

She didn't want to, but the girl wasn't able to suppress a tiny grin. Cali's unexpected wit was contagious. And refreshing from the usual, self absorbed, pity parties or blatant hostility most patients displayed.

"Of course, you don't get your phone or any other electronics back until you're discharged. They lock up your credit cards. It's forbidden to communicate with the outside world. It wouldn't look good to have drug dealers making deliveries," the girl informed her.

Cali patted the back pocket of her jeans, assuring herself the debit card was there. Earlier that morning at the airport, Cali had purchased a bottled water while waiting to board their flight. After her purchase, she slid the card in the back pocket of her jeans, where unbeknownst to the rehab staff, it remained in her possession.

"Do we get to call our families?" Cali was genuinely concerned.

That's a new one, the girl thought. Almost no one wanted any communication with their families since they were the driving force behind their being sent away to rehab.

"Once a week, you're allowed a five minute call. Just to check in. Assure your loved ones you're still alive. That you're not being tortured beyond the normal detox nightmare. You know, preserve your emotional connection with your home base. So, what are you here for?" the girl asked, fully expecting some bullshit vague answer, as usual.

"Heroin. My grandparents brought me here this morning on a red-eye flight from Georgia," Cali answered truthfully. "By the way, my name is Cali Hasting. It's nice to meet you, in spite of our circumstances. What's yours?"

The girl was visibly startled when Cali actually came over and shook hands.

"Well, Cali Hasting, it's nice to make your acquaintance. I'm Yeo Ming. Yeo Ming Hung. So your grandparents were the ones who forced you to come here?" she dug around for the inevitable weak spot.

"No, I came willingly. No one forced me to come here, least of all my MomMom and Pop. I came here because I need to stop using heroin and get my life back on track. Is it okay if I sit here?" Cali gestured to the other bed in the room.

"Take a load off. That one's yours." The girl sat up straight in bed.

It did not escape her attention when Cali kicked off her sneakers before climbing on top the duvet. Unlike anyone else she had ever met at rehab, Cali didn't climb on top the bed with her shoes on or leave them in a heap in the middle of the floor. Instead, she set them neatly at the foot of the bed, tucked out of the way.

All this, the shoes, her apparent honest assumption of culpability for her predicament, and the reference to her grandparents in such innocent and endearing language, calling them MomMom and Pop caused something hard in Yeo Ming's soul to soften just a bit. Her new roommate was vulnerable and Yeo Ming found herself gravitating toward that innocence.

Her tone became more gentle, "You missed breakfast but if you're hungry, we have a fully stocked kitchen that we can access twenty four hours a day. I can show you where it is if you're hungry."

"I appreciate it, but that's okay," Cali turned her offer down. "I don't feel very well to begin with and when I eat, my stomach revolts. I can't remember what it was like when my stomach didn't hurt all the time."

"Plagued by stomach troubles, huh? From the looks of you, it didn't just start. What were you taking before heroin?" Yeo Ming asked.

The girl's malnourished and skeletal appearance did not escape Yeo Ming's keen eye. The gauntness of her face. The way her collarbone was clearly visible beneath her skin. Her clothes much too large for her.

"Mainly, oxycodone and oxycontin. But occasionally, I'd take whatever I could get my hands on," Cali confessed.

Cali never liked the way the pain pills made her gut feel. A hot burning in the pit of her stomach left her in constant fear that any sudden motion would result in vomiting. Lots of it. But then, the throbbing in her knee would gradually subside. The knife-like stabbing pain directly under her kneecap would ease to a point where she could finally feel her muscles start to relax. Then a delicious fog would roll over her, starting at her toes, working its way north over her entire body. Her heavy head and tense shoulders would sink back into the downy soft pillow. She was swallowed into a blissful sleep as she imagined herself floating away, the pain left far behind.

Yeo Ming was intrigued by her new roommate. Apparently, she had never become ensnared by the propensity of most drug addicts for untruths. Cali's honest candor was unheard of in this setting, where almost everyone pathologically lied with the same ease as breathing.

"The oxy probably created a gastric ulcer in your stomach. When you have your physical with the doctor tomorrow, tell him about it. Actually, it's not a doctor, he's a physician's assistant, but he can prescribe some antacid medications to heal it," Yeo Ming instructed.

"Okay, I'll do that, thank you. How do you know about gastric ulcers? Are you a doctor?"

"Almost. I guess you could say, I'm a physician by proxy. I come from a long line of physicians. The trend was broken by my rebellious sister, Chunhua, who is eighteen months older than I. She's a software engineer and a total disgrace to my parents, I might add. So as you can see, not much was expected of me," Yeo Ming made no attempt to disguise the harshness in her tone.

Bending her knees against her chest, Yeo Ming absently rocked herself back and forth on her bed. She couldn't believe she had just divulged so much about herself when she normally kept a tight reign on her private life.

"Careers tend to run in families, don't you think? I want to follow in my Pop's footsteps and become a lawyer like him. It sounds like you should consider carrying on your family's tradition and pursue a medical career since you already seem to have so much knowledge about gastric ulcers and such," Cali pointed out.

Pushing her coal black hair away from her oval shaped face, the waif studied Cali hard before asking, "How old are you?"

"Sixteen. How old are you?" Cali asked.

"Twenty-six," she replied.

"Twenty-six?" Cali's voice shot up an octave in surprise.

"Why is that such a shock?"

"I don't understand. What made you start taking drugs at twenty-six?" Cali smiled when she spoke, making the question seem less accusatory.

Unlike in the therapy sessions where she kept herself guarded, Yeo Ming had an unfamiliar urge to open up to this stranger, "I didn't just start taking drugs at twenty-six. This has been going on for years. I graduated high school at sixteen and was in med school when I first started dabbling with amphetamines. Which led, in turn, to barbiturates to reverse the high when I couldn't sleep for days on end. Eventually, I went after anything in a pill form swallowed with a hefty helping of alcohol. Vodka was my drink preference. It's colorless and odorless, which kept it off people's radars, or so I thought. By the time I was an intern, the course work was almost unrealistic. I refused to accept that I was overwhelmed, just like most of the class, because in my mind, I had to be a shining star. The only way to accomplish that was to pull all nighters, compliments of the amphetamines. If I didn't sleep, that allowed me so much more time to study and complete assignments. I found out the hard way, if I didn't sleep for forty-eight hours straight, I could acquire an impressive amount of knowledge. Long term, though, it's also a sure way to kill oneself."

"It sounds like you got in over your head, but you're here now. That's all that matters. My Pop says everyone makes mistakes. Now you have the opportunity for a fresh start," Cali spoke with true optimism.

"I need a fresh start. This is my fifth stint in rehab and it has to be my last. My family has spent almost a half million dollars on my drug habit. Money that was earmarked for my parents' retirement has been poured down the drain, up to this point."

"Your parents have spent a half million dollars on drug rehab programs?" Cali was incredulous.

"Trust me, it isn't hard to do. A thirteen week stay here costs one hundred ten thousand dollars. A world class program such as this does not come cheap. My pattern is, I stay clean for six, seven months, then I'm right back where I started. My longest period of sobriety was thirteen months, two days. Anyway, my parents are getting old and cannot continue to delay retirement to keep paying for my rehab," it seemed impossible, but Yeo Ming's face filled with an even greater sorrow as she spoke.

"I don't understand. What do you mean this is your fifth time?" Cali was visibly shaken.

"The relapse rate for substance abuse is roughly fifty percent, and that's one of the more favorable statistics. Didn't you know that? Keep this in the back of your mind, all those people you're about to meet in our twelve step sessions, about twenty of them won't relapse. That's it. Everyone else will make rehab one big revolving door. When you get out of here and have access to the internet again, look it up. This time, I'm the one making it, so statistically, that only leaves nineteen of you who won't have to do this again and again. Chances of actual recovery are much lower if the decision to enter rehab is made by someone else. This time, I wasn't forced here, I asked to come. Because I wasn't forced here against my will, I'm confident, I'm getting clean for good," Yeo Ming spoke with conviction.

"This is my last ditch effort. I have no idea why I'm telling you this because up until now, I haven't told another soul what I'm about to say to you. I know my secret's safe with you because who're you going to tell? Recently, I was diagnosed with cirrhosis of the liver, which translates into a death sentence if I don't make it this time. There is no next time for me anymore. Get clean, or die a particularly gruesome death in the next year or two. But I think ninety days here, so far from civilization, I'll actually have a chance for my body to completely detox. Baltimore may have the reputation as the heroin capital of the world, but, let me tell you, there isn't a drug out there that you can't find on the streets of Baltimore City within minutes. Heroin, crack, marijuana, E, all kinds of pills, cocaine. You name it, Baltimore's inner city can supply it. Way out here in the middle of nowhere, I'd guess we're probably forty miles from Baltimore City, so there's no chance of me walking out and not completing the entire thirteen weeks like I've done so many times in the past."

Cali assured Yeo Ming, "I'm only here for six weeks."

"I hate to be the one to tell you this but the minimum stay here is ninety days."

"Oh, no, there must be some mistake. An intervention came to my house last night. He said, it was a six week stay." Cali couldn't conceal the rising panic from her voice.

"Six weeks is pretty common in other programs. In fact, most centers offer outpatient treatment, but not New Light. There's a reason they have the best long term results. It's because they require a minimum ninety day stay. Anything less and those relapse rates are staggering. New Light has an eighty percent success for sobriety five years post treatment which is unheard of. So cheer up, if you really do want to get clean, your chances have just improved dramatically." Yeo Ming left no doubt concerning her information.

Ninety days! Ninety days was more than double the amount of time she agreed to participate in a rehab program. Cali felt a rising sensation of panic in her gut separately from the constant severe stomach ache of heroin withdrawal.

To add to her frustration, it had never occurred to her after these long weeks in Maryland, so far from her family and friends back home in Georgia, she may not be cured. She wanted it to be over. She wanted her old life back. A life full of possibilities and hope. Instead, her mind raced with thoughts of repeated rehab failures. Liver disease. Dying at twenty-six. Hundreds of thousands of dollars wasted.

The pain in her bowels rendered her so helpless that she fell over on her side. A savage twisting inside her body cavity sent a shooting pain up her spine. Collapsed on the bed in a fetal position, a violent trembling spread into the bed, creating a faint tap, tap, tap against the wall. She had to be one of the remaining nineteen. Along with Yeo

Ming, she had to be a success story. Undoubtedly, she knew she'd never have the strength to survive rehab more than once.

"Please, forgive me. I don't feel right," Cali explained.

"You don't look too well. When was the last time you used?" Yeo Ming climbed from her perch on her bed and gingerly sat on the edge of Cali's bed.

"Around two-thirty this morning, right before we left home for the airport." Cali couldn't open her eyes. The light in the room was searing a hole through her corneas, causing intense pain in her eyes.

Unexpectedly, a cold washcloth caressed her forehead before the soft cotton blanket was tucked in tight around her shivering body.

Gratefully, she looked up at Yeo Ming, managing, "Thank you for your kindness."

"You can do it, Cali. Don't let yours drag on for years and years like I did."

Yeo Ming's training left no mistake in her mind, Cali needed immediate caloric intake. When Cali complained of a sudden sharp pain in the soles of her feet as though she had walked across shards of broken glass in her bare feet, Yeo Ming knew this was due to chemical instability. Electrolyte imbalances associated with this level of malnutrition had the potential for sudden death due to cardiac arrest. Most certainly, Cali had already developed some extent of osteoporosis which may lead to pathological bone fractures in the future. Cali was at great risk for infertility, as well as organ failure.

"If it's possible, you look like you feel worse," her words validated Cali's misery. "Is there anything I can do for you? I could get the nurse, but she won't give you any drugs." Yeo Ming studied the girl's ruddy complexion, speckled with bluish spots.

"Thank you, Yeo Ming, but the only thing that will help right now is heroin, so I guess I have no choice but to suffer through this. I do appreciate your kindness. I think I would eventually love to have you as my physician one day. You're very smart and compassionate. No doubt, you're going to be a very successful doctor," Cali's words pierced Yeo Ming's heart.

"A doctor. Yes, that will certainly bring much joy to my parents. I've brought dishonor upon our family name, which is an almost unforgivable act in the Asian culture. Becoming a physician may make up for some of the shame I've caused. After all, practicing medicine is what I've been groomed for my entire life." Yeo Ming broke eye contact as she continued her story, "My father had to use a great deal of influence to prevent the program from separating from me. Separating. That's a much more polished way of saying, kicked out. He told the Dean of Medicine I needed these absences due to a chronic health problem. Under federal guidelines, privacy laws protect all information related to my, so called chronic health problem. Technically, drug abuse is considered an illness. It wouldn't represent a medical institution well to dismiss one of their own due to health issues. So they continue to save a spot for me," her voice mirrored the sorrow on her face.

Determined to feel better in spite of her body's internal revolt, Cali continued talking, "Do you like being a doctor? It has to be very rewarding. Taking care of sick people."

"The public thinks what's depicted in movies about medicine, curing disease, healing people is factual. That's TV, not real life. There's so much out of our control. Noncompliant patients, bad genes, diseases that don't respond to treatments, death. The reality is, there's so much pain and suffering. In spite of our best efforts, there's so much suffering. I think I've already had my fill of it and I haven't even gotten started." Yeo Ming hung her head in defeat before adding, "Anyone with any common sense should be able to see it makes for a rather dangerous situation to give an addict control of a prescription pad."

"What do you want to do?" Cali asked.

"Pardon me?" Yeo Ming was confused.

"You keep saying your parents want you to become a doctor. You've never said a word about what you want. So I'm asking, if you could do anything you wanted, what would you do? Being here, at New Light, this is the end result of following everyone else's dreams, don't you think? This is your life so it should be your dreams you chase after. So tell me, Yeo Ming, if you could be anything your heart desires, what would you be?"

She guffawed at the question, "No one, I repeat, no one has ever asked me that before."

"In my opinion, that question's long overdue. So, I'm asking, what do you want to do with your life?" Cali put emphasis on the word, you.

"A kindergarten teacher. That's what I want to do. Mold young minds. Show them the world. Shower them with love. And have them love me back. Have someone love me back for a change." She stuck out her chin as though offering it for the first blow.

"And you'll be great at it. I can picture it now. All those little kids, learning about the anatomy of the human body. Think of all the little future doctors you'll launch. Most of all, you'll teach them about compassion and kindness."

Yeo Ming let out a tiny, unsuspecting gasp followed by a barely audible, "Thank you."

"I think you should live your life for yourself. Make yourself happy. That should be reason enough to make your family proud," Cali declared before suddenly doubling over at the waist. She cradled her head in her hands. She wanted her stomach ache and the urge to vomit to subside. And her insides to stop quivering. She wanted her skin to feel like it belonged to her, instead of some toxic covering, slowly poisoning her. She wanted to get well.

"Give it a few days," Yeo Ming offered words of encouragement. "Trust me when I tell you, it does get better."

When Cali raised her head, her eyes were bloodshot and glassy. "I want to get clean. I really do. But I just don't think I can do it right now. My mind wants to never use heroin ever again, but my body has another opinion altogether. I know I can ween myself off over the next three, to four, or five weeks. If I take a little less each day, I'm certain I can be completely clean in a couple weeks. Please, believe me, I don't want this to be my life. I will stop taking drugs, all drugs. I just can't do it right now. Right now, I have to get out of here and get myself to Baltimore City."

"Baltimore? No!" Yeo Ming protested. "Don't do it. Everyone knows, the first couple of days of withdrawal are the worst. Don't give up now. You haven't even given yourself a chance."

"Please, I'm asking you to try and understand," Cali begged. Soon, she vowed, soon, she would get her life back on track. Very soon. Just not tonight.

"Cali," Yeo Ming tried to reason with her, "listen to what you're saying. The only way you'll get out of here is if you leave tonight after your last session ends and it'll be dark by then. It's pitch black out there. I don't think you truly understand how difficult a journey it will be. You heard me tell you it's at least forty miles to Baltimore City from here, didn't you?"

"Yes," Cali confirmed.

"Think about it. Forty miles without a car. First, you'll have to make it to the interstate. Then, you'll be traveling for miles and miles by foot through woods before you'll make it to a rest stop where you'll have to convince someone to give you a ride. Trust me when I tell you, the woods out there are extremely harsh. You'll have to navigate over a landscape of impassable terrain in the dark. You can get hurt. There are fallen trees, unexpected gullies," Yeo Ming studied the pathetic teen writhing in pain. "Just look at yourself. You are not healthy. You'll never make it."

"I run for my high school. I know I can do this, Yeo Ming. I have to get to Baltimore."

Reluctantly giving in, Yeo Ming spoke, "I'd like to go on record saying, I think this is a huge mistake. My guess is, if you actually make it off the grounds, you'll have until breakfast tomorrow morning before they figure out you're gone."

CHAPTER 28

"Listen up people. I just got word from the Commissioner's Office, the granddaughter of a sitting judge in Georgia has gone missing. It's believed she's being held against her will somewhere in our fine city. FBI has paid us a visit this morning. I got orders from the Chief of Patrol down at headquarters, they need somebody to show the Feds all Baltimore has to offer. The short straw goes to Detective Gale. Gale, you're on special assignment to them for as long as they need you. Twenty-four, seven. You work whatever hours they need you; overtime is no issue. I'm not sure if somebody's repaying a favor, or if you've royally pissed somebody off." The BPD shift commander in charge of roll call stood behind a small wooden podium as he issued his order, "At any rate, get going. The lieutenant is waiting."

The detective sprang to his feet, his mind racing at the prospect of working with a federal agent as he hurried out of roll call. He was followed by a few congratulatory whoops and an equal number of not so muffled disgruntled comments asking why Gale always rode the gravy train.

This was followed by one booming, "Shut up, Fitzpatrick. Gale's not a hump, like you."

Detective Gale immediately spotted the six three lieutenant in the main hallway, his arms folded over his chest with a do-not-bother-me scowl across his brow. To his right was an equally tall, considerably younger man with an official government identification badge hanging from a lanyard around his neck. He was handsome, well dressed in a tailored navy blue suit. His choice of tie was a loud, flowered, blue and pink, Jerry Garcia knotted high and tight against his collar. He wore expensive looking shoes that were not American made, maybe from Italy. Real GQ looking. Definitely a ladies' man, Detective Gale thought.

"Detective Gale, Major Crime Unit, meet Special Agent in Charge, Walter Kostos. Agent Kostos is a Behavioral Profiler for The Federal Bureau of Investigation, Maryland Division. You are on loan to him, or officially, the FBI, for as long as Agent Kostos deems necessary. Any questions?" Without waiting for the answer, the harried lieutenant continued, "Good."

Satisfied with his introduction, the lieutenant turned on his heels and disappeared. Standing next to the FBI agent, Detective Gale's sports jacket and shoes looked like they were thrift store finds.

The men locked hands in a handshake as Detective Gale offered, "Nice to meet you, Agent Kostos."

"Walter. Call me Walter," the man smiled. Detective Gale guessed him to be mid-thirties. Gesturing around the crowded police station, the detective nodded. "This isn't an ideal place to talk. Too many ears. Follow me."

They walked in silence as the plainclothes officer led them through a series of hallways crowded with police. They walked with purpose, snaking their way through the narrow passageways, ever mindful of so many curious heads turning in their direction.

Coming to an abrupt halt in front of a nondescript door devoid of a nameplate, the policeman paused long enough to say, "Since we're on a first name basis here, you can call me Detective Gale."

Al was merely poking him a little to see if he was stuck with a jackass or not. He waited a beat or two, the whole time studying Walter's face for a reaction. When a wide grin spread across his face, Al chuckled saying, "Call me Al. So tell me something, Walter. Are you housed up in a modern office, a window with a view, and state of the art equipment at your fingertips?"

"I have no complaints," Walter downplayed his spacious work environment, which had the very best money could buy.

On the other side of the southeast district station house, Al unlocked the door to his office. "Welcome. Management had to relocate some brooms," he preempted their entrance to a room the size of a walk in closet. Gesturing his guest to enter first, he added, "It only took me a meager thirty-seven years to climb the ladder all the way to this. I can tell, you're envious, right?"

The dreary room was painted a depressing shade somewhere between gray and army green. The walls were covered with street maps of Baltimore's nine districts. The maps were further broken down into countless neighborhoods, from Fells Point, Greektown, Brewers Hill, Douglas Homes, to Perkins Projects. Yellow, blue, red, and green stick pins pierced the maps, signifying various kinds of crimes. The overhead florescent lighting defiantly buzzed as one tube flickered. There were no windows.

A cheap desk constructed of pressed sawdust masquerading as wood sagged beneath stacks of files that looked as if the weight would eventually cause it to implode. In the center of the desk sat an ancient computer. An equally unimpressive chair was pulled behind the mountain of files, while two mismatched chairs were crammed into the space on the other side of the desk. The chair situated next to the wall housed a towering stack of cardboard boxes, while the chair closest to the door intimidated anyone wishing to take a seat with mysterious stains on the worn blue fabric.

It seemed almost impossible for the room to house any more furniture, yet a metal file cabinet shrunk the space further. More cardboard boxes with lids were piled on top the file cabinet.Walter recognized the room was all business. No family photos. No sports memorabilia. Just an oversized coffee mug bearing a Marines insignia, which had not been properly washed in quite awhile. He respected the care the detective took to shield his personal life from whomever may enter. Potential predators entering this cramped space would never find Detective Al Gale's achilles heel.

"Personally, I've never believed the suit makes the man, so to speak," Walter said as he shimmied his way into the stained chair, making room for Al to slide behind his desk.

"Bring me up to speed." Al didn't waste any time getting down to business.

Walter began, "I have a kidnapping. Cali Hasting's the sixteen year old granddaughter of a sitting Georgia circuit court judge. Cali was being treated for a heroin addiction at a drug rehab facility in Havre de Grace. I have a total of three hits on a debit card in her possession. ATM video on Gay Street shows her withdrawing money and there's a partial tattoo visible on the kidnapper's wrist. We can't make out his face because he's got his head covered with a ball cap and a hood, plus he's positioned himself directly behind the victim. But I have that tattoo. I spent the better part of yesterday at FBI headquarters enhancing the image. Yesterday evening, my agency contacted your police commissioner to access the department's tattoo files in hopes of making a positive identification."

"Oh, sure. The tattoo. It makes sense now. I was wondering why they chose me for this assignment. Here's the thing, you have to understand, my tattoo files are nothing formal. Nothing like you'd find in the FBI files. I'm just small potatoes. I started about fifteen years ago and it's come in handy over the years, catching quite a few perps. Big problem is, I can't get the higher powers that be to make cataloging tattoos a general order. My dream is to see it go large scale one day and have it all entered into our computer's Lotus notes. In the meantime, I bought a fairly inexpensive digital camera out of my own pocket and keep it in the booking area. I get a fair number of pics. A few of my buddies who value the art of investigation get the shots when I'm not around. But I'm lucky if I get one out of every twenty arrests. Altogether, I have seventeen albums with about one hundred photos in each. Better than nothing, right?" Al leaned back in his chair.

Walter couldn't suppress his delight, "Whoa! One thousand seven-en hundred photographs. I'd say that's impressive, actually. You just saved me hundreds of manpower hours combing through tattoo parlors, securing warrants, attempting to get information from disreputable business owners reluctant to give up information about their questionable clientele. How many times have these photos led you to a good arrest?"

"A hundred and twelve. But who's counting?" Al grinned from ear to ear like a little kid.

The middle aged officer jumped to his feet and pulled a cardboard box to the floor. The albums were arranged neatly so the numbered spines were immediately visible.

"Each tattoo is linked to a SID number," Al explained.

Walter interrupted, "SID number?"

"State Identification Number. Everybody arrested in Baltimore City gets one. It follows them for the rest of their life. So, for people with aliases, the fingerprints connect them to their unique SID number. Makes identification a whole lot easier," Al explained. "So what does our tattoo look like?"

Al reached across his desk taking the photo from Walter.

"Death Before Defeet, spelled with two e's? I'd wager this is a prison tattoo," Al deduced as he tapped his thumbnail against his lower lip.

"I don't know much about prison tattoos. I'm not exactly sure what goes into the whole process," Walter confessed.

"They got it down to a science. They get a piece of fruit, like a grapefruit or an orange. After scooping out the fruit, they fill the hollowed out peel with petroleum," Al explained.

"How're they smuggling petroleum inside a jail?"

"You're thinking petroleum, as in gasoline. Petroleum's actually in vaseline, baby oil, skin lotion. They set it on fire and it creates a low burn. They tent a paper bag over it. The color comes from the soot inside the bag. After scraping the soot off and mixing it with more petroleum, they have their ink," Al spoke with years of experience under his belt.

"Fascinating. So, they just light the petroleum?" Walter hung onto Al's every word.

"No, they use a paper clip and a wad of toilet paper. If they roll the toilet paper up real tight, they get a homemade wick that burns long and slow. Then they take something like a paper clip or a guitar string and sharpen it to a point creating a homemade needle they dip in the ink. I've heard they'll melt checkers to get the red. Pretty ingenious, right?"

"They can't spell, but these are the same science majors who cook up meth in their bathtubs. Or mix lethal doses of heroin and fentanyl to sell to kids like Cali Hasting," Walter said solemnly.

CHAPTER 29

Reeling from a lingering confusion as she fitfully transitioned from sleep to wakefulness, Cali bolted upright in an acute state of panic. She didn't know if it was the early morning light slowly seeping along the periphery of the warped boards or the low hum of someone singing to himself. Perhaps it was the combination of the two that shook her hard into consciousness. Unmistakably, the tune was an ancient gospel hymn passed along through the ages. It was a hymn she knew well.

She screamed for help. With every ounce of effort, she screamed and beat her hands against the wall to make her presence known. Hysterically, she screamed for help until she could hardly breathe. Dizzy and hungry for air, her chest heaved. Being sealed inside the sweltering room was like breathing inside an oven. The hot air burned her lungs with each breath but still she cried out for help. Sucking in the humid Maryland air, her lungs struggled to extract oxygen molecules from the hot moisture.

No one came to help her.

Trying to catch her breath, she strained her ears, willing them to hear it again. Within no time at all, the melody returned. This time, she was able to discern the words to the song. She couldn't see him, but what she heard helped paint a picture of the man outside. Like a blind girl, she honed in on her sense of hearing. She realized the cracked and leathery voice belonged to a much older man. His was a generation raised in church, where songs about Jesus were second nature. Arthritic joints transformed his gait to a loud shuffle as the soles of his shoes never entirely lifted from the sidewalk. She heard his feet slowly scuffle along.

Surely, this faceless man was her salvation. He most certainly would be alarmed by what Skeeter had done to her, keeping her captive against her will and call the police thereby putting an end to her misery. This man of God, this man who knew church hymns by heart, could not possibly mean her harm. With a renewed sense of urgency, Cali began to cry out. Hers were cries of agony, indignation, to beg for help.

She screamed louder yet. She screamed until her throat was as raw as if it had been scrubbed with steel wool. She screamed until no more sound came out. She screamed until the old man's singing abruptly ceased.

Still, no one came. Just like that, as suddenly as he appeared, he was gone.

Defeated, she pressed her body against the wall, tucked her knees up tight against her chest as she was forced to endure her prison sentence in solitary. She longed for human contact. Unbearable hour after hour slowly passed for the motionless girl curled into a tight ball. Her left ankle ached from the unnatural weight of the chain and the padlock. A cold sweat soaked through her clothes while the dehydrated muscles in her legs cramped and twisted. A fierce pounding behind her eyes commenced as she listened intently for the old man to return. Using the sleeve of her T-shirt, Cali wiped the constant drip from her nose. Her mouth yearned for just one sip of cool water. And heroin.

She cowered in fear as the day wore on and there was nothing to keep her company but a deafening silence. Why weren't there any sounds of people? She was left with a nerve wracking silence and the glaringly candid examination of her poor choices in life.

This, all this, was the culmination of her own bad decisions. Overwhelmed by disappointment and shame, Cali realized she was long overdue for some honest soul searching. It was the hardest thing she had ever done, taking an honest look in the mirror and viewing herself through the eyes of truth. If only she could turn back time, step back into her charmed world. She was filled with deep regret for the miserable path her life had taken. Over the span of a few short months, she had developed a disregard for everything she once held so dear.

Plain and simple, using drugs was illegal. Her actions were a slap in the face for her Pop, an honorable man who spent his life upholding legal guidelines meant to govern and maintain order and equity. From her earliest memories, she wanted to be like him. How could that be when she showed a blatant disregard for the law, an institution she had aspired to belong to for as long as she could remember, now that her every minute was filled only with the desire for her next fix?

She lied. To everyone. About everything. Where she was. How she spent her days. Why she had such great weight loss. Honor was replaced with deception.

She stole from her grandparents. Not rooting through their wallets or pawning their jewelry kind of stealing. No, she was way more savvy than that. She was much more dangerous because she used her intellect to finagle money from people at her grandparents' expense. Wanting to make sure she was never stranded without money, Pop had generously given her a credit card for emergencies only. Approaching random people at gas stations, she offered to fill their tanks using Pop's credit card to pay the bill in exchange for a fraction of the tab in cash. Cash she then used to buy drugs. Illegal drugs, at Pop's expense.

Money that was meant for her Jeep payment, injected into her veins instead.

She was an athlete. No, she corrected herself, she used to be an athlete. Past tense. Used to be a soccer player. But no longer. Real athletes speak of this intangible code of conduct called heart. It translates into the desire to do better everyday. Don't make excuses. Don't blame anyone else for your shortcomings. It's about respect. Respect for the game. For your teammates. The opposing players. Courage to do the hard things. Integrity is the very foundation of heart. It's the conscience that has no tolerance for cheating or shortcuts.

Her heart was no longer. In fact, she was entirely empty inside. Like a store mannequin. From all outward appearances, her body resembled a girl called Cali Hasting. Others should be warned, don't look closely though, because they'd see she was empty on the inside. It was impossible to know unless they pressed too hard, but if they kept the pressure on for a prolonged period of time, the outer shell would come crumbling down into a pile of dust. She was hollow inside and out. She was a ghost of the girl she used to be.

Hers was once a body strong and vital. Not that long ago, her passion was running. Lean toned muscles told the story of her hours spent everyday sprinting, jogging, intentionally finding hills or stadium steps to conquer. Clean eating reflected in her stamina. A never ending stream of fresh fruits and vegetables.

Toxins found in candy, deserts, or fast foods never crossed her lips. Unlike many of her peers, she had never tried a cigarette. Had never tasted alcohol. No, not Cali Girl, she skipped all that and went straight to oxycodone. Then to heroin. Her picture of health replaced by a body withered, abused, neglected, and malnourished. She was a virtual wasteland.

She used to be happy, awakening every morning with unstoppable exuberance. Her classes were exciting and challenging. When the principal approved of the mock trial club, that small victory fueled her desire to spend her life presenting arguments in hopes of convincing the courts to side with her. That was her dream, to follow in Pop's footsteps and become a lawyer. A trial lawyer. Front and center. Presenting cases with such command, there would be no other possible outcome than to sway juries to side with her clients.

With her high school's government department chair presiding over the mock trial club, Cali was indomitable. Research and preparation instilled the confidence necessary to own the room. She used to be fearless. Until recently, when she became afraid of things that had no reason to provoke fear. Frightened of everyday life. Yet, fool heartedly, she forged headlong into a relationship with a lowlife like Skeeter, someone she should have been terrified by.

Without giving it a second thought, she placed her trust in the hands of the unscrupulous Skeeter. Skeeter, pure evil personified. Why did she allow herself a connection with someone like him, when she abandoned cherished relationships with honorable people, specifically her friendship with Kennedy? People don't exist in vacuums. All her selfish decisions had a profound effect on Kennedy's life, as well. Bewilderment must have surely invaded her everyday thoughts, provoked by a sense of abandonment ever since she made the decision to walk away from their relationship and isolate herself. Hide herself from Kennedy, hide her drugs. Kennedy had no say in the disintegration of their lifelong friendship. Did her best friend rely on empty hopes that today will be the day the old Cali comes back? Or the next day? Or the next?

That was when she realized with horror that she needed to relieve herself. She willed herself not to go. How long had it been since she last used the bathroom? How long had she been here? She couldn't remember anymore. At that moment, Cali could hold it no longer. But where? Her bladder felt as though it would burst. She needed to pass her urine immediately. Panicked, she stood, ever mindful of the oppressive weight of the lock and chain around her ankle.

Holding onto the wall, it took her a minute to steady her balance after spending so many hours folded up tight in a knot on the floor. Her bones felt heavy and stiff. Her right knee throbbed like a toothache which didn't subside when she tried rubbing it.

Desperately, her eyes searched for anything that may substitute as a toilet but there was nothing. The floors were bare with the exception of a thick layer of dirt. Stretching her ankle as far away from the pipe as possible, Cali shamefully lowered her pants. Squatting at the junction where the floor and wall met, she let the hot liquid leave her body. The strong ammonia odor was overpowering. The smell made her gag, causing an upheaval in her empty stomach. Gratefully, she watched some of the dark amber fluid trickle through the joist to the floor below. The remaining urine puddled, ultimately fanning out as the liquid formed numerous tracks in the dirt. Ignoring the humiliation of being unable to clean herself, she pulled up her panties and pants before returning to her spot on the other side of the pipe.

Before Marilyn left, she kept repeating, the longest rope has an end. The longest rope has an end. What did that mean? Was it her way of saying, stay strong because eventually, this situation would be over for her? Or did it translate into, all her evil deeds had finally reaped what she sowed?

There was a time in the not so distant past when she imagined Scarlet's snotty little chides were the extent of wrongdoing. Dismayed by her naivety, she recalled countless tales her Pop meticulously laid out for MomMom and her as they ate their supper every evening together. She had been raised on the legal justice stories her entire life. Sordid tales of lives wasted, driven by the common cores of avarice, lust, power, jealousy. On a rare occasion, there was the commission of a crime out of mere boredom. But never did he allude to this level of brutality.

Prior to meeting Skeeter, she had no real conception such evil existed. Shuddering, she recalled the sinister way his lip curled, revealing yellowed teeth when she pleaded with him not to leave her here. The ruthlessness in his eyes as he gazed upon her suffering with obvious satisfaction.

Defeated, Cali rested her head on her knees as she wondered what form of evil took residence in a man's soul for him to treat another human being with such vulgar malice?

So, was this how it was going to finally end? Dead. Alone. Sealed inside this homemade prison in an abandoned building in a distant city. The sum of her pathetic sixteen years being fear, guilt, pains of heroin withdrawal. A life that, in the end, brought disgrace to the kindest elderly couple, who was the epitome of all things good. Humble, decent people. Her death would seem like a form of relief for all of them. A chance for her loved ones to grieve, accept the loss, get on with their lives. Sorrowfully, she wondered if her body would ever be found.

CHAPTER 30

"Whatcha doing here, huh?" Skeeter appeared out of nowhere.

Surprisingly, for a little guy, his grip around her forearm was a powerful vice. He was hurting her. A faint, barely audible cry of distress caught in the back of her throat. Thankfully, it came out as a squeal, rather than the blood curdling scream of terror she felt. She knew better than to incite his anger any further. Past experience told her, he was capable of anything. Marilyn tried to appear calm, wishing not to betray the clear sense of danger that pulsated throughout her veins, caused her pupils to dilate, making her pant like a hunted rabbit.

Unable to sleep last night, Marilyn lay in bed as she thought about her own plan. She decided to take charge of her own destiny. Starting with tonight when she forfeited a lucrative performance at a club called The Red Maple so she could come see Cali without Skeeter ever knowing. At least that was her plan. It never occurred to her that Skeeter could possibly be lurking about at such a late hour, watching her every move. She didn't see him until it was too late. In fact, until the moment he grabbed her arm, she was completely unaware of his presence. How long had he been standing there, lying in wait?

"Cat got your tongue, huh? I done asked you a question. Whatcha doin' up here without me? If I ain't knowd better, I'd think you're tryin' to double cross me, ain't that right?" his voice was low and menacing. Only separated by less than a foot, Marilyn could smell the rancid breath of someone who had never before visited a dentist.

There wasn't another soul around. Once a thriving neighborhood of homeowners making monthly mortgage payments, the community was ultimately abandoned almost two generations ago. Gradually, the empty buildings were taken over by the homeless and drug addicts. Vacant buildings transformed into shooting galleries. Occupied by squatters. At this late hour, they too, surrendered the dark streets to the cat size rodents that scurried about.

There wasn't a soul to bear witness, but Skeeter wasn't taking any chances. Using the steady grip on Marilyn's arm, he steered her into the inky blackness, nearer to the brick buildings. Everything beyond the shadows was covered in a hazy, yellowed fog, making any activity difficult to discern on these streets. On the entire length of a city block, nearly six hundred feet long, only two miserable streetlights buzzed and strained to emit a faint light, masking his presence until it was too late.

The entire area, further than the eye could see, was post-apocalyptic in appearance. Where once a thriving city existed, rows and rows of three story, crumbling brick exteriors took its place. Entryways blocked with weatherbeaten, peeling plywood, the ignored threat, "No trespassing. Property of Baltimore City", stenciled in black spray paint. The buildings were structurally unsound. Sunken floors exposed to the elements under collapsed roofs. Support beams rotted away. Generations of neglect. Dilapidated houses that became empty shells, the happy memories of better times erased forever.

In a different time, transoms set above the doorways, where the addresses of these once grand row homes were incorporated into the stained glass. The two foot by three foot colorful glass windows could be unlatched from the inside, opened on a tilt to let fresh air into the home. But that was another time in history. In the last twenty-five years, the transoms rapidly became a commodity for anyone looking for quick money. Antique dealers were paying top dollar for these rectangular windows so they could turn around and sell them to the young city dwellers living in the more desirable, renovated neighborhoods bordering Patterson Park. Urban restoration in one part of the city had the opposing effect on the other, as every transom was either replaced by a plank of gray buckled wood, or left as an empty hole above another condemned threshold.

Acres of boarded up, abandoned row homes. Coated in layers of neglect, lay exquisite white marble steps, that half a century ago, women took pride in. Those long ago women used to gather ritualistically every Saturday morning on hands and knees to scrub their marble steps with a stiff brush and a bucket of hot suds. Every Saturday from mid March to late November, without fail, rows of marble steps were proudly polished. It was a different time, a time when people took pride in their homes. Stunning slabs of white marble now buried beneath a blanket of grime and car exhaust remained in place only because they were much too heavy to cart off and sell.

Gone were the old days when small squares of pink or purple candy wrappers stuck to the damp sidewalks. Colorful reminders of playful children that were swept away every morning as women took their straw brooms to their homes' exteriors. The new reality was crumbling walkways in disrepair, missing random chunks of concrete. As far as the eye could see, sidewalks were desecrated with cigarette butts and shards of broken glass. Gutters were cluttered with discarded soda bottles. The streets were littered with miniature empty, plastic baggies that once contained rocks of crack cocaine.

On every block, there was an intentional square of absent side-walk, where orphaned trees lived in patches of brown dirt, devoid of all nutrients. Once a source of beauty, like everything else, the trees suffered the price of ruination and apathy. Roots unable to spread out luxuriously in a rich soil resorted to pushing up out of the earth, tilting the sidewalks above. An aberrance of nature, a few of the trees defiantly sprouted a few haphazard leaves on one side, in spite of themselves, as they hung on for dear life.

"It's so hot today, I suspect to see the devil, himself. That girl's been in there for two days now. She needs some drink. Today, I made grocery. I boiled her sorrel shandy to drink. Made fire and cooked some callaloo and bhaji rice, too. That one in there, she lives far from the kitchen, boy. We don't feed her, give her drink, she's going to die for sure," Marilyn explained. Her bloodstream filled with the pulsating surge of adrenaline driven by Skeeter's hostility was making her feel dizzy.

"She's got a drink. I brung her a Pepsi yesterday," Skeeter was clearly in the mood for confrontation.

Marilyn insisted, "It's gone, I tell you. She's roasting in there. She's like a beached fish, gulping for air. How much monies you think they're going to pay for a dead girl? You've been knowing me practical my entire life. Monkey knows which tree to climb. Think about it. How can I double cross you when the girl is chained up inside? I'm looking out for our best interests, you and me. I'm taking care of our business. If your house is on fire, I wet mine."

For a fleeting moment, Skeeter's demeanor relaxed. His temper appeared to be deflated by the voice of reason.

Blindsided, Marilyn was not expecting the ignition of a sudden, more volatile fury, "Who's the monkey and who's the tree in your little story, huh? Either way, I ain't likin' it, one little bit, understand me?"

"It's island speak. Just our way of talking. Nobody's calling you a monkey. Or a tree," Marilyn stammered, fully aware of Skeeter's dark frame of mind.

"Maybe that voodoo, hoo do, witchcraft garbage you call food is what's gonna kill her. Ever think of that?"

"I made fire and cook Trinidad for her. Better belly bust than good food waste," Marilyn tried unsuccessfully to defend herself.

He twisted Marilyn's arm behind her back, causing her to cry real tears. "You been givin' this a lot of thought, ain't cha?" Even at this late hour, Marilyn wore heavy stage makeup, making the steady stream of tears streak lines of black mascara down her cheeks.

The question was a trap. Marilyn remained silent, waiting for the full scale, unbridled eruption. His mood was quickly escalating and she was convinced it would not end well for her. Like a slap across his face, an insanely large rat scurried over Skeeter's shoe, breaking the spell. Jumping back, he released his grip on Marilyn's arm.

Hugging herself, she massaged the aching bone in her arm. Fear, self pity, and pain filled her. But never did she, for even one second, experience regret for checking on Cali. The girl was looking real bad. Hardly moving. Breathing in short, quick puffs. The trapped air inside was so hot, it felt like the room might explode.

"You ain't tryin' to take her for yourself, are you? Thinkin' about keepin' that ransom money all for yourself? Cut me outta the picture?" Skeeter paced back and forth, like a caged tiger.

"She's in there, right where we left her," Marilyn remained steadfast. "Go see for yourself."

"Yeah, we'll see about that. You're gonna stay right here where you're at. I'm gonna check for myself. If you got any idea 'bout movin', even one inch, I'll bust a cap in your ass right here, got it?"

He reached into the front waistline of his pants and pulled a .38 caliber Saturday night special from his dip. A stolen gun. In a span of five hours, the .38 was stolen during the commission of a crime on the streets of Philadelphia, transported to Maryland via the interstate, and sold to one Jimmi Shiflett in the parking lot of a West Baltimore convenience store.

Marilyn felt the weight of the cool metal against her forehead before she realized what he was doing. The barrel of the gun rested its full weight above her left eyebrow. He held the gun with his right wrist rotated ninety degrees, elbow bent, gangsta style. She squeezed her eyes shut as tight as she could, not wanting his terrifying face to be the last image she saw in this lifetime. Marilyn didn't doubt for an instant his willingness to kill her. He was a ruthless individual. Since birth, something wasn't wired right in his brain.

Everything with Skeeter was unpredictable, so when he suddenly lunged at her with outstretched arms, Marilyn was helpless against her knees giving way. Without warning, he firmly planted both hands on her upper chest before using the full weight of his body to shove her backwards. With her eyes still squeezed shut, she tripped one foot over the other as she stumbled backwards. Tilted off balance, it was impossible to right her feet in time. The momentum was too great to stop the fall. She landed hard against the brick building. In an instant, Marilyn was sliding down the rough brick wall into a heap on the filthy sidewalk, no concern whatsoever for the welfare of her brand new neon pink miniskirt.

The same streetlights that betrayed her by hiding Skeeter from her view until it was too late caught the sequins on her ankle high boots. Purple starlights twinkled from the ends of her outstretched legs sprawled out across the sidewalk. Her tank top pulled crooked across her chest when it snagged on the brick on her way down.

She heard the low snicker of triumph before he stepped over her and made his way into the condemned building where Cali was being held captive. Skeeter left no doubt in Marilyn's mind, it was established, written in stone, Skeeter ruled supreme.

How had she gotten herself involved in this mess? She was a lot of things, many of which she was not proud, but a kidnapper? She had never intentionally hurt another human being in her entire life. Never. And now, a girl was barely alive and she had her fingerprints all over it. Looking at the situation from a realistic point of view, she doubted either she or Cali stood much of a chance of getting out of this alive. Raising her hand eye level she studied her snake ring thinking it wasn't doing its job of protecting her from evil.

That's when it caught her eye, making her wonder with a crushing sorrow, if that was how her life will ultimately be marked. Directly across the street was a makeshift memorial to honor the place of death for a loved one, a friend, a neighbor. To an uneducated eye on such matters, it looked like the remnants of a defunct flea market. Tied to a bus stop sign were several deflated balloons, their once joyful mood expired long ago. Faded plastic flowers were attached along the length of the pole. At the very top, out of a child's reach, was a rain drenched teddy bear in a ridiculous shade of blue. What child would want to hug that straw filled bear? The carnival prize, made in some third world country for a few pennies, lacked the cuddly softness children crave in a stuffed animal.

In the spirit of Edgar Allan Poe's gravesite, where roses and cognac are mysteriously left on the anniversary of his death, at the base of the bus sign memorial was an assortment of empty brown bottles that once contained hard liquor. A farewell toast to a friend. Crestfallen, Marilyn was unable to think of a single person who would bother to memorialize her.

Her thoughts drifted to their days back in juvie when she first met Jimmi Shiflett, AKA Skeeter. Jimmi was sixteen when the judicial system sent him away after launching a brutal attack on a woman. It was a provoked act of retaliation at the request of his mother, Peaches. He was back then and remained today ruthless. Psychiatrists at the detention center wasted no time deeming him a sociopath.

Marilyn heard the plywood covering the doorway slide back, followed by a loud slap on the concrete when Skeeter jumped to the sidewalk below. Sprawled out on the ground was a vulnerable position so Marilyn quickly scrambled to her feet, hopeful he was satisfied Cali was still chained to the pipe. She could finally go home and get some sleep. Lick her wounds in private.

"Good night," Marilyn spoke softly as she turned to leave.

This time, Skeeter's shove was absolutely explosive. Unprepared for the attack, Marilyn's feet seemed to lift off the ground before she landed hard against the brick, her neck snapping forward, then backward, to accelerate the blow to the back of her head against the brick wall. A searing pain shot down her lower spine like a wave of fire. A high pitched ringing flooded her ears. She wondered if her skull was split wide open.

Reflexively her hands grabbed for the back of her head to check for blood. Before she could determine the extent of her injury, Skeeter pounced on her, grabbing her wrists above her head. Pinned against the wall, he forced a knee between her legs, pressing the full weight of his body against hers. In that position, Marilyn remained upright although her legs were numb. She couldn't feel her feet. An excruciating pain filled her pelvis making her fear she may lose control of her bowels at any moment. Skeeter's mouth was less than an inch from her ear, every breath he took amplified as though through a megaphone.

When he spoke, Marilyn expected her eardrum to shatter, even though it was merely a low snarl, "I see you done brung her that Hello Kitty blanket that means so much to you. You two ain't friends now, are you? You try to cheat me out of what's mine and I'll chain you up next to your girlfriend, got it? But ain't nobody gonna pay no ransom for you, ain't that right? If the rats don't eat you first, you'll be goin' back inside when they finally do find you. For kidnappin'."

Marilyn's eyes flew open wide, her heart thundered in her chest.

Pleased by her undisguised, raw fear, Skeeter continued, certain he had her full attention, "Yeah, you heard me. Except this time, I ain't talkin' about no kiddie jail. Freedom gone. Time to get up, time to sleep, time to eat, time to take a shit. You can kiss all that makeup and clothes of yours goodbye. Remember how much you like them communal showers? Think about this, where you gonna get tape, huh? You think they're gonna let you prance around in them short skirts with your Johnson hangin' out?"

Letting go of her wrists with one hand, he forced it under her skirt. Overpowering her, Skeeter roughly grabbed Marilyn by the crotch. Involuntarily, Marilyn let out a muffled squeal of pain. Managing to wriggle one hand free, she tried desperately to claw his hand away but Skeeter's grip only tightened.

"No more Marilyn Mon Yo. Nope. You'll be Marlin the Queen Ho. So you listen up, and you listen real good, I'm the brains of this here operation and what I sez goes, got it? Don't think about gettin' in my way," he warned her.

Thoroughly enjoying himself, Skeeter squeezed Marilyn's scrotum until she passed out.

CHAPTER 31

Al Gale had often heard his wife's friends remark that men were genetically unable to multitask. Yeah, well, they haven't seen this guy in action, he thought. For the past two days, Special Agent Walter Kostos painstakingly studied page after page of tattoos in one album after another, all the while coordinating an extrication strategy. Al was impressed by the agent's methodical approach. A fan of crossword puzzles, words such as steadfast and diligent came to Al's mind as he watched Walter work. Being detailed to the FBI task force was, without a doubt, the highlight of Al's thirty-seven yers as law enforcement.

The first thing on Walter's agenda Monday morning was making sure the agent at Quantico was aware of the partial image of the vehicle outside Old Town Liquors. He was on it. He reassured Walter he'd give him a call as soon as he had something.

Thankfully, Anthony Rock, the judge's law clerk, had the presence of mind to prompt the judge to ask the kidnapper to make all future calls to his personal cell phone. Walter needed the senior Hasting and his cell phone in Baltimore as soon as possible. It was imperative Walter oversaw all calls from the kidnapper. Since Cali had resided with her grandparents, they were vital to the case. He needed them at his immediate disposal. They would have insights that may prove invaluable to Cali's recovery.

Judge Hasting was one step ahead of him. Long before receiving the call from the FBI agent, he and his wife had already booked their flight from Georgia to Maryland and were currently on their way to the airport. Their plane was scheduled to land at BWI in the late afternoon. However, Robert and Maggie were staying behind for the immediate time being to complete the banking transactions. The judge had signed a power of attorney giving his son the ability to withdraw the one million five hundred thousand dollar ransom from various accounts. As soon as Robert secured the money, he and Maggie would join them in Maryland. If all went well, Cali's parents would also be in Maryland sometime later tonight.

When Walter insisted no ransom money would be paid, the judge stood firm. Walter knew he was up against a stone wall when the judge began his sentence with the words, "With all due respect." Cal Hasting wanted his granddaughter back at all cost, unharmed. If one point five million dollars was the asking price for her safe return, he was adamant about paying the money.

Ending the call, Walter quickly placed his next call to the field office, requesting an IT specialist be on stand by. As soon as the Hastings arrived in Maryland, Walter wanted the technology experts working their magic on Judge Hasting's cell phone, every phone call recorded, all incoming and outgoing calls traced. He also needed a silver haired agent to pose as Judge Hasting for the money drop off, if it got that far. One thing was non-negotiable, Cal Hasting was never going to be physically engaged with the kidnapper. Walter wasn't about to put any civilian in harm's way, risking a second victim. If they had no choice but to deliver the ransom money, it would be done by a federal agent.

While Walter addressed his agendas, Al got a copy of the Death Before Defeet tattoo to the shift commander. The lieutenant in charge put the photo on the read out board. Copies went out to each sergeant with instructions to deliver them to the six officers in each of their squads. All police in the southeast district were fully aware of the urgency in this high profile case. Al knew there was a good chance an officer on patrol might recognize the tattoo, Death Before Defeet, thereby identifying the kidnapper.

Feeling his oats, Al asked an officer assigned to the drug unit to review the footage from the blue light surveillance cameras. Beginning in 2007, these cameras were strategically placed in high crime areas throughout Baltimore City. Monitored around the clock by members of the drug unit, activity around the city was live streamed, as well as recorded. Giving the location of the ATM outside Old Town Liquors, Al asked for an examination of a ten city block radius at the time of the transaction. Detective Gale was disheartened to learn the blue light camera project, which cost Baltimore City taxpayers over two million dollars, had very few cameras that actually worked. Regardless, he wanted any available tapes reviewed.

Walter's phone rang as he began to peruse the photo album marked number eleven. It was Nick checking in. He conducted a second interview with the administrator at the treatment facility. In Nick's opinion, she gave the impression of being truthful. After running all of the employees' names through the National Crime Information database, NCIC, everyone checked out clean. He was currently on his way to the southeast police station to join ranks with Walter and Detective Gale.

In the meantime, Walter and Al began contacting Central Booking Intake Facility, Baltimore City Detention Center, Jessup's Correctional Institution, Hagerstown Correctional Facility, all the while uploading the image. No one recognized the tattoo.

According to one artist who owned a tattoo parlor on the corner of Broadway and Eastern Avenue, Death Before Defeet was inked by an amateur. As an afterthought, he was quick to point out, no tattoo artist would ever give out any information on their clientele. Talking to the police about their customers was literally taking bread out of their own mouths. In his opinion, Agent Kostos was wasting his time.

To their disappointment, staff at homeless shelters were reluctant to give out any information about the men they housed. One dead end after another yet Walter continued to scratch at the dirt, determined not to stop until he dug up a bone. Someone, somewhere could identify the owner of this tattoo.

Walter and his new partner had been holed up in Al's cramped office, working tirelessly for hours when Al said, "I've never considered myself to be a gambling man. I didn't think the odds were in our favor, but I think we found him."

Hunched over a picture album, Walter bolted upright in his chair, "What did you say?"

"Death Before Defeet," Al turned the photo album so Walter could see it from the other side of the desk. "We got him, partner. SID number 732178."

Walter sprang to his feet, banging his knees on Al's desk. He raked his fingers through his hair. Spun around in a complete circle before he reached across the desk to high five Al's outstretched hand.

Al's computer came to life as he began frantically typing. "Our kidnapper's name is …Jimmi Shiflett. Twenty-eight years old. Five seven, one hundred sixty pounds. The only alias we have on file is, Skeeter. Looks like our guy's a frequent flyer. Petty stuff, mostly. Over the years, it looks like the public defenders have done a pretty decent job of keeping him out of jail except for a short stint in juvie."

Walter made his way to the other side of the desk, crouching down behind Al's chair so he could also see the computer screen.

Balling up his fist, Detective Gale unexpectedly hammered it hard against the particle board desk. Self reproach in his voice, he confessed, "I should've thought of this before. I keep a computer file on gang insignias. Let's take a look in there." Opening a second screen, Al scrolled through a gang database spreadsheet. "His tattoo doesn't match any of the area gangs. Looks like Death Before Defeet is unique to one individual, Jimmi Shiflett."

"And we just found him," Walter's eyes were bright. "Is it too much to ask, do we have an address?"

"His last three arrests, no known address. But he consistently gave the name of his mother, one Joyce Melton, as his contact person every time he was being processed at central booking." Al's typing fingers were having a hard time keeping up with his brain. "Let's have a look-see at Ms. Melton's criminal history. Ha. No surprise here. It seems Ms. Melton has had her share of brushes with the law. Prostitution, disturbing the peace. Disorderly conduct."

"The apple didn't fall far from the tree," Walter shook his head. "Does Ms. Melton have an address on file?"

"Indeed she does. Her address of record is a stone's throw from here, in O'Donnell Heights. Sixty-three hundred block of Plantview Way."

Walter was already on his phone to the Maryland field office, rattling off a list of vital tactical gear necessary for a hostage rescue when Nick was ushered into the tiny office by the OIC, officer in charge. He needed his list of supplies delivered to the southeast district, preferably within the hour. While Walter gave orders over the telephone, Al took the liberty of introducing himself to Nick. Ending the call, Walter didn't waste any time bringing Nick up to speed on their end of the investigation.

All the stars aligned in the heavens when the call came in from the agent in Quantico. "I have some intel on that vehicle. From the slope of the hood, the curve of the bumper, and the depth of the front wheel well, I can positively identify the vehicle as a Chevy Chevette. That color is called harvest gold. The model years for that paint color were 1976 to 1986."

As soon as Walter shared the make and model of the Chevy with his two partners, Al began searching the MVA database, saying, "There's no vehicle registered in Shiflett's name. Maybe the car parked on Gay Street was just a coincidence and has nothing to do with him."

Impossibly, all three officers squeezed behind the desk and were hunched over Al's computer, searching the MVA database for Jimmi Shiflett's mother, Joyce Melton when there was a knock at the door. There were no vehicles registered in her name either.

A female officer from the drug unit popped her head around the corner, "I reviewed the blue light camera videos like you asked. I got a total of thirty-one images in the ten block radius around Old Town Liquors. You can come on over and take a look if you want."

The policewoman felt like she was in Pamplona, Spain for the annual running of the bulls. Hugging her body against the wall, she barely escaped being mowed down as the three men raced past her to the surveillance video room.

Her computer screen was covered in a checkerboard of images. There was a fair amount of traffic in each of the photos, yet unmistakably, in frame after frame, there it was. A harvest gold, two door Chevy Chevette. About half the photos showed the vehicle traveling westward toward Gay Street, then approximately six minutes later, the same car was captured heading eastbound on Baltimore Street.

Nick said, "That's no coincidence. That Chevy Chevette is our vehicle."

"Can you zoom in?" Walter was practically climbing onto her desk.

"How many people do you see in the car?" Nick asked, wanting confirmation.

"If you get out of my way, I just might be able to enlarge the images," the drug unit officer complained. Like the parting of the Red Sea, the men made a space for her to reach her desk. Putting on her reading glasses, she declared, "Two. A driver and a passenger. From what I can tell, the back seat looks empty. I can't make out their faces or a license plate. If I zoom in any more, the images become too grainy. But I'd venture to say that they're both caucasian."

Nick suggested they email the images to the FBI lab immediately. Heading back to Al's office, Walter's phone buzzed. A distraught Judge Hasting was on the other end.

"Agent Kostos, the kidnapper just called. He said he wants the money in the morning. At seven thirty, he wants me to go to, hold on one minute...." Judge Hasting's voice was momentarily drowned out by an overhead announcement declaring his flight to Baltimore was beginning to board. "I wrote it all down here. He wants me to leave the money at Penn Station located at 1500 North Charles Street in Baltimore City. He instructed me to leave it under the bench outside the men's room, on the outside platform. Train number thirty-nine, heading to New York. He specifically said all the money has to fit inside one black carry-on suitcase. He warned me, no tricks. If there's a GPS tracker or dye packs, he said he'd have no choice but to kill the girl. That's what he called our Cali, the girl. Agent Kostos, my son is making all the bank transactions, so we'll have the ransom money. His plane's arriving in Baltimore at ten twenty tonight. I want to make myself perfectly clear, my wife and I insist the ransom is paid. The money means nothing to us."

Walter listened intently, not divulging any information about their lead on Skeeter Shiflett. If things went awry, if their information didn't pan out, there was no need to involve the judge. Walter was a behavioral specialist and he secretly feared the worst. Skeeter's refusal to call Cali by name indicated emotional distancing from his victim. It's easier to cause harm to someone he ceased to recognize as an actual person. He was more likely to intentionally hurt her or abandon plans with no regard for Cali's welfare. Shiflett's only priority would be to save his own skin if he thought things were going south.

"Call me when your plane lands," Walter told the judge before ending the call.

Walter was convinced Cali's connection to Skeeter Shiflett was happenstance. Walter had no reason to believe Cali preplanned her getaway from New Light with this individual. More than likely, Skeeter stumbled upon her, offering to give her a ride. It made sense to wind up in Baltimore, the epicenter of the heroin trade. All the information they had thus far indicated Skeeter was acting alone.

By all appearances, Shiflett was an amateur, therefore unpredictable. Lacking contingent plans with well thought out scenarios meant he was more likely to make mistakes resulting in his arrest, which also made him more volatile. Because his decisions were rash, a favorable outcome for Cali Hasting was less likely. Confirming his lack of intelligence, his choice for the money drop off was an area filled with security cameras. Shiflett was a wildcard.

"I want somebody on their way to BWI now to pick up Judge Hasting and his wife when their plane lands. And again at ten twenty when the son's plane lands. Let's get two agents to the hotel to make sure Judge Hasting stays put and to guard the ransom money. We need an unmarked car with tinted windows for a stake out," Walter ordered, his mind was going a million miles a minute. "The kidnapper made contact with Judge Hasting. He wants the ransom money left on a train platform at Penn Station at seven thirty tomorrow morning. Get an undercover team there now, disguised as housekeeping. They can use the trash cans to conceal their weapons."

While Nick contacted FBI headquarters, Al reassured Walter, "We got it covered. You heard my lieutenant. Whatever the Feds need, the city'd make it happen."

For the next three hours, the three man team took care of business before they went home to change into clothes for a raid. The three officers agreed to reconvene at nine p.m., sharp.

Just two miles away, Skeeter had spent the better part of the day in his bedroom concocting a plan to get his ransom money. He was jumpy and tense, so he turned on the television as a distraction while he did tricep curls. He wanted his dough, but he still ain't figured out how he was gonna get it.

The local news station was doing a human interest segment on Baltimore's Penn Station. The commentator who talked like she thought she was better than everybody else said it was the eighth busiest rail in the U.S. serving over one million passengers a year. Built in 1911, Penn Station ran thirty trains a day to serve five hundred destinations.

Penn Station, hell yeah! Tossing the dumbbell onto his filthy bed, Skeeter drove on down to Penn Station to case the joint. Slumped down behind the wheel of his car, he watched from afar. There were loads of people, walkin' fast while thinkin' about where they were headed to, not payin' attention to nobody. All of them carryin' black suitcases. Right then and there, Skeeter decided if the old man tried to set him up, if the cops tried to nab him, he'd grab some random kid, stick his gun to his head.

He was brilliant, if he had to say so hisself. People ain't never gave him credit. After he pulled this off, they'd see, he ain't no chump.

By eight thirty, the three officers were pulling off the southeastern police station lot. It was go time and tension in the car was high.

Al eloquently summed up the group's sentiment when he said, "This is when he'll make his move. Everybody knows, cockroaches run amok after dark."

CHAPTER 32

Cali didn't actually hear him slip inside the abandoned row-house. Perhaps she was unaware because, at the time, she was enduring one of the countless fitful nightmares that visited her at random intervals during the excruciating process of heroin withdrawal. Or was it the reward of practiced feet that lightly touched down as he silently darted across the room that kept his presence concealed? It wasn't until he brushed up against her, her leg to be exact, that she became convinced of his existence.

Skeeter had shown no mercy when he left her there, sealed inside that massive tomb. The unbearable temperature inside the row-house made her feel as though the earth had opened up and swallowed her into its molten core. She was deprived the dignity of a toilet. There was no sink to alleviate her desperate thirst. Yet, for Cali, by far the worst form of neglect was her existence being deemed unworthy of a source of light.

Every evening, with the setting of the sun, her terror escalated as she was robbed of her sense of vision. Endless hours were filled with utter blackness, rendering her without sight. Cali felt as though she had been thrust off the face of the earth and catapulted into outer space. Wide eyed, she stared for hours into the black hole where she was being held captive as her imagination magnified her terror.

Alone and afraid in the dark, she found herself longing for the voice of anyone. In the wee hours of the night, Cali hungered for that slight reminder that she was still linked to the human race.

Something had touched her, she was certain. She felt the feathery graze against her lower leg. Peering wildly into the black nothingness, her heart hammered inside her chest. Frozen in place, she dared not stand for fear of rattling the chain against the lead pipe, thereby confirming her presence. Instinct told her to remain very still. No shadow, no glimmer of light from either the moon or streetlights existed inside her imposed vault, yet her head frantically swiveled back and forth as she tried in vain to catch a glimpse of whoever had touched her.

Minutes passed. Trying to establish a sense of calm, she attempted to console herself by thinking she must have only imagined the barely detectable brush against her skin. It was nothing, she reassured herself. Stay calm, Cali Girl, everything's okay. It's probably heroin cravings making your skin crawl.

But deep down, she knew it wasn't true. The darkness may have prevented her from seeing him, but the tiny hairs on the back of her neck felt his presence, nonetheless. Alarmed, her nose confirmed she had company.

Without the benefit of sight, Cali was caught completely off guard by the initial strike. It was the element of surprise that gave him the upper hand. Surprise and the vicious nature of the attack. Seemingly coming at her in every direction, he tore at her clothing, ripping the fabric from her body. Chained to the pipe, she was a caged animal, unable to run away. There was absolutely no chance for her to escape. She had no choice but to fight. The vacant building offered nothing for her to grab as an impromptu weapon of defense. She was the ideal target for this predator. She was cornered, unarmed, defenseless, and worse, blind.

Survival instincts ignited as she fought back with all her might. Her wasted muscles unable to deliver effective punches, she was no match for the savagery. Again and again, he came at her from all angles. He was relentless in the attack, using speed and cunning to overpower her. She felt an unbelievable searing pain in her ankle as her skin and muscle were punctured with something razor sharp, releasing hot sticky blood.

In a last ditch effort to save herself, Cali removed one shoe. Using the heel of her sneaker, she wildly beat him away. The thick rubber sole pummeled him over and over about the face and head. She was absolutely hysterical. Her body flooded with adrenaline, she kicked and punched recklessly. Legs flailing, she fought for her life. This was not how she wanted to die. Not a disgraceful death like this. She refused to succumb without a fight. So, she kicked and punched and slapped for what seemed an eternity. Valiantly, she defended herself for a full six minutes until the coward finally ran away.

Exhausted, Cali collapsed in a tiny heap on the floor, all her strength spent. She was dizzy and disoriented as the room began to tilt, the earth spinning off its axis. Wrapping her arms around her battered body, she struggled to contain her violent shaking. She felt so weak and helpless. She needed MomMom to hold her. She yearned to have her grandmother lovingly rock her in her arms. Tell her everything was going to be fine. Feel her stroke her hair. Have Pop protect and defend her once again. Experience the long lost joy of being surrounded by familiar people who loved her.

Blood pounded in her ears so violently it seemed to squeeze the torrent of tears from her eyes. For the first time, she lacked the resolve to contain her sorrow. Her heart broke wide open. She let loose a pitiful wail of anguish, every hurt pouring out. For the remainder of the night, she was lost in a state of absolute inconsolability.

Somewhere deep in the recesses of her memory, she recalled the phrase, yet prior to the last few days, the phrase held no real meaning for her. But she was there now, this was it, her personal hell on earth. Hell on earth. Hadn't she endured enough suffering? Hadn't she been the cause of unfathomable grief for her grandparents?

One thing Cali knew for certain, he would come back for her. She doubted she would ever have the strength to fight him off again. He would return because he had tasted her. Sooner or later, the rat would find his way to her again.

Having lost all hope, Cali closed her eyes, praying she would never again see another day.

CHAPTER 33

Preparation is the number one key element in any successful covert operation. Anticipation of every possible scenario minimizes hasty missteps. Statistically, rescue of a hostage has a high probability of casualties, so thoughtful planning was essential. In this case, the kidnapper was certainly not a professional, which had both pro and con considerations.

Walter expected Skeeter Shiflett to be less well thought out, not considering the consequences or possible outcomes to each and every move. This guy was not a chess player. His moves were spur of the moment, flying by the seat of his pants, therefore more volatile and irrational. He was much more unpredictable, therefore putting Cali's life in grave danger.

Up until now, his moves didn't adhere to the research which predicted typical criminal behaviors. To outwit Skeeter, the officers had to think outside the FBI's manual of standard operating procedures.

But time was of the essence. If the girl was still alive, chances were, Skeeter's anxiety had heightened to a point where it would just be easier for him to decide to kill her. Her captor would desire less baggage. The three man team agreed they had a maximum of twenty-four hours to spare for reconnoissance. Twenty-four hours or less, then they had to make their move and grab Shiflett at their first opportunity.

The address was located in O'Donnell Heights, a reputed dangerous public housing installation in Southeast Baltimore. It was a place where violence and crime were an everyday part of life. Skeeter and his mother shared an apartment in a two story cinder block building that looked more like a military compound unit than a residential structure. Gray metal bars were welded in place over the windows. Entrances were fortified with heavy doors covered in combat checkerboard metal grates. Rows and rows of the same rectangular concrete building with a flat tar roof were separated by alleys littered with garbage dumped just a few feet from commercial size metal dumpsters. Too much trouble to lift the lid and put the trash inside. Rodents scurried about, snaking in and out of the mounds of garbage as they feasted on carry out chicken and dirty baby diapers.

To the left of the residence, five males approximately nine to late twenties, milled around the basketball courts where the nets had long ago been stolen off the rusted hoops. None of them had a basketball. A steady stream of both foot and vehicle traffic along Gusryan Street first stopped at the corner boy. He stood outside the basketball court, about half a block away. A black kid, maybe fifteen had the uniform of the day on. White T-shirt, black jeans, expensive tennis shoes. He was the bank. Once paid, he held up one or two fingers to signal one or two caps of heroin to the man in charge.

The buyers then pulled alongside the basketball courts to complete the transaction before speeding away. The older man, twenty-seven, twenty-eight, was in charge of the drugs, while the other three divided up various jobs. He kept his gun in the front waistband of his pants, the drugs in empty potato chip bags at his feet.

Two of the kids were runners, bringing back fresh stashes of smack when supply ran low. The youngest one, a white kid, was the most dangerous. Given the title of the lookout boy, he was given a loaded gun to ensure all transactions went according to plan. He was in charge of having the older man's back. Wanting to prove himself a man, he was a loose cannon, only too eager to shoot somebody. Anybody. He wanted to know what it felt like to kill.

Tension in the black vehicle with dark-tinted windows was palpable as they lay in wait. Walter's mind was going a million miles a minute. He noted the time, feeling a small sense of relief that by now both Judge Hasting and his son Robert were safely tucked away in a hotel room with the ransom money.

Adrenaline pulsated through their veins. Their nerves were stretched as thin as the silk weave of a spider's web, just hoping they were in the right place, at the right time. It didn't need to be said, they all knew this was their one chance to recover Cali Hasting. All three lawmen had their heads on a constant swivel as they watched Skeeter's residence and the activity at the basketball court, hoping for a sighting of Skeeter.

They were tired and hungry. Periodically, someone shifted in his seat to alleviate an aching back or cramped calf muscle. The silence was torturous, yet no one wanted to be the first to disturb the mood. The only sound for the last few hours, the inhale and exhale of their breathing. They were at their breaking points when the still was inter-rupted by the alarming sound of Al's stomach gurgling.

Patting his stomach in a futile effort to quiet it, Al confessed, "Sorry, fellas. I ate on the fly today. I'm starving."

"See that black bag on the seat next to you?" Nick twisted around in his seat.

"I do," Al answered.

"Open it. Celeste made some sandwiches for us. There're banan-as, crackers, three bottles of water," Nick instructed.

With overwhelming gratitude, Al removed a plastic container. Snapping back the lid, he found three peanut butter and grape jelly sandwiches, the bread a thick, nutty whole grain. He took one from the top before passing the container to the front of the car.

Letting out a sigh of ecstasy, Al said between bites, "Please, thank your wife for me. You are one lucky man."

"That is a God given fact," Walter agreed.

Granted, Al had just met Nick a few hours ago, but his impression was, he wasn't much different as a man than he was as a boy. Nothing flashy. A decent, wholesome human being. In the end, it was this Average Joe who was the king of the hill. Al liked that.

While the their eyes constantly roamed about, Al's stomach protests had granted permission to speak. Nick began, "I read the statistics. One hundred seventy-five Americans die every day from illicit drug use. It costs our taxpayers well over five hundred billion dollars a year. I know drug abuse is at epidemic proportions, but I just can't figure out what starts it all. Especially for a kid like this. Leading a privileged life. Top notch schools. A family that cares."

Al chimed in, knowing firsthand drugs were the common thread in almost every crime he dealt with, "For years it was thought to be an isolated problem for the poor or homeless. It was ignored the same way AIDS was in the beginning, until it started affecting mainstream America. It sure wasn't on any politician's radar. Once it crossed over into the middle class, costing taxpayers money and jacking up insurance premiums, that's when Washington started taking a long, hard look."

Walter shifted in his seat, his back breaking from being hunched down behind the steering wheel for so long. Setting the night vision goggles down, he rubbed his weary eyes, asking, "I hear you. Is it boredom? Or some catastrophic event, like not getting asked to the prom by the captain of the football team that set this whole thing in motion?"

"If it's adolescent humiliation, then I should've been freebasing in high school," Nick chuckled.

Al was intrigued, "I've got to hear this."

In fact, Al was looking for any diversion to ease some of the tension in the car. Being on high alert, waiting to pounce on Skeeter Shiflett was exhausting. Knowing it could turn into a long, grueling night, the team was grateful for a little distraction to help pass the time.

Walter tilted his head, flashing his mischievous half grin when he asked, "What makes you say that? We were friends at Curley. We were cool. Nerdy, but, cool."

"I didn't start out at Curley. The summer before starting high school, I managed to pester my parents into letting me attend a public school. I was finished with being a career Catholic school student. After nine years of it, I decided, no more ties and sport jackets for me. No more getting picked up after school by my grandmother in her old lady car. I was going to ride the yellow cheese bus like the rest of the kids in my neighborhood. I was going to be cool," Nick reminisced. "So, the first three weeks of ninth grade, I went to Sparrows Point. Didn't you ever wonder why we didn't have the same classes those first couple of weeks?"

"I can't say I recall even noticing," Walter said, knowing Nick's absence going unnoticed would certainly bewilder his partner, who had the memory of an elephant. "I thought we met in Saturday detention, picking up trash."

"That's true, but we both also had world history together, fourth period," Nick reminded him.

"Yeah, I guess I remember that. Continue with your story. You have piqued my curiosity," Walter said.

Both agents adjusted their night vision goggles on the poorly maintained, two story housing unit. It was Al's turn to take a much needed break, setting his BPD binoculars on the seat before rubbing his bloodshot eyes.

Nick continued, "I show up to public school in my green and white polo, khakis, and brown loafers. You know, looking real cool."

Al joined in the banter, "Shirt tucked in?"

"You know it. Shirt buttoned to the throat, I might add. So, we're in music class when the teacher asked each student to tell the class what our favorite song was, and to sing a bar or two." Nick became silent, shaking his head as he relived the humiliation.

"What? You couldn't decide between The Stones or The Grateful Dead?" Al asked from the backseat, enjoying the story.

"I would have been a hero if I would have picked a song by either of them. Nope, I said, The Candy Man."

"The Candy Man? Can't say I ever heard of it," Walter looked puzzled.

"Of course you've never heard of it. No one has, unless you're Nick Filmore or his seventy year old grandmother. The Candy Man," Nick admitted, shaking his head in disgust. "By Sammy Davis, Jr."

Walter's face was blank, "Who's that?"

"There's a name from back in the day. He was part of Hollywood's Rat Pack. Sammy Davis, Jr., Frank Sinatra, Dean Martin. They were from my parents' time, and I'm fifty-six, so, you're talking a few years back. If my memory serves me correctly, he had a glass eye. My mother told me he lost it because he was playing with a coat hanger," Al chimed in, knowing this story had disaster written all over it

"Why would anyone play with a coat hanger?"

"Apparently, sixty years ago, it happened a lot more than you'd think. Evidently, back in the olden days, kids were always running around, losing eyes, left and right, from swinging around wire hangers. They didn't have video games or Nerf guns back then," Al explained.

"Unbelievable."

"But, I can't say I know the song," Al racked his brain.

Nick began to sing softly, "Who can take a sunrise... Sprinkle it with dew... Cover it with chocolate and a miracle or two...The candy man makes everything delicious...You can even eat the dishes."

Al whistled long and low, before declaring, "Sweet mother in heaven."

Silence was imperative on a reconnaissance mission. Detection would not only compromise rescuing the girl but also put them in serious danger. Yet none of the three could contain his laughter. A classroom of hostile teens, clad in denim and black T-shirts glaring at this freak from outer space. They laughed until their ribs ached.

"Even the teacher, who looked like he was older than my grandmother, was speechless," Nick managed, which only threw them into another fit of laughter.

At last, Al used his sleeve to wipe tears from his eyes. "I take it you didn't receive a warm welcome at Sparrows Point."

"I barely escaped lunch period with my life before I called my grandmother and told her to get me out of there. But," his tone suddenly solemn, "heroin never once crossed my mind."

"Do you ever wonder if our parents were ashamed of us?" Nick asked. "Man, I was such a social outcast."

Al did not hesitate for a second, "Absolutely not!" Both Nick and Walter were somewhat startled by his conviction. "I'm not a parent, but I can honestly say, I'd never be ashamed of my kid unless he turned out to be some punk like this Skeeter character."

CHAPTER 34

Defying Skeeter's threats, a battered Marilyn returned to West Lafayette Street to check on Cali. The back of her skull still throbbed from where Skeeter had slammed her head against the brick building. She worried if the muffled hearing in her right ear was permanent. It was painful to walk, her privates were so bruised and swollen. No doubt, Marilyn was making an incredibly risky decision by dismissing Skeeter's warnings.

It was a few minutes after two in the morning, almost two and a half hours since the rat had attacked Cali. When Marilyn moved the wooden slab aside, a suffocating blast of heat struck her in the face, followed by an unexpected swarm of flies. All the windows and doorways sealed off, there was nowhere for the oppressive Baltimore heat to escape. It was easily twelve degrees hotter inside the brick rowhouse than it was outside, and the heat and humidity outside were absolutely unbearable.

Taking her first steps inside the row-house, Marilyn's stomach was assaulted by the stench. Spoiled food left by Marilyn and uneaten by Cali. Of human waste. Rotting human flesh. She froze in her tracks. Was the girl dead? Cooked alive inside this furnace? Recklessly dropping the ice cold ginger kombucha and a plastic container of pigeon peas and curried goat on the floor, she willed her legs to go to the girl. Instinct told her to turn and run away, leave all of this behind. She couldn't do it. Cali needed her.

Marilyn wished she could turn back time and pass by Skeeter Shiflett like a full bus. A cold chill ran down her spine as her she suddenly felt her grandmother's presence. She had a clear sense of her grandmother's words from the grave, "Whatever happens in darkness, eventually comes to light."

Was her grandmother warning her Cali was dead? Marilyn was deathly afraid of dead people. Most island people are. But she had to know. Hastily making the sign of the cross over herself, Marilyn gathered the courage to move forward. Against her better judgement, she stepped into the room with great trepidation. All the while fingering the snake ring her grandmother had given her, she reluctantly put one foot in front of the other until she stood less than three feet from Cali. Shining the tiny penlight attached to her keychain on the slumped over body, Marilyn was certain her instincts were correct. The girl wasn't looking too right. She looked dead.

Marilyn wanted nothing more than to turn and run. Instead, she decided to give Cali one more chance. Making a feeble attempt at rousing her, she shined the bright light directly on the girl's eyelids, without stirring her. Moving the light to her trunk, Marilyn let out a barely audible sigh of relief as she observed the slightest rise and fall of her chest. Cali was breathing. Barely, but she was breathing.

Putting a hand on Cali's upper chest, Marilyn lightly shook her. She was hot, full of fever. Marilyn could feel her swollen heart, pressed up against her ribs, thundering away in her chest. A cold sweat slicked her skin, leaking into her oily hair.

Skeeter picked up on the first ring.

"She's not dead yet, but it is knocking mighty loud on the door," Marilyn blurted into the phone.

"I done already told you not to be stickin' your nose where it don't belong," Skeeter's words seeped out between clenched teeth. He kept his voice low, not wantin' to wake his old lady up. "You better listen good, it's my way or the highway, got it?"

Skeeter was livid. He ain't left no question he was against Marilyn goin' to see the girl without him. She ain't give him no choice, he'd have to rough her up better the next time to make her see who's the boss.

"If you're left in charge, the girl would never eat. When is last time you bring drink? I told you yesterday, it's so hot in here, I suspect to see the devil, himself. You think that judge will pay ransom for a dead girl?"

"It's all figured out. We get the cash, first thing in the morning," Skeeter insisted.

"She'll be dead tonight, I tell you. She's vamping like death. Bring that key. We let her loose, carry her to a hospital," Marilyn persisted.

"Now I know you done lost your crazy, Trini mind," Skeeter yelled into the phone. "This here is my cash cow and I ain't lettin' nobody take what's mine, you understand?"

"We carry her to the hospital. To-night! We've got no choice, Skeeter. We keep her here and we both fry in electric chairs. You get over here now, boy," Marilyn demanded.

It was a quarter after two in the morning when their person of interest, Jimmi Shiflett, AKA Skeeter, made his move. He opened the steel door of his subsidized housing unit and stepped onto the crumbling concrete slab which was a sorry substitution for a back porch. Although it was impossible to see inside the dark tinted windows, Walter reflexively slid down deep in his seat behind the front dash of the car, never losing site of him through his night vision goggles.

"Got him," Al declared, his pulse quickening.

Looking quickly to his left, then his right, Skeeter pulled his black hoodie over his red Chicago Bulls cap. Walter could see the bulk in the front waist of his jeans signifying a gun in his dip. Taking a cigarette from behind his left ear, he cleared the back of his throat and spit a glob of mucus on the ground before lighting the cigarette. The vile act struck Walter like a slap across the face. His father had saved him many years ago from behavior with any resemblance to a thug like Skeeter Shiflett. A bucket on a hot August Sunday morning.

The yellow light flickered across Skeeter's face as he inhaled, revealing sunken eyes and sharp facial features. Taking a long drag, he skittered back and forth like someone allergic to his own skin. He sucked long and hard on the tobacco two more times before he flicked the cigarette across the grassless yard. Red embers somersaulted over the dirt.

"He's the most dangerous kind. He's got nothing to lose," Al observed.

"It's party time." Walter roused his partner, clapping him on the arm. Nick's head was slumped to the side, his mouth wide open. The sugar from the PBJ sandwich, the adrenaline rush of the stakeout, combined with virtually no sleep for the past three days had caused him to crash. Embarrassed for falling asleep, Nick startled wide awake, banging his knee hard on the dash. "Unit six, on the left. Our boy's out and about," Walter said as he handed the goggles to Nick, keeping his eyes transfixed on the suspect's every move.

In one swift movement, Skeeter leapt from the porch, jogging to a makeshift parking spot across the alley. The parking spot was situated at the top of a hill so the alley angled downward until it intersected with Gusryan Street. He yanked open the door to a faded harvest gold 1978, two door, Chevy Chevette and slid behind the wheel. He was coming in their direction.

"That's the car!" Nick blurted out, unable to contain his excitement.

Intuitively, Nick pulled his service weapon clear of the holster. Walter was fired up, eager to trail their prey but when Al rested his hand on his shoulder, he restrained himself from turning the ignition until Skeeter pulled out. Oblivious to the surveillance, Skeeter let the Chevette slowly drift down the hill to the street before he popped the clutch and sped away, unaware of the car behind him.

CHAPTER 35

The human body bestows a most compassionate gift to those individuals teetering on this side of heaven. Entering into a coma, they are spared the physical pains as their organs fail to perform their lifesaving duties. They are graciously unmindful of obscenely elevated body temperatures. The accelerated heart rate of exhaustion causes them no concern as their body deteriorates.

The speed at which the rat bite caused the massive infection to spread throughout Cali's body was greatly accelerated by her severe malnutrition, her drug dependency, the stifling heat inside the row-house, and the way the cells in her body yearned for water. She was unaware of Marilyn's urgent phone call to Skeeter. Cali never tasted the cold ginger kombucha Marilyn brought to her lips. Mercifully, her mind entered a comatose state where she dreamed of Blake.

■ ■ ■

That day, like every day for the past three months had gotten off to a bad start. Cali was late to homeroom. Then when she got to physics, she realized she hadn't bothered to study for a test which accounted for twenty percent of their grade. Just when she thought things couldn't get any worse, when she made it to her chemistry period, she discovered Blake was absent from school. Cali only had one oxycodone left and Blake wasn't there to sell her a fresh supply. By the time evening fell, she was desperate. Groomed with impeccable manners since birth, yet here of late, she barely recognized herself. Her life was a constant stream of behaviors that were so grossly out of character, she wasn't sure what her norm was any longer. She was fully aware showing up at someone's home uninvited was unacceptable behavior but she was desperate. Perhaps Blake could save her from the jumbled roadmap of disaster she was traveling on.

She could no longer sleep. Her skin felt foreign to her, sometimes itching so badly she scratched until it bled. Always feeling jittery and distracted, she had given up trying to concentrate on her school work. Eating was no longer a pleasurable experience because her sense of taste was gone. A pit of fire resided in her stomach. Her days were consumed with unsuccessful attempts at trying to feel normal. She wasn't trying to get high. She just wanted to stop feeling sick all the time.

For the longest time, she stood outside the brick colonial. Blake lived in a well-to-do neighborhood filled with well maintained homes on lush one acre lots. His home was beautiful, with a grand front porch, supported by tall Roman columns. Ivy weaved in and out of a trellis, creating a thick shade of privacy on the far end of the porch. Two ceiling fans provided a cool breeze for those wishing to take a seat in one of the wicker gliders.

At last, she found the courage to ring the doorbell. Cali heard the rich baritone chimes echoing throughout the house. It was Blake's mother who came to the door, invited her inside. She had no more than stepped inside the foyer when Blake's baby sister, Hazel Mae, appeared. She clung to her momma's leg while studying Cali with big brown eyes.

After asking Hazel Mae to show Cali to the kitchen, Blake's mom went to his room to let him know he had a visitor.

Blake's mother paused on the stairs, shaking her head in exasperation while a grin betrayed her, unable to disguise her delight for her youngest child's exuberance. Her heart felt light and happy as she walked to Blake's bedroom, a feeling she hadn't experienced in a rather long time.

A nagging concern for him had weighed heavily on her, interrupting her sleep, robbing her of much joy in her daily life. For the better part of the past six months, Blake hadn't been able to shake the funk he was in. At an age where he should be having the time of his life, he leaned toward spending time alone, rather than with his family or friends.

Months ago, Blake's mom stopped trying to talk to her husband about her uneasiness. Unlike her, he was convinced their son was making a normal transition into adulthood. "He needs a little space to spread his wings. He's got a lot to deal with. Pressures of school and college applications can never be far from his mind. He's sixteen so his hormones are raging. I know you don't like to hear things like this, but I remember when I was his age, I hid a magazine under my mattress. I know he's your firstborn, but it's time you cut that apron string. Trust me on this one, please. Let the boy be."

But, a mother knew. She knew something wasn't right. There weren't any magazines under his mattress; she inadvertently checked every time she changed his sheets. She wasn't afraid of her son growing up and taking the first steps towards making his own way in the world. This is the ultimate goal of parenting, wasn't it? Her husband's theory about an apron string was all wrong. What kept her awake at night were the small changes gnawing at the back of her mind. The amount of time he spent alone in his room. *Always alone behind a bedroom door he religiously took to locking. Where had all his friends gone? She knew she wasn't a doctor, but it seemed to her it wasn't normal for a boy his age to be thin as a rail. When she hugged him every morning before school, her arms embraced a skeleton. And to be so tired all the time. She wanted to take him to the doctor. Children his age get leukemia. Diabetes ran in her side of the family. She wanted him to see his pediatrician. Get some blood work.*

Blake's father was in the family room watching the evening news when his youngest began bellowing orders throughout the house involving milk, brownies, and Blake's girlfriend. Orders based upon, "Momma said."

With all the commotion involving brownies and milk, Blake's father and another sister presented to the kitchen at the same time to meet a lovely green eyed girl with strawberry blonde hair down to her waist.

"Want to hold my doll? We're the same, see? 'Asept she doesn't have any clothes on," Hazel Mae said as she looked down at herself as if to verify she did indeed have on clothing, "and I do."

The little girl held the doll up next to her face for Cali to compare. The brunette doll's resemblance to Hazel Mae was remarkable.

"Our hair doesn't match all the way after I cut my bangs, but Momma said if I cut her bangs too, she's going to take her away for a long, long time."

She reached up her chubby little hand to feel a haircut that could only be self inflicted by a very young child using safety scissors. Cali was in love with the adorable Hazel Mae.

Making her presence known, a lanky girl with a sourpuss scowl, scolded, "No one wants to hold your silly baby doll."

"She's not silly. And she's an American Doll, not a baby doll."

"Same difference."

The harmless tit for tat was immediately put to an end when Blake's father introduced himself to their guest and reminded the girls to put on their best behavior.

But the spirited Hazel Mae wasn't one to give up so easily, especially after she was given a much coveted brownie by her father.

Taking a big drink, unconcerned with her milk mustache, she continued, "She plays with them, too, but she wants to pretend she's all growd up, so it's 'posed to be a secret."

The rise of crimson started in the older sister's cheeks and quickly spread to her neck and ears.

Cali came to her rescue, "Did I tell you, I have one too? I named her Chiquita."

Hazel Mae giggled, her entire body participating so much that she looked like she might tumble off the kitchen stool before she exclaimed, "That's the name of a banana!"

Cali laughed, "I know. Can you believe it? That's how I got her name, off a sticker on a bunch of bananas."

All three girls enjoyed a fit of the giggles, Blake's father appreciating the moment, although he never understood the things girls thought were so funny.

The older girl studied Cali hard with all knowing eyes before blurting out, "I know who you are. Blake told me all about you. He tells me everything, you know."

Cali tried to keep a countenance of calm as she let out a very faint, "You do?"

Did Blake really tell his sister about the pills? How they meet in the woods after school to take drugs together? Why would he do such a thing?

"You're in most of his classes," she stated.

Relieved, Cali nodded. "Yes, I am."

"How can you be in high school? I'm almost as tall as you," the sister observed from the other side of the kitchen island.

Blake's unexpected answer caught them by surprise, "Don't let her size fool you. Cali's mightier than she looks."

He joined his sisters and father at the kitchen island, the four of them occupying the side opposite Cali. A big German Sheppard, the dog Blake ran over with his car, limped closely on his heels. Blake's mom breezed into the kitchen removing the cat, Mr. Pickles, from the kitchen counter.

Without intentionally meaning to, they arranged themselves in a progression from tallest to shortest, so they put to Cali's mind an image of the Von Trapp family. Just like the famous scene in The Sound of Music, the family lined up stair step fashion beginning with Blake's father, Blake, his mom, his sister, with little Hazel Mae bringing up the rear.

Blake's mother's face radiated pure joy. Before coming downstairs, her eldest child hurried to the bathroom, where he washed his face and brushed his teeth. Returning to his bedroom, Blake put on a clean shirt and switched his shorts for a clean pair of jeans. The mere mention of Cali's name ignited something wonderful in her son. He became instantly energized. This was the son she knew best. He was happy. Engaged. Alive.

When Cali asked him if he could help her with chemistry homework, Blake ran upstairs to his bedroom, grabbing his backpack before they drove off in her 1998 candy apple red Jeep Wrangler. A used vehicle her Pop cosigned the loan for. Her first real step into adulthood as she proudly assumed the monthly payments, using her tips from the diner.

Blake's parents stood at the front door, their arms around one another's waists, watching the young couple pull off. Parents overjoyed with the sudden turn in their son.

His father had an ornery gleam in his eye, bursting at the seams, barely unable to resist the urge to say to his wife, "I told you so."

Turning over the engine, Cali said, "I missed you today."

She could see the shine of his huge brown eyes in the Jeep's dark interior.

They hadn't even reached the end of the street before Cali began, "I need your help, Blake. I'm in a perpetual state of panic. Every thought, all day long is centered around taking my next pill. The worst part is, I feel terrible when I take them and terrible when I don't. I don't know how much longer I can take it."

The opioids were ruining her life. She felt sick all the time, but when she tried to go one entire day without taking any pills, she felt so much worse. Her entire life was consumed by something that made her feel bad, both by its presence or its absence. Blake was the one person she trusted to help her.

"Have you thought about talking to your grandparents about it?"

"No," her answer came out more forcefully than she intended.

"Why not?" He twisted slightly in his seat to face her.

"I can't disappoint them. I guess it's the same reason you haven't gone to your parents for help," she gently pointed out. In her peripheral vision, she saw him nod his head.

He asked her to drive to their usual rendezvous point, the wooded area behind their school. Inside the canopy of trees, the air was humid and thick. It smelled like the inside of a plant nursery. They walked in silence to the spot where they regularly met after school, the backpack slung over Blake's shoulder.

Once inside the hollowed out section of trees, Blake told Cali everything. He understood completely how she felt. He felt like the pills were eating a hole in his stomach, causing him to vomit all day long. The back of this throat was always on fire. The entire length of his esophagus burned. His sides ached from all the retching. He tried not eating, but threw up green bile instead of food. His mom was so upset at his obvious wasting away. He recently made the bold move to try something else. It made him feel amazing. His body felt perfect. His mind peaceful. It was rapture. Instant rapture.

She wanted to experience the same sense of euphoria.

"You really should go home and think about it for a few days, Cali. I'm talking about heroin," Blake was brutally honest. "Maybe just re-sign yourself to feeling lousy for a few days and clear your system out completely. Go cold turkey and quit taking anything."

But she was weary beyond words. And desperate. She longed to also feel amazing. To once again possess a perfect body and a peace-ful mind.

"If you won't help me, Blake, I'll find someone who will."

"Don't ever say that." Blake spun around "You know I'll do any-thing for you, but using heroin is serious."

"I understand that. I'm begging you, Blake. Please, help me."

Handing Cali an LED flashlight, he asked her to keep the light steady for him. Blake dug into an inside zipper pocket of the book bag, pulling out a stainless soup spoon, a lighter, a bottle of water, a plastic baggie containing ten or so minuscule plastic vials, a shoe string, and one insulin syringe with an orange plastic cap. Opening one of the vi-als, he tapped out less than a quarter of the white crystalline powder on the spoon. It was no more than the size of three grains of coarse sea salt. To this he added one drop of water. Next, he removed the orange cap from the syringe, using the needle to stir, and thereby, dissolve the white powder. He followed this with heating the undersurface of the spoon with the lighter, cooking the heroin until it completely liquified. He filled the syringe.

He was ready, but she wasn't. She shook her head. Had she come to her senses and changed her mind? Feeling a sense of relief, Blake thought she wasn't ready after all.

Taking his hand in hers, Cali moved them to the open soccer field. To the place where this crazy journey began. Back to the place where Monica made the decision to smash into her while she was defenselessly suspended midair. To the place of an unprovoked act of callousness which resulted in the destruction of a life she once loved. For what? A meaningless high school soccer game. A game.

Lying back in the cool grass beneath a canopy of stars, Cali offered her arm to her friend. It only took a few seconds. Her eyes told him. They grew bright with fascination. The childlike gaze of utter wonderment. No words were required, her beautiful green eyes revealed the rapture.

Pressed against the cool ground, she stared at the heavens above. Far off in the distance, the sound of low rolling thunder followed a sky intermittently lighting up bright enough to resemble flash photography of paparazzi. Crisp cracks echoed overhead as haphazard lightening bolts filled the sky. A summer heat lightning storm consumed the atmosphere with pomp and circumstance. It smelled like rain, yet not a single raindrop fell. Cali was mesmerized by the exploding atmosphere as she bore witness to a phenomena magnificent beyond words.

For the first time since her injury, everything made perfect sense. She became keenly aware she was given a profound opportunity to experience all things in life. A perfect understanding. Undefiled health. Unfathomable happiness. Pure peace.

Cali was grateful for heroin.

CHAPTER 36

When the Chevy Chevette made the erratic stop in the far right lane of West Lafayette Street, Walter followed suit. The consensus in the un-marked police car was, the suspect gave no indication throughout the pursuit he was aware of being tailed. Walter followed the play book to the letter, expertly maneuvering through poorly lit city streets, the headlights in the off position of the departmental issued, nondescript, black sedan. If Skeeter became aware of their vehicle at any time, it was impossible for him to discern the three lawmen concealed on the other side of the dark tinted windows. Taking it out on a stick of chew-ing gum, Nick was clearly on edge as Walter patiently allowed the 1978 harvest-gold two door an entire city block leeway.

Their binoculars and night vision goggles glued to the suspect's back when he emerged from his vehicle, Nick and Al each committed the exact location to memory as Skeeter tilted the wooden plank or-dering, 'No Trespassing', and slithered beneath it into the condemned house. As far as the eye could see, the exterior of the buildings were dilapidated, its inhabitants making a run for it decades ago. Once Nick and Al confirmed the exact row-house Skeeter entered, Walter slowly drove past so his team could corroborate their mark.

Walter continued halfway down the block to set up their staging area. Assignments were quickly decided. Al would take the alley, covering the rear of the house in the event the suspect exited out the back. Walter and Nick would follow the path of Skeeter Shiflett through the front.

Donning bullet proof vests with FBI stenciled boldly across the front and back, the men dressed in haste. Battle grade, black helmets were strapped in place. Night vision goggles attached to the helmets for easy access. Each man was supplied thirty rounds of ammunition in addition to the fifteen rounds in his Glock.

Nick opened the trunk which was a warehouse of tactical equipment. There were bolt cutters, as well as a forty pound battering ram to break down doors, tenderly nicknamed, The Enforcer. Scavenging around in the trunk, he stuck his hand in a cardboard box grabbing stun grenades. They clipped on heavy duty flashlights which were able to project an eight hundred foot light beam. Everyone attached a canister of pepper spray to his tactical vest. Lastly, Nick grabbed the Level IIIA bulletproof shield, while Al radioed the BPD dispatcher, asking for immediate backup to West Lafayette Street.

From this point forward there would be no more verbal communication until the completion of the mission. Giving a nod, Walter signaled it was go time. The team was just yards from their destination when Walter held up his hand, making a sudden U-turn. Both officers followed on his heels. As an afterthought, he retrieved the battering ram and the bolt cutters from the trunk. They could leave them on the sidewalk, outside the designated location, but they'd be readily available if need be. He handed a loaded shotgun to Al.

"Wait a minute," Nick began, "it just occurred to me. Clearly, our priority is Cali Hasting, but we don't want to lose this guy in court on a technicality. Don't we need a warrant?"

Without missing a beat, Al spoke up, "We're in fresh pursuit of a suspect who gained unlawful entry into a building clearly marked with no trespassing. We also have exigent circumstances. Cali Hasting's life's in imminent danger so we have an emergent situation that requires our immediate action. We don't need a warrant."

"Let's go," Walter commanded.

Hidden in shadow, the men hugged the buildings as they ran to their assigned destinations. Walter and Nick gave Al a good twenty seconds to turn the corner into the alley and take up his position at the rear of the house before they engaged their flashlights and made entry.

Skeeter's first indication something was amiss was the muffled clink of the metal bolt cutters on the sidewalk. To the average person, the barely audible sound would have gone unnoticed, but for someone who had spent his entire life one step ahead of the law, the sound was unmistakable. Skeeter knew they had been made. His sense of hearing hair-trigger sensitive, Skeeter grabbed Marilyn's arm, instantly causing her to also become on high alert. Bringing one finger to his lips as a warning not to make a sound, Skeeter held his breath as he listened. When the exterior of the house was suddenly flooded with a burst of light, Skeeter's worst fears were confirmed. The cops were here.

Mere seconds before the FBI agents yanked the plywood off the front entryway, both Skeeter and Marilyn scattered like roaches. Accosted by the revolting stench, combined with the oppressive heat, Nick and Walter hesitated a fraction of a beat. Experience told them the flies swarming about was an ominous sign. If Cali Hasting was being held there, they considered themselves forewarned, she may already be dead.

Walter preempted their entry, shouting, "FBI," in a booming voice. From that moment forward, every few minutes throughout the raid, Walter made their identity known.

The ballistic shield in his left hand, his Glock in his right, Nick led the way. Nick's vision was severely limited since he was looking through a four by ten inch bullet proof window in the bunker. Unlike Walter, Nick had little to no peripheral vision.

As per protocol, Walter gripped the back of Nick's gun belt, forming a tight chain. Just three steps inside, Walter stopped Nick's forward progress, averting a near disaster. Directly inside the threshold was a jagged five by five foot area of missing flooring. Anyone unfamiliar with the building, not immediately stepping off to the left of the entryway, would plummet twelve feet to the basement below.

Their entry was painstakingly slow and methodical. No door, no blind space was to be passed by without inspection. One oversight and Walter and Nick's lives ended tonight. Their footing so near to the hole in the floor was precarious as they stopped at a coat closet. Nick shielded himself and his partner from anyone hiding in the shadows as Walter quickly opened the closet door, gun in his right hand, flashlight in his left. It was empty.

Maneuvering around the sagging floor, a treacherous staircase that no longer possessed a bannister forced them to either turn left down a long narrow hallway, leading to the rear of the house, or proceed straight ahead into what must have once been the main living area. With each step forward, the floor creaked and shifted beneath their feet threatening to give way. Nick felt like a kid on a dare walking to the center of a frozen pond in mid-March. Like the floor, all the interior walls were crumbling, in various stages of toppling over. The house was imploding from years of neglect.

While the agents worked the interior of the house, Al stood guard at the rear. The upstairs windows and back door kept in his sight, Al rested the butt of the shotgun against his shoulder. He kept his feet in constant motion. The sound of grinding glass under his combat boots frayed his nerves as he warded off rats by doing what the foot patrol police referred to as the ghetto stomp.

Long before the man's voice declared, FBI, Marilyn made a mad dash for the back of the house. She had no idea where Skeeter made off to. He just seemed to disappear into thin air. One minute he was standing beside her, the next he was gone. In the rear of the house, there was a kitchen window a city worker did a half-assed job of sealing off. Pushing with all her might, several nails popped loose. Marilyn was able to wedge a space behind the plywood just wide enough for her to squeeze through. Before jumping, she could see the window led to a backyard the size of a postage stamp.

Dropping the eight feet to the yard below, Marilyn practically fell into Detective Gale's arms. Before her feet touched the earth, he had her facedown on the ground. Marilyn was in a state of shock, not at all concerned about her tiger print miniskirt hiked up over her ass from snagging the bricks as she slid out the window. She was unaware of the lavender sequins that stuck to her cheek pressed against the ground, the baubles scattering everywhere when they tore from her ankle high boots. She didn't feel the pain as one of her painted green fingernails ripped, breaking deep down in the quick. Dazed, Marilyn was mesmerized by the thick droplets of blood squeezing from the tip of her jagged nail, leaving a gooey red trail all the way down her finger to pool around her lucky snake ring. In a matter of seconds, her hands vanished from view as they were cuffed behind her back

It wasn't until she heard the policeman speak into his radio that Marilyn let loose her hot tears of despair, "I got one on the ground. Not the suspect. I repeat, Shiflett remains at large."

Walter's left hand in the small of his partner's back felt Nick's muscles tense. They froze in place. Walter was flooded with an oppressive sense of guilt. He was the behavioral profiler assigned to this case, therefore it was his job to get inside Skeeter's head and understand his thought processes. Ultimately, the team's safety was his responsibility. There wasn't any room for the smallest of mistakes on a mission of this magnitude. Every clue left by Skeeter that Walter failed to accurately read put both Cali's and his team's lives in jeopardy. Skeeter had out-smarted him. Walter had erroneously insisted all along Skeeter was a lone wolf when in reality he had an accomplice.

Jolting Walter's attention back to their assignment, Nick took two tentative steps forward. This was no time for second guessing. Nick needed his partner's undivided attention. Getting them back on track, Nick made the unilateral decision to search the main room before making their way down the long, narrow hallway. Stepping forward, they both saw it. In the far corner, a large cast iron pipe extended the entire height of the room, from ceiling to floor. Lying in a small heap, chained at the ankle to the pipe was a very petite, lifeless body. With long, strawberry blonde hair.

They found her. There was no mistake about it, this was Cali Hasting. While Nick ran to the front sidewalk for the bolt cutters, Walter stayed with Cali, checking her labored breathing, feeling for a pulse. She was alive. Barely.

Had Skeeter kept his wits about him and remained concealed be-neath the staircase, he may have gotten away scot free. The secret cubby under the stairwell was virtually undetectable. At a glance, it appeared as a wall, nothing more. In a past lifetime, it was probably used to store Christmas decorations. Skeeter was crouched down in-side, folded up like a human pretzel spying the girl from the shadows.

But as Skeeter watched through the tiny crack of the door as the tall, good-looking FBI agent carried Cali's limp body right past him, something inside snapped. That girl was his ticket to the good life, his chance to rid himself of his pig mother. This was his dream come true and he wasn't about to sit back and watch all his hard work go down the crapper.

Skeeter opened fire.

From the alley, Al heard the first shot, followed by rapid suppression fire. Fourteen rounds, followed by a minuscule pause for a hot reload, then two more rounds.

"Shots fired! Shots fired! Signal thirteen!" Al shouted franticly into his radio to the BPD dispatcher. "Where the hell is our backup?"

Al's next instinct was to climb through the back window, the very window Marilyn had escaped through, but that would be a rookie cop mistake. The team had determined a front entry and any movement in the back of the house would be determined as hostile. If he climbed through the rear window, Al most certainly would be shot by friendly fire. Entering the house from the alley would prove to be a fatal error. Al kept to protocol, the shotgun at the ready in the event Skeeter came blasting his way out the back. No way Shiflett was getting past him.

After being fired upon, Walter made a run for the front door, Cali Hasting in his arms. He left Nick behind firing blindly into the walls. The blasts of gunfire rendered Walter deaf to the sirens descending upon the scene, coming from all directions.

CHAPTER 37

It was the kind of sweltering summer night in Maryland where the thick humidity dripped down the walls. The place was busting at the seams with incoming wounded. It was a typical June night at Shock Trauma, cynically known as the Knife and Gun Club of Baltimore's inner city. Rival gangs on drive by shooting sprees, reckless kids speeding down interstates on crotch rockets, intoxicated males showing off by diving head first into the shallow ends of swimming pools kept coming without an end in sight. Overflow stretchers filled with moaning bodies lined one entire side of the corridor.

The overhead alert sounded, the dispatcher's voice detached, "Trauma Level A in two. Kidnap victim transported by armed FBI agent in unmarked vehicle. Grab and go. Victim extracted from hostile situation receiving gunfire. Sixteen year old, unresponsive, white female. Shallow, ineffective breathing."

"Did I hear her say FBI and kidnapping? Now that's something we don't hear around here every day and this place is a freaking zoo," the older nurse spoke to no one in particular as she emerged from the break room, shoving the last of a cracker in her mouth.

A nineteen year veteran of the emergency department, the nurse called out in her raspy voice as she, along with the rest of her assigned team, quickly moved into trauma bay number one. Between the stress of the job and her pack a day habit, a decade had been added to her face. She knew she should give them both up, Shock Trauma and cigarettes, but she was an adrenalin junkie and she just plain enjoyed a good smoke.

"Possible gunshot wound heading our way," the emergency attending physician, Dr. Edward Euwing addressed his elite team of doctors and nurses. "Somebody call security STAT and give him a heads up. Have him meet us at the doors in the ambo bay to verify this individual's credentials. We can't have an armed person in our area unless we determine he is, in fact, FBI. You two come with me. We'll need to get her out of the vehicle and on a stretcher. Sophia, prepare for the worst. You heard it, people. Let's go."

An immediate flurry of medical personnel, all clad in bubblegum pink surgical scrubs ensued. Everyone assigned to bay number one was already in motion, putting on protective eyewear, checking pockets for surgical clamps and scissors, stretching purple gloves on outstretched hands. A second year emergency medicine resident grabbed the bright orange emergency kit as he, the older nurse, and Dr. Euwing ran for the ambulance bay.

Unbeknownst to the rest of the team, the resident secretly wondered if he'd ever have what it takes to be in charge of an emergency department, any emergency room, much less someplace like Shock Trauma. He had serious doubts about ever being able to fill the shoes of a remarkable physician like Dr. Euwing. Hell, he wasn't sure he was even in the same league with the nurses.

Almost every night, when he finally returned to his sparsely furnished apartment, exhausted and feeling numb inside, the young doctor fretted over his decision to go into this line of work. His best friend from medical school went into cardiology, so he spent his days in some cushy office reading EKG's and doing stress tests on fat, old guys. His friend didn't suffer from insomnia or chronic diarrhea.

But when push came to shove, he craved the excitement. Making a career out of doling out blood pressure medications wasn't for him. The ER was where his passion lay; he just hoped someday he'd be good enough. So night after night, after putting in a grueling twelve hour shift, the young doctor went home and buried his nose in the literature on treating an evolving heart attack, how to effectively manage an airway in an unconscious patient, the steps to insert a chest tube...and on...and on...until he passed out, only to get up the next day and do it all over again.

Sophia, the least experienced member of the team, with eight years under her belt, remained in the room preparing for the worst. She had just pulled the bright red crash cart near the head of the bed when they came busting through the doors. The nurse was riding on top the stretcher, straddling the lifeless body as she performed CPR. The resident ran alongside the head of the bed, squeezing a clear plastic bag hooked up to oxygen that forced artificial breaths into the patient's lungs.

"She's in full cardiac arrest," Dr. Euwing declared as Sophia immediately descended upon the lifeless body. In one swift motion, she cut off all the girl's clothing using trauma sheers, revealing an emaciated and neglected body. The bones of her ribcage and pelvis stretched taut against skin covered in a multitude of sores telling a harrowing tale of abuse and neglect. Bruises in different stages of healing lined both arms. A fairly recent pink surgical scar marred her right knee.

"Do you see this? She's got a chain padlocked to her ankle for fuck's sake," the older nurse called out, her tone incredulous.

For people exposed on a daily basis to a hefty dose of the worst humanity had to offer, the rusty metal chain, which looked like it had been salvaged from a junkyard, bolted to the patient's left ankle rattled their faith in mankind. Her entire leg, from ankle to knee, was angry, red, and swollen. Directly above the chain, two small puncture wounds steadily oozed a foul-smelling, yellowish-green pus. The foot was an unnatural white, as though it had been deprived of nourishing blood flow for a very long time.

"This is why I believe in God. The bastard who did this deserves to burn in hell," the seasoned nurse verbalized the team's sentiments. She wasn't afraid to call it like she saw it.

Sophia adhered two sticky pads, one on each side of the girl's bare chest before powering up the cardiac monitor. The screen on the Lifepack monitor showed something that had no resemblance to a normal pattern. Rather an angry, bazaar, up-down, up-down, child's scribble filled the screen. The patient's heart rhythm was not compatible with life and she would die if she wasn't immediately shocked.

"We've got V-tach," Dr. Euwing called to his team.

Without need for instruction, Sophia called out, "Charging to two hundred joules. Getting ready to defibrillate."

The Lifepack machine made a whirring sound of steadily increasing intensity before it produced a panicked shrilled alarm.

"I'm clear. You're clear. Hold chest compressions," Sophia prompted her colleague to jump off the stretcher out of harm's way.

Sophia pushed the red button, sending a jolt of electricity throughout the girls's battered body. She instantly became rigid as her back slightly arched, lifting her off of the gurney a fraction of an inch. All eyes were on the cardiac monitor, hopeful the electricity restarted her heart. It didn't work. Her heart remained in V-tach, so the older nurse jumped back on her chest, pushing with all her might.

No one seemed to notice when FBI Special Agent Walter Kostos took up residence in the doorway of trauma bay number one. His credentials were cleared by the armed security officer in charge of maintaining law and order in the ER.

Walter's eyes traveled to the chain encircling Cali's left ankle, which looked like it had spent the better part of a decade in the rain or buried in the dirt. Such a heavy duty chain was designed for industrial use or perhaps to contain a rabid pit bull, but certainly never intended to restrain a girl.

Reluctantly, Walter let his vision drift to her body, which was a terrifying, waxy, stark white under the bright overhead surgical lights. Cali looked more like a plastic mannequin than an actual human being. For the first time in his life, Walter understood the desire to kill someone out of vengeance, as a deep seething hatred brewed in his soul for what those savages had done to her. The first rule of law enforcement is not to become personally involved, but all objectivity was lost as he witnessed the fruits of their evil.

Walter wondered why it was so unbelievably hot in there. Weren't hospitals notorious for keeping the rooms ice cold? He felt the steady stream of warm perspiration inside his battle dress uniform shirt. He tugged at the neckline of his heavy Kevlar vest as he watched Sophia use a small, black drill to power a frighteningly large needle through Cali's skin and into the bone. She quickly filled several tubes with bright red blood before attaching the bag of intravenous fluids to the needle in her arm.

Looking at the doctor in charge, Sophia informed him, "I had to put in an IO. She doesn't have any veins. She's all scarred up. Looks perhaps like track marks from IV drugs."

Without hesitation, Sophia made the decision to insert an IO or intraosseous needle into the bone, knowing they are used in extreme circumstances when a patient's veins can not be accessed.

Not much frightened Walter Kostos, but he felt a gripping urge to retreat as he took on the full view of the room's activity. The resident took over chest compressions, two arms pushing the full weight of his upper body down on Cali's bare chest, as the out of breath nurse began preparing medications. Walter anxiously expected to hear her ribs crack from the amount of force required for CPR.

To the untrained eye, the scene resembled utter chaos. People clad in pink scrubs and purple gloves bustled about with minimal direction. The intensity in the room felt like the interior of a nuclear reactor, but in fact, it was a well orchestrated symphony. Walter Kostos respected the obvious chemistry in the way the medical team performed together. There was an air of trust as though every member of the team knew exactly what to do at all times. They worked swiftly, without hesitation. Time meant the difference between life or death.

"Nice work. Causes for cardiac arrest are dehydration. Sepsis or blood poisoning, from the infected areas on her ankle. Her brain may have been deprived of oxygen from a possible drug overdose, so let's give naloxone," Dr. Euwing summarized aloud.

Dr. Euwing, the physician clearly in charge had strategically placed himself at the foot of the bed, which allowed him to observe all the ongoings in the room without impeding anyone's ability to care for the patient. Premature graying and a sag to his skin were well earned for a man who shouldered such tremendous responsibilities.

"She's severely underweight, so we have to consider electrolyte imbalance," the older nurse offered as another cause for the cardiac arrest, knowing her emaciated body was deprived of nutrients and electrolytes necessary to sustain life.

"Are you sure about the age? She looks prepubescent," Dr. Euwing turned to direct his question to the FBI agent.

"She's sixteen," Walter confirmed, surprised by his shortness of breath. In an effort to increase the amount of air in his lungs he removed his matte black tactical helmet. It was a slight relief to unbuckle the chin strap but when he set the helmet at his feet, he almost stumbled forward from being lightheaded. White lights pockmarked his vision. Forcing himself upright, he took several slow deep breaths without feeling any better.

Walter watched as Sophia inserted a long rubber tube between the girl's legs. He felt his stomach lurch as his gaze followed a stubborn dribble of dark brown liquid ooze along the clear tubing before dripping into a bag hanging from the bed frame.

Watching the scant drops of brown liquid, the nurse verified her kidneys had begun to fail as she called out, "No measurable urine."

"We need to give her IV fluids wide open. Sophia, see if you can get a second line in," the resident was finally in the game.

"After you get the line in, let's defibrillate again," Dr. Euwing ordered.

In spite of the frantic scene before him, Walter's mind flashed to his sister and her husband. A young couple who had already accrued a lifetime of financial debt due to the exorbitant cost of repeated in vitro fertilization treatments. A heartbreaking succession of failed IVF attempts. The most sacred human act between a man and a woman reduced to a scientific dehumanization of recorded ovulation patterns and internal body temperatures. Too often to count, he was awakened in the wee hours by a phone call, his sister's soft crying on the other end. Walter's empty reassurances, "It'll take the next time, baby sister."

At the other end of the spectrum were the throw aways. Walter marveled how or why, exactly, does a parent reach the decision to give away a child? From his research and limited conversations with the family, he knew Cali's parents have raised two other children. What was it about this third child that made her unworthy of their love? Did they possess a finite bounty of love that had already been divvied up long before Cali's conception? Questions he knew would never be answered.

"Is there any information you can give us?" Dr. Euwing prompted Walter.

"Her name's Cali Hasting. According to her family, she got involved with drugs about three months ago. Five days ago she eloped from a drug treatment center in Havre de Grace. She was kidnapped and pretty much left for dead. The perpetrators kept her chained up in an abandoned row-house in West Baltimore," Walter informed them, unclear why any of this information was pertinent. "Tonight, my team was ambushed by her kidnappers. They opened fire on us as I was exiting the building with her. I left two officers there and I have no doubt, your emergency room is about to get very busy."

"Hold compressions. It looks like a normal rhythm on the monitor," the look on Dr. Euwing's face was that of someone winning the lottery. Not just someone who won the lottery, but someone who had the one in a million good fortune of finding the winning ticket on the sidewalk. "Do we have a pulse?"

Both the resident and Sophia felt for a pulse, the physician checking the femoral artery located in her groin, Sophia feeling the carotid artery in the neck.

"We have a pulse!" they practically screamed in unison.

Walter reached a hand behind himself for the wall as his head began to spin. In order to steady his footing, he pressed his back against the cool, pale green cinder block wall. His chest heaved as he tried to fill his lungs with oxygen. He was appalled by the way his body was betraying him, yet he was powerless to make it stop. His entire life, he had prided himself on never being the squeamish type. Emotions akin to shame flooded him.

Unbelievably, Walter was a field agent for The FBI, who was physically declining from merely witnessing a medical emergency. During his training at the academy, the agency had taken reasonable steps to prepare him for disturbing images he might encounter during his tour of duty. All candidates were required to witness three autopsies at the state coroner's. Admitting to his achilles heel, Walter specifically requested one of the autopsies was that of a child. Yet today, he felt like a rookie falling apart.

Sophia had initially become aware of Walter's physical deterioration when she drew blood samples from Cali. She was discreetly watching him in her peripheral vision during the entire resuscitation attempt. She noted, in particular, his struggle to breath was becoming progressively more pronounced. As soon as the other nurse loaded Cali onto the elevator for transport to the intensive care unit, Sophia quickly turned all her attention to the federal agent. Grabbing an orderly by the arm, she asked him to bring a clean stretcher into the room.

Performing a quick visual assessment, she was alarmed by his appearance. His skin color was ashen. An abnormal amount of perspiration dripped from his hair and face. Normally positioned directly in the center of the neck, Walter's windpipe and Adam's apple were pushed to one side. The cells in his body were hungry for air, resulting in a heaving chest and very rapid respiratory rate. His neck veins protruded. Agent Kostos was very sick.

It was all he could do to fight the overwhelming urge to close his eyes and sink to the floor. Just one minute, I need to rest my eyes for just one minute, he thought. Closing his eyes, he slumped against the wall.

Feeling a tender caress of a hand, he slowly forced his eyes open. She was standing just a few inches before him. "Buonasera. My name is Sophia."

The silky flavor of her voice rolled over his nerve endings in every part of his body. Her Italian accent excited him. Hell, everything about her excited him. Without a doubt, she was the most beautiful woman he had ever laid eyes on. But she was so much more than physical beauty. He had watched her in her element, helping to save Cali Hasting's life. He was in awe of her calm, intelligence, and compassion necessary to work in such a demanding environment. In that moment, he knew he was not going to let her get away a second time.

"I know you," he searched her chestnut brown eyes flecked with gold, hoping for a hint of recognition. "We were at Jimmy's when the Orioles made that six, four, three double play," he continued to speak in small bursts, fighting to breathe.

She smiled, a smile of intimacy, of something shared. He studied her face, an angelic face he had already committed to his memory.

"Please, sit here. I have noticed you are working very hard to catch your breath. Perhaps, if we remove this heavy vest, it will make your breathing much easier."

He obediently did as she asked, climbing on the stretcher. It was a relief to rest his body, he felt so tired. Reflexively, his hand felt for his Glock positioned on his right hip.

As she helped him remove the bullet proof vest, she made small talk in an effort to keep him calm, "I remember it well. It was a double play. A ground ball was hit to the shortstop in the hole. He threw to the second baseman to get the first out. Then the second baseman pivoted and threw it to first, making a double play. It was a most happy time for the O's. I see, tonight you are not wearing your glasses."

He was instantly rejuvenated knowing she did remember him. Indeed, he had been wearing his glasses that night at the seafood restaurant. He felt his pulse quicken even more, making the room spin.

But a sudden realization instantly deflated his elation, "You never did tell me if you're married."

Pulling the kevlar vest over his head, she could see his BDU shirt was not covered in perspiration, after all. It was a disturbing mixture of sweat and blood, much more blood than sweat.

"May I help you take this shirt off, please?" she efficiently began removing it, not bothering to wait for his reply. As she carefully inspected his torso and arms, she kept him engaged in conversation, "My father and brothers have taught me much about baseball. Men and baseball. It's a love affair that will leave a woman lonely if she does not share the passion."

"You still manage to evade my question." He wasn't about to give up so easily.

She looked closely at his bare chest, while simultaneously running her gloved fingers over his skin. Inch by inch, she slid her fingers through the warm blood, searching for the source of the bleeding. Sophia was patient, not wanting to miss the spot. It took a minute or two but finally she felt it. In the soft area, approximately two inches below his right underarm, was an entry wound the size of a fingertip. A vulnerable spot not covered by the bullet proof vest if his arms were outstretched. Outstretched arms being an expected position when carrying a lifeless girl's body.

"I have no husband, just three brothers. Dr Euwing," she spoke loud enough to get the physician's undivided attention, "we have our first gunshot victim. His lung is collapsed and we need a chest tube right away."

CHAPTER 38

As if falling victim to an evil potion, overwhelming grief transformed the once vibrant and energetic couple into two old people. Like wax figures left out in the heat, their skin looked as if it was slowly melting off. Loose flesh clung to their skeletal remains. The elderly Hasting's emotional suffering had taken root in their physical decline. Robert found the seemingly overnight metamorphosis of his parents surreal. Their palpable grief was consuming them right before his eyes.

Always a robust man, Cal Hasting had become frail and shrunken in a matter of a few days. Robert's eyes were riveted to the imposter swallowed up in his father's clothes. Obviously, his father had created new holes in his belt as he cinched his baggy trousers around his waist. From behind, his head appeared much too large for his scrawny neck to support for any length of time. An overwhelming hollowness settled in Robert's chest cavity as he realized his father had suddenly lost most of his hair.

Robert witnessed the sudden tremor in his father's hand as he placed his arm around his mother's newly rounded shoulders. When she wrapped her arm around his waist, Robert stared in disbelief as her wedding rings spun loosely on boney fingers. His mother's heartbreak evidenced by her being oblivious to the brown shoe on her right foot, a navy pump on her left.

Clinging to one another, each one tried to provide the other with the strength to face what lay ahead as they stood outside the glass door to Cali's intensive care room. Patiently, they listened to the doctor speak as they stood on legs as unsteady as a newborn foal's.

Neither Pop nor MomMom made a real effort to comprehend the doctor's complicated words. The explanations, full of medical terminology didn't matter. Understanding what machine did what or why her tiny body was falling apart was not going to change anything. No medical degree was necessary to comprehend the gravity of the situation. Beyond those doors, their grandchild was barely clinging to life. And they were helpless to change it.

When the doctor said all he had to say, Pop stepped forward, offering his hand. He faced the physician with anguished eyes. His words, heavy like mud, fell off his tongue, "We are most grateful for everything you're doing to save our Cali Girl. If it's all the same with you, we're ready to see her now, please."

"Yes, of course. Follow me."

As Dr. Euwing pulled open the glass door, Pop grabbed onto his shoulder like a drowning man, saying with great effort, "We'd be much obliged if we could go in alone."

Scanning the bank of elevators, Robert remained rooted in place as he waited for his wife. They should go in together, but where was Maggie? How long had she been gone?

As the doctor opened the door, Robert had a sudden revelation about his parents. Scrubbing his face with the palms of his hands, Robert brushed away tears. If their Cali Girl died, he knew, without a doubt, neither of his parents would survive.

Nodding in agreement, the doctor took a step back as the elderly couple entered the terrifying world of an intensive care room. They were immediately assaulted by the smell of hospital grade disinfectant, medications, sweat, unwashed hair, and decomposing flesh.

It looked like a macabre video arcade as rows of flashing neon numbers appeared on monitors above her bed. Trigonometric waveforms depicting vital signs danced across LED screens. Noxious alarm bells chirped nonstop, every alarm a different frequency so her nurses were able to quickly differentiate the heart rate alarm from the ventilator sensor. A rhythmic, muffled hiss from the ventilator forced air into lungs too sick to breathe on their own.

There were so many machines. Compression devices on Cali's legs inflated to prevent blood clots. Six infusion pumps delivered all kinds of medications into her blood stream. A massive cooling blanket tried to quell her fever. Swallowed up in an electronic bed, Cali was barely visible beneath the tangle of tubes and wires everywhere. In her nose, a hard plastic tube hooked to gentle suction emptied her stomach. A clear tube in the back of her throat settled into her lungs. Multiple lines in Cali's neck and both arms were connected to either bags of clear fluids or fluorescent yellow medications that looked radioactive. There was a tube in her bladder. Every trick in the book that medical science had to offer worked tirelessly to keep her alive.

Everything about the room provoked fear. Never letting go of one another, their fingers intertwined, her grandparents walked with purpose. One foot in front of the other, they moved to her. It was clear, this couple would not hesitate to walk through fire for Cali.

When a nurse entered the room a few minutes later, she lowered one of the bed's side rails at Pop's request. Taking great care not to disturb any of the medical equipment, the grandparents took turns gingerly enfolding their arms around Cali as best they could.

Robert remained anchored in the hallway, supposedly waiting for Maggie. From behind the safety of the glass door, he witnessed the scene play out. It should be us in there, Robert thought. We're her parents. We should be the ones who stop at nothing to be at her side. Maggie and I should be the ones dying the slow death of grief, not my parents.

The bell's chime got Robert's attention. Turning his head, he watched as Maggie stepped from the elevator. Her makeup was impeccable. Confidence, poise, and the scent of Channel emanated from her. Her high heels clicked on the tile as she walked to him, her arms full, carting two large cardboard trays of hot coffees, teas, bagels smothered in cream cheese, or egg breakfast sandwiches. He intercepted her halfway down the hall.

"We have coffee, cream and sugar for your father. A latte for you."

Taking her elbow, he steered her toward a small canteen with various vending machines and a handful of cafe tables with chairs. "We can't take this in Cali's room."

Scraping a plastic chair along the floor, Robert plopped down. Resting his elbows on the table, he felt his head was too heavy to hold upright any longer. Burying his face in his hands, he rested his weary eyes. Maggie sat next to him, but not before she covered the seat with several napkins. After all, she was wearing Stella McCartney.

"You really should eat something. Starving isn't going to make her better."

"There's something that's been sitting in the back of my mind and I can't make any sense of it," Robert cut her off. "I'm hoping you can help me sort it out."

Robert's haggard face startled Maggie. She had no idea he would take things so hard. Massaging the back of his neck, she spoke soothingly, "You know, you can talk to me about anything at all."

Shimmying the black canvas backpack off his shoulders, Robert set it on the floor opposite his wife. Funny, she'd never noticed him walking around with a school child's book bag. That looked ridiculous. She made a mental note to purchase a nice brushed leather satchel for him as soon as they got home.

One by one, he removed a total of seven amber prescription medication bottles from the book bag before he began, "This one had fifty oxycodone pills in it. This one had forty oxycodone, plus one refill. This one had thirty hydrocodone pills from our dentist. Here's one from a Dr. Waxter with thirty oxycontin. The last two bottles, from a Doctor Summerlin, each had fifty pills. Dr. Summerlin, why does that name ring a bell?"

Still unaware of the gravity of the situation, Maggie sipped on her chai tea, saying, "Oh, you know Dr. Summerlin, darling. He's been my doctor for over twenty years now. Here, you really should eat something." She pushed the breakfast fare in front of him.

"All these bottles are empty," his voice mirrored the look of exhaustion on his face.

"Hmmm. You know, there's a lovely boutique downtown that sells men's accessories. When we get home, I'm going on a little shopping trip for you. Do you prefer leather in black or maybe an earthy color?"

"Maggie!"

"What, Robert? I'm worried about you. Why are you carrying around trash in a book bag? You look like a hobo. Where did you get all these bottles, anyway?" Maggie was flippant.

"They were in the nightstand of our spare bedroom. The room Cali stayed in. You're missing the point. I added it all up, Mags. There were two hundred ninety narcotics here. All these bottles are empty."

She just stared at him.

"Do you understand what I'm saying? In one month, she took two hundred and ninety pain pills. How many was she taking in a given a day?" Robert questioned her.

"How should I know?"

Robert's eyes lit up. "What do you mean, how should you know?"

"You weren't there, Robert. I did the best I could. You know," Maggie held her chin a fraction higher as she stated, "I can't tolerate anything medical and there I was, all by myself, in charge of braces and ice machines. And revolting bandages. It was so hard, you can't even imagine how hard it was for me."

Just like that, Maggie had clearly turned the tables, making herself the victim.

Taking a deep breath, he took her manicured hand in his, pressed it against his cheek, saying, "You're right, I wasn't there, so I'm just trying to make some sense of it all. How many pills do you think Cali was taking at a time?"

"If I had to guess, I'd say two about every three or four hours," Maggie answered.

He picked up one bottle after the other, examining the labels. "But the directions explicitly say take one every four to six hours, if needed."

"Why are you questioning me about this, Robert? I did the best I could. I have a career, too. I had houses to show. Clients with that much money to spend expect a little hand holding. There were appraisals. Closings. She's sixteen, for crying out loud. She was basically in charge of her own medication, if you want to know the truth," Maggie defiantly told him as she put her tea down. "I have to say, Robert, I don't like your tone."

"You're right. Please accept my apologies." Pulling in the reins, Robert spoke softer, "The prescriptions from the emergency room and the surgeon make sense. It's the medications from all these other doctors I don't understand."

"When her pain medicine was getting low, I got more. That surgeon of hers wouldn't write for any more refills, so I collected on a few favors. After twenty years, my personal physician was more than happy to help. As for this one," Maggie examined the prescription label, "his wife and I play tennis together twice a week. She's quite good, actually. Her backhand's vicious. As a favor to me, she asked her husband to write a prescription. It was so easy."

Maggie checked her nail polish before adding, "I'm not telling you anything you don't already know. We already had this discussion."

Blindsided, Robert was unable to disguise the indignation in his voice, "What do you mean, we've already had this discussion? Exactly when did we have this discussion?"

"The night of the Black and White Gala. On the ride home, I told you how the surgeon said to keep ahead of her pain." Maggie prodded, "I told you Abigail came up with the idea to give her two pain pills at a time. Abigail said it helped her sleep. Does any of this ring a bell?"

Grabbing his own hair out of frustration, Robert pleaded with his wife, "Maggie, don't you get it? The family interventionist..."

"You've never been good at names. Honestly, you should work on that. His name's Mister....."

"What difference does it make? The point I'm trying to make is, he said people can become addicted in as little as a week. One week, Mags. Cali was taking enough pain medication to tranquilize an elephant. I don't think she's going to make it," Robert ran his fingers through his hair. "My parents are devastated. Maggie, I'm heartbroken. What are we going to do? What are we going to do without her?"

Maggie stared blankly at her husband as he suddenly darted from the room, disappearing into Cali's room.

Consumed by their grief, neither Robert nor his parents seemed to notice Maggie never once set foot inside Cali's hospital room. For the next thirty-six hours, while they kept vigil at Cali's bedside, Maggie discreetly devoted her attention to her real estate clientele. She busied herself ordering scrumptious meals which no one touched from a delightful area of town known as Little Italy. She telephoned her girl friends. At a little after seven every evening, Maggie returned, alone, to the hotel to order room service and soak in a hot bath.

CHAPTER 39

Maggie's eyes were wild in disbelief. She shook her head, trying to clear her ears because she most surely did not hear him correctly. For the staff, the equivalent of a lifetime of experience happened at Shock Trauma in only a few years. In fact, it was like being dropped into the middle of a war zone on a daily basis. The things that went on in there were all consuming, continuing to haunt the staff's psyche long after they had clocked out at the end of their grueling shifts. Learn quickly or people die. People's lives were at stake. By far, the worst aspect of the job was the constant delivery of bad news to loved ones.

Whereas a physician in another hospital may have mistaken her shaking her head as a nonverbal answer no, Dr. Euwing recognized the defense mechanism immediately. This mother was refuting the cruel reality that he was burdened to deliver. Maggie Hasting tried unsuccessfully to stop his words. To alter the course of events. His experience also recognized the sudden pallor to her skin as a precursor to fainting if he didn't immediately have her sit. Taking Maggie Hasting by the elbow, he guided her to the tan vinyl chair.

Her husband, Robert, automatically followed suit, sitting like a condemned man. The families of trauma patients behaved in a few predictable ways. Cali Hasting's parents were each suffering their individual feelings of grief in isolation, neither having the strength to connect as a couple. In the flash of an eye, their lives had become a nightmare. Unlike the elderly grandparents who physically clung to one another, Cali's mother and father lacked the strength to console one another. Each was an island unto himself.

Confident Robert Hasting was listening, albeit his head was slumped over, his gaze fixed on a lone gum wrapper that had worked its way under a chair, Dr. Euwing waited patiently for the wife's attention. But she wasn't having any of it. She unexpectedly began to rummage through her purse, blatantly ignoring both the doctor and her husband.

Undeterred, the physician spoke to the the back of the father's head, "As we have discussed before, Cali's developed a compartment syndrome in her left leg, which translates into dangerously high pressures within the muscle tissue. There were several contributing factors. She was lying on her side for perhaps days. The chain around her ankle was too tight, cutting off proper blood flow."

"Chain? What chain?" Robert lifted his head, his expression dazed. He was a man in a foreign land who didn't speak the language.

Although he had previously told the family of the particular circumstances of Cali's history during the initial consultation, emotional shock required frequent reinforcement of information. Dr Euwing reiterated, "Her kidnappers chained her so she wouldn't escape."

"Like a wild dog. Can you even imagine doing something like that? They chained a young girl like a wild dog. How do you get up in the morning, knowing this is what you have to deal with?" Robert spoke in a trance like state trying to reconcile this horrific reality.

Dr. Euwing continued, "The rusty chain was a source of bacteria. It was much too tight, preventing effective blood flow to the leg. There were several abrasions about the ankle which became infected. Since she was lying on a hard floor, there wasn't any loss of resistance, compounded by the weight of her other leg when she lay on her left side. All this resulted in oxygen deprivation to her left leg for quite a lengthy period of time. To further complicate things, there was an animal bite to the leg. The teeth pattern suggests the animal was a rat. All these things combined, the rat bite, along with a chronic state of malnutrition, infected IV drug tracts, high pressures within the muscle compartment have resulted in a life threatening infection throughout Cali's body known as sepsis.

"Our immediate concern is her left leg. We took her to the operating room last night for a fasciotomy which means I cut several long slits in the muscle to try to relive the pressure. The surgery relieved some of the pressure inside the muscle, but not enough. The swelling continues as a result of the infection. So far, we've taken her to the operating suite for three washouts trying to clean out the infection. There's a wound vac in place that sucks out the pus. Infectious disease has her on multiple antibiotics. Cali's kidneys have started to fail, so we've begun dialysis. In spite of our best efforts, her leg remains infected to the point where necrosis, or tissue death, has developed," he paused a moment to let it all sink in as he reminded himself of Trauma's motto, 'Life Over Limb'. Save the patient at all cost. Sacrifice limbs when there is no other choice.

"At this point, we have no choice. We need to amputate her leg." Dr. Euwing felt the familiar flush of goosebumps down his spine as Robert Hasting let out a muffled sound of despair reserved only for families of trauma patients.

"She's only sixteen,"Robert whispered. "Maybe a couple more days of antibiotics."

"I'm afraid Cali won't live that long if we don't take her to surgery immediately. Her condition's extremely grave, Mr. Hasting. I need your signature giving me consent to perform the surgery today. We have an operating room ready for her now."

"Wait a minute. I can't think. If she's that sick, wouldn't surgery be too much for her system to handle? What are her chances of making it through the surgery?"

"If we don't amputate the leg right now, zero. She'll die before morning." He watched the father's shoulders shudder as if he had been struck from behind with a heavy object. "My best estimate is a thirty percent chance of survival with the surgery."

"Oh my God!" Maggie blurted out. "We can't let them do this to her, Robert. They can't even guarantee they can help her. And she won't have a leg if she does. What kind of life is that?"

Robert stared at his wife as though he had no idea who she was before saying, "My parents. We have to tell them."

"They're in Cali's room, but I can have a nurse bring them to you if you'd like them to be part of this conversation," the doctor offered.

In fact, Judge and Caroline Hasting had not left Cali's room for the past three days. Neither one leaving her side to even shower or change clothes.

Maggie suddenly stood, shouting, "No! Absolutely not. Do not bring them in here. I don't care what those two have to say. No one is cutting off her leg. I will not consent to such a barbaric operation. The answer is no. Robert, you will not consider this for one minute!"

She ran to her husband, "Robert, listen to me. Surely, you're not considering this."

"Maggie, you heard the doctor. We don't have a choice. Go ahead, Dr. Euwing, you have my permission to do whatever you need to do. Where do I sign?"

For the first time since they had met, Dr. Euwing looked utterly defeated. "Unfortunately, I can't, Mr. Hasting. Legally, once I became aware of your wife's refusal, I can't provide the necessary treatment for your daughter. In this particular circumstance, I won't perform the surgery without both parents' signatures."

In a moment of desperation, Robert managed to ask the doctor to give them a moment of privacy. Leaving the surgical consent and a pen on a table, Dr. Euwing left the room. Disheartened, the physician closed the door, certain Cali had lost all chances for survival.

Once the physician was gone, Robert took his wife's face in his hands, locking eyes with her. "We have to sign it, Mags. I want to bring him back in here so we can both sign that consent form. You heard him, it's Cali's only chance. We're both on board with this, right?"

"No, Robert, I am not on board with this." Maggie's spine stiffened, ready for a fight. "What's wrong with you?"

"Wrong with me?" Robert was flabbergasted.

"Yes, wrong with you. Have you given even one moment's consideration to how all of this has affected Abigail and Daniel? And what about me? Have you ever thought about me in all this mess? She did this to herself and now she's dragging us down with her. Why can't you see that?" Maggie wagged her finger at him.

"What?" Robert was stunned. Who was this wretched woman standing before him?

"Yes, remember me, your wife? I've given up so much. There were two closings I had to forfeit to be here. Do you have any idea of the money this has cost me? I've been the number one sales agent for the entire corporation, four years in a row. Me, Robert. I did that. That's all been thrown in the toilet, with me giving away my clients. Because of her, I've been uprooted to this ghastly Baltimore City, of all places, without any kind of emotional support from my closest and dearest friends, whatsoever. What am I supposed to tell my friends?"

"Is that what all this is about, how it's affected you?" He knew he was shouting, but was powerless to stop. "It's not about you. Cali's going to die! She's going to die today and we'll bear the blame together if she doesn't have the surgery."

"Oh, no you don't. Don't you dare try to blame this on me." Maggie's eyes sparked with fury. "My conscience is clear. I didn't shove heroin in her veins. It was a choice she made. She's a junkie, Robert, and that's a choice she made for herself. Like a common skid row bum. She's brought shame to this family and I, for one, refuse to feel sorry for her."

"Shame to our family! I don't give a damn what people think about our family!" Robert yelled at her.

"How dare you swear at me! I will not have it. Is this what's happening now? She's turning us all into wild animals. Can't you see that? Don't tell me you don't care what people think. You care what people think, Robert. We all do, it's human nature. You're just too much of a coward to admit it. Tell me, when has she ever tried to fit in with our family? Name one instance when she acted anything like a Hasting. Choosing soccer, a ridiculous sport where she runs around a field chasing a ball, instead of tennis. Or sailing. Golf is a lovely pastime. How about equestrian lessons like Abigail? She's the one who snubbed her nose at attending some of the most elite private schools in Georgia. For what? So she can ride a yellow school bus with a bunch of hellions. Just when it couldn't get any more embarrassing, she gets a job as a waitress. Are you kidding me! She makes us look like a bunch of undesirables. I won't allow her to ruin Abigail and Daniel's lives one more minute. Don't you think people are talking? What am I supposed to tell my friends, Robert? The girl with one leg, the girl with the heroin addiction, I am oh so proud to call her my daughter!"

Changing tactics, Maggie softened her tone. After all, she had perfected the art of manipulation. Since day one, Robert had never refused her anything. She had trained him with the maxim, Happy Wife, Happy Life.

Maggie closed the distance between them, wrapping her arms around Robert's neck. She cooed, running her fingers through his hair,

"We need to count our blessings. Can't you see, we have two beautiful, successful children. Isn't that enough?"

Pulling away from his wife, Robert's voice cracked, "We have three beautiful children. Three children. You want to know what I see? I see our daughter barely alive. Hooked up to every kind of machine imaginable, trying to keep her from dying. And you know why, Maggie? Because of us."

"Us? You want to blame us? Oh, that's bullshit! Pure bullshit, Robert," Maggie's voice had lost every speck of its gentile Southern charm. He had never heard Maggie curse, ever. But they were at a new low in their relationship and if all bets were off, he was ready. "You've always made excuses for her. You coddle her. She chose to be a drug addict. I won't take one ounce of blame for any of this."

Furious he had rebuked her flirtations, Maggie retrieved her Louis Vuitton purse. If she couldn't manipulate him into doing what she wanted, she'd simply leave. The doctor said it, there would be no operation without her consent. Like it or not, she had the upper hand.

"You know what? I'm done with all these shenanigans. I'm flying home tonight. I can tell my friends she died in a tragic car accident. For all I care, she can be cremated here and we'll figure out something to do with her ashes at a later time. We can have a memorial service back home," she announced as she started to leave the room, but Robert was much faster.

In one motion, he pounced across the room blocking the door. Gripping his wife by the elbows, he roughly slammed her against the wall. His face was only inches from hers. Robert had been raised a gentleman, but for the first time in his life, he put his hands on a woman out of anger. He didn't trust himself. He was keenly aware of the foreign sensation of being out of control. He glared at the stranger before him wondering when had she become so hard hearted? He held her there, afraid to let go, knowing if he did, he wouldn't be able to stop himself from striking her across the mouth.

"Cali. Her name is Cali. You never call her by her name, did you know that? And I'm sure you won't admit to your culpability, so let me do it for you. We chose to leave a sixteen year old child...." Maggie turned her head, attempting to shut his words out. Robert tightened his grip on her arms. He was hurting her and he enjoyed it. "Look at me when I speak to you."

He squeezed her flesh until Maggie looked at him directly, her eyes full of venom.

"She's a child and we left her in charge of her own narcotics after surgery. Too much trouble for us to care for our own flesh and blood. We're big important people, with big important commitments. Jobs to go to. Parties to attend. Lunch dates with friends. No time for our daughter. A daughter we basically gave away to my parents from the moment she was born. My parents raised her, Maggie. Not you. Not me. And we were both happy with the situation because we got to continue with the lifestyle that suited us. Nowhere in that lifestyle did we ever carve out a place for Cali."

"I will not apologize for being a successful realtor. For being a respectable member of society. People have surgery every day and they don't use that as an excuse to become heroin addicts," she shot back.

"Those people aren't children left in charge of their own pain medications." To his dismay, tears spilled down his face, spittle flew from his mouth overwhelmed with saliva. Saying the words aloud reinforced the ugliness of the reality. Robert was overwhelmed with shame.

It wasn't the shock of Robert's physical restraint, but the hopelessness of witnessing the emotional collapse of this elegant man that caught Maggie off guard. She was furious and wanted a fight. She longed for a reason to cultivate her indignation and he was giving her plenty of fuel for the fire. But crying. Crying actual tears.

Robert always possessed immense composure, even under the most difficult situations. She was unaccustomed to seeing him not having complete control of himself. Her husband was a civilized man of great wealth and prestige, not some unhinged blubbering sap. His weakness repulsed her.

"My parents took care of her, her entire life. And we were too selfish to take care of our own child for four lousy weeks. One month out of sixteen years. In one month, we destroyed our youngest child because we couldn't find the time, no, that's not true, we chose not to make the time to properly care for our own flesh and blood after she had surgery.

"It was on our watch. Cali needed us. We failed her. We did this to her. You and me. Our beautiful daughter had a simple knee surgery and we were too self absorbed to stay home and take care of her. Then we made the decision to double up on her pain medicine because it was convenient for us to keep her drugged. And then we played ignorant to the downward spiral she was caught up in. You and," the word caught on his lips, "me." Robert sobbed but didn't let his grip on her go.

Through his tears, he stared into her shocked face. "I want the chance to beg her for forgiveness one day."

"Don't be so melodramatic, Robert," she hissed. She enjoyed the shock on his face her words provoked. Her voice dripped with malevolence, "It's me you should be begging for forgiveness."

Without warning, Robert grabbed Maggie around the throat with one hand. Using the weight of his body pressed against hers, he used an old wrestling move to pin her against the wall. He was crushing her ribs. She couldn't breathe. She knew she was going to pass out any minute.

It was a crazed man who whispered into her ear, "Now, you sign this fucking surgical consent form right now, or I swear on your mother's grave, I will squeeze the very life from your body."

Robert tightened his fingers around Maggie's throat until she began to cough and gag. Terror set in as she fought for air. Her eyes glazed against a dusky colored face. He was deranged, a beast Maggie didn't recognize. He squeezed her neck a final time before he forced himself to take his hands off her.

"Sign it. Now." Robert shoved the clipboard securing the consent form in her chest. She choked and gasped for air. Overwhelmed with self pity, she wondered if her windpipe was crushed. For the first time in her life, she was afraid of her husband. Taking the pen with shaking hands, she scrawled her name.

Panic stricken, he snatched the coveted paper bearing her signature. In a crazed state of mind, he ran from the room screaming Dr. Euwing's name. Exhausted, Robert sank to the floor as he watched the doctor, surgical consent in hand, sprint down the hall toward Cali's room.

CHAPTER 40

Everybody who was anybody was going to be there. The Annual Black and White Gala to benefit the Georgian Museum of Fine Arts was the most prestigious event of the year. Five hundred dollars per plate ensured both a handsome donation to the museum, as well as the exclusive attendance of a more desirable class of people. Missing this event was the equivalent of committing social suicide.

Maggie had spent the entire day in preparation of this evening. Ensuring a good night's sleep and youthful eyes, she had taken a prescription sleeping pill the night prior. Sleeping in well past ten, she awoke refreshed and giddy with excitement.

It was only two days after Cali's extensive knee surgery, yet as usual, Cali's post-op care was nothing more than a fleeting thought. Maggie instructed Abigail with making sure to administer her pain medication every four hours around the clock. In exchange for her assistance, Maggie promised a mother-daughter shopping trip at Abigail's favorite designer boutique. Maggie had little time for nursing duties; her day was spoken for. Hair salon. Nails. Makeup appointment at two.

Women poured into dresses meant to accentuate their figures dared not eat. Their stomaches were well trained from the months spent subsisting on lettuce and little else, in preparation for this one evening. More than a nibble here or there would instantly result in an embarrassing bout of colitis. But consuming the right drink, with just a spritz of seltzer, was fair game. And drink they did. Huge silver trays covered with flutes of sparkling champagne or fine wines balanced on the fingertips of young male waiters were quickly snatched. For those partaking in more serious alcohol consumption, two fully stocked bars were set up on opposite sides of the garden.

At the discreet request of the female attendees, particularly those above the age of fifty, all the service workers were male, ages twenty-five to early forties. This was their night and they were determined not a single stray glance was to be wasted on a perky coed. Any hint of lust filled gazes belonged exclusively to them. The vast majority of the male escorts took the ladies' unabashed flirtation in stride. But, as in every situation, there was always a handful of salmon who insisted upon swimming upstream. For the ill tempered, advise was futile, but over the years, many young studs were successfully schooled by the mature bucks.

A powerful businessman chewing on a cigar was overheard by Maggie. "Let's face it, none of us really want to be here. I go along for the ride because it's ladies' night. Payback for doing our dirty laundry and raising our children to be law abiding citizens. It's their annual equivalent of a debutante ball for adult women. My advice, put your dick back in your pants where it belongs and let them have a little fun for a change. In the morning after the hangover clears, well actually let me rephrase that, in the late afternoon when the hangovers start to clear, they'll experience a great deal of guilt concerning their behavior. If you're smart, keep your mouth shut and you will be handed an un-written permission slip to leave the toilet seat up or watch any sport-ing event you choose in the luxury of your own home. We get a free get-out-of-jail card, gentlemen. Depending upon your wife's behavior, it can be good for anywhere from six to eight months."

Maggie and Robert were instantly swallowed up in the throng of beautiful people. Powerful people with obscene amounts of money. It wasn't the men who had climbed the ladder of success, trading their lives for imprisonment inside corporate offices, but their wives who luxuriously bathed in their riches that sparked Maggie's interest. These ladies relished their lives, free of gastric ulcers, because they, not their husbands, were the most brilliant business people to behold. Women who acquired obscene wealth by applying their knowledge of the XY chromosome to their benefit. Woe to those who misjudged them on their inability to decipher the stock market. Their portfolios took root in the form of an ironclad marriage license.

Maggie was the daughter-in-law of The Honorable Calhoun Hasting, descended from a long line of old money. A massive fortune not fully appreciated by his wife, Caroline. More importantly, they possessed an infinite amount of power which, in her opinion, they had no idea how to use to their advantage. They could be rubbing elbows with anyone they desired rather than that nobody Sheriff Earl Mathias. A ridiculous childhood friendship her father-in-law refused to let go. Had he chosen a more savvy mate, rather than that fuddy-duddy Caroline, her father-in-law could have been propelled to a greatness beyond imagination. With a more practical attitude and a few lavish dinner parties, they could have influential people indebted to them, which would only increase their sway. They could basically rule this town.

Maggie was no fool, using her surname to her benefit. The Hasting name almost unanimously guaranteed her as the listing agent for anyone who really mattered. Naturally, people with money gravitate toward people with money. It's a law of human behavior. Her standing as Judge Hasting's daughter-in-law propelled her career to the point where she routinely turned down clientele who would not make it worth her time. Selling million dollar homes was her hobby. She was nobody's fool. With any other family name, she'd be selling three bedroom bungalows to working class people, making inconsequential commissions.

Robert spied his wife across the crowded garden. She had been whisked away by the wife of the CEO of Georgia's largest retirement community, while he was pulled in the opposite direction toward the bar. He caught a glimpse of her as he ordered a single malt scotch, neat.

Maggie was in her element. Smiling, engaged in conversation. The former Miss Teen USA was a vision of perfection. Elegant in a form fitting, black sheath made alluring by a slit that extended to the mid thigh. Bare shoulders showed off toned arms well earned by religious work outs.

Maggie was well aware of the attention she received, albeit discreet. She was a master in the art of allure, giving a mere taste of her sensuality while leaving much to the imagination. She believed in intrigue. Women who bared all for the world to see, females who slept with men on a second or fourth date, those who lived together without benefit of marriage were all fools to be pitied. Evolution was the secret. Since caveman times, men were hunters. Pursuit fueled their desire. Any woman of substance knew, men crave the conquest. It was no coincidence this girl who was once from the wrong side of the tracks was able to snag one of the most desirable men in all of Georgia.

Robert felt his heart swell with pride as he recognized he actually lived the fantasy of marital bliss. His constant travel could have gone one of two ways, discord or the utopia he knew. Plenty of opportunity with a career as an international airline pilot, but he had never once strayed. No reason to. Maggie was both his wife, taking full charge of their homestead, as well as the lover who never once refused him. Upon every return trip home, his first thought never altered, she was a sight for sore eyes. After all these years, he still found her to be the most desirable woman he had ever known. While other men regularly complained of being in the dog house, he and Maggie had never had an argument. Not once.

Feeling Robert's eyes on her, Maggie winked at her husband. He was so naive but that's what she loved most about him. That and his money. After thirty years of marriage, they'd never had a single disagreement. Only a man like Robert, with his head in the clouds, would dare to attribute it to something as simple minded as compatibility. As though they were one and the same. He failed to recognize her as the puppet master.

Maggie was so expert in her ability to manipulate him, he willingly forfeited raising their youngest child. Her obstetrician had said, "After the emergency hysterectomy, the mother failed to bond with the infant. Medications may ease the postpartum depression and help regulate her hormones." When that didn't result in Maggie's yearning for her baby, a psychiatrist suggested perhaps Maggie felt like less of a woman once her uterus was removed. Subconsciously, she blamed the baby. Maggie was fragile. She might hurt herself.

Maggie thoroughly relished the way the Hastings, all of them, tiptoed around her as though she was the emotionally delicate equivalent of a Dale Chihuly glass sculpture. With amusement, she sat back and listened to their outlandish theories on why she displayed such detachment from her newborn. As if her womanhood evolved from some mushy bloody organ buried deep inside her pelvis. Let them believe what they may.

If they only knew the truth. It was ridiculously simple. She'd found her niche. Lugging around a baby would naturally excommunicate her from her social circle. She'd be forced to join ranks with a much younger group of women where she'd be banished to the bottom rung of the social ladder. Maggie already had two children. No way was she letting one little accidental pregnancy ruin her entire life.

Robert wanted to keep his winning streak going. He wasn't about to start any contention on the days leading up to the most important day of the year for his wife. That's why he made the conscious decision not to tell Maggie about the house key or the debit card.

Back at home, Abigail resented being inconvenienced by anyone. She wore her acrid indignation like a badge of honor. And tonight, she had been greatly inconvenienced by being kept prisoner in her own home in order to take care of someone who was technically her sister while her mother was off having the time of her life. Abigail didn't know anything about ice machines or medication. What gave her mother the right to decide she had suddenly become some fucking Florence Nightingale?

Why should she suffer such imposition by someone who didn't even live with them? In the spirit of fairness, a concept completely foreign to Abigail, how did Cali's misfortune befall her? If the little future lawyer in the making was as brilliant as everyone claims, she should have realized the potential consequences of playing a sport like soccer. Selfish. That's what Cali was. Pure selfish. Getting injured and then disrupting everyone's lives like this was plain selfish.

Furthermore, it wasn't Abigail's fault the grandparents took off on some old people's jaunt across Europe. She couldn't understand why her father refused to just call them and tell them everything about Cali's knee surgery. They'd fly home in a heartbeat for their little darling, thereby ridding them all of Cali's woes. Ridding Abigail of Cali.

But her father put his foot down.

He actually said that, "I am putting my foot down. No one is to breathe a word of Cali's injury to therm. It's their sixtieth wedding anniversary and they deserve their time together."

Both Abigail and her mother felt he was serious since he wasn't a man to take an unbending stance on many subjects. Robert had never been the kind of man who dictated behavior for his wife and children.

And what about her worthless brother, Daniel? Shouldn't he be made to share in all this tribulation? But he was safely tucked away at college, probably playing beer pong, naked, not having his life disrupted by this soccer girl.

Begrudgingly, Abigail had finally agreed to give Cali her pain medication. Actually, not such a hardship since it made her loopy, settling her into a daze. But she'd kept that little fact to herself. As soon as her parents left for the evening, Abigail decided to guarantee an uninterrupted evening by doubling up on Cali's doses, giving her ten milligrams of oxycodone instead of the prescribed five. Like clockwork, every three hours, Cali was roused from a sleep so deep no dreams were found. Abigail's annoyed face hovered above her, demanding, "Take these," as she shoved two more narcotics in her face. At three hour intervals, Abigail awoke her sister, repeating the cycle while she spent the evening with a group of nine friends in the game room shooting pool, cleaning out her parents' liquor cabinet, and ordering take out pizza.

"I have a little secret." Maggie giggled, the effects of too much champagne and no food fueling her playfulness. Settling into the passenger seat of Robert's Lexus, she slowly crossed her legs, letting the thigh high slit fall open to reveal miles of bare skin. "We're not going home tonight. I booked a suite at the Hilton. The best part is, it's just down the road."

Her eyes were glassy. She swayed lightly in her seat.

"Don't you think we should get home and check on Cali?" Robert's breath held the sweet woody odor of scotch whiskey.

"No, I do not." An expert at disguising her true feelings, Maggie kept her tone light rather than unveiling the immediate petulance she felt.

Cali had only been at their house for four days and Maggie already had her fill of the girl. It was supposed to be a seamless, uneventful four weeks. But Cali disrupted Maggie's entire life. Starting the very first day. Her in-laws had just gotten on the plane when Cali injured her knee, doing none other than playing that awful game of soccer. It couldn't be a simple sprain. Oh, no. She required surgery the very next day because she tore every last ligament in her knee. ACL. MCL. LCL. And every CL in between. For an entire day, Maggie had to sit in some hospital waiting room with a bunch of wretched strangers while an endless stream of trashy daytime TV tortured her.

Then came the real fun. The doctor was absolutely unreasonable, discharging Cali just a few hours after surgery, who proceeded to vomit in a little plastic bag during the entire ride home. But by the very grace of God, the seats of her Mercedes escaped unscathed. Against her will, Maggie was sentenced to four unbearable weeks filled with electric ice buckets, pain medications around the clock, monstrous braces with hinges. And where was Robert? Safely tucked behind his panels of lights and buttons, flying who knew where.

Maggie forced composure. After all, the Hastings had more money than anyone else in the state of Georgia. And power. Maggie knew she would not hesitate to do whatever it took to maintain the privileged lifestyle they guaranteed her. She breathed in through her nose and out through her mouth.

Robert's words were mildly slurred, "We should be keeping a better eye on her. You said Cali was in surgery over six hours, right?"

"Honestly, it's such a long ride home, Robert. We've both been drinking and if you get pulled over, do you really want to risk your career for a DUI? Trust me, I've taken care of everything. Abigail's there. I told her the doctor said to try and stay ahead of the pain, so she actually came up with a brilliant idea. She started giving her two oxycodone at a time, every three hours around the clock. You'll be happy to know, Mister Mother Hen, I've been texting her throughout the evening and Abigail said she's sleeping like a baby."

Frowning, Robert questioned, "Abigail? What does she know about taking care of someone so soon after surgery?"

"Give your daughter a little credit, Robert. Abigail's a responsible, twenty-seven year old woman," Maggie reminded him.

More accurately, Abigail's a twenty-seven year old child in a woman's body who still lives at home and depends upon us for financial support, Robert thought coyly.

Maggie flashed a perfect smile before reaching across the seat and running her fingers through Robert's thick hair. "Do not fret, my darling, I've taken care of everything, as usual."

It was true. Maggie did take care of everything. The fact was, she loved being in control of their personal life at all times. And Robert willingly went along for the ride. It was the pattern of their relationship. Theirs was a successful marriage, wherein Maggie called all the shots. Rarely, did Robert stand in her way. His wife did not like hearing the word, no. When he was home, he obediently abided by her constant itineraries. Barbecues at home. Tennis dates. Dinners aboard yachts. Drinks at the club. All he needed to know was, where he was going, when was he supposed to be there, and what he needed to wear.

"You know this is the most important night of the entire year for me. Do you really want to ruin it for me just so we can hurry home to watch her sleep?" She gave him her best sultry pout.

He shook his head, knowing he had no one but himself to blame for his wife's spoiled behavior. "Okay. I give." Robert submissively held up his hands in surrender.

Victoriously, she plucked a slip of paper from her evening bag and handed it to her husband. Starting the car, he typed in the hotel's address in the navigation system. Taking a final look at his wife's long legs, he pulled onto the road.

"Did you say two oxycodone at a time, every three hours? That's sounds a bit excessive. What happens if she runs out?" Robert wondered aloud.

The lines in the road blurred as he followed the navigation's directions.

"I'll call my plastic surgeon," Maggie confessed, making it sound like a joke.

"Why would a plastic surgeon prescribe pain medication for Cali?" A beat later, it dawned on him. "Wait a minute, you have a plastic surgeon?"

"My sweet, naive, darling Robert." She tilted her head, looking at him with liquid eyes. "Trust me, he's not about to bite the hand that feeds him. Do you have any idea of the money he's made on the botox parties I've hosted? Not to mention all the ladies I send his way for mommy makeovers."

"Mommy makeover?" Robert couldn't believe he was actually being let in on these guarded secrets.

Maggie was thoroughly enjoying their little cat and mouse game. "Mommy makeovers. Do you really think all those ladies birth a baby and then are strutting around the pool less than a month later in their itty bitty string bikinis without help? I am the most connected socialite in all of Berkeley Lakes, I will have you know. If I endorse a plastic surgeon, then women are climbing over one another for their chance to have him work on them. Keep in mind, Dr. Waxter doesn't accept insurance. He deals strictly with cash payments. He's paid for his vacation home in Palm Beach on the referrals I've sent him alone. I'll give him a ring in the morning. I know for a fact, I can get as much pain medicine as I want, for as long as I want. You have my word, she will not run out of oxycodone."

CHAPTER 41

Robert didn't offer to drive her to the airport when Maggie announced she was leaving. She left without saying good-bye, not bothering to wake him at zero-dark-thirty. Needing to lick her wounds, Maggie caught a redeye flight home, fully convinced Robert would soon chase after her. Even if he stayed until the end, Cali wouldn't last more than a day or two. In the meantime, Maggie could take care of planning the funeral. A memorial service at the country club, followed by an abbreviated graveside ceremony would be lovely. She hoped the weather held out. There was nothing worse than getting your heels stuck in the mud while tramping across a soggy cemetery. She made a mental note to contact the florist who did the floral arrangements for the Black and White Gala.

On the cab ride to the airport, Maggie made the decision to tell her girlfriends she'd been away at a real estate conference. Maggie had no doubt she'd have no problem selling her story. Checking her Rolex, she saw she had time to purchase a silk scarf to hide Robert's hand prints on her neck before her flight departed.

As for the funeral, Maggie decided she would discreetly divulge tidbits of information as she accepted condolences. The Hasting family was much too private to pour out their hearts for all to hear, so no one would expect a detailed account of Cali's untimely passing. Maggie was determined after she was done, the only logical conclusion for Cali's death would be a horrific car accident. Naturally, she'd push for a closed casket, however, if she was stonewalled, she'd graciously acquiesce.

Long after Maggie's departure, Robert began making plans of his own. For the next seven weeks, he, along with his parents, kept vigil at Cali's bedside. Much of his wife's behavior may be attributed to shock or denial. But to return home as though their daughter's life was not in great peril was unfathomable.

Robert let the idea of divorce marinate. He'd have plenty of time to think about it later. Of one thing he was certain, he was never going home again. Maggie could have the house. He bought a condominium, sight unseen, approximately fifteen minutes from his parents, depending upon the traffic. Maggie was right, after all. He hadn't been there. Ever. He had a lot of lost time to make up for.

Every evening, long after they retired to their adjoining hotel rooms, Caroline heard the soft click of a door closing, followed by the elevator chime. She was comforted in the knowledge that Robert faithfully returned to the hospital until the wee hours of the night. At the hospital, he sometimes recounted stories of Cali's ancestors. More often than not, he simply sat in the chair next to Cali's bed while holding her hand. It was the long overdue beginning of a trusted father-daughter relationship.

Unable to sleep, Cal and Caroline discussed their future while staring at the ceiling. Cal was a changed man. Tainted. In good conscience, he felt he was no longer in a position to hold power over the lives of others. He had lost all objectivity. He had spent a lifetime on the bench, giving the benefit of the doubt, reaching in all directions for redeemable qualities for the defendants who stood before him. If

Jimmi Shiflett had been stopped in his tracks years ago, would any of this have happened? The judge's pendulum had swung in the opposite direction and was stuck there. For the first time in his career, he felt some people were beyond reform. People like Skeeter didn't deserve leniency. Slowly, Cal and his wife came to the conclusion, it was time for him to step down. It was time for him to retire.

Cali's recovery got on a new trajectory the day she was able to write a note on a dry erase board. While still connected to the ventilator, the breathing tube in her throat making speech impossible, Cali wrote her wishes to the medical team. NO MORE NARCOTICS!! Her message in all capital letters, followed by two exclamation points. Later that day, the tube was removed from her throat and she began to breathe on her own. Her shocking recovery from that day forward was nothing short of miraculous.

When Cali was finally able to speak in a hoarse whisper, she asked Robert to find her cell phone. Kennedy was beyond words at the sound of her friend's voice. They were right back where they belonged, best friends for life. Kennedy wasted no time spilling all the beans. How she came to Maggie's house to visit Cali right after her surgery. How Maggie refused to let her come in.

Cali's repeated calls to Blake's cell phone consistently went to voice mail. After a few days, Cali finally reached the conclusion he was avoiding her. Who could blame him? In her absence, Blake was able to make a clean break from her.

It took almost a week before Kennedy felt the time was right to deliver the devastating news to Cali about a mutual friend from school who had overdosed on heroin. His sister discovered his lifeless body in his bedroom one morning when he didn't come downstairs for breakfast.

Cali entering drug rehab, combined with the shocking death of a classmate from a heroin overdose gave Blake the courage to finally approach his parents with the truth about his own drug addiction. The week after Cali left for Maryland, Blake entered an inpatient rehab facility in Georgia. He had one more week to go.

Whatever grief Cali felt about the amputation of her leg, she kept buried deep inside. Her focus was getting home. Being able to walk again. Cali was determined when the time came to give her testimony against Skeeter Shiflett, she was going to walk into court with her head held high. Every agonizing therapy session was motivated by that determination. Standing on her own, she wanted to emanate strength. Skeeter would be the face of defeat.

Detective Al Gale came to the hospital to deliver the news to Cali in person. Skeeter's life of petty crime was behind him. He had finally moved up to the big leagues. The charging documents against Jimmi Shiflett were four pages long. He was charged with everything possible from attempted murder of federal agents, kidnapping, extortion, possession of narcotics, to possession of a stolen gun.

Skeeter lay on the eleventh floor of the hospital, six floors above Cali, in the Department of Corrections ward. One wrist was shackled to the bed railing. There was no need to shackle his ankles. During Cali's extraction from the row-house, a bullet from Nick's Glock blasted Skeeter's spinal cord, paralyzing him from the waist down.

Cali was adamant, Marilyn played no role in her kidnapping. According to Cali, if not for Marilyn, she most certainly would have died in that hell on earth. It was the day after Cali's rescue when Detective Al Gale returned to the row-house, discovering the plastic bag stuffed between two joists. At the time, the bag's significance didn't register with him. But after Cali was able to speak, her insistence that Marilyn was innocent got Al to thinking.

The only way to know for certain was for Detective Gale to pay a visit to Marilyn at Central Booking on Eager Street. Cali's Pop insisted upon accompanying him. When the corrections officer brought KT

Shade, SID number 914679, to the interrogation room, Pop requested that she not be shackled to the table. Detective Gale's first thought when he saw her was she looked nothing like the glamorous woman with flowing tresses who slid out of the back window of the row-house. Sitting before the judge and the police detective was a pitiful human being wearing a rumpled orange jumpsuit and thick false eyelashes. Without her wig, her natural hair was close cropped and pixie in appearance. Her chin and upper lip halfheartedly sprouted insufficient-levels-of-testosterone tufts of facial hair. A broken Marilyn sat on the opposite side of the table, her hands meekly folded in her lap.

Detective Gale started, "We tailed Skeeter from his house in O'Donnell Heights to West Lafayette Street. He was the only one in the car. Were you already in the house when he arrived?"

Marilyn nodded, her lips pressed together.

"What were you doing there?" Detective Gale asked but Marilyn only lowered her head, refusing to answer.

"When we were sweeping the house, we found several items. We think those items may belong to you. Is there anything you want to tell us?" Detective Gale leaned forward closing the distance between himself and Marilyn in an attempt to create a sense of trust.

Looking up, Marilyn's eyes were glassy pools of sorrow when she replied, "My Hello Kitty blanket."

Detective Gale nodded before he informed her, "We also found a plastic bag wedged between the floor and wall."

Marilyn covered her face with her hands highlighting nine, long, green fingernails. On her left index finger was a bulky white gauze bandage. It was the finger she injured during her escape out the back window. Tears leaked from beneath her hands and ran down her neck.

"Could you tell us what was in the bag?" Pop gently coaxed her.

Swallowing hard, Marilyn took her hands from her face as she whispered, "Keys."

"That's right. Why?" The detective never let his eyes stray from hers.

"I couldn't find a key that worked," Marilyn explained.

Marilyn's story matched what Detective Gale had discovered — a bag filled with a dozen padlocks and their matching keys. Keys meant to free Cali's ankle. A Hello Kitty blanket mercifully given for Cali's comfort. They also found several plastic containers with remnants of food provided by Marilyn. Cali was right, Marilyn was a victim of circumstances beyond her control.

Without the slightest bit of hesitation, Pop declared, "Miss Shade, as soon as Detective Gale and I leave here, we're going to pay the state's attorney a visit. You have my word as a gentleman, all charges against you will be dropped and you'll be out of here in a few hours."

The Hasting family never knew about the gunshot wound to Walter's chest. By chance, one of the two bullets Skeeter had fired found a very small area directly below Walter's right underarm. With his arms outstretched in front of him as he carried Cali from the row-house, the bullet entered Walter's chest in a vulnerable spot unprotected by the kevlar vest. Once Cali was stabilized in the triage area, Walter had undergone emergent surgery which saved his life. He spent several days in the surgical intensive care unit, a chest tube in his side to re-inflate his lung. Had the bullet been a fraction of an inch to the right, the wound would have been fatal according to Dr. Euwing.

The day Walter was released from the hospital, he made a long overdue call to his dad, telling him, "I found the girl."

"The girl from Georgia?" He rejoiced.

"Yes, the girl from Georgia," Walter smiled into the phone. "And...I finally found The Girl. Her name is Sophia."

THE END

Our heartfelt thanks to Antoinette Manning and Jaimie Pierce Hedrick whose honest critiques and thoughtful insights helped propel our story.

We'd like to recognize our children for their love and support as well as our grandchildren who are the stars of our universe.

A special thank you to John and Antonios Minadakis, owners of Jimmy's Famous Seafood.

ABOUT THE AUTHOR

C. and R. Gale are a husband and wife team who are passionate about observing the smallest details of human behavior. They live in Maryland and are currently working on their next novel.